D0451487

THE BOTTICELLI SECRET

ALSO BY MARINA FIORATO

The Glassblower of Murano

The
Botticelli Secret

MARINA FIORATO

ST. MARTIN'S GRIFFIN ❧ NEW YORK

This is a work of fiction. All of the characters, organizations, and events portrayed in this novel are either products of the author's imagination or are used fictitiously.

www.stmartins.com

Library of Congress Cataloging-in-Publication Data

Fiorato, Marina.
    The Botticelli secret / Marina Fiorato.—1st ed.
        p. cm.
    ISBN 978-0-312-60636-7
    1. Artists' models—Fiction.   2. Art thefts—Fiction.   3. Botticelli, Sandro, 1444 or 5–1510—Fiction.   4. Venice (Italy)—Fiction.
    I. Title.
    PR6106.I67B67 2010
    823'.92—dc22

                                                              2009033892

First Edition: April 2010

10   9   8   7   6   5   4   3   2   1

To my mother, Barbara Fiorato,
who first took me to see *La Primavera*

ACKNOWLEDGMENTS

The Botticelli Secret visits many cities, so I needed help from many people and was lucky enough to get it. Some of those who assisted me are family, some are eminent scholars, some fall into both categories.

I'd like to thank my sister, archaeologist Veronica Fiorato, for her assistance on all things Roman, and my brother-in-law, Richard Brown, on naval history. Also on the family front, I'm indebted to my godfather, volcanologist Alwyn Scarth, for his help with the effects of earthquakes, and my mother, Barbara Fiorato, for tracking down various biblical references, with the assistance of Reverend Roger Wood, who was also most helpful on the subject of serpents in Scripture. My father, Adelin Fiorato, was, as ever, invaluable on the symbolism of Renaissance painting. Dr. Patrick Hunt of Stanford University was most helpful on the matter of the *pavimentum* in the Pantheon, and I also relied heavily on Dr. Antonio Baretta's detailed investigation of the catacombs in Rome. Any mistakes with respect to the above subjects are entirely my own and should not reflect the expertise of those kind enough to assist me.

Special mention must also go to family friend Bryan Clay, for it was he who first sent me a newspaper article about Professor Guidoni's "Botticelli Code," the spark of inspiration for this book.

I must also thank my agents, Teresa Chris and Patricia Moosbrugger, and the team at St. Martin's Press, particularly Hope Dellon and Laura Bourgeois.

We are indebted to the Uffizi Gallery for their kind permission to use their incomparable painting throughout this book.

Above all, I must thank my husband, Sacha, who added to his many roles this time with that of tireless researcher. And, last but never least, my two little cherubs, Conrad and Ruby.

Seven Kings, five are fallen, one is and the other is not yet come;
And when he cometh, he must continue a short space.

—The Book of Revelations, chapter 17, verses 9–10

· I ·

Florence
1482

I

Florence looks like gold and smells like sulphur.

The buildings are massive, gorgeous, and epic. They are made of glowing gilded stone and silver marble. Yet the smells—animal dung, human waste, rotting meat and vegetables left in the gutter from market—would make a tanner blanch. In fact, the city is a mass of contradictions. It is built for giants, with the huge loggias, toothsome palaces, and massy pillars, yet the Florentines are a tiny people and scuttle around the plinths like brightly dressed pygmies. The only citizens that truly fit such a scale are the statues that wrestle their stony bouts in the Piazza della Signoria.

Florence is beautiful and brutal. Her beauty is skin deep; underneath, the blood runs very near the surface. Wondrous palaces and chapels stand right next to the Bargello jail, a place worse than the Inferno. In every church, heaven and hell coexist on the walls. These opposite fates sit cheek by jowl on the ceilings too, divided only by the crossribs. In the dome of Santa Maria del Fiore, our great cathedral, angels and demons whirl around together in a celestial fortune's wheel. Paradise and damnation are so close, so very close. Even the food is a contradiction. Take my favorite food, carpaccio: slabs of raw meat fair running with blood. It's delicious, but something had to die to make it.

On the streets, too, gods and monsters live together. I have no illusions. I am one of the monsters—Luciana Vetra, part-time model and full-time whore. The preachers spill poison about the likes of me from their pulpits, and decent women spit at me in the street. The Lord and the Devil compete for the souls of the Florentines, and sometimes I think the Devil is winning; if you enter the Battistero and look upon the mosaics of the Last Judgment, which bit do you look at first? Heaven, with the do-gooding angels and their haloes and hallelujahs? Or hell, with the long-eared Lucifer devouring the damned? And if you were to read Signor Dante's *Divina commedia*, would you start with *Paradiso*, with its priests and pope-holy prelates? Or the *Inferno*, where the skies rain blood and feckless nobles fry feet first? You know the answer. So there was I, a jade and a jezebel, reviled by decent folk, touting one or more of the Deadly Sins on the street. A lost sheep. Sometimes, though, a shepherd will come among us, one of the godly, selling salvation.

And that's how I met Brother Guido della Torre.

It was not an auspicious meeting. He did not see me at my best. I was *dressed* in my best, to be sure, for I am always aware of the passing trade. But I happened to be sitting on the balustrade of the river, pissing into the Arno. Framed poetically by the saffron arches of the Ponte Vecchio looming behind. In fairness, it would not have been immediately obvious to the good brother what I was doing, as my skirts were voluminous. But I had just come from Bembo's bed, was on my way to Signor Botticelli's studio, and the quantity of muscat I had drunk for breakfast begged for evacuation.

Actually, I'm telling this all wrong—before we go on to talk about Brother Guido, and the right path, let me give you a glimpse of my old life, and the wrong one. Because unless you know about Bembo, and how I came to model for Signor Botticelli, you will never get to understand the secret, and the secret *is* the story. So let's go back to . . . the night before? No; no need to take you through all the depraved sex acts we committed for pleasure on Bembo's part and payment on mine. That morning would be time enough: Friday, the thirteenth of June, an unlucky day for so many reasons. Spring—the right place to start.

2

"Chi-chi?"

Madonna. I hated being woken up after a hard night's work. "Yes?"

"Will you do a favor for me?"

Another one? After the night he'd just had, Bembo should've been doing *me* favors. Over and above our agreed rate, of course. But business is business. I smiled sleepily. "Of course."

Bembo hauled his considerable weight to his elbow and I caught a whiff of his armpit. *Madonna.* I reached for the lavender pomade from the night table and pressed it to my nose. Smiling coquettishly to dissolve the insult, I waited for what came next. It was always hard to tell with Bembo; obscenely rich men reserve the right to be unpredictable.

Benvolio Malatesta.

Fact one, *Fatto Uno*: he was called Benvolio Malatesta, but everyone called him Bembo. Maybe because he had a carefully studied jocular air, like your favorite uncle; a quality totally belied by his utter ruthlessness in business. He smiled and joked a lot but;

Fact two, *Fatto Due*: Bembo was one of the richest men in Florence. He made all his money from importing pearls from the Orient. Lovely things they were: big and fat and as white as an olive is black. He sent little boys with oyster knives to dive for them. Sometimes they ran out of breath or got tangled in seaweed.

Once Bembo brought his finest pearl round for me to wear in my navel when we were fucking (do you see what I mean about never knowing what to expect from him?) Afterward he wanted it back but I told him I couldn't get it out. That was a lie. I tried later in my bath and it came out, just . . . but it hurt a lot. I put it back in there. It fit so well, and now I am known for it—I make it one of the things I am famous for. (Like my tits and my hair.) I always wear gowns with cropped bodices or cut-out holes to show off my pearl. Clients always love something unusual. Especially the rich ones.

Bembo didn't seem to mind. His big pearls were used in jewelery, and the little ones ground down for toothpaste for rich gentlemen or face powder for rich ladies. The pearls made their teeth and skin glow, even when they were as spotted as liver or as raddled as hags. My navel pearl was all good advertising for Bembo. He said that the pearl would pop out one day when my belly grows big with child. (I didn't tell him there's no chance of that happening. Every middle of the month I stuff waxed cotton squares up my hole to stop men's tallow getting through to my woman's parts. It makes me tighter but no one has complained yet.) For one horrible moment I thought that Bembo was planning to get me pregnant. Was he so cock-dazzled that he wanted marriage? *Madonna.* Is that why he let me keep the pearl? But then I came to my senses. A man like Bembo would hardly want to father a brat on a whore like me, for all my beauty: he has a rich frigid wife at home to cool his bed and bear his sons. And he has never asked for the pearl since, though some clients would have cut a girl's navel to prise it out, not caring if she lived or died. Bembo wouldn't do that to me though. He likes me. He even paid me three *dinari* for the night when the pearl got stuck, despite the fact that he couldn't get his gem back. Must have been a good fuck.

Fact three, *Fatto Tre:* Bembo knows a lot of artists. I think it makes him feel a little bit cultured, like one of his pearls, even though he is actually more like the common little ugly oysters that crowd the seabed. He came from nothing, from a line of fishermen, so he is trying to drag himself up to the surface and the light. Like his oysters he is an ugly creature capable of creating beauty, and he does this by his patronage of painters. It's this third fact that he hit me with. And it bought me a whole heap of trouble.

"Will you pose for a friend of mine?"

I was still half asleep. "Which friend?" My voice was a crow's croak.

"Alessandro Botticelli. Sandro."

I vaguely knew the name.

"He thinks you'd be perfect for the central figure for his new panel painting."

I opened one eye. "The *central* figure?"

He smiled and his teeth flashed pearl. I swear Bembo wore his wealth in his mouth. "Yes, Chi-chi. Don't worry. You will be center stage and all the other figures will pale before your beauty." Poetry didn't sit well on Bembo's tongue.

"How many figures?"

"Seven others. Eight in total."

Crowd work. "Doesn't sound very central to me."

His smile widened. "Oh, but you will be, Chi-chi. The whole panel is to be called *La Primavera*—Spring—and you will be the goddess Flora herself."

Still I grumbled. "At least it could have been the Madonna."

Then he laughed. "You, the virginal queen of heaven? The notorious Chi-chi untouched by a man's hand? No and no and no."

I sulked and turned my head. He tickled my nipples to placate me. "Listen, pigeon. Sandro wants you *because* you have known the heat of a bed. Flora is to be experienced, fruitful, with a knowing face—even a suggestion that she is with child. But more beautiful than the day." He knew how to appeal to my vanity.

"And how does *Sandro* know of my charms?"

Bembo collapsed onto his back again and the mattress buckled. He waved his arm to the thin muslin panel stretched like a window next to the bed. I had seen such things before in pleasure palaces and private rooms—a *finestra d'amore*, love's window. Sometimes the host's friends would watch him in a sex act, if the client liked to feel he was being watched. Or another couple would . . . well . . . couple in a chamber on the other side, sharing the sounds of their union. I had no problem with the concept normally—in fact, Signor Botticelli must have had quite a show if I remember some of the positions of last night; but suddenly I felt nervous. Watched by clients pleasuring themselves, fine; watched by an artist who was all set to immortalize me, unsettling.

I sat bolt upright and pulled two ropes of wheat-blond hair over my breasts in an unaccustomed gesture of modesty. Actually, I should tell you *my* three facts since I've now mentioned two of them.

Fatto Uno: I was named Luciana Vetra because I came from Venice as a baby in a bottle. True story; I'll tell you all about it sometime.

Fatto Due: I have lots of golden hair—natural color untouched by lemon juice, before you ask—waist length, with ringlets that have never seen a poker.

Fatto Tre: I have fantastic *tette*—round and firm and small like cantaloupes. And they taste just as sweet according to my clients. But can you really believe what a man says about your breasts just before he spills his cuckoo spit?

"What do you say?" Bembo interrupted my musings.

I crashed back onto the pillows. "I'll think about it." I knew what Bembo wanted. He wanted everyone to see the panel so he could tell them that he'd fucked Flora.

"Perhaps this"—he tapped the pearl in my navel—"will help you think well of my request?" He was wheedling now.

I looked down at the glowing, milky gem and back at him. *That fucking pearl.* I knew I'd have to pay for it one day. "All right," I said. "Give me his address."

And that's how I found myself by the Arno that day, all dressed up on the way to Sandro Botticelli's and badly needing a wee.

3

Unwilling to go all the way back home just for a piss, I answered nature's call, and this was the moment when the monk approached me. He was holding a pamphlet.

I groaned inwardly and would have sent him packing with a well-chosen epithet (I know many), but as he came close I saw that he was, in fact, extremely well favored.

Fatto Uno: he had thick, curling black hair with the sheen of a magpie's breast.

Fatto Due: he had astonishing eyes, the same blue as the Della Robbia roundels in Santa Croce.

Fatto Tre: I could see that he was not tonsured, so he must be a novice (not that full orders would have prevented our coupling . . . If I couldn't rely on a steady stream of monastic clients I would go out of business. Let them take care of their souls; I would take care of mine).

And yet, this baby monk did seem to want to be a part of my salvation. He sketched a cross over my head and wished me peace. Then he handed me the pamphlet. I sighed and said, "Brother, this is no good to me."

His face became lively. "Sister, you may think that the words writ there are not for you." His voice was sweet and low. Cultured. Posh. "But God loves everyone, even the fallen. I think even you might find some assistance from these pages."

I wriggled out the last drops of urine, registered the unintentional insult in "even you," and decided to have some fun with him. "You are right," I said penitently. I took the pamphlet from his hand, wiped my arse on it, and dropped the paper in the churning Arno. "It was very useful, thank you," I said sweetly.

He took in my action and at the same moment realization dawned that I had been relieving myself while he spoke to me. A fiery blush spread across his face and I saw him struggling with his conscience. He badly wanted to leave this thankless slut, but his ministry demanded that he at least *try* to recover one very lost sheep.

He took another pamphlet from the sheaf shoved in the rope belt of his habit. "I am Brother Guido della Torre, novice of the monastery of Santa Croce. These teachings are important, sister, for they speak to us of the salvation of our souls."

Now I was enjoying myself. "Arseholes?" I kept my features straight. "Do you think arseholes are important?"

"Nothing could be more so."

"And do you pray for arseholes?" My tone was earnest.

"Every night."

"And if I was to repent of my ill ways, and follow a life of virtue, do you think arseholes could ever be saved?"

His eyes burned even bluer with a zealot's light. "Surely, sister. For if we pray and strive for all the days on earth, one day our souls will rejoice together in heaven."

I nodded sagely. "So on that day, one might even say that heaven is full of arseholes."

He closed his eyes with joy at the sentiment. "Indeed it would be."

"Then we have certainly found agreement." Poor booby. I

decided to relent. "But despite our accord, your pamphlets are truly no use to me. For I cannot read." Typical monks: printing pamplets for whores who were so ignorant they could not read "cock" on a wall.

"Really?"

"Yes." My early entry into prostitution had given me little time for letters. I did, however, have a fantastic memory—I only had to look at a picture or face to remember it forever. I had trained my mind too—I try, as you have probably noticed by now, to remember three facts about everyone and everything I know. So although I am ignorant of letters, I am not stupid, so don't go thinking that I am.

The monk shook his head, as if he had glimpsed another world. "I'm sorry . . . it's just . . . I have always been around books. They are everything to me. I have read hundreds, and even now"—he blushed again, but this time with pride—"I have been given the honor of becoming the assistant librarian at Santa Croce, even though I have not yet taken full vows."

Now it was I who glimpsed another world. A world of words where the black characters printed on the parchment he held meant more to this monk than the people or places around him. I looked in his eyes and at that moment he saw through me. He knew that he had something I did not, and that for all my braggadocio and insolence, and my guttersnipe ways, I would like to have what he had, and know what he knew.

"How old are you, signorina?"

This was a first. No one has ever called me "signorina" before. I was so shocked that I actually answered truthfully.

"I don't know." Now was not the time to recount that I came from Venice as a baby in a bottle. I decided a little more filth might help me regain ground. "I began my woman's courses last winter, if that helps you."

"Woman's courses?" He brightened, no doubt thinking that I'd already embarked on a program of study.

I let him have it. "I bleed from my cunt once a month." I leaned in conspiratorially and added in a stage whisper, "I have to stuff cotton rags up my *gatto*."

He backed away and blushed again—hotter this time. I liked seeing it. But he was not such a booby after all—he had more in his armory.

"Young, then, but you will not always be young." He was good—he used the ultimate threat to all women, impending age. His hand reached out as if to touch my cheek, then drew back, like one who reaches into fire. "You will not always have the face of an angel, as you do now. Will you still live this way, when you are old, signorina . . . ?" His voice rose in a prompt.

I knew this one. "Luciana Vetra."

He smiled, and was suddenly as handsome as an angel. I could see he had all his teeth, and white ones too.

I narrowed my eyes. "What?"

"It means the light in the glass."

I stared. *This* was why I had been named so. Because I was the baby in the bottle. A glass bottle, from Venice, the home of glass. I saw, now, what book learning would do. And could not speak.

He saw that I was reeling and took his moment. He held my wrist and spoke urgently. "Signorina Vetra. The monks of Santa Croce are running a shelter for fallen women. For was not the Magdalene, most beloved of Our Lord, herself a prostitute? We plan to train women to earn money in gainful professions, and to instruct them in the Scriptures, learn to read, yes, and write too. Then they could find honest work, or even enter our sister order as nuns." His grip tightened on my wrist. "We could help you. *Let the light out.*"

For a moment I saw a different life for myself. I wandered

in the cloister with Brother Guido, psalter in hand, starched wimple framing my face. Perhaps if I improved myself, I would be able to find my true mother, *Vero Madre*, the sweet, kindly lady I had dreamed of for as long as I knew how to dream, the fragrant embrace, the strong arms around me. In my dreams she was beautiful, maternal, and confused with all those images I had seen of the Virgin, whenever I dared enter a church. At every shrine of Mary I saw, I spoke to her as if she were my *Vero Madre*. The monk's words had held forth the prize to me: the shining grail. I could be a daughter to be proud of, instead of a cheap tart who would be better dead and lost forever, than found again in shame. Then I shook my head, more to myself than to the monk. I had let down my guard, I needed to regain the ascendancy. Where was my tough exterior? How had I let him talk to me like this? Why was I nearer to tears than I had ever been? Where was Chi-chi when I needed her? I summoned back my subdued persona. The monk had taken hold of me; very well, I would take hold of him. Quick as a flash I snaked my hand into the folds of his habit and accurately grabbed his cock. "I could help you too, you know," I said, tugging away. "I'm damn sure I could let your light out!"

His eyes widened in shock. He jumped away as if burned, but not before I had discovered something which chastened me further. You should know that I have never, never laid my hand on a man's member and not felt it harden for me. But this monk remained soft as a baby and, to my further chagrin, regained his composure quickly. Worse, his eyes now held pity tempered with a little contempt, as though I'd disappointed him. As if I'd reverted to type. As if he'd seen some good in me in that instant of connection, and I'd proved him wrong. He turned to walk away, and absurdly, I felt like crying again. But by this time a small crowd of rival whores had gathered, and I had to keep my end up. I stood up and bawled at him. "Come back if you change your mind!" I flashed my tits for good measure. "Just ask for Chi-chi!"

He carried on walking, till I lost sight of his black curls in the crowd. My greatest rival, Enna Giuliani, sidled up. With her yards of brass-blond dyed hair, and her lead-painted white skin, she looked like a bad copy of me. If someone had been cast to take my part in a play it would be her. I know that the johns all asked for Enna as a backup when I was not available. She knew I was the most popular, but Enna charged less, so she got more work. The tension did not make for a close friendship. Usually I could deal with the bitch but today my confidence was knocked. Worse, she had witnessed the whole thing, and knew as well as I did that I had failed to get a rise out of the monk.

"Losing your touch, Chi-chi?" she cackled, nudging me with a bony elbow. The raggedy polls around her smirked to see me brought low.

I felt tears prick again. *Madonna.* "You'd know all about that," I rejoined. As I looked at her face, lined beneath the paint, and saw her sagging dugs peeping out of the top of her dress, I felt a sudden chill. The monk was right. We would all get old one day. Enna was twice my age, maybe five-and-thirty, and coming to the end of her use as a whore. She would earn less and less, and finally starve, or perhaps be murdered by those clients who liked their sex a little dangerous. Just one more dead tart, to be found floating and bloating in the Arno. I lifted my chin. Not me. I was on my way to Botticelli's to be immortalized forever as the embodiment of youth. I flounced away.

"Pick up some *borlotti* beans for dinner?" wheedled Enna after me. (I forgot to say—my rival is also my housemate.)

Recovering my bravado, I raised my skirt and farted in her

14

face. "Get them yourself!" I said. The polls snickered at Enna this time, and I left them cackling. Mentally removing myself from their low ways, I set off down the Via Cavalloti to the house of Signor Botticelli, and higher things.

4

Here are the three facts I knew about Botticelli.

Fatto Uno: he was actually called Alessandro di Mariano Filipepi, but was nicknamed "Botticelli" after his corpulent brother Giovanni, a pawnbroker, who was known as *Il Botticello*, "the little barrel."

Fatto Due: Botticelli was a Florentine by birth. He came from one of the poorest *rioni* of our city, Ognissanti. It's so rough even I don't go there.

Fatto Tre: he was totally in the pockets of the Medici. Even Signor Lorenzo de' Medici, the father of our city, a man so great he is known as *il Magnifico,* thought the sun shone out of Botticelli's arse. Apparently the Medici villa of Castello, which you can just see on the hill above Florence when the winter trees drop their leaves, is lousy with Botticelli's frescoes.

A powerful artist then. But I was not nervous as I arrived at his studio. I merely told the acolyte who answered the bell that I was here to be painted. The boy was a *negro,* eyes and teeth bright in his face, and he gave me a look I was well accustomed to as I swept past. The studio itself was light and airy, with more glass in the windows than I had seen in all Florence. At the far end of the room stood a shadowy figure, but I hardly noticed him. There was something else there too. Huge, rectangular, and with color that captured the rainbow. I could see the panel was nearly finished, and it was wonderful. There were seven complete figures there, all larger than life, with a fat baby cupid flying above. All the figures, even the cupid, dwarfed their creator who stood before the panel. The vibrancy of their color made him almost a silhouette. I saw Bembo had been canny with me; the eighth figure—Flora—who was a mere faceless sketch at present, stood slightly to the side and to the fore of the picture. A Madonna of sorts was actually the central figure, already complete and beauteous. She looked exactly as I imagined *Vero Madre* in my head and in my dreams. The sward on which she stood was dotted and studded with amazing flowers that peeped from the grass like fallen jewels. She was flanked by three dancing maidens in white, and a couple of other figures—mythological?—whom I did not recognize. I was well pleased with the work, and must have made some sound of approval, for Botticelli turned and looked at me.

He was middle-aged, perhaps five-and-thirty, with black hair worn long to his shoulders. He was pretty well favored but quite short. And now, thinking about it, the figure on the far left of the painting, the fellow with the sword, looked exactly like the man who regarded me now.

Our eyes were on a level as he studied me. He took hold of my chin, and moved my head left and right, and forward again. Then he looked into my eyes and smiled. *"Perfetto,"* he said. His accent was heavy and a contrast to the beauty before us. But I understood him well enough. *Perfect.* I smiled back. This was the second time today I had had a man lay hands on me uninvited, and, as with the monk, I knew in an instant that Botticelli was not interested in me for sex. He wanted Flora, and I was here to give her to him.

He motioned to me to get ready and I followed his pointing finger behind a screen where a brocaded dress awaited me. The dress had numerous flowers painted onto the creamy white silk. And was beautiful and heavy. The screen told me that Botticelli did not know what kind of woman I was; he clearly thought I had some modesty. He did not know that I would have stripped in the middle of the room in a heartbeat. I put the dress on, shook my hair loose at his bidding, and came forth: Flora personified.

I could tell that he was pleased, though he said little. I knew I was in the presence of greatness as he circled me, arranging my pose. There was a silver ewer of coral roses by the window and he filled my skirt with them, counting them in—twenty, thirty, more—pulling the heads forth so every bloom may be seen. He showed me how to hold the skirtful of roses, my left hand beneath with the thumb tucked away for grace, and the right hand dipping into the blooms as if I was to scatter petals on the sward. I stayed still as a puppet, exactly as he had placed me, and he seemed pleased. Finally, he twisted my hair behind my shoulders. "No need to hide such a face," he said, and I began to like him.

"As to your expression," he said in his coarse Florentine, "I want you to give a tiny smile, as if you have just enjoyed yourself in bed." Perhaps he *did* know what kind of girl I was. I thought about the night before, for I had trained Bembo well enough to please me. He had a little trick with his tongue . . . I thought of the monk doing it to me and my face heated and my lips curled. *"Esatto,"* said Botticelli. *Exactly.* And began to paint.

He painted all day. He said little and I said less. He let me take breaks and walk around, but then was exacting about my return to my pose. I watched the golden motes of light from the windows revolve like the gnomon of a sundial as the shadows lengthened and the room heated with low sun. At last he laid his brushes down and his palette too. I looked at the work and had to put my hands to my face to check it still rode atop my neck, so perfectly was it reproduced on the panel. My expression was replete, comely, and . . . well . . . cheeky all at the same time. No painted Madonna I. Bembo was right. I was a beating heart, a wet sex, a warm bed.

Flora.

The dress was still a sketch, though my hands were complete. "Will you not need me again?" I said, for despite my aching limbs I had enjoyed the day, enjoyed being a part of history.

He shook his head. "No. For I can paint the dress anytime. Such things are commonplace. *You* are a rare Florentine treasure. Bembo was right."

I shook my head in turn. "A *Venetian* treasure," I corrected him.

He raised a brow. "Truly? I have never been to the place, but I have heard of its beauty."

Now I am always a great advocate for my home city, although in truth I know no more of it than the artist does, for I was a mere babe when I was bottled and shipped to Florence. So now I nodded proudly. "Indeed. A city of great beauty, and great trade too. Much greater than Pisa or Naples or Genoa, her seafaring rivals." (Three more cities I had never seen.) Something about Botticelli made me want to seem intelligent, more than just a cheap pair of tits, so I trotted out, verbatim, this slice of travelogue that I had once heard Bembo say. But I had said something very wrong, for Botticelli went white and began to shake.

"What did you say?" It was little more than a whisper, from lips turned tight and blue. His face was ghost-pale, he looked as if he might faint.

What *had* I said? Perhaps the artist was so dazzled by Florence and the slums of Ognissanti that he hated to hear the wonders of other towns. And yet it had been *he* who had mentioned Venice's beauty. I babbled, trying to retract. "Of course, Florence is the fairest city of them all. The Duomo, the Baptistery, your own fair paintings." But it didn't work. He crossed the room in a flash and grabbed my chin again, this time with real violence. I could not breathe.

"Say it again."

I was badly frightened and could hardly speak. My confused brain leaped and circled like a coney as I tried to remember my words. "I said that Venice was greater than Pisa or Naples and Genoa, and—"

His fingers bit deeper. "What do you know of these places? Who told you?"

"Told me what?" I choked the question through gritted teeth, for his hand still gripped my jaw fast.

His gray eyes bored into mine like bolts. "Who put you up to this? Was it Bembo?"

"What? No one told me anything! What do you mean?" For the second time that day, I felt tears prick my eyes. But as quickly as I had been captured, I was suddenly freed. Abruptly he let me go and turned away, as if he were too angry to trust himself. My knees gave way and the painted dress fell about me in a great silken bubble as I sank to the ground. I was shaking still. When he turned back, he was *smiling*.

"I'm sorry, my dear," he said. "Just a bit of fun after a long day. Did you enjoy my jest?"

Now I have seen plenty of bad actors. I live in Florence, don't forget. Dreadful players litter the streets and offend the air with their posturing and wailing. But I've never seen a less convincing performance than the one I was watching now.

He held out a hand and I took it as he hauled me to my feet. "Just a little joke about our maritime states. No need to mention this to Bembo. Get changed, signorina. You can go."

Bewildered, I took myself behind the screen, playing the scene in my head. Something had gone badly awry, but I was more frightened by the sequel to the violent episode than the violence itself—the denial of his anger, the cover-up of any offense. I heard the artist leave the room and the door close behind him. Fear left with him. Then, in the safety of my solitude, hidden from sight behind the screen, I began to get angry. I stripped the dress off as if it burned me, so quickly that I ripped the delicate fish-scale fabric of one sleeve. And cared not. What a waste of a day! I could have been turning tricks in the piazza all daylight long, but now the night had fallen the watchmen would arrest any whores that were not safely indoors in their own beds or someone else's. I'd lost an entire day's income, for I dared not ask for money from Botticelli now. As I pulled on my clothes I fixed my eyes to the wooden panels before me, replaying the conversation in my head, trying to see where I'd erred.

My memory failed me but my eyes did not—one of the oaken panels had a darker line along three sides.

A secret door, no bigger than a Bible, which was a little open.

I pulled it wide and took out the single rolled parchment that was within. I forgot my anger and confusion for a moment, for there before me was a copy of the painting, perfect and complete save for my own face. The Graces were there, the tubby cupid, the martial figure that was the image of Botticelli. The Madonna too; the other figures and my faceless form in the silver dress. Even the same flowers dotted the grass. All that differed from the full-sized panel was the miniature form and the fact that there was a fine charcoal grid dividing the drawing into squares, as if the whole had been captured in a net.

Now you should know that I am not usually one of those whores who steal. Light-fingered tarts are wont to lose their fingers, and working girls that stick their noses in others' money chests or jewel cabinets are likely to have those prying members cut off by the watchmen. Many a pretty polly has been ruined by the loss of her nose, or her pleasuring hand. But today I was angry, and unpaid, and the picture was so beautiful I wanted to take it, just to look at it some more. To mitigate the crime I took the monk's pamphlet from my purse, rolled it, and left it in the panel, closing it with a click. Let the artist look to God for what he'd done to me; done to Chi-chi. I shoved the painting in my bodice and flounced out and past the servants.

The minute my shoes hit the warm cobbles of the sundown street I regretted what I had done. I dithered, ready to go back in there, then I heard the *negro* lock the door and relented. The hour was late—if I didn't get home I'd be arrested by the night watch. I'd give the painting to Bembo in the morning and tell him that it had somehow come to be in my bodice when I got home. Bembo trusted me—always the honest whore.

Comforted, I set off for the market, my perturbation about the stolen picture almost eclipsing my confusion about what I'd said to offend Botticelli. I hoped he would not scratch out my face and use another girl's now for the image of Spring. But I thought he would not. He had liked me well enough, that was clear. And I had liked him, until our inexplicable falling-out.

Anyway, I thought I would set the whole story before Enna when I got home. The scales of our love-hate balance would have to come down on the side of friendship just for tonight, as such a story begged for a good airing. I even wheedled the last of the *borlotti* beans from a market vendor as she'd asked, to put the bitch in a good mood. My purse was empty, thanks to *Signor* Botticelli, but I paid the man with a smile and a kiss on his leathery cheek. No need to overdo it, for the beans would have gone for pig slops anyway, along with all the other market leftovers. The beans were small enough, and some were black, but they'd do well in a stew and would placate Enna and pay for her confessional services. All the stalls were packing up as the sun sank. There's a Florentine saying that if you don't find the Mercata Nuova interesting, then you are dead. Usually I liked to poke around the various stalls, smelling spices and listening to the strange dialects of the merchants plying their tuna or salt or wine, but not that day. That day I was preoccupied, and couldn't wait to get home.

Enna and I shared a cabana by the Arno. It was one of the slum houses that had been built to huddle on the left bank—timbered, rickety, clinging to each other and the shore lest they tumble into the torrent. It was freezing in winter, stank in summer, and got flooded in the rains. (Last spring the floodwater in our cabin reached our ankles and we had to borrow barrels from the coopers' yard to make stepping stones to the bedchamber.) But we were usually bedded away from home anyway, so there seemed little point in spending our earnings on anything better. I hoped Enna had not gone out, or brought a john home, but as I neared the window I heard voices and cursed.

Shit.

She had a client.

Our window had no glass (too expensive, and would just get broken by urchins), just a dun brown curtain we pulled across for privacy. I listened for a while, because if the gentleman had spilled already he might be on his way out. But if Enna was just warming him up, I'd go to the tavern.

This is what I heard.

The man's voice was low and threatening. He said, "You've taken something that isn't yours. I want it back."

Enna didn't sound frightened and I knew they were probably doing some role play. Hell, I've been with fellows who want you to scream as if they're raping you, or dress as a boy while they take you up the back way.

"I don't know what you're going on about." Enna's voice now, rasping like a crow from the pipe she sometimes smoked. I wondered what it could all be about. As far as I knew, Enna didn't steal either; she was too smart. How strange that we'd both become thieves on the same day.

"I'll ask you one more time." The man again. "Give back what you took, and I'll leave you in peace. If you don't, it will be the worse for you."

Now Enna was getting annoyed. I know she doesn't enjoy being threatened, even less so in her home. "*Ascolta,* listen, signore"—her voice dripped with sarcasm—"I can give you plenty of things, and you can pay, and we'll both be better off. But I haven't stolen anything, this day or any other. So unless you want a fuck, you better leave."

The man sighed, but the threat had gone. The sigh was that of a man at a dyer's, told that his coat had been stained green, not blue. A silly mistake, but not a problem. "Very well. Good-bye, Luciana."

My skin prickled.

Fuck.

He wanted *me*.

I waited for Enna to correct his mistake, but she sneezed instead, stopping her words. The door banged and I heard the gurgle of wine—clearly even Enna could be shaken by such things and needed a drink. I waited to be sure the fellow had gone, my heart thudding in my ears and throat. *Madonna.* I better get the painting back to Bembo first thing—it must be important if it had already been missed. The waters of the Arno roared in my ears with my blood. After a hundred of my rapid heartbeats. I walked in unsteadily.

Madonna.

Enna lay on the truckle bed, head cleft from her neck in a gaping red open cunt, only a straining white flap of skin keeping her skull clear of the floor. There was blood everywhere, higher than the spring flood had been.

Then I knew.

The sneeze I had heard had been a knife across her throat.

The gurgle of wine had been her lifeblood pouring to the floor.

I could not move, as the blood carmined the points of my shoes. My body rinsed the stain with a warm stream of piss running uncontrollably down my legs as my bladder collapsed. I slowed my breath and thought.

They wanted me.

I had to go.

5

Here are the three things I took from my house as I fled for my life.

Cosa Uno: the Botticelli parchment, rolled tight in my bodice next to my thudding heart.

Cosa Due: a sturdy cloak of gray miniver, a Yule gift from Bembo.

Cosa Tre: a shard of green glass—a broken piece of neckrim— the only fragment left of the bottle that had brought me here as a baby from Venice. It was hard as stone and curved like a claw. It would make an excellent knife and I shoved it in my garter.

I stepped over the blood and closed Enna's eyes, trying not to vomit in her dead face. If I could have remembered a prayer, I would have said one. All I could think of was *Vero Madre,* so I said the words over and over, like an Ave Maria, invoking my real mother as if she were the Virgin. Then I was out the door.

Safe for tonight. Somewhere I would be safe for tonight. Bembo? Yes; he had gotten me into this mess. I would go to his house, lay all before him, and return the picture. I wanted no further part of it. I wished I could have scratched my image from the giant painting too—I wished I'd never heard of Botticelli. Badly frightened, I pulled my hood tight over my giveaway tresses and headed into the night.

There was the usual press of people on the Ponte Vecchio despite the lateness of the hour. The Florentine day begins at sunset, and here you can see why; whores and night traders began their working day, playing dodge the watchmen, and numerous pairs of well-dressed married couples took the air before bed. I wished I were one of them—usually I enjoy my lifestyle but just for tonight it seemed to me that there could be nothing nicer than the safety of a circle of warm arms, a shared bed—not just for an hour or two—and a good meal. Yet who would ever marry me?

I crept on, unrecognized, and began to climb the hill to San Miniato, that church's bells calling me higher. The half of the city that lies across the old bridge is known as Oltrarno, "over the Arno"; and you can really tell that this is the classy bit. In this exclusive district Bembo had built his flashy new villa, well up the hill from the stews and smells of Florence. Here nothing reached the lofty senses of the hillside residents but a breath of cypress trees and a ring of bells. I knew the way well, but had never climbed the hill on foot before: girls of my talents are conveyed in a carriage (usually performing some lewd act on the way). But fear lent me speed and my heart thumped with my footsteps. Soon enough I breathed the night scent of the myrtle hedges and heard the soft plash of the fountain raining into Bembo's carp pool: I had reached his gates. At my knock a familiar face appeared: Carlo, Bembo's doorman, was as ugly as all seven of the sins, but at that moment I could have kissed him as if he were my *Vero Madre*.

"*Buona sera*, Carlo." (*Uno:* I knew the man's name.)

"How's that new wife of yours?" (*Due:* I knew Carlo was recently married, to a young housemaid, for whom Bembo had given a generous dowry as a reward to his loyal doorman.)

The door opened and Carlo smiled. He carried both hands to his chest as if he were cupping a pair of melons and kissed his hands to his lips. Throughout this mime of marital bliss he said nothing and this is because (*Tre*) he was mute—Bembo took his tongue out, with Carlo's agreement, after drawing up a contract which would see him live in comfort for the rest of his days. See? Bembo was a contradiction, a marriage of kindness and cruelty. I hoped he would not be angry at me tonight. I hid my trepidation with a brassy smile. "Is he in?" I pointed upstairs in the direction of the bedchamber. Carlo nodded.

Thank the Lord. Next question. "And *la contessa*?" If the countess was home, I was screwed. Or rather, not screwed; I would never get to see Bembo if his snooty bitch of a wife was in residence. A shake of the head from the doorman. He moved his hand to touch the bell for the gatehouse servant to show me through the grounds into the house, but I laid my hand on his. "Don't bother, Carlo. I'll just run up and surprise him." My saucy wink elicited a grin. Another flash of the Chichi smile, and I was past, racing through the dark fragrant gardens. The great pond lay before me mirroring the firmament like a dropped looking glass, the golden carp shifting beneath the surface with a flash of moonlit scales. One rose and snapped at a gadfly, and I felt threat closing again. I skirted the lake and fell at last into the spacious Roman atrium. Not a soul stopped me from the shadows and I was up into the muted torchlight of the great stone stairs.

As I reached the oaken door of Bembo's chamber I dipped my head for sounds but could hear naught but my own heart. My knuckles kept time as they tapped for entry—once, then louder. Nothing. Bembo must be asleep.

A plunge of the handle and I was in, to find my erstwhile lover tangled in red velvet sheets, asleep. My addled brain was two steps behind my feet, for I had already tiptoed to the bed and placed my hands on the coverlet before I remembered that Bembo always slept in pearl-white sheets of priceless Egyptian lawn. Never red.

Blood.

My hands were slick with it. Knowing already what I would see, I turned the heavy body and Bembo's head flopped back in a posture never meant by nature. The gaping slash in the throat was the exact fellow of Enna's mortal wound—the same hand, I'll warrant.

Madonna.

My own blood drained from my head and I would have fallen forward, but a rap on the door righted me. I froze at the housemaid's voice. Carlo's wife.

"Master?" A pause. "Master? Carlo sent me to tell you that Signorina Vetra has passed the gate. Is she already with you, or shall I give her refreshment in the atrium?" Another knock. "Master?"

I had, what, two more knocks before the maid entered? I knew she would not hesitate to wake her master—if he had indeed sent for me, he would have meant to be woken for his sport. In an instant I was at the window, out the casement, and swarming down the thick solid ropes of wisteria that snaked up the façade, as fast as a ship's monkey. In truth, I had escaped here once before when *la contessa* had come home unexpected and unannounced. I thought fast this time. I knew that once Bembo was found I would be stopped at the gate. I could not take the risk so I did not drop to the ground, but ran over a low roof and hopped the garden wall, to land with a thud among the silent stones of the cemetery of San Miniato. I felt a presence and gathered breath for a giveaway scream, but saw only a lofty silver heron regarding me with one baleful eye from a stone table. He rose from his tomb like a phantom and flew the wall on silent wings, no doubt to stand sentinel over Bembo's tasty carp. I breathed relief, but only for a moment.

Shit.

Now where?

I had a stolen painting in my bodice, I literally had Bembo's blood on my hands, and would soon be pursued as a murderer, if I wasn't already.

I needed another option. Safety. Sanctuary.

Sanctuary? The word echoed in my memory like bellsong. Who had offered me sanctuary today? Snatches of conversation came back to me like roosting kites. Suddenly I knew where to go. God's house was always open.

I turned the points of my ruined shoes toward the monastery of Santa Croce, to enlist the help of the only man I had ever met who had not risen under my touch.

6

There were three things I knew about the monastery of Santa Croce.

Fatto Uno: Dante wasn't buried there. He died in Ravenna, where his body rots, but they show his tomb in the monastery church of Santa Croce, since it has lately become the mausoleum for Florence's most famous sons. But that most revered of all Florentines is revered in . . . Ravenna. Just one more piece of evidence that the church is one huge con, if you ask me.

Fatto Due: The place was chock-full of well-meaning Franciscans, such as the brother I had come to seek. Franciscans, it seemed to me, did much pastoral work out in the world, for the poor and leprous and other unfortunates. Unlike their chillier brethren, the austere Dominicans of Santa Maria Novella way across town. I'll tell you how I knew that they were more approachable, and that is, though I had never set foot inside the hallowed cloisters of Santa Maria Novella, I had, in fact, been here before. Many times. And that brings me to:

Fatto Tre: the postern brother of Santa Croce was called Brother Malachi, and would occasionally pimp me for the brethren within. Shocking, I know, but the flesh is weak when the willy is spirited, and even those with a calling could forget the Lord for quarter of an hour of prick-play. So I knew Malachi well, and hoped that this pious pander would be at the gate tonight.

The great piazza of Santa Croce was bare and dark, empty even of the pigeons that peck and scratch in the daylight hours. The rough façade of the church loomed out of the dark, giant and forbidding; its door was a dark mouth, its single round window a cyclops's eye. I dropped my eyes from its gaze, for I was badly frightened, and sought the little gate to the cloister, which sat low in the long high wall. Malachi was there, dozing, but waked as I reached through the gate to lift his cowl and crushed my breasts against the wrought-iron curlicues. Straightaway he leered at me, as if he had been dreaming of my face and greeted the reality seamlessly. His leer reminded me of what a dirty bastard he really was, and I called to mind one of the three Latin tags I know: *"cucullus non facit monachum,"* the cowl does not make the monk. (I will tell you the other two in good time—right now I am too concerned with saving my miserable skin.)

"Greetings, Brother Malachi. Is Brother Guido within?"

The odious monk stretched, farted, and leaned against the gate. "We have several of that name in Santa Croce, Chi-chi. Will you take them all at once or in succession?"

I tired of his wit at once. I had walked a dozen miles that night, up the hill to San Miniato, down again to Santa Croce, and had seen two dead souls, one I liked and one I didn't. I needed sanctuary, not sex, and I searched my tired brain for the monk's last name. Something about a tower. "della Torre." That was it.

Malachi's brows almost shot into his cowl. "In truth? The Pisano? I thought him somewhat devout for . . . never mind." He shook his head. "Well, at least he has the money to pay you, and then some, or at least his family does." He turned the key in the gate and I stepped back as it opened toward me. I pushed quickly past the odious brother, but not before he grabbed my tits on the way past.

"The brothers are at prayer," he grunted, trapping me with his bulk. "Don't forget my tithe on the way out. Ten percent, as always."

Madonna. His breath was foul—Christ knew what they fed on here—but I smiled into his drooling face and shot past into the courtyard.

Now I have no time for God, as you know, but I did feel safer at once. The place was peaceful—a cool rectangle of emerald grass like a still lake squared around by perfect loggias of numberless arches. A chapel with a round tower and a quartet of white columns sat at one end like a temple—oddly pagan in this setting. (Mind you, it was built for the Pazzi family, and a more un-Christian bunch I could not imagine. I'll tell you all about them later, as they come into this tale quite a bit.) I skirted round the grass and made my way to the left of the little cloister, and could hear the chanting even before I crept into the nave, soothing me with its peaceful tones. Perhaps the danger was past, and one of those who sang could give me succor.

Even a godless slut such as I could not fail to be impressed by the interior of Santa Croce. It was a massive barn of a church. Every inch of the place was painted, as if the Scriptures were happening around you. Fabulous chapels, all hidden in Gothic arches, huddled at the altar end, their beauties illumined by devotional candles. The brothers, shrinking in their brown habits against the cold, were lined in the nave, cowls down around their shoulders for worship. From the side door where I stood I could see nothing but rows of profiles, alike as peas in the pod, so I could not at once see my monk among them. My throat tightened. There were hundreds of them, a murder of roosting crows. How would I ever find him? Once the mass was over and they were back in their cowls, I would as soon be able to tell one snail from his fellows. I lifted my eyes at the hopelessness, following the pillars to the ceiling, my gaze floating to where the notes of the austere chant rose and gathered like bedtime birds. Stone angels gazed down at me, and I remembered that my monk had a head full of bounteous, beauteous dark hair, like the archangel Michael.

A novice.

Hair.

No tonsure.

I must get up high, see the brothers from above.

And among the angels, as if in answer to a bidding prayer, I saw a walkway, high above the keystones of the arches, spanning the length of the nave. I crept around to the stair and climbed the winding steps to the concealed way; here I could see the brothers from above and study them at my leisure. The awesome aspect of the church below, the frescoes, the tombs, the candles and song rose to meet me. I stared forward at the massive icon of the dying Christ, where he hung sorrowing above the altar like offal. He bent his Judgment Day gaze upon me and I clutched at the balustrade, fearing I must fall. I concentrated on the bowed heads of the praying friars, to stay the wash of terror that had suddenly doused me. Brother Guido must be here, he *must*. I looked along the rows again, this time from above, and picked out the novices easily, the ones without that incongruous bald spot. Two were blond as Venetians.

The third was him.

At once I felt better. He was still beautiful, and taller than all the others save the dark monk that stood right next to him. But his eyes were shadowed with violet beneath, his chin smudged with stubble. He yawned an animal yawn, all white teeth and pink tongue, and I saw that the novice had yet to become used to the earliness of the hour. For this was only the beginning of the Franciscan day—prayers and vigil at three in the morning, to continue at hourly intervals till Compline, and bed before it all begins again. Not for my taste to be sure. And not yet to his. It made him human, and I liked him at once. I kept my eyes on him, not once wavering through the interminable service, for I did not want to meet the eyes of the crucified Christ again. At length the chanting stopped and a monk began to intone Latin from the lectern in a reedy monotone. Another swung the censer back and forth on its chain, and as incense belched forth from the belly of the silver ball, the sweet cloud rose to reach me. The choking scent of the incense, the drone of the monk's voice, the pendulum swing of the censer, the lateness of the hour, all conspired against me. My forehead rested on the cool stone of the balustrade. I had not slept since I was in Bembo's arms, a day away, a world away.

I slept then.

I was jarred awake by a great rustle and shuffle as the monks rose as one and covered their heads to leave the church. I panicked and sought my monk's face desperately, but they were all now cowled, their countenances completely hidden by their deep hoods.

Shit.

I scrambled down from my hiding place and burst out into the cloister before any of them. But I heard the rain of a thousand feet leaving the church. I had only a few seconds alone. Where now? Just in time I ducked into the dark door of the Pazzi Chapel. I hid behind the pillar of the doorway and prayed that no one had business here, for I could now see every passing brother from the cover of dark. I breathed in the newness of the place; I could smell the freshly hewn marble, the varnish of the panels, the clay of the roundels that looked down on me from the dark like blue eyes. Strange that a place such as this was founded by the family that conspired against the Medicis, the Pazzis who plotted and killed the very flesh and blood of our city's fathers. This world *I* now lived in, this world *I* had entered, for I too was now steeped in Florentine blood. My fear returned, greater than ever, and it was all that I could do not to run from this place, this beautiful, peaceful chapel built by murderers. But I forced myself to wait a hundred heartbeats, and then I saw him, passing close, and— thank you, *Vero Madre!*—alone.

I yanked his sleeve and pulled him into the chapel with a strength I did not know I had, and covered his mouth at once against his cry.

His eyes snapped open—blue roundels like the ceramic ones above us—and only when I saw recognition in them did I take my hand away from his mouth. From the instant he saw me and knew me for who I was, I could see that he wished me gone. And I could not blame him. For if he was found alone with one such as myself at this hour, the abbot would bounce his arse out of Santa Croce quicker than you could say, well, arse.

Brother Guido della Torre straightened his garb and composed himself. He had to clear his throat twice before he spoke, and when he did, it was a hoarse whisper. "Signorina Vetra? What do you here?"

Well, at least he remembered my name. I didn't hesitate. Remember, I had been walking since sunset, thinking at every step about my predicament. All the way from Bembo's, descending the hill from San Miniato, I had been thinking about what to say to him. I had considered the options in my head and examined all courses open to me, from complete openness to partial truth. And I was convinced I had reached the best conclusion, one best suited to my usual style of discourse and general disposition.

I had decided to lie through my teeth.

I sank to the floor and took his hand, lifting my eyes to his face like a true penitent. My own eyes, green and sheen as

33

glass, could match his for beauty, and I filmed them with tears. "Brother, I am so ashamed of my conduct today. The truth is, I am lost, and want more than anything to be found, to live in the Lord's fold as the one lost sheep." My metaphor was wanting, so I hurried on. "You offered me sanctuary, and I need it now more than ever." (This, at least, was the truth.) "I came to beg for shelter until I may enter the convent and become betrothed to Christ."

I could see astonishment, disbelief, and deep reluctance doing battle in the monk's countenance. Clearly, he had been willing to help a worthless whore in daylight hours, but had not expected to be saddled with said whore on his own doorstep. His words betrayed his thoughts—to get rid of me as soon as may be. "Sister . . . signorina, I can't, that is to say, nothing can be done at this hour. We are beginning the day's devotions. I must ask you . . . you must see that to be here—" He broke off and sighed. "Signorina, I must ask you to leave quietly, and apply to the postern in the morning."

I toyed with the idea of revealing to him the true nature of the postern monk who would receive such an appeal—Malachi was no better than a pimp. But I threw it out—there was no time for such niceties.

"I'm afraid, Brother, I have nowhere to go. I cannot return to my home." I decided the time had come for threats. "If you cannot help me, perhaps one of the other brothers . . ." I took a step to the door.

He held out a hand to stop me. "Wait." I could almost hear him thinking. My words had been suggestive: the idea of appealing to another—his next notion was to find himself a chaperone.

"Signorina. I think I must lay this before Brother Remigio, my superior and librarian, and one of the initiators of this charitable enterprise. As a man of learning and letters, he designed the pamphlet that I showed you today." Even the dark chapel could not hide the blush that showed me he recalled what I had done with the first copy. (I thought it not the moment to tell him where I had left the second.)

I understood him. He wished to be rid of me, to wash his hands like Pilate and hand me over to his superiors. I was happy; the higher up I went, the more protection I would have. I could pine over the beauteous monk at a more convenient season. The fellow went to the doorway and looked left and right into the cloister. The footsteps of the faithful brothers receded, and there was a muted opening and shutting of doors as they returned to their cells—doubtless for a few hours' rest before their next devotions. Once silence reigned, the monk motioned me to put up my own hood, and, doing likewise, he beckoned me into the cloister. The well-tended rectangle of grass glowed dark green, and the sky above was velvet blue. Ringed by colonnades of perfect arches, the place gave me a sense of peace once more. I felt Brother Guido's hand under my elbow and it was good to be no longer alone.

We tiptoed on silent feet through a pair of great doors to the left of the Pazzi Chapel, to a larger cloister, square this time, with doors leading to each dorter. A stone well marked the center of the quad with a bowed tree leaning over to peer into the depths. The tall monk drew me into a doorway and shielded my body from sight as he whispered instructions. "Signorina, you must stay here," he hissed. "This is the door to my cell, but I cannot take you within, for it would not look . . . well. Nor can I leave you in the open. Stand back into this shadow while I wake my neighbor—the librarian, Brother Remigio, that I told you of."

I knew this was no time for idle chat so I held my tongue and shrank back obediently against the oaken door, fitting my slim frame into the jamb. To be sure, certain parts of me protruded a little, but in all I was pretty well hidden unless someone would come in or out, and as the brother had already indicated, this was his door, so I was safe for the while. I waited.

And waited.

The hard wood bit into my back and I began to wriggle. I counted my heartbeats, then all my teeth with my tongue. I sang all the bawdy songs I know inside my head till I ran out. Then I said all the prayers I know, which took much less time. My limbs froze, and at length, when still he did not come, I was forced to move away from the door, shaking my limbs and waggling my head like one with the palsy. The blood flowed back into my stiff muscles with an exquisitely painful impression of a thousand pinpricks. Still he came not and I stretched my neck, catching sight as I did so of a stone roundel, which sat above the door in carved relief.

It featured a great tower, of arches and columns piled on top of each other, leaning crazily to the right. I knew it, of course, for the great campanile tower at Pisa, which, although only lately finished, was reputed to list heavily to one side, as if fit to fall. Florentines were divided as to the veracity of this tale. Some, like myself, did not believe the story and thought it a feeble lie on the part of the Pisans, in an attempt to aggrandize their inferior city and pull it from the shadow of its great neighbor Florence. Some, who claimed to have seen the thing, merely shrugged and said it was typical of the Pisans, who could not build a pile of shit in a dungyard. I wondered at the oddity of such a carving here, for it was not a particularly religious symbol, and then I remembered that Malachi had called Brother Guido a "Pisano." Was this carving, then, due to the origins of the humble novice that lived within? Surely they would not take the trouble of marking the homeland of each brother who lived here? But the odd carving could not keep my attention for long, for another idea was begging for precedence in my mind. He was not coming.

He had ditched me.

I stamped my foot in frustration, and silently listed all the curses I had heard directed at the Pisans. I had got to "donkey-fucking heretics" when I heard the librarian's door open, and Brother Guido emerged, but alone. I shrank back to my hiding place, but I don't think he would have noticed. He had something pale in his hand and was shaking his head. "Brother Remigio is not there," he whispered, haltingly. "But these—his pamphlets, our pamphlets—are scattered all over his cell."

He thrust the thing at me. I knew it at once for the twin of the ones I had seen that day, and went cold.

They were here already.

They knew.

I took Brother Guido's arm urgently. "We must find this brother. Where would he be, if not abed?"

"I know not." He shook his head, bewildered. "I followed him from prayer and was hard upon his heels when you . . . apprehended me. If he is not in his cot, then he must have gone to the library, or mayhap the scriptorium, for some private study of his own."

"And where are these places to be found?" I rapped out the question.

"Across the cloister."

"Let's go."

I took hold of his sleeve and pulled him across the lawn. The time for concealment was past—much better, now, to be in the safety of the open, where no one could approach us without declaring themselves. We headed for the tree and the well in silence, but as we neared this central point Brother Guido spoke again, this time in a voice pregnant with relief.

"All is well," he said, "he is here."

At first I could not see where he was pointing, but then I realized that what I had thought to be a tree bending over the well was, in fact, a tall monk, with a curly poll like Brother Guido's, leaning over the water in silent contemplation. I felt a sudden disquiet. He was awfully still, had been since I had first spotted the "tree," some half hour ago. We drew close, and I could see that the librarian, too, had a pamphlet in his hand. With palpable relief, Brother Guido touched his brother's shoulder and said his name.

The librarian's head detached from his body and fell down the well.

Faced with such an awful occurrence, we did not move or speak for fully seven heartbeats, but stood, mute, looking into each other's eyes, our faces mirrored in horror. Only the terrible splash as the head met its rest in the depths prompted me to grab Brother Guido and force him down behind the well and its attendant corpse. The monk's face was moon-pale, his lips moving in prayer or catechism or I know not what. He turned his eyes on me, and as he fixed me with his terrified gaze, his words began to form sense. "Begone, I cannot help you. Take your devilry from this place and leave me be."

Now, I have been accused of many things in my time, but "devilry" is a new one. I had to get him to focus on my problem, but the only way I knew to get a man involved in a woman's plight was to highlight his own plight. And he had a big problem to contend with—I may not be book learned, but I am smart and I could see exactly what had happened. I let him have it. Grasped his cowl tight around his neck. "Now listen to me, you cowardly sack of Franciscan *shit*," I hissed. "My life is in danger and if you won't help me, fine. So much for your pastoral care, but now is not the time to examine your conscience. Know instead that earlier today I stole a painting, and since then, three people are dead in the search for it, including your brother librarian here." He began to ask a question, but I was in full flow. "They have come here in search of the pamphlet that I left in place of the painting when I stole it. They are coming to look for you. Your brother, here"—I looked at the headless corpse looming above us—"God rest him, was taken for you. He sat with you in the church, his cell is next to yours. He keeps these pamphlets in his room. He is tall like you, slim like you. He has . . . had . . . dark curly hair. The only thing they missed is that as the senior librarian, he is tonsured and you are not. But he was cowled, as were you all when you left the church, and if I had not taken you aside, they would have found the right man." I caught my breath and I let the facts sink in, and his face, already blanched, now took on the sickly hues of terror. "Aye, you know I am right," I went on. "They made a mistake, as they did before tonight when they killed my friend in place of me. But they do not care who they kill, be they ever so lofty"—my voice cracked as I thought of Bembo—"and will not stop till they get what they want. They think you are helping me, and now, believe me, you damn well will. Now gather your wits and get us out of here."

This last seemed to focus his mind. When he spoke, it was brief and to the point. "The herbarium," he said, and we set off at a run, before I could tell him I had heard footsteps in the arches as we talked.

Brother Guido led me to a low door in the wall and we were through into a fragrant garden, planted in a maze of box hedges. Without stopping for conference we climbed as one over the peach trees that espaliered the retaining wall, and we were down into a slop of drainwater, which soaked our feet as we ran back into the piazza of Santa Croce. At once we darted down a side alley and ran till we reached a quiet square where we could rest and see the approach of four narrow alleys. We sat at a little water fountain, drank to cool our burning lungs and rest our bursting hearts. The sky was lightening, and we would soon be discovered.

"We must away." Brother Guido echoed my thoughts.

"Where?" It was all I could do to gasp out the syllable.

"I know a place which will welcome us. It is not far, but a hard climb."

My heart sank, but terror rose and gave me the strength I needed.

"Take me there," I said.

7

Leaving Florence in search of sanctuary was perhaps the hardest part of the whole night. Under a gray smear of a sky, we made our way through the slums of Ognissanti and began to climb the hill to Fiesole. Ognissanti, as I already told you, is a shithole. And the former home of Signor Botticelli. A fitting home for the bastard, if you ask me. Shanties and shacks cramp together, grays and browns, assorted in size and shape like a grin of bad teeth. And the residents! More than once the sight of a monk and a girl together elicited a leer or a gesture from one of the hideous citizens, who seemed to have been belched up from Signor Dante's hell. The whole place stank, too, of the numerous tanneries and their attendant sludge. Everywhere eviscerated animals were stretched out in unlikely starshapes like guilty souls on the rack. I lost my shoe in a suck of mud where the Arno had burst its banks in spring, but was too tired and terror shredded to care. My fine shoes with the golden points had already had to contend with piss and blood tonight; meet it was that the mud should take one. I threw its fellow after it and saw the monk eyeing me.

"What?"

He shook his head. "That may not have been wise, signorina. The way is long and hard."

I narrowed my eyes. "How long?"

"Above five miles. And upward." He made a weak gesture up the hill, to where an indistinct skyline was a silver thread emerging from the dark. I shrugged, with a bravado I did not feel, and trudged after him barefoot. My feet stung on the path, proving the brother's point—but I had already lost one shoe before I flung the other; what was I to do, walk the hill with one foot shod and the other bare? I raised my chin and caught him up—no mean feat for he was tall, his stride was long, and his pace quick.

"Where exactly are we going?" I puffed.

He did not turn. "To Fiesole. There is a Franciscan monastery on the hilltop there—they will offer us sanctuary and sustenance until we may calculate our most expeditious course of action."

I garnered three things from this speech.

Qualcosa Uno: Brother Guido no longer had the notion of ditching me. His use of "we" and "our" warmed my chilled heart. But,

Qualcosa Due: he was angry with me. And I could not blame him. One minute he was safe at Santa Croce, with nothing more to worry him but what volume he would read in the morning, and the next minute he was running for his life with a prostitute who had needlessly placed him in mortal danger. Oh, yes, and,

Qualcosa Tre: his style of speech was somewhat different from mine; he would never use one syllable where three would do.

I trudged beside him in silence for a spell, but as the ground began to rise behind the city I had to ask him to stop as my feet were blistering. The look he gave me was not unkind, and he helped me to sit in a broom bush for a little. I wiggled my sore toes, thinking that these poor members were not designed for such expeditions. I had always had such pretty white feet—even that fiend Botticelli had remarked upon them as I had held my pose as Flora. I remembered, too, soaking my feet in a golden bowl of rose water at the house of a minor Medici, when the silver Turkish slippers he liked me to wear in bed had rubbed them raw. Now they were a mess, and fat tears of self-pity swelled in my eyes. The monk swam into view as he knelt before me. "Signorina" he said, haltingly. "May I offer, that is . . . in an effort to alleviate your suffering, to offer you present relief . . ."

To my surprise he was holding out to me his own sandals, rough leather paddles with a simple thong apiece to hold them on. But I only had to try one against my foot to know that I might as well have worn a pair of twin shrimp barges from the Arno, they were so large. The difference in size between the monk's feet and mine elicited the first smile of the evening. My grin broadened with the thought that he must have a big cock.

Below us the kites wheeled around the great dome of the cathedral, the striped marble turning it to a great tiger sleeping in the half-light, sated by the hunt and waiting for dawn. Beside it the lantern tower of the Medici palace, home to Florence's greatest family, stood crowned with teeth like a crocodile's gaping jaw. Brother Guido hauled me to my feet and I could sense him softening toward me—gaining an understanding that I had not wished for what had happened, that I had fallen into this pass by foolishness, but now wished it away, like someone who has jumped headlong into a well and realizes his mistake on the way down. I thought of saying somewhat of this to the brother, but then remembered that my metaphor might have unfortunate recollections for the fellow; I saw again his friend's head bouncing down the well shaft in Santa Croce, and heard the attendant splash. So I kept my peace and let him speak if he would. And at length, he did.

"Well, Signorina Vetra, you'd better tell me exactly what happened today. Try to leave nothing out, for there may be important circumstances which might mitigate our culpability when we attempt to clear ourselves of this business."

I turned wide eyes upon him. "You think we'll be able to get out of this?"

He nodded beneath his cowl. "I'm certain that if all is explained, the thing can be put to rights."

I saw that his confidence had risen with the terrain, and felt it in myself too. The road snaked ahead, and pointed black cypresses pierced the sky, like a rank of spears defending us. Regiments of vines stood in serried ranks, hiding our progress and providing a pathway. The vine leaves were glossy in the fading moon, night purple with a bloom of blue chalk. I craved the sweet globes of the grape harvest, but it was too early in the year; the vines were naked. My stomach was light but my shoulders were heavy with the burden of secrets. If I recounted the entire story to the monk, he would share the weight with me. The field mice, roused by our step, scuttled over my bare feet, making me giggle. Our breath smoked as we panted, but I was warmed by my miniver and the exercise. I even forgot my poor feet for a spell. Aye, as we climbed up the blue hill away from Florence, the sleeping tiger and the tower of teeth, I began to feel safer, and wondered, briefly, if we were mistaken to feel so.

But my companion, too, sounded positively chirpy as we climbed into the lightening sky. "Yes, Miss Vetra, we are not entirely friendless. The abbot of this monastery we seek now is an old friend, and my family, of course—" He broke off. But not before I had divined that he was very well connected, and might be of some influence. He waited, and I plunged into the silence with an account of what had passed that day, the commission to become Flora for Botticelli, the glories of the painting in progress, the artist's sudden anger. I told him of my thievery of the smaller painting from the panel, and, somewhat shamefacedly, of my mischievous replacement of it with the pamphlet Brother Guido had given me. I then told, in muted tones, of the murder of Enna and Bembo, that in the first instance my identity was mistaken, and in the second, I was wanted for murder. The tale was long, and by the time I had told it, my throat was as raw as my feet. But we had come some considerable distance in the telling, and were now among the lush villas that sat on the hill, where, as at San Miniato, the rich roost loftily above the city. The way had improved, and I peered curiously through the high gates and arches to elegant, peaceful courtyards with shaped trees and ornamental lakes.

Once—I had to look back to make sure—I glimpsed a giraffe, striding slowly in the blue predawn, bending its long neck to nibble at a myrtle hedge. I turned to Brother Guido, to share this fantastic sight, but the monk was thoughtful once again. I thought at first that his anger had returned, but a glance at his noble profile told me that he was considering carefully what he had been told. I considered the tale myself—and concluded, with a sinking heart, that it sounded like a tale told by an idiot; a fantasist and lunatic. But the brother, who had seen the evening's conclusion to the day's beginnings with his own eyes, seemed in no wise inclined to doubt my story. Continuing his steady pace, he eventually broke his silence. "Even the most judgmental listener would have to concede that, but for a moment of madness and mischief on your part, the sequel to your transgressions was far in excess of the relative proportions of a fitting punishment."

His bookish language was beginning to irritate—only when

I looked at his handsome countenance could I begin to forgive. "Meaning?"

"In short, signorina, these forces that pursue you are clearly concerned with a greater crime than a stolen painting."

I digested this in silence. "What crime?" I asked, truly bemused, but before he could reply I spied a monastic mass of gated high walls and a steeple, and grabbed the brother's arm. Our journey was surely over.

"*Vero Madre* be praised!" I cried. "Is that the place?"

He shook his head no. "This is San Domenico, the great Dominican monastery and spiritual home of their order."

I had had enough. "Could we not beg sanctuary here?"

The perfect profile hardened as the head shook again. "No. They would no more shelter a Franciscan than they would shelter one such as yourself . . ." He blushed in the dawnlight, and hurried on to cover his mistaken slur. "That is to say, their order is the only one they recognize, and they follow their rule with strict observances. Our destination"—he pointed skyward again—"sits there, at Fiesole." I followed the finger to a small golden building above us, crazily perched on the crown of the mountain, with a hundred steps leading to the cloister.

Fuck.

I'm afraid I was not the best of company on the final climb. I was so convinced that San Domenico was our destination, I could not bear even a short distance beyond. My feet bled, I groaned and bellyached, and begged to stop at every step. Our plight and my story were both forgot as we trudged to our goal, and the brother was merciless in his pace. "The dawnlight begins to spread in the valley," he explained, "the umbra of night is retreating up the hill—we are more visible with every second. Onward."

But neither his poetic speech nor his warning could move me farther. I had neither energy nor will to complete the final climb. As we reached the stone staircase of the little hilltop monastery I collapsed, weeping, on a stone bench at the foot.

"Just a moment," I begged. "At least let me put myself to rights before I meet your abbot. You must see the sense in that?"

He let me sit then and rub my feet, moaning with pain as I once again examined their cuts and blisters, magnified a hundredfold from when we had stopped before. After a moment the monk sat beside me, but only when he gasped did I look up and see what he had seen.

And I ceased my bellyaching.

For there below us Florence was laid out like a glittering carpet of gold, wrought by a thousand Persian infidels. The Duomo was now no tiger sentinel, but a warm copper bell, the Arno a twisting ribbon of gilt. A city of fable and infinite beauty in the brand-new light of the day. We stared in silence, shoulder to shoulder, while a feeling of escape and companionship warmed us with the sun at our backs. I began to pat my wild mass of hair into place in preparation to meet the abbot. I rose before my friend, but he held my sleeve. "Don't you think it's time you showed me?"

My filthy mind ran the gamut of everything about my person he might be asking to see, before my middle brain reminded me that never, with look or gesture, had he shown any interest in me beyond the irritation of my presence. No, I knew him to be truly devout, so had to ask further. "Show you what?"

"What this is all about." He half smiled. "The painting."

I sat again and drew the rolled canvas from my bodice. It was warm from my breasts and somewhat besmottered with sweat, for which I blushed. But he did not seem to notice and unrolled it tenderly in his long, ink-stained fingers, fingers that were clearly used to handling documents of great price. I looked, not at the painting but at his face as he took in the figure of Flora, Venus, the beauteous trio of dancers, the martial figure with the sword, and orange grove encompassing all. He looked for a long, long time in silence, with an expression of almost religious revelation. Saint Paul cannot have looked more ecstatic on the road to Damascus. I found myself, once again, thinking about what he would look like in bed. (Brother Guido, I mean, not Saint Paul; from what little I know of Scripture, I am convinced that that apostle would certainly have been resistant to my charms.) Then he turned and looked at me with his startling blue eyes, full in the face for the first time that night.

"It's beautiful," he said. He looked back at the picture in his hand then Florence below him, and then the picture again. "Beautiful," he repeated. "I don't know which is more so."

8

Even I had to admit that the Franciscan monastery at Fiesole was a place of peace and beauty. Glowing in the breaking morning, small and perfectly perched on the high hill, the place seemed set in amber, a preservation of an earlier age. We had been to Dante's hell; now we had climbed the heights into the poet's paradise. Certainly it is true to say that I have never been as happy to see a place in my life. When we reached the head of the wide golden staircase set into the hill, and I found balm for my torn feet on a hundred stone steps warmed by the healing sun, I surveyed the perfect little cloister, the tiny chapel, and the cells beyond, and responded to the sacred peace in my own way. "Thank *fuck* for that."

Brother Guido shot me a look of ice. "Watch your tongue, signorina. You are in God's house now."

"I'm sure he's heard it all before." My flippant nature surfaced as, once again, I began to feel safer. Brother Guido, on the other hand, seemed to have become more edgy, as our interview with his friend the abbot approached. I began, suddenly, to doubt his influence, else why would he fear an application to a man he claimed to know well?

The place seemed deserted and I knew that we must have come at a time of sleep, when all the monks would be in their cells, or at prayer, when they would all be packed tight as sardines in the monastery church. (I do know a little of the holy orders, for, of course, I was raised by nuns, but we do not have leisure to speak of that now; more later.)

At last we saw a lay brother hurrying across the quad, and I knew our moment had come. Brother Guido gripped my arm till it hurt. "Head down and no talking," he said. "Remember all we discussed." And with that he strode across the dewy grass to intercept the brother. After a brief conference I was beckoned over and the good monk led us through an arch into an even smaller quad, just as pretty, this one boasting a clear round pool, in which a myriad of golden fish switched and flashed. We were led to an oaken door, and the lay brother knocked and entered ahead of us. I tucked my chin to my chest as Brother Guido had told me, and drew my hood so far forward that I never saw the lay brother from first to last, merely heard, in a Sicilian accent, "My Lord Abbot will see you now."

I clasped Brother Guido's skirts, as I had been told, and followed in his wake into a light and airy chamber empty of all save a chair, a scribe's table, and a crucifix. The window, crisscrossed with diamond quarrels, looked out into yet another tiny quad, and I boggled at the geography of the place; it seemed passing small but in fact fitted together like a series of concentrick squares, one fitting inside the other like a Russian's doll.

The abbot rose from his chair and greeted us, with a word I didn't know, and Brother Guido replied in the same tongue. I stole a quick look at the old fellow and became aware at once of three things.

Qualcosa Uno: he was white haired and smiling, like a kindly *nonno.*

Qualcosa Due: his voice when he spoke mangled our fair language as I have never heard. Such strange stops to our beautiful vowels, and jerky consonants like a soldier's drum. I had been prepared for this accent on the climb, however, for the abbot was an Englishman by birth, known as Giles of Cambridge. I knew now he had greeted my friend in English.

Qualcosa Tre: his eyes were the blue of day-old milk, with a smoky film that lay over the orb, pupil, whites, and all. And that's when I realized that Brother Guido's scheme, which we had discussed all the way up the hundred steps, had a good chance of working.

For the abbot was blind.

After that I could look all I wanted, so long as I remembered my part well when the cue came. Yet it was not so much what I saw as what I heard that astonished me. And it was not the accent but the content of the lines that gave me pause. The dialogue went thus.

"Lord della Torre!" began the old fellow. "What an honor! How are your family, your good uncle?"

I shot a look to my not-so-humble companion, through eyes narrowed to arrow slits. *Lord* della Torre? Never in all the oblique hints at wealth and influence had I suspected that Brother Guido *himself* was a *signore*—a nobleman. Hmm. I was unsure whether to be pleased or dismayed by this revelation but, on balance, decided that it could only be good for me if Brother Guido was a rich young lordling. He might, in truth, be able to save my hide after all.

Brother Guido himself ignored me, and did not seem overly discomfited by the revelation. He evenly replied, "Well, my Lord

49

Abbot, well. But I beg you to remember that I am now become a novitiate of Santa Croce, and go about the world as Brother Guido." Brother Guido knelt to kiss the abbot's ring of office, and my eyes rested on the handsome cabochon-studded cross. *Madonna,* that must be worth a few florins. I watched carefully, rehearsing for my own obeisance. Yet the conversation continued.

"Yes, yes, you have joined our family in God," said the abbot with obvious delight at the correction. "Of course. You will forgive me, I did not notice your robes." The abbot smiled in a way that showed his acceptance of the blow that God had dealt him; so comfortable was he with the state of blindness that he was happy to make a joke of it. I began to like him, but was jolted out of my reverie like a player who hears his cue.

"And may I present Brother Lucius of Salerno?"

Brother Guido's voice concentrated my mind. I rolled the sleeve of my miniver high, so the abbot would not feel such exalted furs. I had wrapped Brother Guido's humble Franciscan rosary around my wrist, threading the wooden beads through my fingers where the abbot would feel them as I took his hand. I bent to the hand I held, old and rough as parchment. I barely brushed my lips against the ruby cross, mindful as I was of the softness of the feminine mouth. The old man saw nothing amiss, though, and the pleasantries continued.

"Brother Lucius is laboring under a vow of silence at present," explained Brother Guido, "but asks me to greet you and pay you his respects. He is truly penitent, my lord, for he has come all the way from Santa Croce barefoot."

The abbot nodded and smiled his charming smile once again. "My eyes may have failed me, son, but there is naught amiss with my ears. I could hear at once that of the two pairs of feet that entered my chamber, one was shod and one was not. You are welcome, Brother"—this to me—"a true pilgrim indeed." He nodded thrice, slowly and thoughtfully, then uncannily turned his rheumy eyes in the direction of Brother Guido's voice. "And now, my son, how can I assist you?"

I waited, with a butterfly flutter of nerves, for Brother Guido to lay our whole history before his friend. But once again, I was to be surprised.

"My Lord Abbot, we ask no more than a bed for a day and a night, before we continue forth into the world."

"Such a thing is easily given."

"And such humble victuals as you give to the other brothers."

"Granted," said the abbot, opening his hands with a generous gesture. "I divine that you are both tired, and therefore I will excuse you from the normal observances of our rule. You may sleep the day through, and I ask only that you attend mass at Matins before you leave." He waved away Brother Guido's thanks. "Brother Tommaso will show you to your cells. I wish you a good rest, Brother Guido, and you, too, *Brother* Lucius." I lowered my head again as the Sicilian lay brother reentered the room. But as we followed him through the cloister and up a dark stair to the dorter, I could not help hearing the playful emphasis on the second "brother" the abbot had uttered in his dismissal, and reflected on the fact that there were some things that the blind could see very well.

The Sicilian brother had more keys than Saint Peter, and he took a little time to find the correct pair on the huge iron ring he wore on his knotted belt and unlock our twin cells. Brother Guido and I had time for a whispered conference behind our hands in broad Tuscan, which we hoped the Sicilian would not understand.

"Why didn't you tell the abbot?" I hissed. "He seemed lovely. I thought he was your good friend?"

"He is."

"Then why, *my lord*?"

Brother Guido ignored my sarcasm. "I'll tell you tonight."

Then the door was open, stopping all further conversation, and I spotted the little truckle bed in the corner of the room, below the inevitable crucifix. I felt such a longing for bed as I have never felt, not even for my noblest clients' most stuffed and feathered four-posters. I had registered what Brother Guido had said, but frankly, I was too tired to care.

9

"Well?"

I had slept the day through, and the light velveted to night outside the window of the little cell. The single candle brightened, and the flame fluttered as I plumped my hands onto my hips, and stood looking down at my monkish friend with a questioning stare. In answer he vacated the single chair that his room held and motioned me into it. Brother Guido himself took the truckle bed where he had lately slept twelve hours round, just as I had done next door. He pressed his long hands together as if in prayer. "All right," he said. "I did not reveal your circumstances—our circumstances—to the abbot because I believe that you have . . . inadvertently . . . made a discovery of significant portent."

My face must have looked as blank as my unpainted countenance on the image I had stolen, for he swiftly simplified his terms. "You found something out. Something they do not want you to know."

"What?"

"I do not know."

"And who is 'they'?"

"The dark agencies that pursue us, and are determined to wipe your knowledge clean."

"But we don't know anything!"

Brother Guido sighed and chose a tone in which he would address a simpleton. "*I* know that, but *they* do not know that we do not know."

My head hurt. I felt like a simpleton. "Wouldn't it be better to come clean and beg the protection of the abbot?"

"Sanctuary is not what it once was," said Brother Guido sadly. "You know yourself that the flower of the Medicis, Guiliano, was cut down in the cathedral by the diabolical Pazzi family."

Ah, yes, that reminds me. I said I'd tell you about the Pazzis, didn't I? The Pazzis, in whose chapel I had so recently sheltered at Santa Croce, had hacked Giuliano de' Medici to bits, while he was at mass in Santa Maria del Fiore. Local reports said that they stabbed him twenty-nine times and hacked at his head until it split like a melon.

"Well . . ." I amended weakly, "perhaps we could explain to . . . you know . . . *them* . . . explain all this."

He was agitated now and rose to pace the tiny room. "Explain to whom? We do not even know who seeks you. How could we ever be safe again? How could we return to Florence, be we never so protected, without fear of our lives? That every footfall is an assassin, that every dish is poisoned, that every winter chill is the kiss of a knife?"

I considered this. Brother Guido painted quite a picture, and no, I did not particularly want to live as he described. "Then what are we to do?"

"We must use the only advantage we have."

I did not much feel that we held any advantage. "And what is that?"

"They are afraid of us."

My laugh was a donkey's bray. "*They* are afraid of *us*?" I was incredulous. "They have chased me round Florence butchering my acquaintance—and yours—and yet *they* are afraid of *us*?"

"Yes," he said simply. "Our supposed knowledge threatens them. And so, we must truly possess that knowledge to keep them at bay. The secret is our hostage, and we may be able to use it against them, to barter for our safety."

"But . . . but . . ." My boggling brain could barely form a sentence. "We don't *know* the secret."

"Yet."

"*What?*"

"We figure out what they think it is that we know."

"And how do we do that?" My voice was laden with scorn.

Brother Guido smiled. "You have the key to the puzzle right there." He pointed directly to my chest and I wondered briefly how my tits were going to help us out of this. He flapped his hands impatiently. "The picture."

Frowning, not understanding, I drew the painting from my bosom again. It had been crushed by my sleeping form, and I flattened it out on the reading desk, securing the rolling edges with a candlestick and a Bible.

Brother Guido came to my shoulder and his shadow loomed large. The painting lay, golden and perfect, in the pool of candlelight, every detail singing out in the dark cell. Brother Guido lowered his voice, almost with reverence, but his tones were no less urgent. "You have been pursued all this while because you took this painting."

I swallowed the panic that rose in my throat, spun to face the monk. "Then I could give it back! I'll go back to Botticelli's— the abbot will give us an escort—I'll return it . . . say sorry. I was going to give it back, to Bembo, and then Bembo was . . . is . . ." My torrent of words faltered as Brother Guido began to slowly shake his head. "Don't you see?" he said. "You cannot go back. For even if you returned the painting, you would still know the secret. You cannot unlearn what you have learned."

"But I don't know the secret!" I almost screamed it. "I could explain that I don't know . . . and . . ." This time I stopped myself before Brother Guido could hush me, for I knew it would be no good. I was only a whore—a good one, but still a whore—and they would sooner kill me than take the chance that I was lying. Plus, I had seemingly passed on my knowledge to another, a man of God, who was not as alone in the world as I. I sat down, heavily, before the picture. "All right" I said. "Then how are we to solve this puzzle?"

The monk began to pace behind me again, his robes whispering on the stone floor, his feet beating time. "I think our pursuers believe that you know something about Botticelli's painting. About the *Primavera*. That you saw something when you were there that day."

"But I *didn't!*"

"So you say. But from what you told me, Botticelli became— somewhat agitated—when you were sitting for him."

My mouth curled at the understatement. "That's true."

"I think you saw something in the room, or in the painting, and referred to it unknowingly."

"There was nothing in the room."

"Then it must have been the painting."

"But the painting is still *there,* we don't have the real thing. It's bigger than a warship's sail."

Brother Guido impatiently tapped at the parchment I'd flattened on the table. "Yes, but *this,* signorina, is a *cartone,* a perfect miniature copy of the panel that Signor Botticelli is painting. The faint grid that is drawn across the figures is to assist the transfer from this small parchment to the vast space on the panel. The artist will carefully measure and study what each square contains, and then transfer the information to a larger square which he will have mapped out on the wall. You see?"

I did see. I remembered from Botticelli's studio a net of strings stretched across the vast panel. And told Brother Guido of them. He nodded. "Yes. Sometimes the grids of ropes are stretched across a frame, and then candles lit behind, so that the shadow of a grid is thrown onto a wall. Artists have different ways of working, but the principles are the same."

I tired abruptly of my art lesson. "All very interesting, and I'm sure you have a point."

"It's this. What we have here is an *exact* replica of the *Primavera, exactly* as it will look on the final panel, down to the smallest detail. The only item missing from the inventory is your face, and we have the original here." The ghost of a smile. "I'm saying that whatever Botticelli is hiding in *his* painting, whatever allegory or code he has placed within it, is within *this* one too."

I began to see.

"So, we need to figure out what the message is, and *that* is how we may get ahead of the game."

I took issue with the brother's choice of words. I didn't think the events of the last day seemed much like a game, nor did I see how we could figure out what the painting "meant." But as my options were narrowing, I decided to humor the fellow. He certainly seemed enthusiastic, and not at all afraid—he was excited by the challenge and looked almost as triumphant as if he had solved it already, his handsome face aglow in the candlelight. Fucking intellectuals.

"We have a few hours before mass, and then we must go from here. So let us begin."

We transferred the painting to the floor, and I brought the candle from my cell. Darkness thickened outside as we studied the painting in its twin circles of light. It was incredibly detailed, and crowded with figures, and I knew not where to begin.

Brother Guido echoed my thoughts. "Let's begin with the simplest aspects, and we will move to the imagery and allegory in due course."

I cleared my throat in an attempt to conceal the fact that I did not know what at least two of his words meant. "Yes, yes, let's do that."

A wave of his hand invited me to begin.

I swallowed, hoping I would not appear too ignorant. "Well, there are eight figures. Nine, if you include the little flying dwarf."

"Cupid. Eight adult figures and a cupid. Good."

His praise encouraged me. "There are two men and the rest are women."

"Six females and two males. Good."

This was easy. "One of the men is a . . . blue tree goblin."

He snorted with laughter and turned it, too late, into a cough. "Forgive me. A *what*?"

I was crushed after my good beginning. "He looks like a tree goblin," I protested huffily, pointing to the figure on the far right of the painting. "He's blue. And he has wings, and he's in the trees."

"Very well." Brother Guido composed himself. "Forgive me. I didn't at once recognize your somewhat—pagan— identification. And?"

I responded to his pompous tone by becoming as crude as I knew how. "And he's trying to fuck the girl who's puking flowers." I pointed to the maiden in white who had a stream of blossoms flowing from her mouth. He winced at my language.

"He seems to be attempting an abduction or . . ." He cleared his throat. "A . . . rape." He looked sideways at me, but I'd heard much worse in my time. And been paid to hear it. "Good. And what of the other male?"

I looked carefully, for the first time, at the martial figure with the sword. I started, then looked again.

The monk saw my astonishment. "What is it?"

"It's him! It's Botticelli."

"Are you sure? It's a self-portrait?" Brother Guido craned in, so his curls brushed my cheek.

"Yes!" I said, breathless suddenly with the closeness of him (you should remember, I usually get tumbled half a dozen times a day, and I'd gone from sundown to sundown without a man). I had to concentrate hard to return to the matter at hand. "It's the very spit of him. That day in the studio I noticed it before. He's even wearing the ocher-colored cloak that he wore when he painted me."

"All right." The brother moved away again, to rub his chin thoughtfully. I missed his nearness. "Well, that must be significant. Let's return to him later. What of the other figures?"

"Well, the one in the middle, the grand lady, looks like a queen or a Madonna"—I kept the comparisons to *Vero Madre* to myself—"and next to her—the pregnant one—is, well, me."

"Flora. At least we have one identification. And I think the other, the queen as you dubbed her, may be Venus, goddess of love."

I nodded, as if I, too, had been thinking the very same thing. "And then here are three maids in white." I studied the graceful trio. "It looks like they are dancing."

"Good. I think so too. They would appear to be the three Graces of Roman mythology."

I began to feel better. "And there are lots of flowers on the ground, and"—I peered closer—"oranges in the trees."

"Excellent."

I sat back, flushed with triumph. I turned to the brother. "What did you get?"

"Well, the thing immediately put me in mind of the *Stanze*, an allegorical cycle of poems by Angelo Poliziano, who is the favored poet at the court of the Medici. The allegory expounds on the metamorphosis of spring into summer, which would seem to be commensurate with the title of the piece, *Primavera* meaning Spring. Now, one would *assume* that the figures on the *right*—clearly depicting the rape of the shepherd girl Chloris by Zephyrus, the god of the west wind, and her subsequent transformation into the goddess Flora, the figure which you depict—begin the scene, and that the scene is to be read from right to left as most allegorical paintings are. But the presence of your friend Botticelli on the left of the picture, next to the three Graces, gives me pause. Although his appearance as Mercury, the winged messenger associated with the month of May, would seem to give credence to my first theorem, I think that the manner in which he holds his caduceus high, and stirs the clouds clockwise, indicates that the picture is meant to be read another way, namely, clockwise from *left* to *right*. Moreover, if you look very carefully at the slices of landscape *behind* the figures, the land on the right is the golden color of summer and autumn, and on the left, the colder, fresher hues of spring and early summer. But although this may indicate the direction the painting must be read, and that all the figures are immediately (almost too obviously) identifiable from well-known classical tropes, I must confess that its deeper secrets are hidden to me." He paused to draw breath, and shook his head in puzzlement.

I suddenly felt a little less clever. And more confused than ever.

So it went on for hours.

Mercury and Venus were the only figures wearing shoes. The leaves framing the head of Venus were laurels, indicating the patronage of Lorenzo de' Medici. Two of the three Graces wore jewels, one was unadorned. And so on and so on. Our eyes were hollow and shot with blood, our brains stuffed with detail, our throats hoarse with chatter.

The sky had already begun to lighten, and I was hungry for breakfast and a jug of beer.

Brother Guido stood, suddenly. "We're approaching this in the wrong way," he stated firmly. "We are no nearer to divining the true meaning of the piece. Let's leave the painting for a moment and go over your time with Botticelli again."

I sighed and swore, for we'd been through my interview with the artist a hundred times.

The brother ignored my language. "What did you say just *before* he became enraged? Tell me word for word, and don't leave anything out."

"It was just idle chatter."

"About what?" he persisted. "Perhaps you mentioned something that was in the painting? One of the figures or flowers?"

Madonna. "I tell, you, I didn't," I protested. "I told him what I told you, that I'm from Venice, and that it is a city of great beauty, and great trade too."

"Anything else?"

"I said something about Pisa and Naples or Genoa, her seafaring rivals."

The monk suddenly knelt by me and took my shoulders, with the same urgency but more gentility than Botticelli had done earlier. "You mentioned those three cities, and no more?"

"Yes—well, Venice first of course."

"But you mentioned Venice in isolation? Then grouped the other three together?"

"Yes."

"And Signor Botticelli did not react to your mention of Venice? He showed no anger or vexation?"

"No, he was all charm. In fact, it was he who first sang the city's praises."

"But he became enraged when you mentioned Pisa, Naples, and Genoa in the same breath."

"Yes."

"You're *sure*?"

I was. *"Yes, I tell you."*

His eyes began to dance. *"Three,"* he crowed. "Three cities that are doing the same thing. Three maidens that are doing the same dance. You said yourself, they could be the *same girl*. Three Graces, three cities. Maritime powers. Luciana, you did it!" He spun me round in a mad dervish-like whirl. In the delight of the moment I barely knew that it was the first time he had used my name. Childlike as he, I bent over the painting again. *"Cities,"* he said. "They're all cities. Each figure represents a *place*."

My blood pounded in my chest, I was no longer tired. "And which other cities?"

"I know not. But I do know that something is afoot." Brother Guido's curls stood out from his head like those of a dark angel; his eyes were blue fire.

"But what?"

"War? Trade? Hidden treasure?"

Now he was really getting carried away.

"But we'll soon find out. And one thing is sure—*they* think we know already. That is why we are tangled in this coil."

I looked again at the three beauteous maidens, innocently dancing their strange measure, revolving for eternity in their graceful trinity. "Which is which?" I mused, almost to myself. "Which of the three Graces is which city—Pisa, Naples, Genoa?"

He examined the painting again, calmed a little. "Let us look carefully. What do you notice about them?" He glanced sideways at me. "I would venture you have danced a measure or two in good company, signorina. I imagine you are a dancer of great grace and beauty. Might you see something in their attitudes or postures?"

He was right of course. I *am* an excellent dancer, and *have* danced many a measure in the greatest of Florence's houses, before being taken upstairs to dance quite a different measure in the bedchamber. But even in such houses, I rarely receive such gallantry, and was suckered into giving the Graces my full attention. "Well," I began. "Their hands look a little—strange."

"How so?"

"Well, I know three things about courtly dancing.

"*Qualcosa Uno:* when you dance in a ring, you tend to keep the hands low, as is seemly for a woman in company. But here, the hands of two of them are lifted high, their gaze is lifted to their hands, and the hands themselves twisted into an odd attitude above their heads, in a manner that would not be—well, usual in polite circles." I felt a little odd speaking of what was seemly, when I, clearly, am not, but I do know a little of manners, even if I do not actually have any.

"*Qualcosa Due:* in a roundel such as this, the trio should all face the same way."

Brother Guido nodded slowly. "Perhaps the message is in the hands. The gaze of the left-hand Grace is directed at the clasped hands. Perhaps they are trying to tell us something—make a shape of some kind?"

I looked and looked until I was near cross-eyed, and the monk did likewise.

"Not unless they are trying to tell us about a duck, or some other fowl, for the life of me I cannot see any other shape depicted by those fingers." I rubbed my eyes.

"Perhaps they are spelling something?" Brother Guido mused, too tired to notice my feeble jest. "Do their hands make a letter? If not in the Arabic, then the Cyrillic script, since classical figures are thematic here?"

I had no thoughts on letters, Arabic or otherwise, for I cannot write. I left him to that particular line of inquiry. My tired mind wandered, to be brought back by a swift question.

"You said you knew three things about dancing. What was the third?"

Madonna, he was quick. "*Qualcosa Tre:* your gaze should be lowered modestly to the ground. You should never look directly at a gentleman, even if he is your partner in the measure. You should never meet his eyes, no matter what pleasures you intend to exchange later. Yet the middle maiden"—I pointed—"while her sisters gaze at the hands, is looking directly at *him.*" I traced my finger left to the face of Mercury, as played by Signor Botticelli.

"You're right!" exclaimed Brother Guido. "She is gazing at him intently, as if she would say something."

"Or as if she wants him in her bed."

The brother blushed. "I think she is the key," he said. "It's her. She alone of the three is connected by her glance to Botticelli. Let us turn our eyes upon this central Grace, and only she. She conceals the identity of the first city. Pisa, Naples, or Genoa. We must search for any letter, or mayhap coat of arms, concealed about her person."

Once again, I was stranded on the sandbanks of my ignorance. I knew naught of any of the three, save that they all went to sea and were packed full of merchants and sailors that sometimes washed up in Florence to unload their wares between my legs. But, to show willing, I looked again at the flame-haired maid, seeing in her glance at the handsome Mercury something of my own desires. My tired eyes traveled from her red head to the white hands clasped above.

And then, I saw it. A shape swam into my tired view.

'Twas not what was there, but what was *not.* The space in between the hands, the strange, swanlike clasp of the dancers, described exactly a shape I had seen only yestereve. A strange trick of my spent brain took me back to the doorway of Brother Guido's cell in Santa Croce, where I had shrunk into the shadows of a silent cloister, the darkness shielding me from mortal danger. And there, above the doorway that held me, in a stone roundel was carved a tower. A tower that *leaned*.

"*She's* Pisa," I said. The strain of the night brought a gurgle of laughter from deep within, rising, unstoppable, from my throat. "She's wearing the tower on her *head*."

Brother Guido bent over my pointing finger. He, too, began to laugh, a deep, musical sound, strange in its unfamiliarity.

"So she is." Then, softer, "So she is." He shook his head. "That I, who call Pisa my home, did not see this, when I have grown under the shadow of that very tower. The shape, the incline, all is exactly right. Even the bell tower at the very top is described precisely by the negative space between the Grace's fingers. What an ass am I, a blind, foolish ass! And as for you"—he turned with a smile that warmed me from head to toe—"there are many things to be learned besides what we may find in a book."

I returned the smile, feeling almost bashful, which is not like me at all. "And now?" I asked, already dreading what he would say.

"Pisa. We're going to Pisa."

"We're *going* there?"

"Yes. For two reasons. One, my uncle is a great man in the city and may help us. Two, we are endangering my Lord Abbot for every hour we stay here. For if the assassins trace us to this place, they may believe we have shared our knowledge and decide to murder him too."

"Is the same not so of your uncle?"

"No, for he is a man of great power and consequence."

I snorted unattractively. "So was Bembo."

He nodded thoughtfully. "Well, if our timing is right, we may be able to meet him without revealing ourselves."

"What *can* you mean?"

"You'll see," he replied enigmatically, and then lifted his head as if he smelled music. "D'you hear? The bells are ringing for Matins."

"Stay a moment." I pulled his sleeve. "We have identified Pisa as the central Grace. But what is to say that she is the *beginning* of the whole puzzle? There are many figures here. We cannot run off on this goose chase to Pisa for the sole reason that she is gazing on Botticelli with bedchamber eyes."

Brother Guido smiled. "We *can* be sure, for it is not lust but love that shows us the way. Love is blind, but look, Luciana, he shows *us* how to see. We follow the arrow." This time it was my turn to follow the point of a finger. Brother Guido indicated the fat flying cupid, with the blindfold covering his eyes. I watched further as the monk's forefinger traced Cupid's fiery arrow, which pointed directly to the ornamented head of the central Grace.

Flame-haired, as if the arrow had set her bright head alight, and crowned with the tower of Pisa.

We sat through the mass in the freezing chapel. Our flesh numb on the stones and our minds numb with discovery. Cowled once again in my cloak of miniver, I stole a sideways glance at Brother Guido. He was praying hard—really praying, as if he meant it. In the refectory after, I sat at the long tables among the ranks of silent monks, all eating in a polite, restrained manner as one of their number read from a holy text. Relieved that I would not have to talk, even to Brother Guido at my elbow, I shoveled bread and dried cod into my cowl and glugged my quota of beer, and felt oddly optimistic as we left the table to take leave of the abbot. We stood once more outside the little golden monastery; a day had come and gone and come again, and we knew much more than when we had arrived. Florence, the eternal city, still glittered below us in the valley. Were the assassins that sought us still there or closer at hand? I shivered and turned from the view to see the abbot approaching, followed by his little Sicilian monk holding two dancing ponies on a leading rein. The kind old fellow made us the gift of the two cob ponies in return for a promised benefice from the della Torres; Brother Guido promised to petition his uncle on our arrival in Pisa. As Abbot Giles of Cambridge said an affectionate farewell to Brother Guido I straddled the neckbone of my pony like a man and winced.

The old abbot reached up to me. "Brother Lucius, there is something in the saddlebag for you. But best to open it when you are down the hill." His sweet smile reached his blind eyes but he turned before I could thank him, and hobbled back to the cloister.

By the time our mounts reached the bottom of the hundred stairs my crotch was already aching for all the wrong reasons as my pelvis bumped on my pony's neckbone. When we rounded the corner I bade the brother wait while I opened my saddlebag. Inside was a fine sidesaddle for a lady, tasseled and pommeled and a comfort to my aching groin.

My smile lasted me all the way out of the Arno Valley, but as I turned to look my last at the city I'd lived in and loved in, I wondered if I'd ever see it again. As we rode seaward Florence was a little pain under my heart.

· 2 ·

Pisa

IO

I wasn't that impressed by Pisa when we finally got there, for three reasons.

Ragione Uno: It was pissing with rain.

Ragione Due: everything was a bit like Florence but a lot smaller. The same river Arno ran through the center but in a slower, narrower stream; the palaces that lined the banks seemed smaller and less opulent than their Florentine counterparts, and the people, too, seemed smaller and less polished than their elegant cousins (excepting my companion, of course, who would stand above all men anywhere he went).

Ragione Tre: my arse was as raw as carpaccio and my sex so numb from my pony's neckbone that I was sure I would never feel pleasure in fucking ever again. And to think I called the blasted animal "Pene" (penis) in the first place because at least that way I would get to ride one every day. Brother Guido looked thunder at me when I shared this little joke with him as we jogged along—he in turn dubbed his mount something pious: Aquinas, after one of his favorite writers or something. Anyway, I was being paid out for my jest now. I was in agony.

Don't get me wrong, I was very glad to be in Pisa, after a seemingly endless trek through the Florentine hills. I used to love the view of the hills from the safety of the city, when they are misty and blue green and far away. But clopping over them on a reluctant pony, when every step feels like you are being shafted by the entire Florentine army, all at once, is no joke, I can tell you. Particularly when the hills at last gave way to the Pisan flatlands, stale, level marshes with a salty stink and a dun color, stretching as far as the eye could see, and depressing the spirits till I felt as low as the landscape. Add to that the stink of cowshit, the flies in the daytime, and the mosquitoes at night. I itched all over and was now more bites than flesh. I am definitely a city girl.

But the city of Pisa, when we finally reached it, seemed no more than a pale imitation of my Florence, a city that I loved more with each step I took away from it. Now I didn't recall all the fear and the murder and the blood—only the golden palaces, and warm baths with rose petals floating, and hot salty food for my greedy stomach. I certainly tested Brother Guido's devotion as I constantly whined and moaned and complained for the entire journey. He showed great restraint, the bastard, not even giving me the satisfaction of a sparring partner, but as we approached the city and I began to criticize his beloved home, I could see my barbs were beginning to penetrate. I am a bitch, it is true, but before you pass judgment upon me, remember that I was saddle sore, mosquito-bit, starving, bone-cold, and soaked to the skin. And I hadn't had a man for five days. Oh, yes, and was on the run for my life.

As we crossed the Arno, its surface torrid with the pelting rain, Guido drew his cowl closer over his head, to shut out the tempest and my complaints together. He soon found a solution to my griping though, an irritating catchall answer to my constant questions.

"Where are we going?"

"You will see."

"Where is this famous tower? Is that it?" I pointed to a rickety crenellation on the river, dilapidated and listing, hung with filthy linens to be cleansed by the rain. Brother Guido's blue eyes flashed, but he ignored my insult. "You will see."

"Well." I was relentless. "This certainly is a beauteous city." My argument was assisted by a wight who dropped his hose and pushed out three turds into the river from his bare arse. "Where is all this miraculous architecture?"

"You will see."

It worked. I could get no more than that single phrase out of my monkish friend, and at length we came to a great wall with an arched gate within. Above the arch was a great stone shield bearing the Medici arms of six great balls in a ring. The arms made me feel oddly at home. But I was about to see something that I had never seen in Florence. As we went below, Brother Guido said the single word, "Now."

And I did see.

As we passed the gateway the rain stopped abruptly, as if delimited by the wall. The sun shone and a glorious rainbow arced above the most beautiful sight I had ever seen in my short life.

Madonna.

There, set into a deep green meadow studded with diamond raindrops, towered a holy trinity of the finest buildings ever seen. I slid from my mount, mouth slack with wonder. In the bright sun the white Cathedral was a dazzling marble casket, the Baptistery a perfectly balanced round jewel of a building, crowned with a filigree diadem. And most fantastic of all, the campanile, leaning at an impossible angle. The fabled tower reached into the sky with layer upon layer of perfectly arched loggias, slender galleries, and arcades of snowy white, spiraling round and ever upward in their lofty measure. All in all, the place was a miracle of balance and beauty, and as I dimly heard Brother Guido smugly telling me the place was called Campo dei Miracoli—"the field of the miracles"—I could only nod feebly in agreement. All were on an immense scale, as if a race of giants had come to this green garden to build their wonders.

"Magnificent, is it not?" said Brother Guido in an ecstasy of understatement. "And beyond"—he pointed to a long blind wall—"is the Camposanto, the cemetery, a perfect rectangular cloister boasting many wonders within. The soil for the foundations was brought from Golgotha, yes, all the way from the Holy Land." I still could not speak as we walked forth among the great buildings, but I sensed that I had somehow been forgiven. "Well, Luciana," said the monk, "your obvious state of awe mitigates your earlier churlishness somewhat. For here is the true glory of my city, which took three centuries to realize. They say that this *campo* perfectly represents our journey to God. It is said," continued my friend with enthusiasm, "that in the Baptistery we are baptized to faith, in the Cathedral we celebrate it, in the Camposanto we await resurrection, and in the tower"—he pointed high—"we reach up to the divine heights of the Kingdom of Heaven."

I allowed Brother Guido his triumph and forgave him his wordy explanations, for the place was truly a marvel, made unique by the crazy collapsing campanile. The monk echoed my thoughts with his next speech. "I find the tower is rendered more beautiful, not less, by the imperfection of its stance. And you can see at once, can you not, from the shape and the incline, that the tower is indeed the edifice that Botticelli's Graces describe in the *Primavera,* with the negative space between their clasped hands."

He was right, the relationship was exact. We were certainly in the right place to begin our quest. Now at the base of the tower, I was frightened and exhilarated at once by the sight. To look directly up at the structure was to feel as if it could fall at any moment and crush me flat. Excited at last to speech, I asked a single question. "Can we go up?"

Brother Guido seemed pleased by my continued enthusiasm, a welcome contrast, I'll wager, from my humor of the last few days. "Yes," he said. "If you are not afraid."

I was afraid. "Of course I'm not. Why should I be afraid?"

"Because they say the thing will come down in under a year. Mind you, they've been saying that ever since it was built."

I shrugged, but in truth would have been sorry to see such a splendid structure fall into rubble—sorrier still if I was within. But I tied my pony by the tower's dark door as Brother Guido did likewise, and kilted my skirts ready for the climb.

"There is a stair within," he said. "We must look for anything which tells us of the tower's connection with the *Primavera*. And take care. The incline, together with the circles you must describe with your feet as you ascend, can be somewhat disorienting."

Brother Guido was not wrong. Before we even reached the second gallery I already felt as if I had had a couple of bottles of Chianti. But I was enjoying myself—not just from the sensation of drunkenness, which all seemed so long ago, but because my spirits rose, too, as we climbed. My feminine wiles returned as I clasped Brother Guido's arm, giggled to punctuate my steps, and fell against his body as oft as I could. 'Twas not much for one as prick-hungry as I, and his complete indifference offered me little comfort, but it was better than naught. Most delightful of all, though, were the glimpses of the green fields below, and the beautiful sight of the Duomo and Baptistery laid out in a great white cross below. At last we reached the top, and I could admire the view of what was, I had to admit, a breathtaking city. For long moments we lingered, the painting all but forgot, enjoying the scene below, with the ant-sized humans scuttling about between the great white behemoths. At length, though, I noted a gathering crowd, as the ants became a swarm and began to congregate in a square far below. "What's going on?" I said, pointing, my breastbone squeezed against the warm stone balustrade as I strained to look.

Brother Guido, in a fatherly gesture of protection which touched me not a little, grabbed the tail of my skirt. "Take care." He moved beside me to look. "Ah. They're getting ready to begin."

"Who is 'they'?"

"Among others," he said, "my uncle. And they're getting ready for the Gioco del Ponte, which is held on this day every year. I was hoping we'd be in time." He began to move toward the doorway of the gallery, to begin the long descent.

"And what is the 'jocco del pointy'?" I called after him.

He glanced back with a teasing smile. "You will see."

I followed Brother Guido down the tower, but this time he was so far ahead that I saw no more than a flutter of his coarse brown habit at the turn of the stair, or heard the patter of his sandals on the gallery below. But at last we reached the outer door that led us out onto the *campo* and we were untying our mounts when I saw it.

"Look!" There was a carving, just beside the lintel of the tower's door, a pin-sharp relief in the white marble, its angles newly chiseled and freshly cut, the lines of the design black in the strong sun. It was a ship: a fine ship with billowing sails and a sturdy crenellated forecastle, riding atop curvy waves so cleverly rendered that you could swear the petrified ocean was undulating before your eyes. "Does it mean something?" I wondered aloud. "For it was the stone tower cut above your door in Santa Croce that led me to see the tower in the *Primavera*, the very tower we now stand beneath."

Brother Guido shrugged. "A ship," he said. "Quite commonplace. Pisa is famous for its maritime might; it is a regular emblem in our art and architecture."

"But this carving is *new*—you can all but smell the marble dust." I once serviced a stonemason in Florence, who covered my best gowns in the snow-white dust of Carrara marble. If he hadn't paid so well, I would have been quite annoyed. But the smell—the sweet, almost burnt smell of fresh-cut marble—that same smell crept into my nostrils now.

But the brother was already on his pony. "It cannot be. The tower was finished more than a century ago."

I mounted Pene, but as I followed Brother Guido I looked back more than once at the stone ship by the door until it receded from sight. The carving, and its newness, together with Brother Guido's assertion of Pisa's maritime might, gave me an odd feeling. I followed his swift trot into the main thoroughfare as the crowd grew thicker and louder, and by the time I had remembered where I had heard such sentiments before, the noise and the press of people was too great to shout to the monk. Three maritime states. Pisa, Naples, Genoa. They were the words I had said to Botticelli.

The words that could get me killed.

I I

At length the crowds were so jammed either side of us that my legs were pressed painfully into Pene's sides, and the pony began to fart most noxiously in protest. I noticed with amusement that the crowd behind his arse began to disperse a little to avoid his foul winds. Brother Guido took down his cowl and turned to yell at me.

"Follow me to my uncle, he will see us well seated."

"Where is he?" I bawled. I could not hear his answer but saw his jabbing forefinger point.

Madonna.

We had come at last to a large square, colorful as a parrot, with scenes and frescoes painted on all the square houses around. The buildings themselves were crazy colors: canary yellow, saffron orange. And the people themselves were dressed in such bright weeds to match that they dazzled the eye: sashes and ribbons, quartered tunics in clashing hues, and shining silver helmets of a military style.

I craned to see what Brother Guido could be indicating, and I saw, set above all the chaos, a high platform decorated with flowers and ribbons. On a central, thronelike chair sat a large, handsome fellow, with a twisted velvet cap and a silken surcoat. His long legs in their party-colored hose disappeared from the knee down into a veritable sea of fine greyhounds which wound about his feet, barking at any that passed. His household stood about him, offering wine and meats, in livery near as splendid as his own. But though the finery piqued my whore's interest, as a woman it was the fellow's countenance that held my attention. His face had a high magenta color of good living which set off the startling blue eyes. Brother Guido's eyes. And but for the blurring of age, the face was Brother Guido's too.

The uncle.

Brother Guido hailed his kinsman from the crowd, and I felt at once uneasy, for it had been our notion, decided on the road, to approach him unseen, not in so public an arena. But I knew that Brother Guido felt safe in this place, for it was his home, and that help was too near at hand for him to hold back. His uncle's face split into a delighted smile at the sight of his nephew, and a single motion of the lord's hand was enough to send the largest of his retainers to part the crowd and reach our mounts. This giant of a fellow bowed to Guido and took our leading reins, bellowing at the crowd to make way. In less than an instant I was seated in the loge at the nobleman's left hand, holding a cup of *very* fine Chianti and receiving an introduction to Lord Silvio Gherardesca della Torre. He kissed my hand most courteously, though Christ knew what I must look like, all bedraggled and besmottered from the road. Nor did he inquire of my relationship to his nephew. Instead, he showed a gentlemanly courtesy as he presented his giant to us. "This is Tok, my Hungarian mercenary, who did save you from the crush of our good citizens. He saved my life once, in my campaigns in Lombardy, and now wishes he hadn't." The giant did not smile; indeed, it was not clear if such an expression would be possible for him, as his face was a maze of scars. His eyes were as small as his head was large; hard and dark and round as twin cannonballs sunk in a battlefield. He might have been any age from twenty to forty, but his mass and his scars made it impossible to divine. We thanked him guardedly.

"It wass my pleasure," Tok replied, bowing slightly, "and vil be my pleasure to protect your persons in any way I can, during your stay with my lord."

His strangled, guttural Tuscan was hard to make out, and I suspected he had once taken a blade to the throat, perhaps in his master's cause? But there was no doubt that with the wine warming my belly, the protection of this monolith of a mercenary, and the kind attentions of his master, I was beginning to feel much better. I quite liked Pisa. The people seemed charming. The customs quaint. I took another slug of wine as Lord Silvio conversed with Brother Guido, who was now as comfortably seated as myself, but on the right hand of his uncle. I wondered what they were saying—how would Brother Guido explain my person, my presence at his side? I caught his glance once, and he smiled and nodded, as if to reassure me that we were at the end of our journey and were safe and well. I began to relax and look around me. Below us there was clearly some local spectacle unfolding, as the center of the square began to empty. Marshals ran into the space to organize two teams, and buglers cracked their cheeks to blow a fanfare.

Lord Silvio leaned close to address me, and I stiffened briefly, thinking that he might interrogate me about my presence alongside his chaste nephew. But it became clear that he merely wished to explain the festivities to me. Whatever interim explanation Brother Guido had given him, it must have satisfied his curiosity for now, although their brief conference could not possibly have included all the details of our adventures. I stopped worrying and became conscious of the warmth of Lord Silvio's licorice-scented breath on my ear and throat, which made me tingle still further. Yes, Brother Guido's uncle was certainly an attractive, mature man, and as we conversed I gave him the benefit of all my most practiced flirtations. Though I wished I'd had a mirror to correct my appearance.

"Signorina," began the lord, "you are about to witness one of our oldest Pisan customs, instituted in our fair city by the emperor Hadrian himself. The Giugno Pisano, or Pisan games, end with the Gioco del Ponte." I recognized the words from those Brother Guido had spoken on the tower. "It is an old rivalry between the parties of the Cockerel"—he pointed to a gaggle of young men dressed in red and orange—"and the Magpie." This time he indicated the opposite team, on the far side of the square, wearing pied tunics of black and white. "You will notice that my own man, Tok, is dressed for the Cockerels, for that is my own team, even though, as the lord of this place, I must not be partisan." He smiled an attractive smile, and I could see that, despite his middle age, his teeth were still good.

To be truthful, I cared not for games, but would certainly enjoy the sight of four-and-twenty prime specimens of manhood tussling, while Lord Silvio's servants plied me with wine. As if we lived in a fairy tale, a golden carriage with gilded wheels and panels painted in the della Torre colors appeared at the foot of the loge. Lord Silvio himself handed me in, and settled me on the velvet cushions. He took his place beside me, with Brother Guido opposite, and told me, "You, Signorina Luciana, shall be my mascot for the day, and a lovelier one I have never seen."

My tomcat's grin was frozen by the dour look on Brother Guido's face. "Cheer up," I whispered. "He probably means that I'm wearing a dress of red and orange, the colors of the Cockerel party." For indeed my travel-stained dress had once been a handsome gown of those hues. Brother Guido did not look convinced, but the carriage jolted and we were off. I saw him thaw a little as the carriage passed through the streets, for even *he* had to be enjoying the fact that, in a matter of hours, we had been transformed from a couple of freezing pilgrims to the fortunate favorites of the local lord. Brother Guido began to point out well-loved landmarks with his uncle, and in his usual wordy way, he began to acquaint me with the spectacle that we were about to see. At last I could see the glittering silver Arno, bright as a new ribbon in the sun, so different now from the mire of sludge I had crossed earlier in the hammering rain. Then I had been atop a skinny pony. Now I rode in a golden carriage. The day was certainly improving. The crowd, meantime, was parting like the Red Sea, and Brother Guido explained, "You may see, signorina, that the crowd is dividing to the north and south banks, to indicate the ancient historical opposition between the parties of the Mezzogiorno and Tramontana."

I did notice, but I noticed, too, that he had become more formal with me in the presence of his uncle. We had become "Brother Guido" and "Luciana" on the road (he would never call me "Chi-chi"), but now I was back to "signorina." Before I had time to ponder this, he went on.

."The people are getting ready to support the colors of their own *magistratura,* or court. The *magistratura* is the political-military organization of a city quarter or of the team which participates in the Game of the Bridge."

God, he could be boring. It was fortunate that he was so pretty. I stifled a yawn. "So what actually happens in this game?" I just wanted more wine. I didn't even care about my appearance anymore, which is very unusual for me.

"Essentially, each team must push a large battering ram weighing more than seven tons across the old bridge—this one we are approaching now—while the other team tries to stop them. It is a wonderful contest where elements of folklore fuse with the proud warrior tradition of the parties, where each bank of the Arno fights for sovereignty over the bridge."

These Pisanos were clearly insane. "Are you actually telling me that all this spectacle is to do with two bunches of dressed-up men pushing a large log over a bridge, while the other lot try to push it the other way?"

Brother Guido visibly deflated. "Yes."

Madonna. But I was aware of Lord Silvio's amusement as he watched us, and quickly returned to my flattering mode. "How wonderful! And what a fitting . . . celebration of the might of this great city," I finished weakly and felt my praise had been unconvincing.

Indeed, Lord Silvio had detected my scorn. "The people enjoy it, and always have. It is their only chance for a real, honest-to-goodness scrap. You see, Pisa has little to do with landlocked combat, but at sea, well, our maritime forces cannot be matched, even by such cities as Genoa and Naples."

And there it was again—that trinity of seagoing cities, bringing a small chill to my day like a cloud passing over the face of the sun. In truth, I had all but forgotten the *Primavera,* and now felt the whisper of danger again. But uncle and nephew smiled their twin smiles and our carriage drew in to the center of the bridge, where Lord Silvio was well placed to adjudicate the heats. As far as the eye could see, crowds lined both banks of the Arno, dressed in their partisan colors, cheering themselves hoarse. I watched the first few heats, enjoying the sight of young men straining against each other to push the massive phallic rams over the bridge. But even the sight of the bulging muscles began to pall, and I soon saw that the mighty mercenary Tok was (literally) carrying the Cockerel team to victory for the Tramontana side of the river. He had followed us on foot from the Piazza delle Sette Vie, leading Pene and Aquinas on their reins, but still had the energy to join the fray with enthusiasm. His bulk and strength made the huge battering ram seem as light as a matchstalk, and the opposing team fell a dozen times at its mighty prow. I watched as he skillfully smashed his ram at the Magpie's team, once dispatching three young men at a time, to be carried into the crowd by their womenfolk and patched up by a hovering apothecary. Yes, Tok was a bull of a man, and with his protection I felt proof against any assassins that the city of Florence may have sent after us.

Toward the end of the interminable contest, I retreated into the golden carriage to enjoy the wine and delicacies handed through the window by the servants. I was nearly asleep when I was jolted by the reentry of Brother Guido and Lord Silvio, their shining faces telling me that the rooster party had won the day. I quickly showered them with congratulations, and joined in as best I could with their detailed analysis of the stratagems and heats. When there was a pause at last in the self-congratulation, I asked, "And are there more delights to the day?"

Lord Silvio smiled. "The best of all. Now comes the feasting, for it is the eve of our saint's day." Now he was talking my language. My stomach growled in anticipation.

"Saint Ranieri," put in Brother Guido, "was a great man and fine musician, who put all his wealth aside to become a humble hermit in the service of God." His eyes shone again, this time with devotion not triumph, and I saw that Pisa's patron saint had been more than a little inspiration to the young lordling to put away his inheritance and take orders in the church. But I had no time for liturgy right now; I wanted to hear more about the feast.

"At my palazzo"—Lord Silvio waved his hand down the bank of the river, where the great houses were already studded with diamonds of candlelit windows—"we will hold such a feast as you have never seen. My guests will enjoy the finest dishes, and you, signorina, as a friend of my well-beloved nephew, will be the guest of honor."

I was practically salivating by the time the carriage drew to a stop at a fine, square palace right on the river. Once again the lord himself alighted and waved away his footman so that he might personally hand me out of the carriage. I lurched down the steps and smiled happily as I righted myself. "What a wonderful day!" I slurred into his face.

The lord seemed pleased. "You like Pisa, then?"

I had had the best part of two bottles of Chianti and nothing to eat save a few salted anchovies and a handful of apricots. I liked everything at that moment. "Yes." I spoke carefully, trying hard to control my drink-numbed tongue. "It is a very. Fair. City."

He lifted my chin with his gloved hand, in a tender gesture, and shot me through with the eyes that were so like Brother Guido's. "Much fairer now, signorina. Much fairer now." He turned with a flourish of his cloak and started up the torchlit steps. "Come. Let's go in. We'll feast in Saint Ranieri's name and enjoy what the night brings." He offered me his arm and caressed my form with unmistakably hot eyes. By contrast, Brother Guido looked like thunder as he followed us into the palazzo. Unseen, I allowed a small smile to play on my lips. 'Twould be an interesting night indeed.

12

"What, in the name of God and all the saints, do you think you are doing?"

We were now in a sumptuous bedchamber, clearly a lady's. There were delicate diamond panes of glass in the windows, which showed a fine view of the twilit Arno. A four-poster bed with a red and gilt coverlet invited me, and a finely worked tapestry of the Garden of Eden adorned one entire wall. I could not have been happier. Back in luxury's lap where I belonged, I could not care less about the silly *Primavera* and its silly secrets. What were they to me, Principessa of Pisa? I had found Eden indeed, but there was a serpent in my Paradise, in the shape of Brother Guido, lecturing me as if I had just munched the apple and caused the fall of man.

It was the nearest I had ever seen Brother Guido come to anger, after all that I had done to him. Even when he had heard his best friend's head splash into the well of Santa Croce's cloister, he had not reproached me for my stupidity. Nor had he ever blamed me for my inclusion of his own person in this dangerous escapade. My drink-addled mind ran through any transgressions that I might have committed that day, but came up empty. I thought I had been perfectly charming. "What do you mean?"

The answer was a surprise. "Flirting with my uncle like a common—" He stopped himself. "You are tempting him into sin and dishonoring the name of my aunt."

"And where is your aunt? How have I injured her?"

"She has been dead these ten years past."

Shit. I had made a gaffe, but that only made me even more bullish. "Ten years!" My exclamation came out as a neigh worthy of Pene. "Jesu, let the poor man have a little fun before his dotage! He has grieved enough. And in case you had forgot, I *am,* in fact, a common whore."

He looked sad. "I hoped you may have left that life behind, that the one good to come from this whole misadventure might be that I could lift you out of that life, just as I intended when first we met." Then the anger returned. "And whatever *you* may be, *he* is a respectable man, and overlord of this town. It is not seemly. You are damaging his position."

"I'm just getting him to *like* me, so he might be more inclined to help us!" I lied, for I had enjoyed the male attention and the promise of more. If I couldn't have the nephew, the uncle would do for now. I'd happily butter his trumpet for a few florins, but sensed I shouldn't admit this. I swiftly turned the debate around. "And what about you? I thought we were concealing our presence to protect your uncle. We came from Florence in two days on a couple of old ponies—do you not think those that seek us might do likewise? Are you not placing him in danger by consorting so openly with him?"

This last came home to roost. Brother Guido sat on the coverlet, face drained of color, the humble brown stuff of his habit making a contrast with the silken sheets of the four-poster bed. He sighed the anger out of him. "You are right," he admitted. "I have been most rash. I was so relieved to see him, and so thankful for his help, that I allowed myself to accept his protection openly, and his hospitality too. I have, indeed, placed him in danger, and broken my fast, and enjoyed the spectacle of the day when I should have been at prayer. I had no right to reproach you. It is *I* who have sinned. And God will scourge me for it." He turned his blue eyes on me, now beseeching. "What are we to do?"

I sat beside him, feeling bad. "Take heart," I said. "We are now under his protection, and under the protection of that pet mercenary of his."

"Tok."

"The very one. Let us make the best of it. We will feast tonight, or *I* will," I amended hastily as he shook his head, "and when the guests have gone we will show your uncle the painting and ask him the best course of action. We are openly in his household; well, let it be known, and let us appeal to him for all the help that we may."

He nodded. "You are right." He stood and looked from my window into the dusk. The bells rang out in the darkening city and brought him out of his reverie. "They are ringing Vespers," he said. "There are but two hours until the feast—make yourself ready as best you can, I will see you downstairs." He pulled up his hood and made to leave the room.

"Where are you going?" I asked, suddenly panicked.

"To mass," he said, "there is a little church, hard by here, called Santa Maria della Spina. There is a reliquary within, which bears one of the original *spina*."

I showed him a blank face.

"A thorn from the crown of the crucified Christ. I will pray before it and repent of my sins, as *he* did with *his* last breath." He gave me a specter of a smile and was gone. For a moment, I felt disquiet—although we had fought, I did not want to be separated from my only friend, did not want any ill to befall him on the dark streets. All this talk of last breaths was making me nervous. But as I turned to regard my reflection in the looking glass, I forgot my fears.

Madonna.

I looked like an escaped lunatic. My dress, once the finest I owned, put on five days ago to please Bembo, was crusted with mud and sweat, and the dyes had run in orange rivulets down the cheap silk from the rainfall. My hair was a bird's nest, standing out from my head and straggling down over my back and shoulders, looking more like straw than gold. My fine miniver cloak was now matted and greasy as a wolf's pelt, and my face had been tanned from my journey to a disgusting peasant brown (so far from the porcelain white I was used to), so my eyes shone out like green jade glittered with drink, like a moon-mad crazy. I could have screamed. How could I have mingled eyes with Lord Silvio when I looked no better than a leprous beggar?

I had to do something. I pressed one hand to each cheek, to stop the spinning of my head, and looked around the room. Luckily, the lord (or rather his servants) had thought of everything a lady (or, well, me) might need for her toilet. There was a large copper bowl of tepid water, with days-eyes floating on the surface, and a jug to pour it. There was a bone-toothed comb, such as Bembo had brought me once from Constantinople. There was a little sandalwood chest with a dozen little drawers, containing such ointments, pastes, and unguents as I knew that other ladies used to enhance their looks. I had never needed such things before, but today the case was desperate. Finally—I clapped my hands with glee—there was, draped over the bed chest, like a snakeskin waiting for a body, a wondrous gown of green and gold.

Two hours later I was transformed.

I had spent the first hour combing out my madcap hair and

dousing it with water. After it was thoroughly combed and rinsed, I squeezed out the water and twisted the wet mass up onto my head, there to dry while I worked on the rest of me. I could already see, as I began to wash my face, that the blond tendrils over my ears and forehead were already drying and curling up into their accustomed ringlets, fair and fluffy as a day-old chick. Good.

Now for the body. I was caked in mud and sweat and smelled like a week-old haddock. One sniff of my own crotch almost made me faint. I used the rest of the water, and the rough flannel provided, to rub every inch of my tanned flesh till it was rosy with health and cleanliness. I even spat on the pearl in my navel and rubbed it till it glowed. Then, cleaned and wrapped in a silken robe, I did something which I know will disgust you. I picked out the flowerheads and drank all the water I had washed in.

Now before you judge me, hear this. My housemate Enna—God rest her rotten soul—said she once fucked a Spaniard who told her that if you have drunk overmuch wine you should drink the same volume in water, and in a little while you will feel much refreshed. And he was right—I did. (I must say that was a valuable little piece of advice he gave Enna. He also gave her crabs, but that was her problem, not mine.)

So when the bells rang for Vespers I was ready, sober as a friar, taking an inventory of my new persona in the looking glass. My hair now shone in a rippling sheet of gold to my waist, softened by the curls that framed my face. I had rubbed an ointment into my skin that I had found in the cabinet, which had a fine sheen to it, as if a million tiny flakes of gold had been mixed within. Although still tanned, my flesh now glowed as if something ethereal. The green and gold gown clung to my body, which was somewhat thinner than I would have liked from my days on the road, but the famous Chi-chi *tette* were still there, thankfully undiminished by my trial. The gown was cut cleverly so that my breasts were concealed and revealed in equal measure, in the best of taste. I had no jewels, so I took the days-eyes I had saved from my bathwater and twisted them in my hair. My reflection was breathtaking, but the flowers reminded me of the *Primavera* and my role as Flora in that painting. I took the *cartone,* the miniature copy of that picture, from the bodice of my old gown, and tucked it safely down the front of my new one. Tonight, Brother Guido and I would share the secret of the *Primavera* at last, and finally we would have an ally. With a mixture of fear and excitement, I turned from the looking glass and went downstairs.

The grand white marble stairs of the palazzo led directly down into a spacious salon where the splendid-looking guests were already gathering. As I descended I could see a rainbow of silks and velvets, birds of paradise in their saint's-day finery. There was a hum of chatter, as the Pisanos gobbled away to each other in their odd dialect like so many turkeys. A hush descended along with me, and I saw, among the white blobs of upturned faces, Lord Silvio and Brother Guido. (I sighed relief as I saw my friend unscathed.) The former nodded with appreciation, the latter let his chin drop with slack-jawed amazement at my transformation. I could not blame him, really, for he had never seen Chi-chi in her full glory—by the time I had sought him out at Santa Croce I was already panicked and blood spattered, and on the road I had been naught but a bedraggled harlot. Now, he appreciated the full force of my beauty for the first time. I felt a little tingle of pleasure. Could I begin to hope that I would one day turn him from God to the pleasures of the flesh—my flesh? Well, if not him, then there were many men in the salon, as I mingled through to my host, that cast such appreciative glances at me I knew I could turn a good few tricks this night if I got the chance. And about time too—I am not accustomed to being prick-starved for as long as this.

I hid my profane thoughts behind a mask of smiling innocence as I greeted Lord Silvio and his nephew with propriety fitting to the event. Lord Silvio had clearly heard a little of my history by now, but he kindly did not allude to my actual status in life. Instead, he showed his superior manners by courteously weaving a little fantasy about my origins as he led me to the dining solar.

"Signorina Vetra, tonight you resemble the finest ladies of the Venetian court, for it can be stated plainly that no lady who waits on even the doge himself can boast a fraction of your charms. You are an ornament to Tuscany."

I smiled as a servant drew out my chair. "Your nephew told you, then, that I hail from Venice."

A nod. "He did. And I can heartily believe it. You resemble the very best of the northern type, with your blond tresses and light eyes. In fact, I once knew a lady in Venice who resembles you very closely. She—" He broke off. "No matter. Let it be said that you certainly have no rival, neither in that state nor this."

He then turned to address the ever-present Tok, who was hovering at his shoulder. They both seemed to be discussing the empty chair at the lord's right hand, and I was able to turn to Brother Guido on my left.

"Did you tell him anything about the painting?" The words burst forth from him like poniards.

I rolled my eyes. I knew he was a man of the cloth, but surely he could make an effort to emulate his uncle's manners? "Luciana, you look incredible in your finery," I corrected sardonically. "I could scarcely believe it was you. How privileged I feel to be your escort this eve."

Brother Guido's smile was small. "You know that we holy

brothers do not think of such things. Our minds are occupied by higher matters, and the only beauty we mark is that of the Lord God and his beloved Son." He crossed himself.

I snorted unattractively, then smiled at the servant that poured me wine. "Really. Well, you looked fairly appreciative when I was coming down the stairs. Or was that God's skirt you were looking up, while your mouth caught flies?" It was too easy. He reddened.

"I . . . was merely surprised at the alteration in your person, no more, I can assure you. And allow me to counsel you against the sin of vanity, for it is a heinous fault and can lead you into ruin."

I sighed. "In answer to the question that came before the sermon, no, I did not ask your uncle about the painting. I thought there too many people gathered."

He nodded and made as if to continue, but I had a question of my own. "The empty chair at your uncle's left, is that for his son? For you have a cousin, do you not?"

"Yes. Niccolò. But no, he is not yet here."

"Then where is he?" Another thought struck me. "And where was he all day, for that matter? Surely he should have been at your uncle's side for all the festivities?"

"He is at the university."

"Where? Padua, Bologna?" I named two of the three universities I know. The third, here in Pisa, would not explain his absence.

"No, here in Pisa." He smiled wryly at my surprise. "He is expected tonight, as you see." Brother Guido's voice was heavy with irony.

"But will not come?"

Brother Guido shrugged, and I could see his reluctance to speak ill of another man, especially a kinsman. But I saw more dislike in that shrug than I had ever seen him express, and more censure than he had ever given, even to those nameless ones that had murdered our friends. "He is not, perhaps, as mindful of his duty as Lord Silvio might like. But as an only son, he may act as he pleases and still be assured of preferment."

"Why?" I was belligerent. "I have heard of many cases when an undeserving son is disinherited in favor of another. Why does not your uncle do that?"

Brother Guido looked me full in the eyes, with his blue gaze. "Because the only other potential heir that he loves and trusts decided to become a monk."

Madonna. I saw it all now. Silvio loved his nephew Guido better than his own son, Niccolò. Niccolò was undeserving, but before Silvio could elevate Guido to the status of heir, Guido found his calling and took the habit. "And does . . . your uncle not try to dissuade you from your path?"

"All the time," admitted Brother Guido ruefully. "For you see, he has in every way been a father to me. I lost my parents to the plague of 1460—I was too young to mourn them. My uncle schooled me and raised me, taught me all that a young noble should know. He was always mindful that fate had given him the inheritance that could have been mine, for he was a younger son, and my father's death had given him the city. Thus he treated me with no less favor than his trueborn son; at times, with more," he admitted, and shook his head. "I do not say it was right, and certainly it fostered no great love toward me in my cousin's heart. But as I grew and read widely of the Scriptures and others of my uncle's devotional books, I heard God calling to me. I agreed to enter the Franciscans as a novice, with my uncle's blessing, for a year—to consider my calling before taking full vows. But my mind is now made up," he finished with resolution.

I looked back to Lord Silvio and felt sorry for him. Yes, I, a humble jade, looked up at a great lord and felt sympathy. For here he was, in his own house, sitting between a no-good whore and an empty chair on *his* saint's day, staring into space as his son humiliated him with his absence, while his well-beloved nephew was lost to him as an heir. I pressed Lord Silvio's hand to recall him to himself and began to praise the placement of the table, determined that he should enjoy his night.

And indeed, there was much to praise, without my having to perjure myself. Each course that followed was more magnificent than the next. I stuffed myself happily with hare's testicles, so small and smooth that you could swallow them whole, fresh-caught *lipioti,* tiny octopus with two tiny front teeth, sharp as barbs, which you must remove before eating them, and coal-black pasta made with the ink of a squid. Then there was a positive menagerie of stuffed meats on the groaning board; little deers and immense boars, roasted and sewn back into their skins, eyes staring glassily at those that had come to devour them. There was even a peacock, cooked and mounted with his glorious green-blue tail replaced to fan out as a centerpiece. I ate until my dress bit at the seams, and drank heartily, and laughed with Lord Silvio, and had a thoroughly good evening.

Brother Guido, I noted, ate nothing and drank only water, for he intended to fast. A platter of oysters, which he had told me upon the road were his favorite food, was placed before me, for the three of us to share. Now I never eat oysters, don't ask me why—I think it's partly to do with the fact that they make the pearls, like the one in my navel, and partly because they remind me of swallowing a man's seed, which I have to do enough in my line of work without doing it in my leisure time too. I pushed the gold platter toward Brother Guido. "Go on," I tempted him. "Your favorite."

He looked at me as if I were the Devil in the wilderness, pressed his full lips together into a line, and shook his dark curls. "I must not," he said. "I am fasting in honor of Saint Ranieri who did inspire me to my calling."

"Surely oysters don't count! They are Lenten fare, peasant food!"

He shook his head again. "From daybreak tomorrow I may eat again, but not before the saint's day dawns."

I shrugged, and moved the platter toward his uncle, for I would not have the righteous monk suffer the pains of denial needlessly, whatever you may think of me. But as I moved the plate I swept some of the nobbly shells into my lap, there to conceal them in my apronlike overskirt. He could not eat till morning? Well, then I would save half a dozen for his breakfast. His uncle, meantime, ate heartily of the rest of the plate; clearly the love of these ugly shellfish ran in the family.

After the oysters came the sweetmeats, and I stuffed myself once again with meringues, marchpane, and little pastries from the Orient. And then came the climax of the feast; two servants carried in a most wonderful pudding made exactly in the likeness of the leaning tower, the white sugar artfully describing the layered arcades and colonnades, even the bell tower on top. The thing was placed on the table, where it leaned authentically, amid a burst of applause from the guests. Brother Guido and I exchanged a look. Seeing the tower again, remembering the very shape that the Botticelli's Graces described with their hands, reminded us that the hour had come when we must share what we knew. Even the steady presence of Tok at the lord's shoulder did not prevent a sudden shiver. The sugar tower was soon demolished and the platters carried around. I saw, as had happened all evening, that the empty place by the empty chair was served with a platter as if an invisible guest sat there, and the plates and delicacies were beginning to mount up like a scullery sink. On the other side of me, Brother Guido refused his plate, and I admired his abstinence in the face of such delights, as much as I admired the beauty in his stoic face. The pudding was delicious, but as I enjoyed the burst of sweetness I became aware at the same time of a sour little pain just below my heart at the thought that, in under a year, Guido della Torre would take full vows and be lost to me forever.

At length, the final guest had gone, and the two della Torres and I were closeted together in the library tower of the palazzo, a fine room with four glazed windows looking to the four points of the compass, and the rest of the walls lined with books. Lord Silvio was clearly as fond of reading as his nephew. I had never seen so many books in one place before. The three of us hunched around the well-lit reading table in the center of the room, like a trio of generals perusing a wartime map. Lord Silvio looked at the painting for long moments before speaking. His face inscrutable, he tapped his left thumb on the table as if beating out a measure. This digit was adorned with a golden thumb ring, decorated with nine golden balls, and the ring sounded in my head like a bell. I was ready to scream when at last he spoke, and when he did, it was to say something entirely unexpected.

"It is *indeed* beautiful. They said it would be." And then, hurriedly, "I have heard of Signor Botticelli's work but have never yet seen an example. And you *stole* it, signorina? Right from under the fellow's nose?"

I hung my head, but the lord smiled.

"I cannot censure you, having seen it. Anyone would want such a thing."

"Others do want it," Brother Guido interjected grimly. "We were pursued through Florence and are perhaps hounded even now. Both of our closest friends have died in our stead,

and one of Luciana's . . . clients"—he choked over the word—
"in pursuit of this painting."

Now Lord Silvio's brow furrowed. "But they have the original. Signor Botticelli has his painting; this is just the *cartone*,
surely?"

Brother Guido nodded, his shadow nodding agreement in
the candlelight. "Yes. But what we fear, Uncle, is that they do
not merely desire the return of the *cartone*. We believe that the
painting contains a message, and they think we know what it
is, and they wish to eliminate our very beings, for fear of our
knowledge."

"It looks like an allegory of some sort, certainly," agreed his
uncle. "Perhaps . . . it puts one in mind of the *Stanze* of Poliziano . . ."

Madonna. Not him too.

"So I thought also," put in Brother Guido eagerly, "but
there seems to be a deeper, political meaning. Signor Botticelli
was moved to great anger when Luciana joined the names of
Pisa, Naples, and Genoa in her discourse."

"Pisa, Naples, and Genoa?" The lord turned his eyes on me,
not lustful now but thoughtful. "These are all great maritime
states."

"Exactly. And we believe that it is these great cities, not
goddesses of allegory, that are represented by the three Graces
here."

Lord Silvio peered closer. "And which figure is Pisa in this
theorem of yours?"

Brother Guido pointed. "Here, above the figure of the central Grace, the joined hands of the Graces describe exactly the
edifice of our leaning tower."

Lord Silvio shrugged. "An interesting coincidence surely,
but no more."

"And furthermore, this blinded figure of Cupid points his

arrow exactly at her head. Here is where the quest is supposed to start."

Now Lord Silvio studied his nephew. "Quest?"

"Yes. Into the meaning of the painting. Three of the figures are cities. What do the remainder represent? We have stumbled on a secret, *zio,* and someone does not want us to know what it is."

Now for something really odd. Lord Silvio burst into a volley of false laughter, so loud that it rang around the walls of the library tower. But a heartbeat before he had given way to mirth, I had seen another emotion in his eyes.

Fear, naked fear.

We waited for his hilarity to pass, and when it had died he clapped us both on the shoulder as if we were drinking companions. "Nonsense," he said, still smiling broadly. "There is no secret here. These are the three dancing Graces of classical mythology, and no more. You must let this matter drop and return to your lives. I have a much better solution for you than chasing hither and yon, trying to get to the center of a labyrinth of your own making. Why not simply return it?"

Brother Guido sighed with exasperation. I could tell he was disappointed, that he had expected to find an ally in his uncle. He had not expected our great breakthrough to be dismissed out of hand. "Those that seek us would find us in a heartbeat if we return to Florence. And even if they did not, the commune would try Signorina Vetra, and she would lose her nose; perhaps her hands too."

I swallowed at the thought of the brutality that could be meted out by the state. I had been so concerned with the unlawful assassins that pursued us, I had never stopped to think what the recourse of the law would be. But Brother Guido had known and had tried to protect me. *Madonna.* I would never work again without my nose or my pleasure-giving hands.

Lord Silvio nodded, and then a sudden notion lit his face. "There I can help you, both of you. There is one man of Florence, that if you gained his pardon and protection, no man would dare gainsay." He met his nephew's look. "Yes," said Lord Silvio simply. "Il Magnifico, Lorenzo de' Medici himself." He said it as if he were uttering the name of God Almighty.

Now, I only knew three things about the ruler of our city-state of Florence.

Qualcosa Uno: he was stabbed during the Pazzi conspiracy, but escaped while his brother Giuliano was butchered in the cathedral.

Qualcosa Due: he was a banker and therefore richer than Croesus.

Qualcosa Tre: he writes poetry in Tuscan, hence his association with Angelo Poliziano, his poet friend that everyone keeps going on about.

Clearly, by the look on Brother Guido's face, I had underestimated the reach of the man.

"And you could . . . petition for us with him?" he asked his uncle.

Lord Silvio thought for a moment. "I can do better than that. He is a firm friend of my heart, and I will take you to see him on the morrow."

I spoke at last. "Back to Florence?" My heart felt a great gladness and terror at the same time.

He smiled. "No need. He has a palace here, in Pisa, that great palazzo with the red and white brick, that you may have seen today. One whole bank of the river—the Lungarno Mediceo—is named after him and his family. His heralds have given it out that he will be here in residence for the saint's day, tomorrow. Or, I should say, today." For it was well past midnight.

Brother Guido and I gabbled our relieved thanks. Surely, il

Magnifico could protect us. I was already thinking of how I would dress my hair, for what greater feather in my cap than an assignation with the greatest of the Medicis. I had all but forgotten my earlier attraction for Lord Silvio, when he took my hand to lead me down the stair. "I shall see you in the morning, then, nephew," he called over his shoulder to Brother Guido. "And you, signorina," he murmured in lower tones, "come to my chamber when the bells ring for Lauds."

My heart and my cunt thrilled at the words. I was to be bedded after all, and was safe from danger too. I pressed his hand with joy, but 'twas short-lived, for Brother Guido heard.

"My lord!"

Lord Silvio stopped in his tracks.

"You cannot importune Signorina Vetra," began Brother Guido heatedly. "It is not seemly. Think of the saint for whom we celebrate."

Lord Silvio smiled indulgently. "Guido, Guido. How can you, a man of the cloth, understand the ways of the flesh? Besides, God gave us our bodies and our sensations to enjoy. To deny ourselves would be the greater sin."

"I? Not understand?" brayed Brother Guido. "Of course I understand. D'you think because I wear this"—he grabbed a handful of fustian draped over his chest—"that my heart does not beat, that my blood does not flow, that my senses—and yes, my bodily lusts—do not thrill in the face of beauty?" He looked at me then, his face contorted with agony like a damned soul, his eyes shining with tears. "To take the vows is not to *numb* all feeling, but to feel them just as fully yet *deny* bodily pleasures and devote yourself to God. For one night, I ask you to do the same."

His uncle turned once again to go, clearly anxious to avoid argument with one he so loved. But Brother Guido spun him violently round by the shoulder. "If you will not think of God, then think of my aunt, the mother of your son, your dead *wife*." He placed a biting emphasis on the word. "You cannot so dishonor her in this house!"

The shout echoed around the walls, just as laughter had done moments ago. I looked fearfully at Lord Silvio, now sad and still and dangerous in his silence. He spoke in quiet, measured tones that did not for a moment conceal his anger. "My wife was dearly beloved, as the Good Book says, but has been dead for ten years. My son is a weaning milksop, not fit to bear our name. And my nephew"—here two pairs of angry blue eyes mingled in stares that were eerily alike—"should have a care how he tells his uncle how to act within his own walls." And then the sadness drowned the anger. "I'm alone, Guido. With you gone, is there to be no comfort left to me?"

Suddenly he was not a great lord anymore, just a man of middle years, alone in the world despite his wealth and consequence. I felt sorry for him and I know Brother Guido did too. We stood, still as statues, with the painting lying between us in the glimmering light, forgotten in this family conflict, the graceful figures witnesses to what was said. Lord Silvio broke the spell. "Guido, I will see you in the morn. Signorina, later."

I nodded, not sure what to do, afraid of angering either. Brother Guido was silent but once his uncle had left the tower and descended the stair, he suddenly yelled, *"No!"*

But it was too late. The word and the slam of the door at the foot of the stairs came together.

Now, I expected pleas and exhortations from Brother Guido not to meet my assignation, but I got neither. He was gone too, without a word, slamming the oaken door as he went. I moved to roll up the painting and place it in my bodice. I felt sorry for Brother Guido, and was interested to hear that at least he still had a man's feelings and not those of a eunuch. But I had an empty cunt and an empty purse, and nothing would keep me from my appointment that night.

Nothing, that is, but the lord himself. I waited excitedly in my room, pacing by candlelight, waiting for the bells to ring for Lauds and the servant to fetch me. I had washed my nether parts with rose water, and drawn a silken thread through my teeth to cleanse them from the feast. I had emptied the oysters from my skirt into the copper ewer, which had been filled with fresh water, to keep cool for Brother Guido for morning. One sniff of my skirt, though, and I cursed my kind gesture, for it stank like a fishmarket. I rinsed the overskirt and put on a silken chemise instead. The stuff was so fine that my body was clearly visible beneath, but I cared not—easy access is no bad thing in my game. When the bells rang at last, there was a soft knock at the door and I arranged myself prettily on the bed, in case Lord Silvio had come to fetch me himself. But Tok entered, filling the doorframe with his massive bulk, telling me in his weird Tuscan that Lord Silvio sent his apologies, was indisposed, and must defer our meeting. *Shit.*

"Indisposed?" I questioned in my haughtiest voice. "In what manner?"

The mercenary didn't miss a beat. "He iss unwell. Somesing that my lord ate at the feast, mayhap."

The fellow closed the door before I could question him further.

Fuck.

I threw myself back on the pillow and said every curse word that I knew. *Indisposed,* indeed. My lord had clearly had an attack of conscience due to the mewling and canting of his pious nephew. A pox on Brother Guido. I hated him.

I raged for a while, then got below the coverlets, as I knew I must try to sleep. I must be beautiful for my audience with il

Magnifico. But I could not. As I twisted and turned in the gorgeous sheets I reflected that even if Lord Silvio was truly ill then he could not feel worse than I. To be promised bed play and then denied it was so much worse than never having the offer. In truth, I had slept better on the road, in sheep shacks and cow barns, home to fleas and great dollops of shit, than in this luxurious solar. The sky was a watery gray before I gave in and resorted to my unfailing method for inducing sleep. I let my hands drift down my smooth belly, over the pearl in my navel and between my legs to find instead the "pearl" that resided there. As I stroked and arched, I thought of how mine and Lord Silvio's encounter might have gone, but when the sweetness flooded me it was his nephew's face that I pictured, and the same countenance swam before my mind's eye as I drifted at last to sleep.

I slept heavily, and late, and when I woke it was to a crescendo of knocks to my door. A glance at the window told me that I had slept the day away. I rose slowly and ran a dry tongue round my teeth. Would that I had another ewer of water to drink, but the copper by my bedside was swimming with Brother Guido's oysters and I nearly vomited at their fishy stink. I staggered to the door to admit Brother Guido himself.

He greeted me guardedly, clearly not sure how to confront one that had bedded his uncle. I motioned him to come in. "You can crack a smile if you like," I said, "for I spent a night as chaste as you did." (Well, nearly; unless you count my fingersmith's hands beneath the covers.)

He breathed relief. "I am truly glad that your heart, or my uncle's heart, found room for repentance."

I toyed with the idea of letting him think that I had made a sacrifice on his behalf (I could always use the favor for bargaining later), but then decided that if his uncle were ill in truth, my lie would be discovered. "Aye, his heart," I said wryly, "or mayhap his stomach. He was ill in the night, according to that monster that serves him."

Brother Guido was all concern.

"Did you not know?" I asked, softer now.

"No," he said. "I have been all day at the Duomo, hearing a cycle of masses for the saint."

"Well, even you must have prayed enough to break your fast now." I motioned to the copper bowl of water and the oysters I had kept. He actually smiled as he sat down on the coverlet, ready to enjoy his deferred feast. " 'Tis most kind of you, for in truth, I am famished." He raised the largest to his lips just as a knock sounded.

Tok entered at my call, and regarded us both for an interested instant, before delivering his tidings. "Lord Guido. I haf been up and down this day to find you. You must come to your uncle. His illness is worse and he iss sinking fast."

Brother Guido dropped the oyster like a hot coal, and we both hurried after Tok.

The mercenary strode ahead down a paneled passage and through a quiet courtyard with a fountain at the center, mutely arching in the gathering dusk. At the far side he opened the oaken door to his master's rooms. The bedchamber was dark, as the drapes were drawn, and there was an evil shit-smelling stench, overlaid with woodruff and incense from a burner, to keep the evil spirits at bay. On the bed, twisted in silken sheets, and pale and hollow as a shell, lay Lord Silvio, already much changed from the man I recalled from last night. His flesh had a greenish pallor, his breath came in labored rasps. On his forearm, three stone-colored leeches lay in a row, glistening fatly and undulating as they gorged on infected blood. I knew, from one glance, that I was destined to see yet another dead man. Out of respect that I rarely show, I hovered at the door, but close enough to hear the last conference of the kinsmen.

I expected Lord Silvio to express his great love for his nephew, to express sorrow for their argument of the evening before, or even to make one last impassioned appeal for Brother Guido to leave the church and accept his inheritance. But the words I heard bore no relation to any of these. Lord Silvio scrabbled for Brother Guido's cowl with a pale hand and said, quite clearly, *"Muda."*

Brother Guido visibly started. "Are you sure?"

Lord Silvio nodded. "Muda. *Muda."* Then: *"Follow . . . the light."* Then all clarity left him; he tried to repeat himself but failed as the spittle ran down his ghostly cheek. Brother Guido gentled him, pressing his hand to his uncle's slowing heart, and I saw a glint of gold as the dying man slid the ring from his thumb to his nephew's. At that instant the door opened, and an elderly priest entered with the last things needful for the final rites. Lord Silvio, seeing that a stranger had entered, attempted speech no more but lay back, as if spent. Brother Guido silently took the oils and wads from the priest and anointed his uncle himself, wiping the libations away as he prayed for his kinsman's soul. Lord Silvio's face was drawn in a hideous rictus grin, but as his clawed hand drew the sign of the cross on his dying chest, peace relaxed his countenance. He was dead.

I withdrew from the room with the priest, to allow the della Torres a last farewell, and as the confessor blessed me and left I thought about what I had seen. To begin with, I could not fully comprehend our new predicament. I didn't think, at that moment, of how we were right back in the shit, having lost our one protector. Nor of how we would petition Lorenzo de' Medici without a sponsor. Nor did I reflect on the, frankly, bizarre final words of the dying lord. I thought of Brother Guido. Guido who had shown such bravery and nobility in the little scene that had just played out that I felt shame for my lewd thoughts. He was truly holy, and I should not wish to wrench him from the path he had taken. And yet, as I had watched his long hands stroke the holy oil into his uncle's forehead, and heard his low sweet voice pray, and watched his dear serious face witness the passing, I had thought him truly the angel I had compared him to, and felt more strongly for him than ever. For the first time I saw the danger I was in, not from the assassins of Florence but from my own sensations and desires.

At last the door opened and Brother Guido came out into the light, blue eyes blinking but tearless. My condolences and questions were cut short. "We must go," he said.

"Where?" I thought, instantly, of the painting. Were we to run again? Or would we pursue our audience with Lorenzo, even with Lord Silvio gone? But there was another matter at hand.

"I must break the tidings to Niccolò." He twisted his uncle's ring where it rode, unaccustomed, on his thumb. Twisted, twisted.

"Who?" In all the drama, I had forgot.

He looked at me then, and the last rays of the sun turned him to gold like the ring as he answered. "His son."

And so ended the seventeenth of June, 1482, the feast day of Saint Ranieri, as the next day began.

13

Tok led us through the darkening streets, still crowded for the saint's feast day. I kept my eyes on the burning torch he carried, following it like the star of the Nativity, trying to make sense of what had passed. Brother Guido was taciturn, pressed into silence under the weight of the heavy news he carried. I grabbed a handful of his habit, for the mercenary moved fast in front and I was fearful of being left behind, but still he said nothing. I was anxious to ask for Brother Guido's interpretation of his uncle's last words. What was Muda? And how was Brother Guido to "follow the light"? Was the last a blessing for Brother Guido's chosen path, the holy light of divinity and a life in the church? I dared not ask. For one thing, Brother Guido's preoccupied countenance forbade speech. And for another, I was not sure how much of what had passed he wished his uncle's mercenary to hear. So I kept my peace, and at last we reached an odd destination: a matching pair of great houses, connected with an arch set on a bias across a corner, making the two into one. The connecting wall of the house boasted a clock, and I would have stared longer at this rare wonder, but Brother Guido moved swiftly inside. We climbed a dark stair, and then entered a chamber of such opulence that my dark-accustomed eyes blinked and filled with water.

This place, a suite of rooms more elegant than any student surely had a right to inhabit, was almost more sumptuous than the della Torre palazzo itself. The beauties of the room—the plush cushions, the gilt sconces, and the velvet draperies—were the first things I noticed.

Qualcosa Due: a white pasty youth reclining on a golden chaise.

Qualcosa Tre: a small boy, black as ebony, lying atop him, his head bobbing at the older fellow's groin.

Brother Guido, innocent that he was, did not, I think, know at once what was happening. But I lowered my head to hide a smile, at the same moment that Tok let loose a guttural shout of laughter, which he turned into a cough. It was the first time I had seen a glimmer of humor from the wight, and as we shared an amused look, I began to like him better.

The tableau on the couch rose up and broke apart, and

Niccolò Gherardesca della Torre (for it was he) casually tucked his cock back into his hose as he greeted us, as if he had been doing no more than scribbling a late-evening essay. The little *negro*, who cannot have been more than eight, slid from the room, giving us an evil glance from almond-shaped eyes as he went.

"Well, Guido," began Niccolò in a nasal pipe. "Or should I say Brother Guido? You have finally come to pay homage to your coz. Tok told me you were visiting our fair city; I had expected your tribute before now."

Really? I had not seen Tok as a social creature, but apparently he had been running hither and yon, informing his lord's heir of our doings. Now it does not, as you know, take me long to form an opinion, and I disliked Niccolò on sight. He had the family features, but it was as if an indifferent artist had attempted to set down Brother Guido's face, and then left his work in the rain. The features were blunted and irregular, the noble nose angular, the chin so weak as to recede into the student's neck. The lips were an unhealthy purple, permanently wet and formless, and the mouth was surrounded by little white spots that denoted an unhealthy lifestyle. His voice broke when he spoke, changing like a weathercock between boyhood and manhood, and his humor, too, seemed by turns falsely charming and childishly vicious. Shorter than his cousin and younger too, Niccolò nevertheless browbeat the monk with his higher rank, and Brother Guido, mindful of propriety but clearly reluctant, bowed to his relative. However, his words were barbed. "And I, cousin, expected I might see you at the feast at my uncle's house yester evening." Brother Guido fairly spat the words that reminded the boy of his duty.

"Ah, the feast. Yes, I was otherwise engaged, I'm afraid." Niccolò's pale eyes, weak in color as a winter sky compared to my friend's summer blue, went to the door through which the catamite had left. "But I hope my absence did not ruin your feast. Nor the tourney that preceded it." Tok *had* been busy with his information. "And who is this little poppet? Very pretty." Niccolò's eyes flickered over me without interest. I shifted a little, wondering if he could smell the fishy fumes from my oyster-soaked skirt and would mistake the odor for the similar one of sex. He did. "Broken your vows already? Or is she a little gift for my father's grace, to win yourself some favor?"

Brother Guido flinched at the mention of Lord Silvio, visibly swallowed his dislike, and took his cousin's hand, a gesture which sent Niccolò's pale eyebrows right up into his neatly dressed bangs. "I bring grave news, cousin. I'm afraid my lord your father is . . . dead." The word choked Brother Guido a little and even my stony heart melted, not for the son but for the nephew. Nevertheless, I waited for the tears and lamentations of the della Torre heir: perhaps he would throw himself prostrate and sobbing, over the couch he had recently defiled? I did not expect what came—the smallest ghost of a smile playing at the corners of the weak mouth.

"Dead, you say?" He picked up the jewel he wore about his neck and tapped it on yellow teeth. "Really."

Brother Guido did a very bad job of hiding his shock and disgust. "There is more. He said"—the monk lowered his voice—"his last word was 'murder.' "

Niccolò seemed intrigued. "Murder? The English word?"

Brother Guido nodded. "Yes. For remember that we had an English confessor, some years back, Brother Giles of Cambridge? He taught my uncle the language, to further his business dealings, and taught us English in the schoolroom too? I'm convinced that my uncle spoke English as a code at the last, so that others might not know his meaning. He was telling us he was killed by another's hand." Ah, *that's* why I didn't have a clue what he meant, for I have less English than a Scotsman. But as

Brother Guido slid his blue eyes to the door, where Tok lounged in the doorframe, I suddenly knew that it was not from myself that Lord Silvio wished to hide the meaning of his final words. "And then," Brother Guido continued, "then he told me to 'follow the light.'"

I waited for Brother Guido to mention the gold thumb ring that Lord Silvio bequeathed to his nephew at his last, but nothing more was said. Now I thought about it, Brother Guido kept his left hand beneath the voluminous sleeves of his habit— well out of sight. I shrugged mentally—mayhap the monk wished to hold on to this keepsake of his uncle's and feared that to reveal it would be to lose it. (Fair enough.) My thoughts were rudely interrupted as the new head of the della Torre family laughed in earnest, an unpleasant honking sound that would have sat better in the throat of a Christmas goose than a new-dubbed lord. "Murder? How priceless! My father murdered! Perhaps I did it, did I?"

We were silent as he enjoyed his own wit.

"No, I'm afraid I did not, though ofttimes I thought of it." Niccolò coughed twice to collect himself, and wiped his streaming eyes. "Now, cousin, I am going to give you an object lesson in why I am the intellectual of the family, with an academic education, and you are fit for nothing but wearing out your sandal leather pacing the cloister."

I felt stung to retort that Brother Guido had read more books than any fellow I had ever met, but Niccolò seemed absorbed in his own rhetoric. He fitted his thumbs in the facings of his gown like an attorney-at-law. "What did my father actually *say* with his last, unlamented breath?"

Brother Guido shifted his feet. "I told you, he grabbed my cowl, pulled me close, and said, 'Murder.' He said it twice, and then said, 'Follow the light.'"

"Murder?" said Niccolò, still playing the lawyer's part. "Or *Muda*?"

Brother Guido's dark eyebrows drew together "It . . . I suppose . . . he may have said that word."

I hated to agree with Niccolò, but his rendering of his father's last word did sound more authentic.

"It did sound more like 'Muda,'" I put in. "I mean, I have no English to speak of, unless you count curse words I learned from the merchants I've screwed, but . . ." I trailed off.

The cousins still locked eyes as if I had not spoken and Brother Guido filled the silence. "Why would he say 'Muda'? What does it mean? I have never heard the word."

Niccolò smiled grimly. "My dear coz. Just because you have not heard a word, does not call its existence into question. It is a word, and a place too. *This* is the Muda." He gestured outward and circled his weak wrists to encompass the chamber.

"This room?" Brother Guido's confusion was apparent.

"This building, this house, this tower in which we stand. It is named the Muda." A hateful smile played on Niccolò's lips.

"I don't understand," Brother Guido faltered.

Nor did I.

Niccolò flourished his surcoat like an attorney, enjoying himself. "Let me furnish you with a little local history, since you have clearly been gone too long. This tower was the very place where our distant ancestor, Ugolino della Gherardesca, was imprisoned for treason with his two nephews. In this very room they were starved for ninety days, in a state of desperate gnawing hunger." Niccolò moved closer, his voice heavy with threat. "You must remember the tale, cousin. The *eldest* of his nephews"—he gave the word a deadly emphasis—"feeling himself near death, begged his uncle to gnaw on his flesh to sustain himself. And so here, in this very room, Ugolino ate his beloved nephew *alive*."

There was no mistaking the malice now. I shivered as in my mind's eye the finery melted away and the tower was once again a cold stone prison where such unspeakable things came to pass. Niccolò's pale eyes glittered, enjoying the vision, and I felt my friend to be in danger and thanked the stars for the presence of Tok.

But Brother Guido met his cousin's gaze unwaveringly, with a courage that made me like him even better. "Of course I know of the tale. Ugolino's atrocity was well documented in the Thirteenth Canto of Dante's *Inferno*, when he meets the poet in the seventh circle of hell." I could have cheered as Brother Guido won the book-learning contest. "I merely did not know that this place was named Muda."

Niccolò, discomfited, broke his gaze and turned away, and the company relaxed somewhat. "Well, now you do," he rejoined weakly. "I am glad to have been the instrument for your instruction. And now that you have been enlightened, even a person of *your* limited faculties must see that my father merely meant that you must come to the tower of Muda to tell me of his passing."

"And the light?" Brother Guido fought back. "Perhaps in your august knowledge, you have a notion of what my uncle meant by 'follow the light'?"

Niccolò had lost interest. He waved the question away. "Tok's torch guided you here, did it not? I don't know. Now, I have matters to attend to. Fabrizio!"

The black child came back into the room so quickly I knew he had been listening at the door. I regarded him with contempt. An accomplished door-listener, like myself, knows well enough to leave it a few heartbeats before entering the room when summoned; it's much less obvious.

Brother Guido took the hint. "I will leave you alone with your *grief*," he said with emphasis, and bowed with barely concealed disgust.

We were halfway out the door, and Niccolò had already begun to stroke the boy's hair when he fired his parting shot. "Oh, and coz? Do stay at the palazzo—as my guest—for we have much to discuss. Family matters, you understand. Don't go anywhere, will you? Tok, see that he doesn't."

Brother Guido and I both saw the look that passed between Tok and his new master as the door closed. *The king is dead, long live the king.* We both knew that the old order was gone and the new regime was in place; the favorite nephew was now cast down and the black sheep of the family exalted.

I knew as well as Brother Guido that Tok had been assigned to kill him.

14

Once outside, we meekly followed Tok for a little while, but it needed no more than a look and a little pressure of the hand to send me dashing into the dark crowd at Brother Guido's signal. We snaked through the packed side streets, and only when we came to the riverbank, and were sure we'd lost our escort, did we lean against the balustrade, gasping for air. At last I managed, "Where now?"

Brother Guido shook his head. "We can't go back to the palazzo," he said. "Our best hope is to go downriver to the Medici palace, and petition to see Lorenzo ourselves."

"Without your uncle's introduction?"

"What choice do we have? We must hope that the family name is enough. And we have the painting as collateral. Come."

We ran as fast as we could down the Lungarno Mediceo, weaving through the dark shuffling shapes of the saint's-day revelers, until we saw the red mass of the Medici palace in the dying light. As I craned up at the house that loomed from the darkness—immense, forbidding, and the color of meat—I felt an extreme foreboding which almost made me open my bowels there and then. I grabbed Brother Guido's sleeve.

"Don't," I panted. "Something isn't right."

"Many things, signorina. But we must do something. We cannot run forever." He approached the grandiose steps lit by torches, where two armed guards were talking to a third man, maybe a tradesman or jongleur. But there was something familiar about the great height, the width of the shoulders. The giant turned.

The third man was Tok.

"It's them!" he shouted to the guards. "Quickly!" And he gave chase.

Shit. How had he gotten here ahead of us? We turned as one and fled back to the river, trapped by crowds at either side. (What were they all waiting for? It was as if they had all gathered to witness our capture.)

Brother Guido led me quickly to a small private pontoon. He fumbled with the rope of the only moored boat as Tok thundered down the little pier, the planks bouncing under his weight, the two Medici guards following behind. In a flash of a blade I pulled the green glass knife from my hose and sliced the rope; one grateful glance from Brother Guido later, we collapsed in the bottom of the boat, panting like summer dogs, our lungs and limbs still aching from the chase.

As we drifted into the midstream of the dark river we saw Tok, bent double on the pontoon, looking murder at us as we slipped from his reach. As Brother Guido fished two splintered oars from the bottom of the bark, I felt confident enough to wave sweetly as the giant became a pygmy, and then a bend in the river took him from our sight. "And now what?"

Brother Guido was manning the tiller in an attempt to keep our vessel in the fast current. He shook his head, dark curls clinging to his forehead with the sweat of our pursuit. "For the first time," he said, "I have not even a notion of how to proceed. My uncle—our one protection—is gone. I signed his death warrant the instant I sat with him at the festival. They knew from that moment I would show him the *Primavera*. You were right. We should have approached him more covertly."

This was no time for triumph. "It was the oysters," I said, sharing with him at last the growing notion I had had since yestereve. "The golden platter at dinner was meant for all three of us—the family trencher for the head of the table."

He nodded with comprehension. "Then we must thank the Lord that neither of us ate them—you because of your dislike and me because of the fast. The saint did save me."

Perhaps. But I shivered to think how close he had been to eating the oysters I had saved for breakfast—only Tok's interruption had saved him from his uncle's fate. Ironic now that Tok had been sent to kill us by Niccolò who, had he been a dutiful son and attended the feast, would have eaten from the same platter and died too. *Madonna,* my head hurt with the mathematics of murder.

Brother Guido spoke again. "If it had not been that way, they would have got him somehow. And now we have been prevented from our audience with Lorenzo, the only man who could pardon us. I know not what to suggest. Nor where to take you. We are drifting, literally and metaphorically. We are a leaf in the current, and we must place ourselves in the hands of God."

I had no intention of letting God run this. "We can't give up!" I said. "There must be somewhere we can go!"

Brother Guido looked me in the face. His eyes held no fight, his gaze was dull and dead. "No," he said. "It is ended, but for a miracle."

I cast desperately about me for a solution but could see nothing but the strange landscape of dark houses lining the Arno on either side. Then, like the pinpoint of the polestar, a light appeared in one window. Then another. Then all the way up and down both riverbanks, each window, each door, each terrace and balcony, was filled with torches or candles. Every lamp was lit, every rush dip given fire, every tinderbox struck. Could this be to do with us? Could this be the hue and cry that Tok had started to find us? No, surely not, for the whole city was suddenly alight, one glorious constellation. Then, as we watched, the lights flooded the river like stars falling to float on the dark water, as the crowds that lined the riverbank set little paper boats onto the tide, each little vessel carrying a single candle. This fairy flotilla drifted along with Brother Guido and me downstream until we were surrounded by the little flames like fiery lily blossoms. I smiled with delight, despite our situation, and saw Brother Guido smile too. "Is this our miracle?" I asked him.

"Of a sort," he said. "'Tis the festival of lights, the Luminara, held each year on the eve of Saint Ranieri's day. I should have remembered that . . ."

He stopped, as if choked, and I scrambled to his side, dropping my oar overboard in my anxiety, fearing he was suffering a seizure. Quitter he may be, but he was the only ally I had left in the world. In the golden glow from a million lights, there was enough illumination to see how pale he had suddenly become. "What is it?" When he did not reply I took his shoulders and shook him like a doll. "Brother Guido? What?"

"The light!" he said, turning eyes on me that were now brighter than any torch in Pisa that night. "Follow the light!

My uncle is showing us the way—his last words to me was our escape route."

My heart began to pound again. "But where are they going? Where does the light lead?"

He pointed downriver. "To the ocean," he said simply, as we followed the numberless floating torches that were leading us to the sea.

Very soon, before the city's bells had rung another quarter, we began to see that our destination was not the open water but a place somewhat closer. For a trick of the current made every torchboat gather in a wide tributary, a sort of millrace, that lay like a lake at the foot of a tall, castlelike building. A bend in the river at this very place meant that the torches stopped, the fiery lilies pooling in a lake of fire, which was a beauteous sight to behold.

I felt three things at this point.

Cosa Uno: wonder at the sight.

Cosa Due: relief that we were not to set out to sea in a tiny wooden bark that only had one oar and was already sploshing with bilgewater.

Cosa Tre: a growing fear that we would be set alight. But soon it became clear that the hundred thousand torches were being doused by someone, or something, for the pinpoints of light were going out as they reached shore, as quickly as they had been lit. As our boat drifted in, we could see that numerous dark figures, each with a bucket, were dousing the candles as they came. I assumed that they were employed by the commune, to lessen the risk of fire on this dry spring night, but something silent and secret in the watchers' manner made me hold my tongue, and sink down into the bottom of the boat at a single motion of Brother Guido's hand. We bobbed into the bankside bulrushes and crept from our vessel onto the marshy bank. Brother Guido pulled me low in the bushes.

"Where are we?" I whispered.

"That is the Fortezza Vecchia, the old castle. See the crenellated tower high above?"

I looked carefully through the leaves. "You said the old castle," I whispered. "What is it now?"

"The Arsenale."

Even I knew what an *arsenale* was. I had slept with enough shipbuilders in my time. But I also knew that they were, usually, dependent on daylight for their constructions and did not work at night. "What's going on?"

Brother Guido shrugged, beckoned. Bent double, we crept from the undergrowth to the foot of the fortress and followed the line of the curtain wall, secret in its massive shadow. As we drew close we could hear sounds of building work—hammering soldering, and sawing—and the shouts of workmen, which by some acoustic trick had been unintelligible on the silent water.

"The curve of the river, and the thickness of the old castle walls, must conceal the noise from the city," whispered Brother Guido. He pointed up and we passed through a little doorway. Above us there loomed the derelict tower of the old castle, with half a spiral stair and rooks roosting in the eaves. We climbed as high as we could, away from the deafening cacophony, and at length reached the top of the tower. At our backs Pisa glittered like the firmament of Venus. But before and below us lay a sight belonging to warlike Mars.

On a man-made lake inside the massive ruined castle was a flotilla of immense ships at various stages of construction. With sturdy prows and crenellated forecastles, they resembled exactly a sight I had seen only yesterday. "The ship on the tower!" I whispered to Brother Guido in a sunburst of revelation, and he nodded hard and repeatedly. He had seen it too—the exact design of these warships had been etched onto the Leaning Tower of Pisa, and sat carved above the door of that great edifice. A clue, a cue, a code writ in stone. I felt it in my ribs as sure as day that this fleet of vessels was somehow connected to the *Primavera* and the *cartone* I held firmly in my bodice.

I watched the torchlit workers, hundreds and thousands of them. The sailmakers swarmed over the great ships like ants, the smelters and welders were as busy and hot with their hammerings as blacksmiths in hell. The smell of cedarwood was strong in my nose, the tar for the ropes, and the canvas of the sails. Then Brother Guido tapped my shoulder; I turned to look and there, beyond the fortress where the river was dark, was the dusky shape of another ship, and another beyond that, and another beyond that, as far as my eyes could strain into the night. Had the torches progressed farther down the river they might have fired the whole armada and reduced them to charcoal. These ships were complete, ready, and finished right to the last detail. The closest ship's crow's nest was next to the tower where we stood, and nearly as high. The flag of Pisa, emblazoned with the city's cross, fluttered so close I could have caught it in my hand. *Madonna*. What was going on?

My gasp was a little too loud. Shouts were given from below and the shipbuilders began to point. Half a dozen ran to the stair.

"The river!" cried Brother Guido, and took my hand, as if to jump into the dark deeps.

I yanked his arm nearly from its socket. "You're crazy! It's too high!" I hissed, for we were a good forty feet from the inky water. "Here." With a great leap I jumped riverward but made it to the crow's nest of the nearest ship and held out my hand to Brother Guido. "Jump!"

He leaped, became tangled in his habit, and scrabbled at the edge of the crow's nest platform. I grabbed both his hands. "Don't panic!" I looked into terrified eyes. "I have you." Although in truth my poor shoulder tendons screamed from the strain of his weight. "Find the rigging with your feet!" I gulped as his sandals scrabbled on the newly tarred ropes and found a foothold, but no sooner was he stable than I was down and past him, swarming down the rigging like a monkey. If we could reach the bank before they reached us . . . *if we could reach the bank before they reached us* . . . I was down on the deck, but footsteps sounded on the gangplank. "We're trapped," I mouthed at the following brother. "The hold, quick!" I swiftly located the entrance, lifted a grille behind the mainsail, and dropped below, with Brother Guido following so hard behind that he almost squashed me. We rolled behind a pile of sacks and lay still, breathing as low as we could. We could feel footsteps above, see planks buckling under men's weight, and hear voices questioning. The flare of a torch flooded through the grille, as the watchmen searched the hold from above. I knew if they came below, we would be discovered; but after a cursory wave of the torch, footsteps sounded on the gangplank again, as the searchers moved to the next ship.

After a long moment, Brother Guido made as if to rise, but I held him back—we must wait till they were well clear. I resolved to count a thousand heartbeats, but had only got to three hundred before I felt a jolt, and an odd sensation in my stomach. I sat bolt upright. "We're moving!" Brother Guido leaped to his feet. "Quick!"

We scrambled to the deck, but by the time we reached the ship's side rail, there was already a stretch of black water between us and the bank too wide for any mortal to jump. We turned slowly, both knowing what we would see. A half-circle of torches surrounded us, each one illuminating the ugly countenance of the sailor that held it. Tanned, scarred, and practically toothless to a man, wrinkled and knobbled with muscle as a bag of walnuts, they did not look welcoming. *Fuck.*

The tallest and ugliest of the collection approached, clearly the captain. He shone a torch in Brother Guido's face, while his mate did the same service for me. Except the first mate's greeting was to grin and fondle my tits. I spat neatly in his face, an instant before his captain fetched him a ringing slap. The first mate turned to spit out a tooth, shrugged, and resumed his torch-holding duties, seeming to hold his captain no ill will. *Madonna.* They were roughnecks indeed.

Brother Guido, bristling at the insult to my person, obviously decided to begin on the offensive. "I am the nephew of Lord Silvio della Torre," he announced, as if he had just stepped before the pope himself.

The Capitano did not seem impressed, and said with great economy, "So?"

"And I demand that you let us go in peace."

The Capitano sucked on a hollow tooth, and rubbed his dry beard till the lice ran, their little pewter bodies visible in the torchlight. If ever an apothecary strayed aboard, he'd have his work cut out. "Can't do that," was the reply, not noticeably hostile, merely matter-of-fact. "Once you're here, you're here."

"And where is *here,*" spat Brother Guido, gaining courage from the captain's indifference.

"*Here* is the fleet of the Muda."

I saw Brother Guido's eyes flare open with surprise, then close instantly as the Capitano hit him with the butt of his torch.

Just an instant before the first mate did the same to me, and all went black.

15

I was aware of three things.

Cosa Uno: somebody had a headache.

Cosa Due: someone was groaning like a doomed steer at a butcher's yard.

Cosa Tre: when I opened my eyes I thought that I had not, for it was so dark at first. I lay still for a moment, long enough to know that the headache was mine, and I was the one doing the groaning. I remembered the blow to my head, and knew from the rolling motion that we were on board ship. We? Yes, Brother Guido was there. I rolled against his soft bulk when the ship pitched, but he lay still, unconscious.

Dead?

The notion pulled me to my elbow as my head beat time with my heart. I nudged and shook the monk till his head rolled on his neck, but the black eyelashes fluttered and the blue eyes flew open. "Luciana," he said. A statement, as if he had dreamed of me and woken to the reality seamlessly, with no surprise. "Where are we?"

I had only woken a moment ahead of him, but I'd already had time to work this out.

"Back down in the hold."

He rose, too, at that, groaned, looked about him. Typically, his first concern was for me. Also typically, he couched his kind inquiries in a manner that even the most knowledgeable apothecary would find hard to follow.

"Do you have any abrasions about your cranium? Is your vision tolerably intact?"

"I don't know what you just asked, but I'm fine," I replied, as cheerfully as I could. "I have a headache that bangs like an African's drum and a mouth as dry as a ship's biscuit. But other than that, still alive. You?"

He rubbed the back of his head, and then scrutinized his pale hand for blood. "Fine too. For now."

"For now?" His words chilled. "Do you think they'll kill us?"

I heard, rather than saw, him shake his head. "Not at once. I think they have a job to do, and this fleet—the Muda—has to reach its destination on time, and we are merely an inconvenience."

"Do you think they know about the picture?"

"No. I think all this is connected to the *Primavera,* but they do not know that *we* are connected to it. Let us hope they will take us where they are going and set us free."

A wan hope indeed.

"Our first course of action would be to conceal our consciousness from our captors."

"Eh?"

Dimly I saw him raise a moon-pale finger to his lips.

"Not let them know we are awake. We may hear something of our fate."

It seemed as good a notion as any, and my pounding head invited me to lie down again anyway. So we resumed our lifeless postures and waited. And waited. All seemed silent above, no footfalls, no conversation. I began to wonder if the Capitano and his hideous mates had set us adrift and then abandoned ship, to leave us alone on a ghost ship. I had heard of such phantom vessels that sail the Spanish straits with no earthly crew. Eventually, I was so tired and worn-out with fear that I was nearly asleep in truth when we saw a torch flare through the grille of the hold and heard voices.

". . . would just be throwing good money after bad, and you know how I hate to do that."

It was the voice of the Capitano—a man that had once been cultured, perhaps wellborn, but his voice sounded as if it had been choked with weed and barnacles, like the hull of a ship, and cracked with sea air.

"Looks like we killed them anyway." A younger voice, unschooled, ignorant, not the first mate who had hit me.

"No. Berello has been hitting people over the head for years—if I want him to kill someone, he'll kill them."

"So now what?"

"Keep 'em. If the lad is a noble, we'll take him to Don Ferrente, might be a ransom there. And the lass is so comely that she'll sell for good money in the market."

"Might make the trip a bit more fun. Haven't had a fuck since Famagusta. Dirty little Turk who gave me lice."

I held my breath for the Capitano's answer. Now I'm a jolly girl who likes a good time, but being worked over by a crew of ugly, lice-ridden seamen for no money is not my idea of one.

"No. If she's a virgin we'll get much more. Don Ferrente himself might take her, but not if she's been poked by the likes of you. Keep your prick in your pants or I'll chop it off and feed it to the sharks, and tell the other lads the same."

The crewman sounded chastened. "Aye, aye. Will we feed 'em?"

"Why not? Not the good rations. But we don't want her starved. Keep her tits juicy. And if he's somebody—Della Torry, was it? Might be a bit awkward if he dies before we reach . . ."

At this the footsteps faded and we were left both relieved and frustrated. We waited for silence, then began to whisper, Brother Guido's voice warm in my ear.

"Well, at least we know we will be fed, and that we are in no present danger."

I found his ear in turn. "Wonder where they're taking us though. Shame we just missed it. If it's not one of the cities in the picture, we'll be off our course."

"It *must* be one of them." Brother Guido spoke with certainty. "The fleet, my uncle, they're connected. Something has been set in train, and we are to be carried along. I assure you in the name of Mary and all the saints that we will be going to Naples or Genoa, and as soon as we see some sunlight, I will know which."

I was impressed but too tired to ask how he could possibly

divine our direction from the sun. Everyone knows that the sun is a great fiery ball that moves around the earth—it is never still, so how could it be any kind of marker? Presently we began to move around, in the hope that food would come if the crew knew that we were awake. But after long hours of walking from one end to t'other of our pitchy prison, feeling wooded walls and naught else, we observed a gray dawnlight begin to seep through the iron grille above. We could now see our jail, ten feet square of space, with the grille set so high above that we could never escape without a rope or ladder. They knew we were safe down here, trapped like lobsters in a pot. We sat down again, regarding the hole we were in, considering our options, realizing we had none. We were at the mercy of the brigands that walked above us. Ignorant of our fate, we were too afraid to plan, and fell to bickering the morning away. At length we subsided into a sulky silence, and this was how we greeted a new phenomenon: bright sunlight suddenly flooded through the grille trapdoor of the hold, and a square of golden light began to crawl down the wooden wall of our prison, gradually, gradually sinking to the floor as the ship sailed its course. Brother Guido was up, swift as a fox, craning below the grille to see the sun's position. I stood beside him but could see little—after a night in the dark the sky was too bright for me to behold. Brother Guido looked about him, frustrated.

"What do you need?" said I.

"I need a marker of sorts—a stylus, pen, charcoal. We are nearing the middle of the day and I must take a measurement."

I raised a brow. "I don't think you're in luck."

"Hmm."

He lurched to the larboard side—the left—and began to prise a glob of tar from between the clinkered planks of the hold. The ship was new, so the tar was tacky and the monk rolled the mass into a long stylus and spat on the end. He gazed at the floor, and where the light hit the board at the extreme southern edge of the grille he made a neat cross with the black tar marker.

"What the fuck . . . ?"

He held up one long palm in my face, to silence me, and held the other hand to his heart. He was counting. Long moments passed, then he suddenly made another mark, where the light from the same point now fell in a new position. He then connected the two points with a line, drew a third, seemingly random point, and connected the three to make a triangle. Then he drew a circle neatly within the fattest part of the triangle and began to write numbers against the adjoining points in his cramped and wiggly hand. I got bored and stared up, hoping for provisions to be sent down, but my daydreams of salt beef and ship's rum were soon interrupted—Brother Guido sat back on his haunches, face flushed with his calculations in the light of the new day.

He had his answer.

· 3 ·

Naples

16

"It's Naples." He spoke with great confidence. "We're going to Naples."

I groaned inwardly. I'd hoped never to have to go to the savage south. "Are you sure?"

"Positive. We're sailing at seven degrees of latitude, in a southerly direction, at twelve knots. A goodly rate. The wind is favorable." He scribbled more numbers. "We'll travel ninety leagues a day at the least. With a following breeze, we could reach up to one hundred seventy leagues." He scribbled still, and muttered some calculations under his breath. "We should be there in three days."

"What!" I could not countenance three days in this hole, but Brother Guido seemed fairly cheerful, damn him. "Take heart. They will not harm us. They spoke of taking us to some southern potentate—'Don Ferrente' they named him. We must just hope he is a man of honor and will treat us with kindness." I thought of remarking at this point that all I had heard of the south was that it was full of criminals and vaga-bonds, who fucked monkeys when women were in short sup-ply. But Brother Guido was in full flow. "We know my uncle meant me to be aboard this fleet, for he told me to follow the light to the Muda, which I did. Perhaps he meant all along for me to go to see Don Ferrente. And at least we have now, surely, left behind the assassins that pursued us from Florence to Pisa." He looked confident and almost happy. "In any case, we have already passed one night aboard. We must simply resolve to use our faculties and prepare an investigative mentality for what we might find in Naples."

I raised my brow at him.

"I meant only that we should peruse the *Primavera* further and concentrate on the third Grace for any signs of how this southern kingdom might be connected to this plot."

I hated him at that moment.

"But we should wait till they have fed and watered us. For then we may be sure that they will leave us alone for a while, for us to begin our conference."

I was slightly cheered by the thought of food, for I am a girl who thinks of my stomach more than almost any other part of my body. But the feast that eventually arrived was never going to satisfy my greedy organ—an unseen hand threw down a couple of ship's biscuits and a quart of water in a goatskin, which tasted more of goat than water. Even this mean repast revived us a little, though, and we retired to a bright corner of the hold to examine the painting, which was thankfully unaffected by our adventures.

"All right," said Brother Guido. "Let us consider the three Graces together, since they are so intimately connected, and then we must learn all that we may about the one we identify as 'Naples.'" He glanced at me fondly. "Why don't we begin with your observations, signorina, as that methodology seemed to work last time?"

I registered swiftly that he had begun to name me formally again. Clearly he only called me by my given name when he was off guard. I sighed. "Fine," I said. "But try not to be so fucking rude if I say one of them looks like a tree goblin this time."

He suppressed a smile despite my profanity. "Very well."

"I suppose I am to give you the benefit of my layman's opinion, then you steam in with your academic bullshit."

Now he definitely smiled. "As you say."

I looked closely at the three graceful maidens with their hands entwined. "Well," I began. "I don't know if it's because we are aboard ship, or because we already know that they're maritime states, but they look like their dresses are, well, watery. You know, sort of see-through, and swirly, and glistening."

"Diaphanous."

I shot him a look. "The right-hand Grace has her sleeve blown back by the breeze and it looks sort of like an angel wing." I stole a glance at the monk, lest he deride me for my fantasy, as he had for my tree goblin pronouncement.

He peered, doubtful "All riiight." He dragged the word out like a strand of hot glass.

"And their hair too. It looks sort of windblown, as if by a sea breeze."

"Good. What else?"

"As we said before, they're dancing. They're sort of stepping *in* toward each other, not pulling away. Their weight is on their forward foot, like this."

I got up to demonstrate, and knew that I cut a graceful figure in the bright hold as he watched me. Then the effect was ruined by a sudden lurch of the ship, which sent me tumbling to my arse. Gentleman that he was, Brother Guido got up to right me, but I had already taken my seat, and covered my shame by carrying on. "I guess that could mean they are banding together in a huddle."

"An alliance! A maritime alliance!" He almost shouted it. "They are completely linked together and absorbed in each other. Except, no."

"What?"

"Pisa. The other Graces are looking at each other, but she's looking directly at Botticelli, in the ocher cloak, as we said before."

"And," I said, noticing for the first time, "she's let her gown slip from her shoulder, an old trick."

"To entice his interest?"

"If that means to get him to screw her, then yes."

"But look," Brother Guido said, ignoring me, "*he* has a bare left shoulder too, as he wears his cloak flung across him in the classical fashion. In his persona as Mercury might she not be mimicking him, to show their connection?"

"Or maybe her gawking at the artist is just to make it really clear that *she* is the starting point of the puzzle?"

Brother Guido rubbed the back of his neck, where the Capitano had slugged him. "Well, let's leave that to one side for now. We are getting ahead of ourselves, for I think that Botticelli—Mercury—is one of the *last* figures in the quest."

"Why?" I challenged belligerently.

"As we discussed in Fiesole, he stirs his caduceus—cloud stick—clockwise to the *right*. And the landscape, seen in thin slices through the trees, moves from cold blue on the left to golden yellow on the right, with the coming of Flora."

"Hmm," I said doubtfully. "Well, the other thing I was going to say is, they're all wearing pearls, which are the fruits of the sea!" I said triumphantly, feeling my own pearl where it rode in my navel.

Brother Guido looked closer. "I can see that the right-hand and left-hand Graces are wearing a rich brooch and fine pendant on a chain."

"On her hair," I put in triumphantly.

"I beg your pardon?"

"On her hair. Look closer." I was beginning to enjoy myself. "The left-hand Grace is wearing a brooch pinned to her bodice.

But the right-hand Grace wears her pendant on a plaited lock of her own *hair*."

"You are absolutely right!" He flashed me his rare and dazzling smile, all the reward I wanted ever. "Both pieces are adorned with rubies too. But where are the pearls on 'Pisa,' the middle Grace?"

I pointed smugly. Clearly, in matters of fashion I could be of use. "Look, they're woven into the collar of her gown. Seed pearls, much less valuable, but still pearls."

He nodded. "Perhaps the richness of the jewels denotes the relative wealth of the three states? Perhaps Naples and Genoa are richer than Pisa."

"Really? The south?" I shook my head. "I heard that when the goat's udders are empty they drink her piss, they are so poor."

"I cannot concur with those particulars," he said dryly, "but in essentials you are right. The northern states are richer. That cannot be the reason."

"For all we know, Pisa may be wearing a brooch but we can't see it, because she has her back to us."

Brother Guido looked at me blankly, clearly unable to appreciate my logic. Then he shook his head as if my statement were a bothersome fly. "Well, we cannot get into the question of what may be present but unseen in what is, in fact, a fictional representation of an imaginary tableau. Philosophical though your question is."

Now it was my turn to look stunned. I had never been accused of being philosophical in my life. "I'll tell you something though. The jewels look real."

"Real?"

"Yes. Real. Everything else looks, well, made-up. Fantastical. But the jewels on the two Graces, they look *real*." I pointed. "Look at Naples's pendant—the dark gold setting, the ruby in the center; three pearls hanging with the right weight and shadow, topped and tailed with white gold." I'd picked up plenty of jargon from Bembo.

Comprehension dawned. "You mean that everything else is a trope, sorry, a type drawn from Botticelli's imagination, but that the jewels are *actual* jewels, that actually exist, taken from life?"

"Yep." I hadn't really meant all this exactly, but I am never one to shy away from taking credit.

"So . . ." You could almost see Brother Guido's mind leaping ahead of his more sluggish tongue. "You think the Graces are *real people*."

All right. "Yes," I said. "Why not? I am real and I sat for Flora. May not these three maids be real people too? Maybe not Pisa. I think she is a type—'trope,' did you call it?—and she is looking at Botticelli to show that she leads the way. But the other two, on the right and left, are real ladies. Look, they even look like 'people'—their features are quite distinct from each other."

"You're right. I know that at first we thought they were almost interchangeable in their similarity. But I think at first glance one is supposed to garner that impression, so that the discerning viewer sees that the 'cities' are similar in nature, that is to say, *maritime*. But when one looks closer, one sees that the places are quite different. The devil is in the details. Clues, Luciana, we're being given clues."

I warmed at the use of my Christian name. "So who are they?"

"At one of them I can guess," he said. "For here on the left is a face once seen and never forgotten. I saw her, long ago, when my cousin and I went to Florence with my uncle, God rest his soul. We were to attend a tournament given in honor of Giuliano de' Medici, Lorenzo the Magnificent's unfortunate brother."

(You remember, he was the one carved up by the Pazzi family in the cathedral.)

"She was there, watching from the loge, looking like Guinevere."

"Like who?"

"Never mind." He was lost in his reverie. "She was as beautiful as the day. She was Giuliano's mistress, Simonetta Cattaneo."

I jolted. "The 'pearl of Genoa'?"

Now he started in turn. "You have heard her called so?"

I laughed. "All the time. It was Bembo's sales pitch when he was hawking his pearls. 'There you are, my lady,' I mimicked my dead client, 'there's only one pearl more beautiful, and that is Simonetta Cattaneo, the pearl of Genoa.' I remember it well, for when she died of the consumption he was quite put out, for he had to think of a new slogan."

I smiled at the oddities of my old lover's ways, but then looked up, fearing Brother Guido would disapprove of such callousness. But he was too excited to note it, if indeed he had even heard.

"It all makes sense! I thought at first that they were wearing white because they were—virgins . . ." He choked on the word. "I mean that in the vestal sense"—I shrugged—"but now I think they are *deceased*. You were right about the angel wing. The right-hand Grace and the left-hand Grace were real women, who are now *dead*."

"All right," I said. "So we know that the left-hand Grace is Genoa, as she is a portrait, we think, of Simonetta Cattaneo."

"I'm sure of it, now I have studied the face."

"And look! She wears a pearl above her forehead! There could be no clearer sign!"

"Indeed. I have never seen a larger. 'Tis settled."

I thought of flashing him my midriff, but did not think I should upset our current amity.

"Well," I went on, "if she is Genoa, and we are definitely heading for Naples, then she's the *last* figure of all, not the next."

"Precisely. So we know where the hunt ends, at least."

I could not bear to think, for the moment, of the journey that stretched ahead, all the way to alien Genoa, at the other end of our great peninsula. "We know a little of the figure of Genoa, then," I continued, "but absolutely bugger all about Naples, which is where we're about to wash ashore."

"You're right," Brother Guido agreed, visibly descending from our recent triumph. "Let us concentrate on 'Naples.' To recapitulate: she is dead; she wears a pendant on her rope of hair. She is very fair."

I shrugged. "She's all right"

He smiled. "You might even say the fairest of them all."

Now I was getting annoyed. "That miserable milk-skinned moppet? Are you blind?" Any fool could see I was much better looking.

"You misunderstand me. I merely meant, she is very fair-*skinned*." Brother Guido ceased his teasing. "More so than the other maids."

"Oh. Oh, I see." I cursed my lack of poise. "And much blonder too."

"So, in summary, our clue would be a blond, white-skinned maiden, dead, who is connected to Naples. Hmm."

For once, Brother Guido looked flummoxed and began to rub his neck again. He looked so crestfallen that I attempted to cheer him. "Isn't this where you gallop in with your book learning?"

But even this fail-safe did not seem to lift his spirits. He gave half a smile. "I'm not sure it would be of much benefit in this case. Your own observations, taken from the *Primavera* itself, are worth far more."

'Twas a great compliment, one that should be repaid. "But I'd *like* to hear."

He settled to his elbow, stretched out like a Roman senator, and I did likewise. The sun was lowering, and I settled down as if I were a child hearing a tale at bedtime. "The three Graces are a well-known classical theme of antique texts, identified by Horace, Hesiod, and Seneca as Aglaia, Euphrosyne, and Thalia. They were three sisters who signify mutual benefit, for one sister gives, the second receives, and the third returns the favor."

"Then," I interrupted, "it seems that the idea of an alliance is not such a stupid one. Otherwise why is this fleet of ships— the Muda, as I suppose we must call it—heading to Naples?"

He brightened a little. "It's possible."

"There you go! And what more do you know?"

"Actually, more relevant to us than these august writers is the fact that Marsilio Ficino wrote a letter about the three Graces to Lorenzo di Pierfrancesco de' Medici."

"Hang on. Who, wrote to who?"

"To *whom*."

I flapped my hands impatiently and he took the hint and carried on.

"Marsilio Ficino is a fine poet at the Medici court."

"I thought that was Polly something. The one you and your uncle went on about?"

"Poliziano, who wrote the *Stanze,* on which I believe the *Primavera* to be based. Yes, he is the poet laureate, but there are many poets at Florence's court. It is a seat of great learning."

"So, this Ficino fellow wrote to Lorenzo de' Medici about the Graces?"

"Not Lorenzo the *Magnificent*. Lorenzo *di Pierfranceso* de' Medici, il Magnifico's ward and favorite young cousin. The one that lives at Castello. Men say Lorenzo the Magnificent is closer to Lorenzo di Pierfranceso than to his own sons." He looked suddenly desolate, and I knew then how much the loss of his beloved uncle grieved him. I tried to place his mind back on course.

"All right. So?"

"Lorenzo di Pierfranceso is Botticelli's patron. He has commissioned many paintings by him; I'd be very surprised if this *Primavera* was not one of them."

Light dawned. "And what did the letter say? Wait, tell first—how do you *know* about this letter?"

"I am an amanuensis."

"An ama-*what*-sis?"

"An amanuensis. A monastic copyist. Because these poetic letters contain beautiful prose and verse of great merit, Lorenzo di Pierfrancesco lends them to the monastery of Santa Croce."

Once again I was impressed by his accomplishments, more so because I myself couldn't write "bum" on a privy door.

"We copy them in the scriptorium and bind them into volumes to be kept in the library and appreciated by the ages yet to come."

"So what did it say?" My voice was slurred and drowsy.

I was prone by this time, and the light had faded. We had talked the hours around, and my eyes fought sleep. My last consciousness was his soft voice in the dying day.

"*Sol autem inuentionem uobis omnem sua luce quaerentibus patefacit. Venus deniqe uenustate gratissima quicquid muentum est, semper exornat.* 'The Sun makes clear all your inventions by its light. Finally Venus, with her very pleasing beauty, always adorns whatever has been found.'"

At the last, I could swear he gently touched my cheek.

I slept.

17

I woke to the sound of retching and the sickly sweet smell of vomit. Brother Guido was hunched in the corner, doubled up as he expelled his insides. In the pewter light of dawn I could see his matching gray pallor. Concern overrode my disgust and I jumped to my feet.

"Shit. Are you all right?"

"Fine." He waved me away, clearly shamed of his state. "'Tis the seasickness." He spat neatly once more, then as is often the case after a bout of vomiting, he clearly felt instantly better. "My cousin Niccolò used to tease me about it mercilessly when we were children." He gave a weak smile. "It was a great joke to him that the heir of a maritime state could not countenance a rough sea."

"But you were fine yesterday."

"Did you not hear me?" he said. "A *rough* sea. The waters are different today, the wind is up, the ship pitches and rolls."

He was right. I could not have approached him even if I had wanted to, for when I tried to walk, the floor lurched and I lurched with it, as if jugbitten. I smiled, enjoying the game. And presently got the hang of it. "Look!" I cried, dancing about the tipsy hold. "I have my sea legs!"

Brother Guido regarded me balefully as he crept along the wall and sank to his haunches far from his leavings. "You're very cheerful. Let us hope it does not get worse."

"Worse?" I was happy and confident as I knew this was our last day on board. "It's only a squall, surely."

He rolled his eyes in sockets hollow from his travail. He had almost a full dark beard, and his pallor and weight loss made him look much more like a religious ascetic than an angel. "I suppose so. In fact, the waters around the straits of Naples are notoriously rough, as the currents of the seven seas converge as you round the sheltered edge of the peninsula. I did not mention it, thinking it would fright you, but you are finding out for yourself." He sighed. "At least we will get there faster, as we are being blown into port like an acorn on a millpond. It's a following wind."

"There you are then!" I crowed. "We must ride it out as best we can, and then the time will come to leave this accursed ship and the bastard rats that sail it. Depend upon it—tomorrow night we'll be in silken sheets in the palace of Don Ferrente." I skipped across the planks and patted his shoulder. "Take heart." I used a phrase of his own. "Perhaps I am showing you my true Venetian colors, for they say each Venetian is born in a storm, and therefore we must have the best seafaring stomachs of all." I was cock-a-hoop, the dangers of the crew above and the city before me forgotten. I just wanted off this fucking boat.

An hour later I desired it even more. Brother Guido and I were rolling about like peas on a drum as the ship pitched alarmingly. Each time we rolled under the grille we were doused with a briny splash of seawater which stung the eyes and stole the breath. We were both vomiting copiously, I even more than he; I made no more boasts about being a sea-hardy Venetian. We could no longer puke neatly in the corner, but threw up everywhere, over each other and ourselves, with only the seawater to cleanse our misery and shame. We were bruised and aching, thrown from fore to aft, from larboard to starboard. Presently, horrifyingly, the hold began to fill with water to our ankles, then our waists. I knew not what would happen if the merciless brine soaked the painting, but could no longer care. With the storm bellowing outside, we could neither speak nor hear. Soaked and shivering, Brother Guido and I clung together like souls in hell. All shame disregarded, all differences forgot, 'twas as if we were one person. I knew I would die that same hour, but that I would not die alone. *Born in a storm,* I kept thinking. Venetians are born in a storm. Born in a storm, died in a storm, the circle complete. The water rose more and Brother Guido began to pray—but as the cold sea seeped up to my bodice, his eyes flew open. He gave a cry; the screeching winds and falling torrent made him mute, but I could see by the shape his lips made that he had said the name of the *Primavera*! I no longer cared for the painting that had brought us to this pass, but I cared for him. For his sake, with chilled fingers I fumbled with my bodice and took out the waxed roll, held it high above the roaring torrent. He looked desperately around for a way to salvage the parchment, and the answer floated up past his chest—the goatskin gourd. Dextrously he rerolled the parchment, small enough to push through the neck of the gourd, and shoved in the wax cap tight. Then, being the taller, he wound the gourd's leather strap around his neck and hung the goatskin around the back in his cowl. I knew as well as he did that if the water reached there we were dead anyway.

But soon our relative heights ceased to matter as we began to float then, our feet leaving the floor, higher and higher. Or did the ship sink lower and lower? I could no longer tell. I had no rudder, no compass, no longer knew starboard from larboard or up from down. I feared for my friend as his brown fustian habit accepted the weight of the water, turning black and heavy, all but dragging him down. But soon our heads were pressed against the grille, the waters rising still as we gasped for air. The painting would be saved, but we would not; we were rats in a trap. Our faces were crushed by the cold iron of the grille and the warm flesh of each other. In my last act, I pressed my chilled lips to Brother Guido's because I did not want to die without showing him I loved him.

At that moment three things happened at once.

Cosa Uno: the freezing iron lifted away from our faces as the grille was raised.

Cosa Due: unseen hands hauled us to the storm-battered deck.

Cosa Tre: Brother Guido della Torre kissed me back. Hard.

Before I had time to countenance this triple miracle, I was being dragged forward, downward, I knew not where. I held on to Brother Guido, unable to open my eyes against the lashing sea spray. I felt myself being lowered over the side of the ship—surely we were not to swim for our lives! But no, my numbed feet felt the bottom of a craft. The sinking ship, doomed on its maiden voyage, protected us from the bite of the wind and spray, and I could see that I was now in a curracle with Brother Guido and the Capitano. All other souls, it seemed, were doomed, and so were we if we set forth bounded in this nutshell of a boat. But the menfolk took two oars and pulled away from the wreck, myself crouching like a figurehead in the prow of the curracle. As we pushed forth, we left the lee of the ship and I looked the storm in the eye. *Madonna.* My hair whipped around my frozen face like Medusa's snakes, whispering saltily with the brine that rimed my locks. I could see with brief sharp pride that Brother Guido pulled the oar strongly and competently to match the Capitano's stroke, and reflected that even the worst Pisan sailor must be better than the best of other men. I held on to the boat's sides till my muscles cracked, as we rose to the top of waves high as dark mountains, then sank down again, lurching into the inky depths like damned souls falling into the chasm. Lightning ripped the sky, as if a black arras were being rent to reveal a heaven of silver; paradise was glimpsed in an instant and then snatched away from us. The wind stung my face so I turned back, just in time to see the flagship of the Muda being swallowed by the sea, the masts sinking at the last till the Pisan pennant fluttered for the final time and was gone.

Exhausted, I curled up in the bottom of the boat, not caring what happened now. The spray and the cold stole my consciousness away, and I passed out, with Brother Guido's kiss still printed on my lips.

Woke to a warm sun, a glassy sea reflecting the blue sky like a mirror. All around the boat were ships' planks smashed to matchwood, and clothing curling and floating in the water like a laundry.

My oarsmen were both prone in their seats. For the second time in a day's span I feared that my friend was lifeless. My heart quickened—no, Brother Guido lifted a hand to swat away an errant fly, then settled down again. Asleep. Exhausted. The Capitano, on the other hand, lay with his bloody mouth open, showing neither breath nor life.

Well.

That is how Principessa Chi-chi arrived in state to the southern kingdoms. Marooned in a curracle, with two unconscious men. Both bearded and battered and bruised and bloody. One as ugly as all seven sins, and dead as a Friday fish. The other as beautiful as the dawn and gloriously alive. As if the deceased Capitano had considered my wishes, my left foot was bound to Brother Guido's right with a cuff-and-chain arrangement. I thought of searching our captor's corpse for the key, but the thing caused me no discomfort, and I'd really rather not do an unpleasant job when I could wait for my friend to wake and get him to do it. I gazed on Brother Guido's sleeping face and drank in his beauty, the memory of the night before beating in my temples and throat. I noticed, as an afterthought, that the gourd with the *Primavera cartone* in it still hung safely round his neck, but I wasn't even sure I cared. Perhaps after last night we could forget the whole puzzle and settle down here where no one knew us, drink wine and eat olives and raise beautiful children. I gazed on their father's face and enjoyed my fantasy.

At length I looked forward from the prow and saw a sight that pleased me almost as much. Curved and glittering as a necklace cast onto the sands was a perfect crescent of a bay. Above it sat a glowering blue mountain which smoked a little from its peak as if it were a new-made dish pulled lately from the oven. Little white houses huddled on the beach like pearls, and farther up the slopes, great palaces studded the hillsides like rubies.

"Naples," said a voice from behind me.

Not Brother Guido's voice. A voice of brine and barnacles.

Shit.

The Capitano was alive.

18

My expression of horror did not go unnoticed.

"Sorry to disappoint you," said that graveled voice ironically as he straightened in his seat and spat a couple of teeth over the side. "And I expected at least a thank-you for saving your skin. I realize a kiss may be pushing it; 'tis true I do not look my best, just now."

I narrowed my eyes against the sun and him.

"Are you expecting me to believe that you saved us, through the goodness of your soul?"

He smiled a bloody toothless smile. His mouth resembled that of a monstrous toddler who had shed his first teeth but not yet gained his second. He spread his rough hands. "My motives are as lofty as my reward is like to be."

I had to admire his honesty. "Ohhhhhhhhh. *That's* it. You think you can get a good price for us with your patron . . . Don . . ." I struggled to recall the name.

"Ferrente," he supplied. "Of course. Maybe not so much you, though I must say when you're bathed and dressed you'll have no peer. But your boyfriend . . . he's a noble, so he said."

"He is not my—" His smile widened and I stopped.

"Well, you looked pretty cozy when I pulled you out of the drink."

"What happened to your crew?" I said, anxious to deflect attention. I looked at Brother Guido, hoping for some support, but he slept on.

"Dead."

"*All* of them?"

"I should think so. Ship went down, didn't it? We got the only longboat."

His callousness took even my breath away. "Don't you care?"

"Not really." He shrugged. "The rest of the fleet will be coming—they were too far behind us to be wrecked. And even if they *were* wrecked I could always pick up another crew. Especially in Naples. Busy seaport, you know. Busy." He nodded, as if he were discussing the pleasant weather, not the death of his entire crew.

"Hang on. Are you saying they were alive on board, but then you left with us and let them go down with the ship?"

"They weren't all alive. Some got washed over."

"Yes, but . . ." I'm not sure why I was arguing with him. "Didn't you want to bring your first mate, or that fellow that got crabs in Famagusta, or . . ."

"Berello and Cherretti? They're not going to fetch me any bounty with Don Ferrente. A couple of poxy seamen. No, I've done better with the princeling and the mermaid, thank you very much."

"So you left them to die?"

"Yes." The Capitano collected my expression. "What do you care? You're alive, aren't you? All you knew of Berello was that he hit you round the head."

"Yes, but . . . he's your friend—was your friend, wasn't he?"

"I've sailed with him these twenty years. But friends are a luxury for the rich. If Don Ferrente pays out, mayhap I'll have the money to buy a few."

"But . . ." I stopped. I looked at Brother Guido where he slept. Although I had barely known him twenty days, let alone twenty years, I knew that I would still never desert him. Yet it was useless to canvass such a subject with the Capitano. Instead, I resolved to find out what he knew. "These ships, brand-new, so many of them, what are they for? D'you know?"

He spat over the side with precision. "No. I was paid to bring a fleet of 'em to Don Ferrente."

"And that's all you know?"

"They don't pay me to know more. One thing I *do* know—less you're told, less trouble you're in."

I couldn't fault him there, but remained silent, frustrated that he could not tell me more of the purpose of the massive fleet. But while the Capitano and I had been busy with our discourse we had drifted much closer to shore, and I could see more detail of our destination—lemon trees with sun-bright fruits and dark glossy leaves, bundles of nets drying in the sun, glittering with dewdrop diamonds of water. I knew that we were no longer in immediate danger, for such an unscrupulous, single-minded man as the Capitano would not only keep us alive but actively protect us until he got his payday. I was almost enjoying myself—the day, and the view, lifted my spirits. But to be perfectly honest, the fire that really warmed my heart was the memory of the kiss I'd shared with Brother Guido. In that moment, even though I'd been on the point of death, I'd been happier than I'd ever been. I knew then that he did not entirely belong to God, not yet; that I had reason to hope. And I realized then, too, that I'd never known what it meant to really want one man and no other. I'm not saying I've never enjoyed my work—hell, a good swive is a good swive, but my *heart* had never been captured before. Last night, I thought my heart was about to stop beating forever. But actually, it had never really begun to beat, not till that moment. Now I was truly alive, and ready for anything that fate might bring, so long as we could be together.

I looked back to my sleeping love and suddenly felt afraid of his waking. Would he remember that he had kissed me? What would he say? As if I had bidden him, he stirred, groaned, and sat straight, blinking in the light. His eyes were as burning blue as the high curve of the sky, his pupils tiny pinpricks, and when he looked at me I knew he remembered because he was instantly scarlet, as if dipped in boiling oil. And I knew my face burned too.

The Capitano looked amused, missing nothing. "Good morrow, *Brother*," he said with emphasis.

Brother Guido winced. "Where are we?"

The Capitano waved his hand. "Very nearly at the port of Naples. My hometown, actually. Now you're awake, I thought I might prevail on you for a little rowing, since you gave such sterling strokes last night. I would've asked your girlfriend, but we were having such a pleasant chat, and besides, she doesn't look too strong. We'd have gone round in circles."

I began to get the measure of the man. He was not without humor, but he was utterly without compassion. In his battered face his eyes were as little and cold as a fish's. I felt a shiver despite the warm sun, for I knew that the moment we ceased to be of use to him, or if he did not get the expected price for us, our lives would be straw to him.

Brother Guido did not rise to the Capitano's jibes; in fact, his face was inscrutable as he took up the oar and rowed silently. He said so little on the way into the bay—and then only inquiries as to direction or speed of his stroke, all addressed to the Capitano—that I knew something was badly amiss. He would neither address me nor look at me. I sighed. That was the worst of these religious types, and I should have expected it from him tenfold, knowing him as I did.

Guilt.

We pulled into the bay and I could see on closer inspection that Naples was a pretty shabby place close up—the houses not so white, the aspect not so fair. A dwarf trotted along the harbor and tied up our boat for us, biting the coin that the Capitano flipped him. The midget handed us all out of the boat, and as I set foot on land for the first time in days I could have dropped to the ground and kissed the filthy sand, so glad was I. In fact, I nearly did take a tumble, as my legs felt most peculiar—the ground underfoot felt insubstantial and uneven, and my body wavered as if it were still at sea. All this was not helped by the manacle on my left foot, for Brother Guido and I had to shuffle along with an odd gait, bound together in an awkward fashion as if we took part in a May Day caper. Yet my "friend" made no attempt to steady me; it was the Capitano who grasped my elbow. "Landsickness," he said, "it'll pass." And together we made our way up the wharf into the town, and the streets closed around us.

I was struck by a wall of noise. I was confounded by a rainbow of colors. I breathed a hundred different smells. My senses were assaulted all at once. Naples was like nowhere I had ever been. I had stumbled into an Arabian bazaar.

From our first steps we were constantly harassed by Gypsies and locals alike. The streets were a casbah of yelling hawkers, selling their bright wares—food, beads, fishes. I even saw a collection of human skulls for sale, staring ghoulishly from their stall. I saw, too, shuffling lines of slaves manacled just like us, pretty girls in a string, or strong men, or housemaids, all tied together like chattel. I knew this would be our fate if we did not please Don Ferrente. The place was lawless, noisy, confusing, menacing, a city of thieves. Yet we were embraced by the residents as they waved us into their shops and even homes. Once the Capitano led us into a dark doorway and bought a skin of wine for a coin. As we drank in turn (Brother Guido refused as I knew he would), I looked about me. The whole family, six of them and a babe, were there in one room—bed, earthpit, cooking pot, everything. 'Twas so dingy it was a relief to get outside. "Do they *all* live there?" I bawled at the Capitano, above the noise of the populace. "Yes," he bellowed. "It's called a *basso*. The whole house in one chamber."

Madonna. To cook, shit, fuck, and sleep in one room, with the babes looking on? Even Enna and I had lived better. I strove for something nice to say, remembering that he was a local. "Good wine though."

The Capitano nodded. "White wine, called Lacrimae Christi, tears of Christ. The grapes are grown in the shade of the volcano"—he pointed up to the hunched blue mountain above us—"and the precious salts that come from its belly flavor the wine." I had heard, of course, of such mountains that breathe fire and molten rocks. I cast a nervous glance at it, but the volcano was a sleeping dragon today, smoking calmly into the blue sky.

Down below, there was no such peace. There was noise everywhere; music could be heard constantly, in a cacophany of styles. With every step we heard the drone of popular songs, sung in nasal tones. One particular song I heard everywhere, perhaps a dozen times on our short journey.

Jesce, jesce, corna;
Ca mammata te scorna,
Te scorna 'ncoppa lastrico,
Che fa lo figlio mascolo.

Peer out, peer out!
Put forth your horns!
At you your mother mocks and scorns;
Another son is on the stocks,
At you she scorns, At you she mocks.

The Neapolitan tongue was near incomprehensible to me, especially as ortolans and gaudy parrots screeched from the eaves in competition. The song seemed to be about *snails*—that couldn't be right. "What are they singing about?" I asked our captor.

"Cuckold," he said briefly. (I knew what that meant—it was when a woman fucks another man behind her husband's back.) The Capitano made an odd symbol with his hand, with the first and little fingers extended like horns while the middle pair of fingers were held down by the thumb. "Here, we make the sign of the Devil's horns. It wards off bad luck," he said.

I began to look, and I saw the symbol being made everywhere, all around me—by the black-clad widows who sat three-deep on a crumbled wall, to the olive-eyed babes spinning their tops in the dust. I noticed Brother Guido saw it too, and he crossed himself in reply. Thus the sign of God negated the sign of the Devil, as if to ward off such heathen beliefs. I smiled at him but got nothing in return, so turned again to the Capitano. "Why, what bad luck are you expecting?"

"I'm hoping that when I marry, my wife won't cuckold *me*."

I could not wish him joy in any future union, but since

Brother Guido was not speaking to me, I carried the conversation on. "You're not married then?" said I, trying to sound surprised.

"No, but I'll take you, honey tits, if you're asking. If Don Ferrente doesn't want to suck on them himself, that is."

I shot him a look of loathing, sorry I had bothered to converse with him, but he merely laughed.

"Come on. You can't hate me that much. You woke first in the boat, did you not? You could have tipped me over the side while I slumbered, and been rid of me for good."

Damnation, that's what I should have done! Fuck, fuck, *fuck!*

He saw my expression and his grin widened. "Why didn't you?"

"Because I didn't think of it in time," I admitted stiffly.

He laughed again. "Well, at least you're honest."

I looked to Brother Guido to see how he would react to this exchange—the casual contemplation of murder. But he had drawn into his shell as completely as the snail of the song. I saw him telling his rosary beads through busy fingers as we walked, his mouth moving constantly in prayer. *Huh,* I thought. Probably trying to pray the taste of me away from his lips. Good luck. A kiss from Chi-chi is not so easily forgot. I felt sad though—in our time of danger we had never been closer, and now, even though we were shackled together, we could not have been further apart.

We pushed our way through the maelstrom of hurrying citizens and I reflected on how little the people were. They seemed no bigger than the midget on the wharf who had tied our boat, and were swarthy and saturnine, not like the tall, willowy blondes of the north. It was hard to see how the pearl-pale lady from the *Primavera* would find a home among such a people; she was as different from them as a greyhound from a pack of curs. Like myself. I looked down on them, in many senses.

Yet the place was clearly a mass of contradictions. For as many walls that were daubed with crude drawings like a cave of the ancients or painted with slogans that even made *me* blanch, there were niches with Madonnas and saints everywhere. At every street corner was a shrine of devotion, each clean and well respected, with well-tended flowers or neatly trimmed candles. I noticed, too, that among the varied merchandise on sale in the streets, the apothecary drugs and the body parts and the stolen wares, were hundreds of scenes of the Nativity, carved from wood, some painted, some plain, and all exquisite, clearly a local specialty. Naples was a place of contrasts, a city crammed with the filth and the faith in equal measure. Like Brother Guido and me: the faithful and the filthy, joined by accident, and rubbing along together as best we could.

Soon we began to climb a hill away from the harbor and I noticed, as in Florence, that when the ground rises, the ruffians fall away and the district gets a little nicer. The heat, however, was oppressive when we climbed out of the shade of the streets and the market awnings. I began to sweat freely. Now I could see our destination looming over the town—a red castle, grand and spreading, with twin turreted towers joined by a grand white marble arch. As we drew closer, I knew it was time for action—we would never get out of this pass if Brother Guido remained as mum as an oyster. As we reached the castle gates, and the Capitano stepped forward to bribe the guards that crossed their halberds in our faces, I pinched his arm. At last he looked at me, but like a mortal who looked upon the demon who had damned him.

I got mad.

"Look," I said. "Wake up and act like a man. Whatever happened on that ship, we're alive and we have the *cartone*. Use your wits and look about you. We need to charm this man, Don Ferrente, or the quest ends here. Act as if you are a person of consequence, for pity's sake, for you've been as dull as Doomsday since we landed on this rock."

In reply he merely shook his head.

I gave up. "You're pathetic," I spat. "All right, fine. Act like a mewling milksop. I couldn't expect any action from you. Why you can't take charge of the situation I don't know. I suppose it will be up to *me* to save our skins, as usual." And I swept along in the Capitano's wake. I knew the last swipe was unfair, for Brother Guido had saved our bacon more than once on our travels, but I wanted to say anything that would shake him out of his guilty torpor. Not that it worked.

As always when I am about to meet a new and powerful man, I worry about my appearance. My skin felt tight from the sun, and dry from the water, and when I licked my lips I tasted salt. My hair still fell in salty ropes that whispered as I shook them back, and had dried almost white blond in the fierce heat. I was soon to feel even more of a peasant, as the Capitano led us through room after room of the most sumptuous chambers I had ever seen. Everywhere there were courtiers milling in their gorgeous costumes, but strangely, all the clothes and jewels, and the decorations of the walls, were only in black and white. By the time we had passed through the third or fourth antechamber, filled with haughty black-and-white courtiers who stared down their noses at us as if we were driftwood that had washed up on the beach (which we were), I had begun to think that my sun-dazzled eyes had lost their ability to see color. The hues of the rainbow were completely absent from this place. Without knowing I was doing it I was looking at every lady for a resemblance to the right-hand Grace, the fair lady we had identified as "Naples." Even though I knew that the dame had to be dead according to our deductions, still I looked for her spectral spirit walking among these courtiers. But all the ladies at this court were dark-haired, black-eyed Spaniards, and none of these magpie ladies came close to the moon-pale delicacy of the right-hand Grace. "Why are they in black and white? Did somebody die?" I whispered to the Capitano.

He shook his grizzled head. "'Tis not mourning but fashion," said he. "You are in the court of the Aragonese, and they think it becoming to wear only black or white."

Madonna. "And . . . Don Ferrente, he is one of the nobles at this court?"

"Hardly." The Capitano's sneer was unpleasant. "Don Ferrente is Ferdinand the Sixth and First, King of Aragon and Naples."

A *king*. Shit. Typical, that once again I was destined to meet a great man when stinking like a ferret and looking like a porcupine in a thunderstorm.

At last we passed through an immense pair of doors to the grandest room of all—a long gallery with walls of intricate carvings—tiny pieces of ivory set into dark ebony to make the most fantastical shapes and patterns. Neither the bone nor wood were of any great value, but the workmanship that had gone into the panels, which stretched as far as the eye could see, made them priceless. In the center of the gallery stood an imposing figure, dressed all in white, leaning on a vast black fireplace in a noble attitude. The huge grate was empty on this burning day, and in the embers of the last fire crouched a man in simple black, on a three-legged milking stool, whittling a block of white wood so the snowy curls sprang from his fingers into the grate.

The man in white was speaking a language foreign to me, presumably Aragonese, but as my ear attuned I could make out a couple of words and could tell that Spanish was none too distant a cousin to Tuscan. The white man's serf grunted in reply, but did not look up from his carving, a breach of manners that would have had him beaten in Florence.

We walked down the gallery softly, ignored by the black and white pair, but the white lord turned as we drew close.

"Capitano Ferregamo," he said, teaching us the Capitano's name for the first time. "I see you survived the recent storms. Congratulations. Can the same be said for the fleet of the Muda?"

Ferregamo bowed low and spoke in a voice so humble I scarce recognized it. "Only the flagship lost, as far as I know, Excellency. The others will follow today or tomorrow, for we were a good league ahead. We had to put to sea early, for reason of these intruders you see."

"You have brought some bounty for Our Grace?" The white-clad monarch had an odd quality to his voice, a strange sibilant hiss like a snake.

"Indeed. The man is a noble from Pisa. The woman his doxy, but a beauty that I thought might please His Majesty?"

His Majesty? Was this white fellow *not* Don Ferrente? Were there yet more chambers to traverse before we reached the room of the throne? The snake man spoke again. "But your 'nobleman' wears a monk's robes," said he, circling us with interest, holding a white pomade to his nose as if we smelled (which we probably did).

"He is no monk, Excellency. I caught him embracing this woman aboard ship."

I flashed a look to Brother Guido and saw him hang his head in shame. The black-clad servant in the fireplace carved away, his knife whistling through the air, the shavings jumping away from his fingers, chip, chip, chip.

"Hmmm." Snake-tongue smiled. "But he did not take her virginity?"

"Not aboard," asserted the Capitano with conviction. "I'm sure of it. They were watched constantly."

This gave me a jolt. Watched? Had the Capitano seen us take out the *cartone* and heard our council on the painting's meaning? No; I willed my heart to slow. The Capitano would not have undertaken such a watch himself, and all other hands were dead. I vowed, though, to tell Brother Guido to have a care of the painting when we were next alone—if we lost that, we were done for.

Snake-tongue looked at me speculatively. "All right. She may do. What say you, Majesty?"

The man crouching in the fireplace spoke with unexpected command. "Let me see her."

I turned astonished eyes on him. He? *He* was Don Ferrente, the King of Aragon and Naples? He was dressed in a simple black gown without ornament, and he hunched like a serf over his horny, carving hands. But his gaze was gray steel and his nose had a noble hook—not a man to be trifled with.

If this was unexpected, then what happened next was more so—the man in white neatly ripped my gown from my shoulders. Caked with salt and dried stiff, it tore easily to expose my chest to my waist. I thanked *Vero Madre* that I had passed the *Primavera* to Brother Guido; otherwise it would have been lost. I stood still as three men gazed at my naked charms, Brother Guido averting his eyes. I knew how to work such a situation, though; I arched my back and wet my lips, and wished for a colder chamber to harden my nipples. If my breasts were the only way to save us, then fair enough; they were equal to the task.

"All right," said the king. "I'll take her. Not the man, though. I've enough nobles in this place, and most of them are a nuisance."

I turned horrified eyes on my friend as the white man motioned to me to cover up. Surely we were not to be divided!

The Capitano was wheedling now. "I thought, my lord, that there might be a ransom."

The king regarded Brother Guido, who looked like a beaten man. "I think not. Just sell him, Ferregamo. You are not usually so fastidious."

The Capitano sank down to our feet to unlock us. Our feet were parted, but I clung to Brother Guido's habit. If only he would speak.

"No!" I begged. "You can't take him. He's important!" I felt ridiculous. And I love him! I added under my breath.

The Capitano dragged Brother Guido to the door, and I watched, appalled, as I looked my last on him. In despair, willing him to speak, I crossed myself, speaking the only language he heeded now—the sign of God, his God whom he had wronged by kissing me. God whom he returned to like a lost sheep. At last, at last, he acknowledged me, and replied to my gesture with one of his own, a most extraordinary thing—he made the Neapolitan sign of the horns, the gesture we had seen all morning, to ward bad luck away from me, wherever I would end up. His uncle's thumb ring flashed gold and I turned away, sick with fear of being alone in this court of chess pieces without him. But as the great door opened the king stood for the first time. "Wait!"

It was a command. The king strode down the black-and-white gallery, took Brother Guido's left hand, and looked closely at the thumb ring. He studied the bright gold band, with the nine gold balls encircling it. The king raised his own left hand, where the twin of Brother Guido's ring rode on the thumb. My eyes widened. Another ring! Don Ferrente looked my friend in the face. "Who *are* you?"

Brother Guido's reticence fell away like a mask, and I saw him draw himself up so he looked the king full in the eye, at that moment a king himself. Fixing Don Ferrente of Aragon with the truth of his blue gaze, he said clearly, "I am Niccolò della Torre, heir to the states and dominions of the city of Pisa."

The extraordinary king shook his head as if he had just received a stinging blow, then smiled a smile that transformed his face.

"My *lord*! Forgive me. I did not know that you were coming yourself!"

"I thought it best, especially at this time," replied "Lord Niccolo," feeling his way.

The king nodded. "Indeed. Indeed. *He* did not say . . ."

"*He* does not know. I thought to surprise him at the coming event."

Another nod. "Of course. Of course. Forgive me, forgive me. Forgive my treatment of your person, of your consort." This with a smile at me. "But why these holy weeds?"

I could see Brother Guido thinking fast and admired him greatly. "You perhaps have not heard of my father's untimely death. Foul play it was, and I left the city as soon as I could, under the cover of night and in the habit of a simple monk."

"Your father is gone? I am so very sorry. Lord Silvio was a fine man, and truly, you have the look of your father. His bearing, his looks."

It was true, Brother Guido did resemble his uncle more closely than did his cousin—the man he was pretending to be. But what did he mean by this deception? What benefit could there be of pretending to be what we were not?

The king went on. "Your father told you everything, I suppose?"

"Of course. I am his heir in *all* things." Brother Guido spoke with heavy significance.

"Then the players have changed, but the game is still on," said the king, calling chess to my mind once again. My head spinning with this web of deception, I had to concede that the tactic was working, for the room was suddenly full of servants who were being given orders to see to our comfort. A gaggle of handmaidens led me from the room, and a group of menservants did the same for Brother Guido. The Capitano was dismissed with orders to see to his fleet, given a heavy purse by the man in white. He left without a backward glance, his transaction complete, no more sorry to leave our company than we were to lose him. Then I forgot him at once, for I heard the king say, "You will have the best chambers that my castle can offer, my lord. Your consort will be in an adjoining solar for your comfort and pleasure. Please forgive my major-domo for touching your property."

" 'Tis already forgot, Your Highness," said Brother Guido, inclining his head in forgiveness at the white-clad minister.

"You are most gracious. Although, in truth, I have three mistresses myself, and a wife too, and if someone would take one off my hands 'twould be a blessing."

The two "nobles" guffawed, like men, and I noted that Brother Guido was a gifted actor. I marveled at this new fellow; could it be only a few moments ago that I had berated him for his inaction, for his uselessness, for his lack of invention?

"Perhaps you will do me the honor of traveling north with my court tomorrow? Since we are both invited to the great occasion 'twould be foolishness not to go together."

Brother Guido, though he must have been as confused as I, played along. He inclined his head. "I'd be delighted. Of course, my retinue will be waiting for me there."

The king personally saw us to the door; his majordomo, now wearing a smug smear of a smile, took my arm as if I were a queen. I looked at him snootily—I would not forget he had ripped my dress.

One thing more would confound my ears before we left

that chamber. For as we took our leave, Don Ferrente said to his majordomo, nice and loud so we could hear, "Santiago, I charge you to look after this my most honored guest. For Lord della Torre here is, like myself, one of *the Seven*."

19

I was taken from the room by a pair of Moorish beauties who showed me to what appeared to be a bathhouse. They stripped my torn and salt-caked dress and I slithered into the milky water, which lay like smoky green glass below Roman columns and capitals of stone that looked as soft as sugar. One maiden tossed in jasmine blossoms and the other washed me gently with porous sea sponges, even in the most intimate places. Although I've never been into that sort of thing (though of course I would oblige with a little Sapphic posturing if a client paid for it), I must admit my body was in paradise for these moments. My mind, however, was tossing on a stormy sea, and I could almost have screamed to have been parted from Brother Guido at such a time, when a thousand questions crowded my mind. My body was at peace, but my brain was in turmoil. Who, or what, were "the Seven"? Or rather, if Don Ferrente and Niccolò della Torre were two of them, who were the other five? What did the thumb rings mean? What was the newly dead Lord Silvio's connection with Don Ferrente? What "great occasion" were we invited to? And what the merry hell did the *Primavera* have to do with it all? I tried to still my racing thoughts, for I knew that Brother Guido would be getting similar ablutions from his menservants, so I would have to wait patiently for an audience. I only hoped the monk had managed to conceal the painting from his servants.

At length I was clothed in a loose shift and taken to my room, an airy chamber with a door that I knew adjoined my "master's." The slaves fussed around me and I could not wait for them to be gone, although they brought fruit, rolled herrings, and cooled wine in a clay jar of crushed ice. They told me, in their odd Neapolitan dialect, combined with a great deal of dumb-show mime, that the tiring women would be here soon to dress me for dinner. Throughout this entire discourse, my ears strained for sounds of my friend next door, but I could only hear occasional moans and cries that confused me greatly. If I had been listening at the door of any other man on this flat earth of ours, then I would have thought there was a little self-abuse going on, but with Brother Guido I knew that there was no question that he was "taking himself in hand." Alone at last, burning with curiosity, I listened at the door but the room was now silent. Almost sure that there was no one now within, I did not knock but entered at once.

He was there, alone, facedown on his ornate bed, his visage turned to the wall. His habit lay in a heap at the foot of the bed. The knotted belt, I noticed, was not there. The brown fustian had collapsed in a crumpled pool as if its occupant had shed his skin. And indeed he had. For Brother Guido's back was slick with blood, striped again and again with the sting of a whip. I knew three things then.

Cosa Uno: Brother Guido had used the knotted belt of his Franciscan habit to scourge himself for his transgressions.

Cosa Due: without counting, I knew that there were exactly forty lashes on his back, the number that the vengeful Romans had laid on the back of Christ on his death day. My questions died on my lips and I withdrew, stricken. Brother Guido turned his head at once, caught, but when he saw it was me two crystal tears fell from his bright blue eyes, across his noble nose, to fall on the silk coverlet. *Lacrimae Christi*. I knew the third thing:

Cosa Tre: I had done this to him. I had tempted him like a siren of the sea, he had kissed me back with what he thought was his last breath, and he could not forget that he had done so. Stricken, I closed the door, not knowing what to say.

20

I sat on the coverlet of my bed then, watching the bay through the window. I must have sat so, not moving, for some time, for the bells rang twice as I sat, motionless, growing cold as the sun went down. I told myself I was thinking about the *Primavera* and the puzzle hidden in the painting, but in truth I thought of Brother Guido all that time, lying motionless one door away, silently hurting, all because of what I'd done. Could we ever go back to the way we'd been? Or had our relationship suffered a sea change from which it would never recover? Chi-chi, with her confidence and bravado, had deserted me once again and I was just a girl sitting alone with her thoughts: Luciana Vetra, homeless, friendless, and motherless. Never had I needed *Vero Madre* more; to feel a pair of loving arms around me, and a soft kiss to the top of my head. For once I did not crave the heat of a man's embrace, but the strong circle of a mother's arms. Now, you should know, if you have not already guessed, that I never cry; not since I was a baby in a bottle, when the glass sent back my cries to my own ears so magnified that I thought I'd better stop for my own comfort. But now I felt as if the tears may come at last, and even though they did not, it seemed that Bembo's pearl had traveled from my navel to my throat, there to lodge forever no matter how many times I swallowed.

The glittering diamond necklace of the bay below turned to jet as the vista darkened, and I barely blinked when the slaves returned to light the lamps. As the room warmed to light behind me, I heard a soft voice and turned around at last.

Three ladies stood in my chamber, all in black. Like a murder of crows. But there their funereal likeness ended, for they all had pretty faces and merry eyes and smiled a trio of smiles that were eerily alike. In fact, they reminded me of nothing so much as the three Graces, but alive not dead, clad in black not white, and as dark in countenance and feature as the Graces were fair, just as the bay outside had turned from bright to black with the end of the day. The women introduced themselves as Eulalia Ravignano, Giovanna Caracciola, and Diana Guardato. I instantly forgot which was which, but smiled with a welcome I did not feel.

"And you are the ladies of the bedchamber? Come to dress me? The slaves said you would come."

One of them smiled wider than the other two. "We are come to dress you indeed," she said in clear Neapolitan, albeit scattered with Spanish hisses like a basket of snakes. "But we are not tiring women. We are freeborn ladies of the court of Aragon."

"And we all share a special relationship with Don Ferrente," put in the second.

"Not unlike the one you enjoy with Lord Niccolò," added the third.

Now this last I doubted, unless the three ladies were on the run from Florentine assassins after stealing a painting and enlisting the help of a total stranger who was a monk masquerading as a nobleman. But I had the drift of their hints.

"You are his mistress . . . es?"

They nodded as one.

"*All* of you?" But as I said it, I remembered that Don Ferrente had admitted as much himself, and owned to a wife too. I didn't need to wait for the nod this time.

The ladies were friendly and full of life—they fluttered around me chirruping in Spanish and lifting my chin and hair, circling my waist with their hands, and discussing, clearly, what I should wear. I knew them then for what they were—not crows but blackbirds, with their beady black eyes, blue-black hair, and their heads cocked to one side as they considered my charms. But their sense of fun was infectious and I felt Chi-chi come home to roost as I joined in their discourse when they reverted to Tuscan. I felt that we were all very much alike, for what were they, in truth, but high-class whores, be they ever so noble? Bawdy and witty, they discussed their bedsport openly and asked me intimate details of my liaisons with my own lord. I could not tell them that we were as chaste as Christmastide, so had to improvise with details of my other professional couplings. They all seemed to share each other's opinions, and finish each other's sentences, with a fluency that suggested that they spent all their time in each other's company. Clearly, from their stories, they shared Don Ferrente's bed together too, all at once rather than in succession. On the subject of my "master" they were of one mind.

"By the field of stars, he's a fine gentleman."

"I have never seen the like."

"He makes the others here at court look like washerwomen."

"Excepting our lord Don Ferrente, of course."

"By Saint Jude, I cannot wait to see him in his hose and codpiece! I'll wager he has a fine leg, and a fine foot too."

They cackled together. I smiled but could not confirm their guessings, for of course I had never seen Brother Guido in hose.

"Never mind him for now," said the one who I think was called Eulalia. "Let us dress this dove as our master commanded, to equal the beauties of her lord."

"Shall not be difficult, for she is favored like an angel."

If they but knew. "Ladies," I began, "there is no need to assist me. I can dress myself, if you give me a gown."

They laughed again. "La, no, my dear!"

"'Tis true it is below our place to dress you . . ."

"But our lord Don Ferrente knew we would welcome the chance to adorn such a beautiful bird. 'Tis a project we would enjoy."

"For believe me"—they spoke still in strict turn—"this court has few enough beauties, for most are old widows with swollen bellies and slack cunnies."

I could well believe it. For even this trio of attractive women were of a variety of shapes and forms, and each had their failings. One had thick wrists, another snag teeth, and the third, as she bent close, had bad breath that copious use of oil of cloves had failed to cover. I could only assume she did her lord Ferrente's service below the covers, and not face-to-face. All, too, were well into their middle years.

"For the queen likes her own beauties to shine forth, undiminished by those of others," they explained.

Now I was curious. "She is very fair, then, the queen?"

"Yes, indeed. Giovanna of Aragon is a great beauty," said Diana generously, with the others nodding agreement.

I was curious as to their relationship with the queen, for although I had been betraying noblewomen by fucking their husbands for a good few years now, I had never actually *known* the ladies. What was it like to live under the eye of the woman who knew you were warming her husband's bed?

"Oh, we *like* her."

"She is lovely."

"I am proud to bear her name," said the one who was clearly Giovanna. "On our shared saint's day she gave me a rosary for my missal."

I was curious. "And she is faithful, to Don Ferrente?"

"Oh, yes. Without question. He is not a man to be trifled with, for he can show great cruelty and violence to those who betray him. Certain of his rebellious barons have been recently murdered on his orders, some of them friends since the cradle. And for women it is even worse."

"In Sicily, my dear, if you betray your husband with another, your husband can beat you to death with the full support of the law."

I swallowed. The strains of the Neapolitan song drifted back to me from this morning, carried on the chimes of Vespers. *"Jesce jesce corno,"* indeed. If a man strayed, he was a horned snail in a comic song. If a woman strayed, here in the hot and passionate south, she was as good as dead. The king slept with three different dames every night right under his wife's nose, but a queen had to be beyond reproach. I thought hard on this as the ladies fluttered around me once more, pulling and pushing me, twisting strands of hair, applying ribbon and jewels, lacing my bodice. I had ever lived outside this law, outside the strictures and proprieties that governed other women. I had been turning tricks since I was old enough to bleed. Could I ever live this way, as a "decent" woman, so strictly policed in all her behavior? And what of love? Did that simplest and strongest of feelings have a place in the noble world of court? Did the king truly love the queen; *could* he love her, when he shared his favors so widely? And yet if he did not, why would he care if she took another lover? It was all most confusing. It was fortunate, really, that I was *not* a noblewoman.

I was so deep in thought that I barely noted what I was being dressed in until they pulled me to the looking glass. I gasped.

Once again, as in Pisa, I was transformed. But they had made me into a dove among the blackbirds—I was dressed from head to foot in white. My dress was stiff with a thousand seed pearls and stood out from my waist in a hugely full skirt like a bell. A delicate ruff of lace adorned my shoulders and framed my face, now pale again from days belowdecks. My hair was more blond than ever, bleached of its color by the sea salt and sun, twisted up into ripples by the ladies with the same pearls pinned into my locks. My skin was as pale as the gems that adorned me. I had been transformed into the very Grace whose identity we sought here in Naples. And then the notion chimed; in Florence I had been Flora. Here I was one of the Graces. Was I destined to inhabit all the ladies of the painting in turn?

Despite my spectral beauty, however, I knew, too, that the Chi-chi glitter in my eyes was back. I was a honeypot, a walking temptation for all the men of this court. Why, then, was I not excited? Why did I not plan, as I usually did, for some hot and licentious union with a random fellow this night?

I knew, of course. *Jesce jesce corno.* As I followed the ladies to dinner, an alien thought struck me. I had ever been a faithless slut, but I knew now that there was only one man I wanted, and if I could but marry him, then I would never stray.

21

The ladies led me through a dozen piebald presence chambers, in a procession of other magpie courtiers until presently the space opened out into an enormous banqueting hall with elegant cross ribs arching high above in an elegant spider's web. Arranged across the room were three long tables, making three sides of a square. A servant led myself and my three companions to the central table, where we were placed at either end, leaving room, I supposed, for the royal party. Seated and alone again, I scanned the room for Brother Guido but could not see him in the sea of black and white. When all were settled, the musicians sounded from a high gallery, and I looked up to see the buglers crack their cheeks like the four winds. Two doors opened at the end of the room and the royal party arrived at last. They were a glorious sight, but like the rest of the court, I only had eyes for their noble guest.

He was unrecognizable from the broken Christ I had seen bleeding on his bed this afternoon. He was clean-shaven. His hair trimmed and curled to shining blue-black ringlets. His face was glowing with health, the warm hue of an apricot. His blue eyes shone from his tanned face and swept the room with a noble mien. He was attired in black, his night-velvet surcoat adorned with a scattering of chips of jet, but his voluminous velvet sleeves were slashed to show a blouson of snowy white beneath. His legs were clad in tight black hose, showing calves and thighs that could have been hewn from marble, so firm and long and finely muscled were they. (Me being me, my eyes, of course, strayed to his codpiece, which seemed to boast of so substantial a manhood that my cheeks grew hot. I could not believe then that I had grabbed his prick the first time we met, would give anything to do it again now.) His attitude and expression were all stern nobility, and he wore his power like a mantle. I wondered that a humble monk could dissemble so, but my fickle woman's heart wanted him more than ever. I saw now, at once, what he could have been if he had accepted his uncle's legacy and felt sorry for the path he had chosen. Now Pisa would suffer under the yoke of an unworthy *finocchio*—the real Niccolò. Lord *Guido* della Torre, on the other hand, would have clearly been a true Prince of Pisa, a noble sprig without peer. He was magnificent.

And I was not the only one who thought so. Even Queen Giovanna—whom I had to admit was indeed beautiful in her dark Aragonese fashion—mingled eyes with him when he kissed her hand in tribute. For this woman, whose chastity was beyond reproach, to show such blatant interest was a testament to Brother Guido's charms. I looked quickly to Don Ferrente, but the king was settling into his chair and greeting his guests and had not seen the exchange. Then Brother Guido was at my side, and I felt my hand raised to his lips. But his eyes did not meet mine as they had met the queen's. My hand dropped, burning, to my lap and my cheeks flamed to match, and yet as he took his seat beside me I knew he had noticed my beauty, and that he was just as affected as he had been when he saw me descend the stairs in Pisa.

He, too, was clearly thinking of that night, for, as if he had caught the echo of my thoughts like a distant chime of bells, he said, "How charming you look tonight, Luciana. Truly, I'm honored to have you as my companion."

The very words I had teased him with omitting as I had descended his uncle's stair. The blue eyes sparkled now, and I marveled that they could hold so many expressions. So bleak was his stare when I had entered his room earlier, yet so lively with humor now. I divined that his good mood must have a reason; perhaps in our time apart he had made some significant discovery that took us a little forward in our quest.

Whatever the reason, I was glad.

It was quickly clear to me that I was in for an enjoyable night, for three reasons.

Ragione Uno: Brother Guido was drinking, as I had never seen him do, clearly in an effort to support our charade, for as a nobleman on a nonfast day he would be expected to enjoy the wines of his host.

Ragione Due: we were to share the same dish, as I was Pisa's acknowledged consort, and all couples were sharing a platter, as was the norm in high society.

Ragione Tre: Brother Guido was closely observing other

nobles and their courtesans around the tables, and aped their behavior with me, leaning close, sharing morsels, and whispering in my ear. It mattered not that we spoke together of a stolen painting; the closeness itself was enough. I was happy to play along. For this afternoon, in his chamber, he had looked at me with the eyes of the damned across a yawning chasm that seemingly could never be breached. Now, although we were merely players in a play, I felt I had crossed the valley and scaled the battlements—was it too much to hope that I might, one day, be admitted to the citadel?

While I mused, Brother Guido spoke at length to the king on his right, but the roar of chatter was too great to hear what they said. When he turned back I bent close to his perfumed head, and as once before, his warm hair tickled my cheek. "Did you find out anything about the Seven?"

"No," he breathed at me. "He was speaking of how this is a better residence for such feasts than his old abode, Castel Capuano across the bay. This place, Castel Nuovo, he inherited from his dead father, and he said that such bereavements can bring joy as well as grief. He alluded to my own loss."

Here, I am sure, Brother Guido presented a very suitable countenance of the grieving son, for he cared more for his uncle than the real Niccolò ever had. "Anything else? What's the celebration that we're all supposed to be attending?"

"He didn't say, but he did imply that tonight's feast is in honor of someone or something. He's making a toast; mayhap we'll learn more then."

"And the *cartone,* is it safe? Where is it?"

He patted his shimmering, jet-studded chest. "Here."

It looked suspiciously flat—as if nothing lay under the nap but his smooth broad muscle. "Still in the goatskin?" I asked with narrowed eyes.

"No. I told them to take care of the gourd for it contained

relics of my dead father. The Spanish understand such things, and my lord king did send me a jeweled leather pouch, flat like a pocket, meant for the carriage of relics on the person. I effected the transfer, and the *cartone* is safe. Not damaged by our travels, nor like to be in the future, for the pouch is sturdy and proof against water."

My shoulders dropped in relief. "Thank *fuck* for that. 'Twould have been a fine pot of piss if we'd come all this way and—"

Brother Guido shushed me with a flap of his hand, for the king stood up to speak and the room fell silent in three heartbeats. Tall and aquiline, Don Ferrente cut an impressive figure in his head-to-toe black. "My dear friends," he began, in his gravelly, Aragonese-accented Neapolitan. His white smile accepted the whole room, and from the corner of my eye I saw his trio of mistresses *and* his wife all looking up at him with adoration. "We are here, as you know, to celebrate the betrothal of the cousin of a dear friend."

There was a rumble of dissent around the room, which surprised me—I thought the king well loved. Mayhap he should murder a few more barons in the future.

He held up a hand to stay the protests. "No, no, my friends. Lorenzo de' Medici has given our kingdom pain in the past, and we have not always been on good terms. But since his visit to me earlier this year, and the tribute he paid to me, all past wrongs are forgotten. I consider us to be as brothers—we do not always agree, but we are bound together by blood." There was now laughter, and the hecklers seemed satisfied. "And for this reason we celebrate today the betrothal of his dearly beloved cousin Lorenzo di Pierfrancesco de' Medici, and Semiramide Appiani, of the House of Aragon."

My dull brain struggled to keep up. Lorenzo il Magnifico had recently fallen out with Don Ferrente, but had come here himself earlier in the year to make good. His cousin, Botticelli's patron, was to be married to a member of Don Ferrente's family. Was this alliance the "tribute" il Magnifico had made to the House of Aragon? "Wonder what they fought about?" I whispered to my consort. "Must have been serious, for il Magnifico to offer his cousin as a marriage prize?"

"Shhh!" Brother Guido hissed, for the king was speaking again.

"And we have the honor to be invited to the nuptials, a sennight from today."

All right. Did that mean that Lorenzo di Pierfrancesco would be traveling south to marry at the home of his bride? Where in the stinking south would we be bound next? I felt a strange foreboding.

"So we raise our glasses to the health of the bride and groom, to the benefits of our alliance, and for the progress of our court on the morrow to the wedding. In fact, 'tis not so bad a thing that we shall be absent from Naples for this little while, for, as you all know, our Blessed Saint Gennaro's blood did not liquefy this year."

Now this I did not understand at all. I looked around the court for signs of laughter at a joke that was too lofty for my understanding. But there was nothing but grave nods of assent, which set the noble heads bobbing like corks in a barrel. I looked back to our host impatiently. *For the love of* Vero Madre, *just tell us where we are bound!*

"So I give you our sojourn to the beauteous city of *Florence*."

My wine was already in my mouth and I spat it straight back out in a rainshower. Brother Guido gripped my arm till it hurt and the court stilled and looked to me, the king included. "Hiccups," I murmured. "Sorry."

The king's quizzical glance thawed to a smile. "Such things are easily forgiven in the face of such beauty."

I relaxed outwardly, but my innards were in turmoil. *Florence?* Were we to return to the lion's mouth, and certain death? I looked hard at Brother Guido, but his sunny countenance remained unchanged, and he patted my hand in assurance. I looked down at my lap, trying to suppress my feelings as the king continued.

"And now, I will reveal a little gift that I have made with my own hands for the happy couple, a great honor to show my friendship to the Medici family."

With a flourish the ever-present majordomo Santiago whipped a black silk napkin from a bumpy object in the center of the table. It was a carving, beautifully rendered and quite finished, of the Nativity scene. We all craned closer. It was a little wooden miracle, for every detail was present. The babe, laughing, held up his starlike hands to the Virgin who knelt in devotion. Every particular was perfectly rendered— every strand of hair, every jewel in the crowns of kings; even a robin sang from the eaves. From the glow of the white wood I recognized the woodwork that the king had been whittling earlier that day, and remembered, too, the hundreds of Nativity scenes I had seen for sale in the streets. Not one of those rivaled what we marveled at now. As the court murmured its approval the king spoke again, with visible pride. " 'The day-spring from on high has visited us—' "

" 'And Kings shall come to the brightness of thy rising,' " finished Brother Guido, as if completing a password.

I held my breath, lest this be seen as insolence, but the king smiled again. "Indeed. You know your Scripture. Very fitting, for a leader of men." Here he spoke out to the whole room. "Christ was the greatest leader of all, for did he not show us all the way, on Calvary's hill? Tell me"—he turned again to look at Brother Guido—"what do *you* think of my gift?" Don Ferrente inclined his head with mock humility, fully expecting a compliment.

"I think, *'timeo Danaos et dona ferentes,'*" replied Brother Guido, his eyes icy, his face a mask of pride. He was clearly speaking Latin, and he translated for the lack-learned, myself included, in a ringing voice. And that's how I learned the second of the three Latin tags that I know, and could scarcely believe the insolence of its meaning: "Beware of Greeks bearing gifts."

This time he'd gone too far. The court gasped in unison, and I looked with horror at the king, who stared back at my companion, steely and unsmiling. I dug Brother Guido viciously in the ribs. What the hell was he playing at? Pride and arrogance were all very well, but in a just measure that would convince that he was really Niccolò della Torre. Blind insolence was another thing—was he trying to get us killed? And he censured me for spitting my wine!

Don Ferrente gave a series of throaty gulps and Santiago jumped up at his elbow with wine. But the king waved him away, eyes streaming. Was he so incensed by his guest that he was having some sort of fit? But no, Brother Guido had judged his reply aright; Don Ferrente was *laughing,* and his court of sycophants did likewise until I felt I was in a pit of yelping jackals.

"Very good," chuckled the king, "very good. My honored guest makes a play on my name. *Dona ferentes, Don Ferrente,* 'bearing gifts.' Very good." He sank to his chair, speech over, still murmuring the jest and giving little shouts of laughter. I understood then that the king was powerful, merciless, even dangerous, but not very clever. He admired scholarship, and aspired to it, and Brother Guido had seen that. I had to give him credit. He had finished the biblical reference and made a Latin joke that Don Ferrente would just about get, and so endeared himself to the king, who was now slapping him about the shoulders.

" 'Tis a trifle, my gift. Just a trifle," said the king, waving his hand in a dismissive manner at the carving which had started all this, waiting for the inevitable contradiction from his guest. Now, it seemed, a compliment was necessary.

"Not so, Majesty," rejoined Brother Guido, more than equal to the task of flattery. "For although other gifts may have a greater value in their materials—gold, jewels, and suchlike— your carving is so exquisite that the value is immeasurable, lying as it does in the quality of the workmanship."

Even I, born flatterer that I am, thought that Brother Guido might have overcooked it. But the king was all smiles.

"If you admire it so much, perhaps I will make one for you, at your upcoming nuptials. The dogaressa's daughter, is it not? A fine marriage prize!"

At the same time that Brother Guido inclined his head in agreement, I literally jumped with shock about a twelveinch in the air. *Betrothed?*

For the second time that night the king looked askance at me. Brother Guido covered quickly. "My fair consort has a particular love for this air that your musicians are playing. She is anxious to dance, for she has a great talent for it and cannot stay still when the music calls!"

I smiled and nodded along—it was either that or protest that I had the palsy. I thought we had gotten away with it, but the king nodded and clapped his hands. "Excellent!" he called into the sudden silence. "A measure! Play the air again," he charged his musicians. "Our guests will honor us with an exhibition dance in the Pisan style."

I looked murder at Brother Guido, but in fairness he did not look too happy either. I was comfortable in my own skill for I had not lied when I had told him I danced well, that night when we had first discussed the Graces' attitudes. I had no idea, however, how well schooled a monk would be in the forms of dance. He could look the part, which he did, but he may have two left feet.

I need not have worried. The musicians played a simple, slow pavane and we circled around each other with matching skill, alone in the middle of that vast space, a raven and a swan taking a measure. I was pleased and surprised—he had clearly been brought up with all the needful skills of a young princeling before he had entered orders. I would have begun to enjoy myself, were it not for the latest revelation, a subject we canvassed in hissing whispers whenever the dance brought us together. "So you are . . . Niccolò is . . . betrothed?"

"Yes."

"To the dogaressa's daughter? From Venice?" Oh, the irony.

"Yes. It was settled before my cousin went to the university."

My thoughts wheeled with my person as we turned away from each other and described a wide circle of the room apart, before joining hands again. "But he is a *finocchio*! Queer as Christmas!"

Brother Guido rolled his eyes. "Really, Luciana. You, in your former circles, must have divined that a preference for . . . the company of boys does not preclude a man from a tolerably happy marriage."

It was true. I had known many such in the noble society of Florence—men who had never approached me or my fellows, men who Bembo said had a *matrimonio bianco*—a white marriage. "But what about love?" I blurted, thinking again of what I had learned this afternoon: that the nobility seem to hold no store by human feeling. "Is this poor maid to be shackled to a

174

cruel fellow with no interest in her person? No . . . bedsport?"
I could not think of anything worse.

"You are talking like a simpleton. The compensations of
such a match are great—he has lands; she does too, and a shipping fortune to boot. I thought you understood such transactions. Love does not enter into the case. And if it did, I doubt
whether you yourself would have made much of a living in
your former profession."

He was quite correct. Marriage *was* more about business
than feeling. But it wasn't right. "It's not right."

"I never said it was. Such transactions of noble heirs like so
much exalted cattle is morally abhorrent to me—it's one of
the reasons I entered Holy Orders in the first place, else the
maid of Venice would have been destined for my bed, no
doubt." He grimaced like a gargoyle. "But happily, human love
is no longer my concern. I know only of divine love as every
monk should."

I toyed with the idea of telling him how many of his order
I had screwed in the hallowed precincts of his own foundation. But I thought I had a more exalted argument. "Fra Filippo
Lippi was a monk," I said, naming one of Florence's most
famous artists, "and he married a nun, and had a child!"

Brother Guido shrugged delicately. "Some there are that
leave the order and enter worldy life. But not I. I hope to strive
for divine love, in a state of chastity, for the rest of my days."
He did not quite meet my eyes. "And besides, I cannot pretend
to understand such an emotion anyway. Human love, and the
excesses it drives people to, is a mystery to me. What is love,
anyway?"

I did not quite believe his protests. That dying kiss he had
given me, on the sinking flagship—not acknowledged, not
mentioned—had more to do with human feeling than he
believed. Or human passion at any rate. Not for nothing had

he striped his own back in penance like the Christ. But he had asked an interesting question, and I thought I knew the answer.

"Love is when you like someone so much you have to call it something else," I stated, pleased with the notion. My friend did not look convinced, so I returned to the earlier theme. "And when is the wedding to take place?" My confused mind could not at once separate Brother Guido from Niccolò—I almost felt it was the former who was to be married, not the man he impersonated.

"I know not. 'Twas all settled when I was at Santa Croce. But unless it is in the next few days, I am quite safe from the horns of matrimony."

The dance ended and he bowed, hiding a smile. I did not see what was so funny, and burned with curiosity as we returned to the high table, where the king clapped enthusiastically and his toadies followed suit.

"Capital!" he cried. His Majesty reached for my hand and I made a courtesy as he kissed it. He seemed loath to let it go so I took Brother Guido's seat and sat happily next to him, for I had some questions.

"The lady who is betrothed to my lord . . ." I began.

The king inclined his head indulgently. "The dogaressa's daughter?"

"Why is she called so? Why not the *doge*'s daughter?" For I knew that "doge," meaning "duke," was the title of the ruler of my former city of Venice, and "dogaressa" the title of his wife.

"For the reason that the mother and daughter are said to be as like as two peas in a pod. And added to that, the dogaressa is a remarkably strong-willed lady—she hauled herself up from the streets, for she was once no more than a courtesan. She is reputed to rule her husband; they say that beneath her fine gowns hangs a prick and her balls clang together like a ring o' bells, for the doge has none." He chuckled, with a confidence that suggested that no one would dare slander *him* in this way. But I was not concerned with the politics of the situation. "And is she fair? The daughter, I mean?"

Now he smiled, amused that a businesswoman such as myself should feel the sharp thorns of jealousy; after all, for most loyal mistresses, a marriage did not mean the end of a relationship, as his own ménage proved.

"As to that, I cannot say, for she has been shut in a nunnery for these many years. But what I can tell you is that her mother is as fair as the first morning in May, so beauteous that she goes about often in mask in the Venetian fashion, else, it is said, the city would grind to a halt while the citizens stop in the streets to stare at her. So the daughter must be likewise if the reports are true."

My face must have been sour as a lemon, for now Don Ferrente laughed openly. "But you should not be downcast. Be she Venus herself, she would be as a candle to the sun next to you. They say daughters are like pancakes—the more you make, the better they get. Well, in that case I say that your father must have got a dozen daughters on your mother before he sired you."

There was Don Ferrente in a nutshell; a learned compliment referencing Venus followed by a sally about pancakes. The man was a king and a commoner, learned and ignorant all at once. But whichever way you sliced it, he had paid me two compliments, so I beamed, sunlike again.

"Indeed," he went on, "'tis a pity we may not all choose our wives with our hearts." He patted his own queen's hand in a way that suggested there was indeed a great affection between them. "For you could not do better than this dove, Lord Niccolò."

Brother Guido, taking his cue to join the discourse, nodded graciously in acknowledgment of the compliment to his taste.

"For she is la Fiammetta personified."

Now it was Brother Guido's turn to jump and spit his wine. "I beg your pardon, Your Majesty?"

The king, thinking that the noise of the feast had drowned his words, leaned closer and shouted across me. "I said she is the image of the Lady Fiammetta—the golden hair, white skin, dark arched brows." His hands sketched my attributes in the air as if he carved again.

Brother Guido, looking ill, nodded weakly.

"As a learned man like myself, you will appreciate this . . ." began the king, proving me right about his intellectual vanity. "Did you know that Giovanni Boccaccio did in fact first become inspired to write of the Lady Fiammetta right here, in a church in Naples? 'Tis said he caught sight of my own ancestor, Maria d'Aquino, daughter of the House of Aragon, at mass, and became obsessed with her beauty. Ever after he wrote of her as Fiammetta, his muse."

I looked back to Brother Guido as if I watched a game of tennis. He had recovered himself with his customary speed. "I have heard of the fabled lady, of course. And I am tolerably familiar with the writings of Boccaccio." The latter I believed, I wasn't sure about the former. "You must be very proud of your literary heritage, Your Majesty."

He could not have said anything to better please the king— this bandit who would be a scholar.

"I'll warrant you have a fine library here, Majesty," Brother Guido went on, in a voice that told me his question had a purpose beyond mere flattery.

"I do, I do." The king nodded, while I wondered where this direction tended.

"Might I impose upon you to let me borrow the *Elegia di*

Madonna Fiammetta, this evening? You have put me in mind to read it again with fresh eyes, now that I know the lady was your illustrious ancestor."

The king looked like a dog that had suddenly discovered he could lick his own balls. "Of course! Gladly. Santiago!" But the majordomo had already disappeared in search of the volume. "But if I were you, my lord." The king beckoned and Brother Guido bent close. "I would close the book after a while and enjoy the real thing." With a saucy nod at my tits the king rent the air with laughter as he displayed the other side of his character. The scholar retreated behind the ruffian once more.

As soon as he may, Brother Guido excused us from the feast and I grumbled all the way back to the chamber, for I had not finished my wine. Once there, however, I too was excited to resume our quest, for a small volume lay on my lord's pillow: a leather book bound in red buckram with the cover chased in gold. "All right," I said, as Brother Guido took up the book with trembling hands. "Take me through it again. This writer, Giovanni Boccaccio—"

"Who lived above a hundred years ago and wrote the *Decameron,* along with other great works—"

I let this pass, as I had patently never heard of it. "Saw some woman in a church here in Naples—"

"Apparently Maria d'Aquino, Princess of Aragon."

"And started writing about her."

"She became his muse."

"And in his books he called her the Lady Fiammetta."

"Correct."

"And the one you've got there is Fiammetta's life story."

"It's the *Elegia di Madonna Fiammetta*—the *Elegy of the Lady Fiammetta.*"

"And you think Maria d'Aquino, or Fiammetta, or whatever

you want to call her, is the dead woman we're looking for, the woman in the *Primavera*?"

"The 'Naples' Grace. Yes," he said simply, unfolding the *cartone* from the pouch at his chest, and staring intently at the left-hand Grace.

I took the painting from him and did likewise. "So what are you looking for now?" His long fingers were riffling through the pages of the book in a practiced fashion.

"Anything. A description. A clue. Listen." One of his long digits rested on a line of dialogue. "'Her hair is so blond that the world holds nothing like it; it shades a white forehead of noble width, beneath which are the curves of two black and most slender eyebrows . . . and under these two roguish eyes . . . cheeks of no other color than milk.'"

"All right," I conceded. "It sounds like her. Now what?"

"I propose to stay awake and read this volume tonight. Then by daybreak I may have found something."

I looked at him and then the book. It was a slim volume, but even a fast reader would take hours to chew through it. And he suddenly looked desperately tired, the excitements and dangers of the day telling on his face.

"Or," I suggested, "we could just find out the name of the church where they met and start there."

He smiled relief. "Once again, your practicality conquers my intellect. You are right. Let us rest, for I sorely need to sleep, as do you."

I stood in the door long enough for him to have to ask.

"In your *own* bed," he said with emphasis.

Worth a try. I backed out and closed the door. When I returned to my solar I took a last look out of the window at the bay below. The moonlight turned the necklace of Naples to pearl. The moon seemed to shine unnaturally bright tonight—I hoped it was not an ill omen.

22

First thing in the morning we sought Santiago. We tracked him down to the long gallery, where he fixed us with his perpetual oily smile. Now that we were honored guests nothing was too much for us.

"My good fellow," began Brother Guido imperiously. "Signorina Vetra and I are minded to attend mass, to pray for Lorenzo di Pierfrancesco's upcoming nuptials. His Majesty Don Ferrente mentioned a certain church last night—where a local legend took place, to do with the writer Boccaccio, with whose work you were kind enough to furnish me." He spoke casually, his offhand reference to the writer pitched to excite no suspicion. "Could you tell me, is the place far?"

Santiago, however, nodded and smiled with great significance. If he had been a less subtle creature I could swear he would have winked at this point. As if Brother Guido had asked him to procure him a small boy, he answered archly, "Ah, yes, of course. My lord and I expected you might like to see . . . the church," he said with a knowing emphasis. "'Tis not far into the city, to the northeast. Take the Via Nilo, for there lies an interesting Roman statue—a representation of Old Man Nile, who is said to speak to beautiful ladies as they pass." The majordomo sketched an elegant bow at me. "In the face of your charms, Doña, he cannot possibly remain silent."

My smile matched his for insincerity.

"And the name of the church, once again?" Don Ferrente had, in fact, never mentioned the name, and once again I marveled at Brother Guido's skills as an actor.

"San Lorenzo Maggiore," supplied Santiago with a heavy significance.

"Ah, yes." Brother Guido nodded. "I remember yestereve, that the church seemed a fitting place to offer our prayers, as it is dedicated to the saint that named both il Magnifico, and his cousin that is to be married."

Santiago bowed so low that it was impossible to see his reaction to this. He left us with a flourish, but turned at the door. "One thing, my lord."

We both held our breath.

"The wedding party leaves for the north at the Angelus." And he was gone.

"The Angelus?" I asked as we left the castle.

"A single bell that tolls at noon every day here in the south." Brother Guido looked sideways at me. "Don't worry. The sun is still low. We have plenty of time."

But the monk had misread me—I was not afeared that we would miss the wedding train, I was afeared that we would *catch* it. I still could not believe that we were to return home, back to danger.

As we walked through the precincts of the castle we noted the great preparations that were taking place, as there was a bustle of black-clad servants packing and carrying trunks of silks and victuals hither and yon. We left the main gate and took the northern coast path into the city. We were both clad in the austere black day clothes brought by our respective servants. Although the Moorish bath girls had come to attend me, of the three mistresses of the king there was no sign. I suspected they were so jug-bitten from the night before that they would not rise before the Angelus woke them. I noted now that the clothes, though plain, were well cut and suited my escort very well. I hoped he thought the same of me but suspected he had not even noticed the contrast of my white-blond locks with the black velvet, which suited me almost as much as my white attire from yestereve. For all the world we resembled a respectable couple going to mass. As the streets closed around us we felt it safe to talk.

"D'you think Santiago knows what we're up to?" I began.

"I don't think so. He seemed to think he knew *something,* but I don't believe it's anything to do with the *Primavera.* More likely it's something to do with the Seven."

"Maybe he listened to us talking last night."

Brother Guido shrugged. "It is true that the Spanish race is not averse to a little espionage. Spying," he amended for my benefit. "But what would he have heard? We only really discussed the painting under the cover of the noise of the feast. Last night we were talking about Boccaccio and Fiammetta, and that much we told him ourselves." He thought for a moment. "He did tell us something of interest, though. It can be no accident that the name of the church is 'San Lorenzo,' the name shared by Lorenzo de' Medici and Lorenzo di Pierfrancesco."

"Yes, but there are churches called 'San Lorenzo' all over this land." I panted, for his long stride forced me to trot to keep up. I noticed that my companion always walked faster when his thoughts were racing. "The saint is well loved."

"Surely. But Lorenzo de' Medici is called the 'great,' the 'magnificent.'"

"*Maggiore!*" I cried, light dawning. The same name as the church.

"That's right. And he is the cousin of our groom-to-be, Botticelli's patron. I wonder if Botticelli was trying to finish the *Primavera* in time for the wedding?" he mused.

"The event definitely has some significance, outside of just a happy family gathering."

My brain, like my feet, struggled to keep up. "Are you saying that Lorenzo di Pierfrancesco is one of the Seven?"

"I'm not sure," admitted Brother Guido carefully. "But I do know that this church must hold the answer to at least some of our questions. So I need you to exercise all your faculties of observation and deduction."

"You mean keep my eyes peeled and my wits about me."

"That too."

This was more like old times—him using long words and me using short ones. With the climbing sun on my back and Brother Guido by my side I could almost forget the threat of our imminent return to Florence hanging over us. We walked for a spell in silence, and as I noted the saints and Madonnas peering from their niches to mark our way, I was jolted by a remembrance. "What did Don Ferrente mean last night, when he said something about some saint's blood? Not being *liquid*?"

"Ah, yes. The 'miracle of San Gennaro,'" he replied promptly. "The serving men who dressed me told me all. Three times a year at the cathedral here they hold aloft a vial of the blood of their saint, San Gennaro. The vial contains solidified, clotted blood; but after many minutes of prayer and beseeching the blood miraculously becomes liquid, and is shaken for all those at mass to see. The citizens queue for a sennight to kiss the vial. This most recent time, however, the blood did *not* liquefy, which is seen locally as an omen of bad luck."

I considered this. "What happened last time it didn't?"

"The volcano erupted," he said briefly.

I eyed the smoking blue mountain above us with a skeptical glance. It seemed peaceful enough. "And you believe all this?" I asked, fighting to keep the cynicism from my voice.

Brother Guido shrugged. "Miracles are a matter of faith, and when you have faith, everything is possible. But it matters not whether I do or don't, for the servants do, and all the court, as you saw. They truly believe that ill luck will befall the city, and that is partly why the king is so keen to progress north. For by the time they return, it will be time for the blood to be tested again, mayhap with a better result."

I shook my head but kept my peace. Such fancies were not in my lexicon, but I did not want to insult my friend, when we had returned to our delicate balance of comradeship. I changed the subject. "Are we even going the right way?" I ventured.

"I believe so. See," he said, pointing, "there is the statue Santiago mentioned."

"Ah, yes," I said with a curl of my lip. "Old Man Nile who talks to pretty girls."

He smiled in reply. "Well, whether he does or not, this is the Via Nilo. We must be going in the right direction."

We drew close to the statue and I could see better the form—an old man indeed, much worn and pocked by the elements, clearly many centuries old. But for all that, the reclining attitude was remarkably lifelike, and when I looked into his slumberous eyes, I did feel great wisdom there, and that he could almost speak. Without knowing why, I lingered, and let Brother Guido gain a few steps ahead, before I whispered to the old stone man. "Greetings," I said shyly, feeling foolish.

"Look behind you," he said. It was a voice as deep as gravel and as old as time, but quite distinct. I felt the ice and heat of shock flow through my veins in turn—surely the stone man hadn't actually spoken? But despite myself I turned. That's when I saw him for the first time—the creature that would haunt us.

A leper—for those were the weeds he wore—lounged against a fragment of a Roman pillar, his wasted claw outstretched for alms. But his attitude of beggary was just for show, for he was looking straight at me, with eyes I would never forget. Almost silver, his orbs burned from his head and shot me through with terror as if they were twin blades. For a heartbeat our gaze connected and he knew he was seen, and vanished behind his pillar. I could have followed him then, but could not wait to remove myself from his malign presence. I ran to catch my friend, did not stop to thank the statue who had alerted me to this evil thing. For as I ran I suspected three things that I could not prove.

Cosa Uno: the leper had been following us since Florence.

Cosa Due: he had killed Enna, Bembo, and Brother Remigio, and Lord Silvio too.

Cosa Tre: he had been assigned to kill *us*.

I grabbed Brother Guido's black sleeve to speed him along, adding to the impression of a couple late for mass. But he noticed my agitation at once.

"What's amiss?"

I did not slacken my pace. "I'm just concerned that we may not have time for our search. See." I nodded to the blazing blue heavens. "The sun climbs already."

He matched my stride then, and presently we found our church—a noble building in sand-colored stone with a lofty spire. After the brightness of the day, the gloom within blinded us and we fumbled about like noonday moles, but it soon became clear that we had missed the mass. There was no one within save a single robed priest at the far end of the nave, extinguishing the candles from the service. We exchanged a relieved glance—'twould be so much easier to explore the church as a couple of pilgrims rather than as part of the congregation at a crowded mass.

"All right," whispered Brother Guido. "Look hard—anything to do with a lady, or a lock of hair, or a jewel such as we see in the painting. There *must* be some clue within this place that connects it to Fiammetta. Perhaps the tomb of the real Fiammetta, Maria d'Aquino. Or some reference to Boccaccio."

We began a slow and thorough tour of the place, circling each pillar and pew, stopping at every plaque or monument. After one circuit it seemed our search would be in vain—the only lady present was the Holy Virgin, the only tombs those of Neapolitan knights of old.

"We're missing something," insisted Brother Guido, his voice low, his eyes on the distant priest. "Perhaps we should ask . . ."

"Wait!" My eyes had been idling upon a stone carving on the wall. "Here's a lady!"

We moved nearer and Brother Guido peered closely in the candlelit dim. He moved his long fingers over the carving, in an attempt to make it out better, then shook his head. "No good," he said, his voice colored with disappointment. "'Tis Saint Veronica, for see, here is Christ carrying the cross, and she wipes his brow with a cloth."

He was right. Chastened, I looked farther up the wall as my companion moved away. "And what of these scratches above? What do they mean?"

"Scratches?" He turned.

"Yes, see, a point and a line." I moved my fingers over the deep indents scored into the stone: *V* and *I*. "Here."

Then I saw his eyes do that odd thing that they do when he has a revelation: they burned such a bright blue that they almost lit the gloom. "Not scratches," said he. *"Numbers."*

Now, as I said before, I cannot read, but I do know my numbers—at least from one to ten, then my knowledge becomes a little sketchy. Working girls need to know about numbers, for money comes in numbers, does it not? "Those aren't numbers," I scoffed. "At least, the line could be a one, I suppose, but the point is more like an arrowhead, or—"

"*Roman* numbers," he interrupted me, urgently. "In Roman

numerology, the characters are different from the Arabic numbers we use in everyday life. Here, the point or *V* means five, and the *I* is indeed a one. This is a *number,* the number six."

My mind was as dim as the church. "But why is *this* carving named six? Are you sure it isn't *V* for Veronica?"

His eyes burned even bluer. "Because it's one of a *series.* Saint Veronica wipes Christ's brow. *Six.* This is the sixth station of the cross."

"Ah, yes."

"You know of the stations?" He seemed skeptical.

"Convent educated. The stations are the steps that Jesus took toward his death on the cross. There are fourteen in all," I said smugly.

"Then see here"—he moved to his left—"another relief— carving, sorry—of a man who takes the cross from Christ to help him with the burden. Simon of Cyrene carries the cross for Christ—the *fifth* station of the cross."

"So?" I was lost. "What does this have to do with Fiammetta?"

"Forget Fiammetta." He flapped his hands impatiently. "We were working from the wrong clue. If this is *five,* and the next is *six,* then there must be a—"

"Seven!" I almost shouted the number and Brother Guido turned on me.

"Be silent!" he hissed. "Remember, we saw a priest as we entered—we do not want our business known."

"Shit, sorry," I mumbled, but I was too excited to truly repent. "Come on." We moved to the right, past Saint Veronica, to the seventh station.

"Christ falls for the second time," whispered Brother Guido, indicating the fallen figure below the burden of the great cross. "And here." His fingers traced upward. *"V-I-I,* the Roman number seven."

"All right," I breathed, my eyes on the beaten figure beneath the cross. "Now what?"

"Perhaps a door or a passage? There must be a way to open this panel!"

"Maybe the cross itself?" I whispered urgently.

"It has fallen sideways to make an *X*," he noted. "Perhaps *X* marks the spot?" Brother Guido almost smiled. "Worth a try."

We pressed the cross, first he alone, then I too. Our urgency so great and our hopes so high that we did not heed our fingers pressing intimately together in the task. Then, frustrated, we pressed and pulled every part of the carving, even Christ himself, before standing back, beaten.

"Surely," I said, in a last desperate attempt. "It is the *number* that is important. The seven."

"You're right," agreed Brother Guido rapidly, and before I could even reach out, his strong fingers were on the *VII* pressing and manipulating. I heard before I saw—the *V* depressed inward and the panel opened in a grating of stone upon stone. It was not as you might expect, the sound of a portal that had not been opened for centuries, but rather one that had seen recent use. Inside was a door with a rope hoop for a handle with a fob hanging upon it.

The rope handle was plaited hair.

And the fob was Fiammetta's jewel.

It was the exact one from the painting, with a trinity of hanging pearls and a ruby set in gold. My heart was in my mouth with triumph, and I turned to Brother Guido, my slow smile matching his. "This is it," he said, always one for stating the obvious.

"Well, come on then, what are we waiting for?"

He placed a hand on my arm. "Wait," he whispered. "First, let us ascertain the whereabouts of the priest. If he observes our exit, then the secret is revealed."

I saw the sense of this. "Hold hard then. Won't be a heart-beat." I nipped back to the aisle to check on the robed figure—he was still tending candles at the far end of the aisle, but as if my gaze had bidden him, he turned and straightened. My heart began to thump painfully. He was . . . very tall for a Neapolitan. And his robes looked, well, *fuller* than a humble priest's. The figure began to stride down the aisle toward me and I was suddenly rooted to the spot like a coney in a fox's gaze. His black robes swirled around him, his cowl fell back a little, and halfway down the nave a shaft of godlight struck his hood and caught the light of his strange silver eyes.

It was not the priest of San Lorenzo.

It was the leper.

Realization freed my feet. Quick as a cat, I was back at the doorway. "He's coming," I hissed urgently. *"Move!"* There was no time to explain; let Brother Guido think I feared no worse than the interference of a nosy priest. I yanked at the loop of hair and felt the plait pull open a portal, to reveal a twist of stairs falling below. As Brother Guido and I plunged down the steps, the door closed behind us, silently, completely, without a chink of light to tell our pursuer where we had gone. I pictured the leper turning around and about in the dim church, his robes whirling, unable to countenance our disappearance. I should have been exhilarated; we had confounded the threatening specter who shadowed us by disappearing into thin air. But I was unsettled and could not forget the silver eyes that held the promise of death in their gaze. We clattered down the dark steps, plunging into deeper gloom; we were entering Hades but I felt no fear: we were leaving behind a figure above who held much greater terrors for me.

At the foot of the stair the space opened out again into a massive cavern, a cathedral of rock. We stopped, breathed heavily and looked around. I don't know what I expected—buried treasure perhaps, or the other members of the Seven playing dice together. But I certainly did not expect a gloomy cavern, colder than Candlemas and wetter than Whitsun. "You think Don Ferrente meant us to see this . . . this cave?" I ventured.

"Not a cave," he corrected. "Look carefully. For *this* place was built not by nature but by man. See—pillars, here and here. And a well, and a Roman arcade."

Sure enough, as my eyes adjusted, I saw as he did. Forms and shapes of a buried city. "What *is* this place?"

"A place that was once called the new city, and is now the old. Neapolis, Roman Naples."

We walked the underground world with wonder. The hairs on my neck prickled as we trod the streets of the ghostly city, passing the pillars of a market, noting iron rings where horses had once been tethered, fragile arches spanning above. All lit by a gloomy greenish light coming from up ahead. I trotted after the striding monk, not wanting to linger. "You think this is a secret way known only to the Seven?"

"I do."

"What makes you think that no one else has found the passage?"

He stopped abruptly and I almost barreled into the back of him. "Fiammetta's jewel," he said briefly. "I imagine it was placed there for a pair of reasons. One, that it is a signpost to those who can read the painting—*id est,* members of the Seven."

I ignored the Latin but took the point.

"Two—it is a test: a way to maintain the security of the portal. For if a common thief or vagabond found the passage he would steal the jewel at once, for it is a thing of great price. The Seven, as I hope to prove, are all exalted men—kings and princes. Those of the Seven who pass through the doorway leave the jewel where it hangs. If one day it is gone, then Don

Ferrente and his conspirators know that somewhat is amiss—that their secret is revealed and they must be on their guard."

"Then what are they protecting? Why all this secrecy?"

"Let us find out, shall we? There must be a way through," concluded Brother Guido, "for the light is coming from somewhere."

In truth, though I found the place eerie—a place of the long-dead—I was glad to be safe belowground, glad to be out of the silver gaze of our leprous pursuer. Shortly we came to the source of the light as the Roman streets opened out onto an immense cavern with a natural lake, and that cave opening directly to the sea. At that moment it did not even occur to me that we were trapped. For spread out before me was a fleet of ships, more ships than I had ever seen together, even on that fateful night in Pisa. Here were hundreds, perhaps thousands, all crowded together, hidden from sight and approachable only by sea. But, unlike the old fortress in Pisa, there were no sailors or shipwrights here, no crew. All was silent, and secret, and vast. A waiting fleet, seen by no eyes but ours. I whistled.

"Then we have our answer," said Brother Guido in a low, awed voice, "clearly war is planned, on a massive scale."

"Could Lorenzo di Pierfrancesco be plotting against his cousin Lorenzo, with the King of Naples, and your uncle, and"—I quickly calculated—"four others?"

"I know not. One way to tell would be to attend the wedding as planned and see if Lorenzo wears a ring upon his thumb."

"So we must return there then?" I said, a burst of joy and terror in me. "To Florence? Home?" The word held none of the comfort that it should.

He looked at me as if he, too, felt my divided heart. "We had to go back someday."

"Why?"

"Because of Flora," he replied briefly.

"Why?" I repeated, my eyes on the fleet before us.

"Come on, Luciana. *Flor-a. Flor-ence*. The figure in the *Primavera* is Florence's most beauteous citizen—you—covered in flowers. Flora. Flora is Florence."

I could see the logic of what he said, sweetened as it was by the compliment. We did not need a lengthy conference to come to that conclusion. "But there is somewhere else we must go first?"

He nodded. "One figure, that of Venus, stands between us and Florence. One city, before Lorenzo di Pierfrancesco's wedding." Brother Guido sounded as if he knew more than he told, but did not press the point, and before I could prod him further his mind took another tack. "Indeed, there must be some reason why these fleets are hidden, deep down here in the south, where a northern state such as Florence could never guess what might is being amassed against them. It would explain why my uncle, if we are to assume his culpability, did not just leave the fleet in Pisa. It is too close to Florence and would be seen by those coming for commerce to the seaport." He thought for a moment, clearly troubled by his uncle's involvement in anything less than honorable and by his own masquerade as his cousin, his own involvement. "Don Ferrente *meant* for us to see this. *That* is why his snake, Santiago, was being so knowing this morning—he *knew* there was a hidden passage from the church of San Lorenzo Maggiore through Neapolis to this cavern—volcanic probably. A fantastic, vast harbor created by nature, unseen by all those above—a perfect place to conceal a secret armada—but a secret that all those who can read the painting would know."

"All of the Seven," I put in.

"Precisely. But it is likely that Don Ferrente and any others of the Seven have been down here regularly, to see the ships amass, to make their plans. For this place is only accessible through the church, or from the open sea. This is where our friend Capitano Ferregamo would have been instructed to bring the ships when he arrived from Pisa. It's where all the others that were *not* wrecked would have come."

I scanned the topmasts and saw, at the mouth of the cave, perhaps a hundred ships flying the cross pennant of Pisa. "Look!" I cried. "There they are! The Muda, the very fleet we saw being completed not a sennight ago." I looked about me. "Why aren't they guarded?"

"No need," rejoined my companion. "No one knows they are here save the Seven or the sailors who are in the pay of the Seven."

We walked forward to survey the amazing scene—and I marveled again at the difference between this fleet and the one we had seen in Pisa—here there were no shipwrights swarming like ants, no carpenters. No tar-monkeys. These ships were ready. But 'twas a ghost fleet with no one to sail it. "And where are those sailors?"

Brother Guido shrugged. "Disporting themselves in the port no doubt."

I nodded knowingly. "Rum and whores."

"As you say," he replied wryly. "There is a great enterprise afoot—lives will be lost soon enough—they are doubtless enjoying their leisure while they may."

"Jesu. What has your uncle gotten us into?"

He refrained from replying that it was, in fact, I who had gotten us into this.

"I don't know. But it's up to us to get ourselves out of it." He pointed out to the ocean. "See, the sun climbs. If we are to return to the *castello* before the Angelus, we must away." He turned back. We had seen what we had come to see, and headed back as if to return to Neapolis and thence the church of San Lorenzo.

And thence the leper.

It was time.

I put my hand on his arm. "Not that way." I told him what I had seen—the Old Man of the Nile's warning, the malevolent leper by the Roman pillar, the same leper in the church above, following us, observing us from beneath his cowl with his silver eyes.

For a moment I heard nothing but the whisper of the tide and the groan of the ships pressing against each other in the swell, then Brother Guido spoke.

"But even if he *was* there, what makes you believe that *he* is the author of all our woes and has followed us all this while?"

I shrugged. "I just do."

"But that is not logical. You say he has a threatening presence, yet this is surely an impression assisted by his stature, and the fact he is swathed in robes and a cowl with his features bandaged—"

"It's his eyes," I insisted.

"And you say," he went on smoothly without pause, "that his eyes have a strange quality—almost metallic. Perhaps it is so, for God makes man in many differing castes. But you must see how irrational you are being. We know not what this unfortunate's business is with us. He could as easily be a friend as a foe. For you have not actually had any discourse with him, have you?"

"Of course not," I scoffed, "as I'm fairly sure that *our* first conversation would be *my* last."

He took my hands, and I realized with the touch of his fingers how cold my blood had run since I had seen the leper. "Luciana. Suppose you are right. Suppose this figure had some malign intent. Who are his paymasters? If he has indeed pursued us from Florence, then how is it that we are, and have been for some time, successfully playing the part of my cousin and his courtesan? If this person knows our true identities, why have we not been revealed to our hosts?"

I shrugged, sulky now. "All I know is, he scares the shit out of me. And if you're so sure he's no threat to us, why don't you walk out of here right now and back to San Lorenzo, and make your courtesies? Perhaps you could shake him by his leprous hand."

"I am not saying that he is *no* threat to us."

My voice heated. "And who killed Enna, and Bembo, and Brother Remigio by the well, and even your uncle?"

He blanched. "I did not assert, as you know, that there was no foul play in these cases. I think, as I said at the time, that someone thought we had learned the secret of the painting and wished us out of the way."

"So what do you think happened to *those* assassins?"

"That we lost them on the voyage to Naples. There was little chance that we could be followed across the high seas, for *we* did not even know where we were bound, and even if someone had followed us aboard ship, the flagship went down with all hands."

"The rest of the fleet got there well enough, though." I made a sweeping gesture at the multitude of ships anchored before us.

He turned to me, his blue eyes troubled as a stormy sky. "Very well. Supposing I accept your assertion that to return to the church is death. 'Twill have to be the sea. Can you swim?"

I nodded, breathless. "Can you?"

"No."

"Oh, for fuck's *sake*!" Now was not the time to question how a young nobleman could have been raised on the coast without learning to swim. How could I tell my companion I'd rather head into the blue sea that rose and flung itself at the mouth of the cave in an ecstasy of spray and crashing waves? That I'd rather carry him through the brine myself than have to return to that dark crypt and meet once more the silver eyes of the mysterious leper that had followed us here? "We will have to go seaward," I said stubbornly. "We'll have to steal a bark or something." But the way was impossible. Angry cobalt waves at the cave's mouth now swelled to tidal proportions to confound us. We would be dashed from the rocks and claimed by the sea, swimmers or not. We skirted the thousand ships and stood huddled together on the foamy shores of the lake as the spume licked at our boots. "We're trapped," I admitted gloomily.

"Not so," said Brother Guido gently. "We must repair to the church and brave the fellow if he is indeed awaiting us. Time is short—we *must* return else we will miss the royal train north."

I knew he was right—but my cold dread weighed me down like the seawater that had soaked my velvet skirts. I stumbled as I tried to turn, and fell to my knees in the surf. I shrugged off the monk's helping hand; while I was down there I thought I may as well pray for a miracle to keep me from that church and the gaze of those silver eyes.

You will know, by now, that prayer is not a custom with me. In fact, if the Lord had a spare moment in his day I doubted he would heed a lost sheep such as myself. But, incredibly, a miracle came. The vicious elements that ruled this place now smiled upon us and offered a marvel. In a moment of eerie calm, and sudden silence, the sea began to retreat— sliding back and over the sands like the tide going out in the time it takes the heart to beat. In an instant, the waters were gone. We looked at each other, baffled.

"God has smoothed our path," said Brother Guido, smiling. "He has taken the sea away from our feet, as he did for Moses."

I had never thought myself a second Moses before today,

but my companion spoke the truth; the water moved from our sight almost to the horizon, leaving nothing but a calm blue line between earth and sky.

"Never mind all that," I interrupted his biblical musings. "Let's go."

Behind us the ships in the hidden lake sank down till they were almost graveled, their timbers and ropes whining and creaking in protest. They were saved from grounding only by the shallows of the natural reservoir, retained within the enormous cavern by a lip of rock at the mouth of the cave. We clambered over the retaining shingle and scrambled down to the sands—instantly dry and golden in the noonday sun.

'Twas hard to countenance what we saw; it was not just low tide, but as if a sea had never existed on this shore. "What has happened to the ocean?" I breathed, unwilling to break the sudden quiet.

Brother Guido shook his head in wonder. "I know not. Perhaps it is a thing of custom here—a sudden riptide that takes the sea away. At the mud flats of Pisa, sometimes the seas withdraw at an ill moon. But I have never seen it occur with such rapidity, nor completeness."

The sand was flat and gold as a wheatfield, and the sky as blue as Mary's cloak. It was a peerless day, and at another moment to stroll along the sands thus with the man I loved would have been my dearest dream. But all was not right. The sun was too bright, the sky too blue. Everything seemed too— well, *real*. And furthermore there were no birds singing; even the seagulls—whose constant yakking and mewing I'd endured for three days now—were silent. There was not a creature on the beach despite the sudden retreat of the sea, not a worm's cast, not a stranded herring. The air seemed strange, viscous, as if 'twas an effort to walk through it. I tried to express somewhat of this to Brother Guido. "The air seems, well . . . *solid,* not liquid as it usually is."

I expected him to scoff at me as he had many times before, but he glanced about and nodded.

"I know what you mean. Like the saint's blood."

I remembered the legend of San Gennaro—remembered the bright moon last eve, and now the sea had drained away like water from a ewer. Portents, omens, signs. I shivered despite the heat of the day, and my steps quickened. We walked the short distance to the port and, by strange chance, entered the city once again by clambering upon the jetty where we had landed a day ago. This time, though, no waves lapped the wooden pier, and no citizens thronged the dock. We took the same route through the market, but today doors closed as we passed and the black-clad widows pulled their veils across their faces. Lethargy had replaced lechery, calm had replaced chaos. Curs skulked in the shadows, their barking silenced, their heads on their paws. Today the sign of the Devil's horns was everywhere—every citizen from the oldest graybeard to the youngest child made the sign with their hands: little and first finger extended, and middle fingers held by the thumb.

We climbed the silent hill to Castel Nuovo and were let pass at the gates. Inside the castle courts I looked forward to a return to normality, but here, too, there had been a sea change. Outside the keep a dozen gold and black carriages lined in wait. The black horses stood still as statues, but rolled their eyes to the whites, their flanks dark with sweat. They did not shift in place or flick manes or tails at bothersome flies—for, incredibly, there were no flies to swat away. Brother Guido and I walked grimly forth to join a waiting Santiago. Now there was no argument about whether we would or would not return home to Florence with the king. Whether we went all the way there or not, one thing was for sure: we had to leave this eerie place in those fast carriages or face we knew not what. At Santiago's gesture, we followed him to the royal carriage. We needed no second invitation, for I felt more and more uneasy. Brother Guido wrenched open the gilded door of the third carriage, with the elaborate cognizance of the House of Aragon upon it. We climbed inside and almost fell into the laps of the king and queen. They nodded, but their tongues were silent, their smiles muted. They felt it too.

As I caught my breath I looked to the bay below and marveled at how hidden were the cavern and the fleet—had it not been for the riddle of Fiammetta we would never have known it was there.

But as I looked to sea I saw something else.

The ocean was gathering in an enormous steely mass on the horizon, a wave of such biblical proportions that it seemed all seven seas were rising to crash upon the hapless city and sweep us from the coast like insects. Fishmouthed in horror, I pointed seaward and my noble companions followed my finger with their eyes. It was enough.

"Drive!" bellowed Don Ferrente. As the order left his lips three things happened.

Cosa Uno: the twelfth stroke of the Angelus struck.

Cosa Due: the angry sea rushed home upon the city.

Cosa Tre: the driver's whip cracked and the earth did too.

An immense rumbling shook the ground beneath us and the castle walls round about. I looked to Brother Guido, horrified, my teeth rattling in my head and my ribs shaking in my chestspoon. Masonry began to fall from the fortress, and we lurched forward at a pace that would be frightening were it not that every hoofbeat took us farther away from this falling place. It felt as if the end of the world had come, but our horses sped down the drive and hurtled out of the castle gates, needing no further cuts of the whip. As we rattled around like polenta in a stockpot we wordlessly regarded the scene below. The vengeful tide seemed set to consume the bay as the waters curdled and seethed on the shores, greedily snatching boats from the harbor and shacks from the hillside. I clasped Brother Guido's arm hard enough to hurt, in genuine fear for my life as the horses bolted through the ruined city. I felt his hand squeeze mine in return. I knew at that moment that he felt death approaching too, but I understood also that he had forgiven me for what happened last time we stared doom in the face. In the town below, buildings collapsed before our eyes, crumbling from their foundations upward as the earth continued to shake in violent tremors. More than once we were nearly flattened by falling masonry; the carriage before us overturned in the dust, our terrified horses swerving and pitching just in time. We did not see what happened to the passengers, but there was no question of stopping, not if we were to live. In some places hardly one stone remained standing above another. As we passed San Lorenzo Maggiore somehow I registered that part of that church had fallen in a heap of stone, the tower standing firm like a chimney as gray dust climbed into the sky like smoke. I offered a silent prayer that the terrifying black specter with the freezing silver eyes had surely met his end within. Everywhere were the sounds of screams and shouts and the sights of citizens running with their homes piled on their backs, snaillike, the *corno* of the popular song. Firestorms broke out everywhere in little pockets which threatened to spread, and I knew that in such a sun-soaked, arid place the city could soon be reduced to cinders. I understood now the power of the blood of Saint Gennaro—not just religious hocus-pocus, which I had snorted at with scorn at last night's feast. His blood had the power to shake the earth and drain the seas. His blood had not liquefied this year so he had given his people fair warning; he had told his people of impending doom.

And doom had come.

"The city gate!" yelled Don Ferrente to his driver above the chaos. "We must climb the hill away from the city." He pointed to the glorious triumphal Roman arch we had passed through on the way to San Lorenzo.

Another rumble entered my ribs as the ground shook again. As we hurtled to the gates, rubble rained upon the silk canopy of our carriage, ripping the roof and powdering our heads as the queen and I competed in our screams. Still the faithful horses pressed on, skirting the human disaster, the fallen masonry, and the keening women kneeling and crying by the road. I could not let myself think of what they had lost—we just had to reach the arch and quit this place. We passed the statue of Old Man Nile and I was glad that he, at least, had survived this to live a thousand more years. I blew him a kiss for his earlier warning as we sped past, but this time he was silent, shocked into slumber by the wreck of his citadel. But I knew by the very sight of him that we were nearly at the city gates. The wedding carriages thundered round the corner in a maelstrom of dust, skidded through the great arch and began to climb, and suddenly we were away from the chaos, high in the hills, the earth still once more and the cursed city below us. I wondered that the sun still hung in the sky.

We shook the rubble from our heads and masonry dust flew from Brother Guido's curls, giving him a smoky halo. Our carriage slowed to a more sedate pace as we climbed the cliff road, and the sight of green plane trees and olive groves soothed my pounding skull. When my ears ceased their ringing I found my tongue. "What just happened?" I gulped, my voice hoarse from screaming. "Were we fired at from below by sappers? Were a thousand cannons turned upon us?"

Don Ferrente smiled, seemingly unaffected by our narrow escape. "It was not men but the old gods who shook the earth. I have heard of such shakings before, but did not know they could come so strongly." He calmly brushed rubble from his velvet sleeve and glanced through the window back at the ruined coastline. "The Romans held that Neptune, god of the sea, was the 'earth shaker,' and it was thought that he was the bringer of such quakes. It is the disturbance of the earth, of course, that causes the seas to retreat and then return in the giant wave you witnessed."

"Such a tremor has happened *before*?" I asked, goggling.

"Here in Naples an earthquake interrupted Emperor Nero's stage debut as a musician, a thousand years ago," put in Brother Guido eagerly. "Pliny wrote of it. Nero thought the gods had slighted his talent."

I withered him with a look. I might have known that the monk would add his two florins to the case.

"Well, well." Don Ferrente broke in, and I saw that he did not appreciate Brother Guido's superior knowledge. "The gods may have cursed Naples, but they saved our noble skins at any rate."

"Only I don't believe in gods in the plural," rejoined Brother Guido, who never could leave well enough alone. "It is our *singular* God, our Father, who did save us from disaster."

"To be sure, to be sure," said Don Ferrente airily. "And now, we may go to give thanks in his spiritual home on Earth—our next destination." I heard Brother Guido catch at his breath, but all I could think of was how seemingly unaffected the king was by the near-ruin of his adopted kingdom, not to mention the loss of one of his own carriages. I hoped the doomed coach did not contain his trio of friendly mistresses. The loss of Santiago, however, I could bear without too much grief.

"We cannot risk taking the coast road in such an event," the king went on smoothly, "in case some further shocks occur. We will go east and pick up the Appian Way."

Now I caught Brother Guido actually *smiling*, the unaccountable man. "The Appian Way," he repeated as if in a dream.

Don Ferrente nodded his noble head. "The road that will take us all the way to—"

"Rome," finished Brother Guido, and his smile widened. Only I heard him add under his breath: *"Just where we need to go."*

· 4 ·

Rome

23

Madonna.

You will not believe me when I tell you.

I, Luciana Vetra, Chi-chi the common Florentine harlot, am a guest of the pope himself.

I swear on *Vero Madre* that it's the truth. Here I stand, on the battlements of Castel Sant'Angelo, the Vatican's own riverside castle. I look down at the low summer waters of the Tiber, a sluggish silver ribbon snaking through the hills. I look across the river to the church of Saint Peter, pure gold in the last light, greater even than the Duomo in Florence. I am here as the guest of the prince of that great basilica, the most powerful man on this peninsula, His Holiness Pope Sixtus IV.

Now, I don't have to tell you that, before this evening, I couldn't even have told you what the pope's name was, no, not even if you'd bet me a keg of Marsala. But nor do I need to tell you, for you have traveled with us long enough, that Brother Guido has furnished me with all the necessary details and many unnecessary ones too. He is in a ferment of excitement, chattering like a barbary monkey privily in my ear, for this is the pinnacle of his religious career, to be here in the citadel of the pontiff, the head of his order and all the others too. *Jesu.*

We entered Rome in the early evening, after a sennight on the road. We suffered none of the privations that we had encountered on the road to Pisa from Florence, and the trip could not have been more different from our floating prison aboard the flagship of the Muda. Our carriages were comfortable, food and drink plentiful, and the wayside places where we rested were luxurious. We broke our journey either in the hillside palaces of nobles friendly to the king of the south or at wayside inns, which Don Ferrente's men commandeered completely, throwing the established guests out on their arses. 'Twas a fine sight to see the hoity lodgers ejected, lugging all their traps with no servants to help them, grumbling at the inconvenience, struggling down the Appian Way to the next watering hole. I settled into their nests with the mischievous pleasure of a cuckoo, and wondered again what it would be like to be truly noble and to have real power, instead of being a humble whore who was merely playing the role.

As we drove through the city's gates at last, I marveled at the scale of the place—massive square buildings shone gold in the sun, places which were on a scale I had never seen, not in Florence or even in the greatness of Pisa's Field of Miracles. These were the dog days; the Dog Star rode high beside the sun, and the sun shone long and late, but even she was vanquished at last. Gold turned to silver as the light grew old over Rome and the night began. The palaces and civic buildings, castles and churches, took on the sheen of fairyland, for the city was a very opal: a place without peer, for a race of princes.

My impressions were cemented by our arrival at the Castel Sant'Angelo, a huge, crenellated wedding cake built of terracotta brick, a red rook in our chess game. Perched on the banks of the sluggish river, the place was more a fortress than a palace of pleasure, yet our chambers were nonetheless sumptuous, our welcome warm. The wedding party was assigned the entire top tier of the castle, and we fed and watered in fine style in our own dining chamber. Brother Guido and I took the air after dinner, both, without speaking it, looking for a place to be alone. We had snatched some private conference along the road, but the ladies all roomed separately from their men along the way, and the only time Brother Guido and I shared together had been in the royal carriage under the eyes of the king and queen. Here we had shared the odd whispered conversation but had not dared to discuss the *Primavera*. And, for the last few days, when it had been revealed that the pope had invited us to his own castle, with a promise of an audience before we left for Florence, Brother Guido's whisperings had been nothing but excitement at meeting the father of all the church. He prayed so much that I thought his tongue would fall out, and knelt at every roadside shrine till I felt he would wear his knees to the bone. I feared that Don Ferrente might become suspicious of him, for Niccolò della Torre did not, I am sure, have much of a reputation for religious devotion. Back in the carriage, I reminded my friend by my actions and stern looks to remember to act his part. I lolled against him like any doxy, pressing my tits in his face and whispering reprimands in his ear as if they were sweet nothings instead of sour somethings. (In this, I have to admit, I was pleasing my own sensations as much as considering our safety.) He corrected his outward behavior, but I knew by the time he reached the city, he was in a fever of religious ferment. My pent excitement matched his own, but I was differently charged: I was ravenous to talk more of the painting at last and to know where this great city fitted into our puzzle.

On our evening *passeggiata* we found the perfect place for our conference—the highest battlement of all, manned by two frightening-looking guards who paced the perimeter continuously. They did not challenge us or question our presence there, and I supposed they had been briefed of each guest's identity and were well used to noble guests taking the evening air to admire the view. Now, though, I turned my back on the vista, as I had once before on Fiesole's hill, and returned, at last, to business.

"Are we secret enough?"

Brother Guido looked around, the keen breeze riffling his curls. The moon was full that night, and his face had a pearly sheen of an angel once more. "I think so, for the guards are a good hundred paces away, and here we cannot be observed or overheard."

"Get it out then."

He knew that, for once, I was not being bawdy. He reached into his jerkin and pulled out the *cartone*. Together we flattened the painting on the balustrade and gazed at the central figure—Venus, as we had dubbed her, now identified as Rome. I asked the question that had burned my poor brain for a week. "How did you know?"

"That Venus is Rome? There are so many clues I hardly know where to begin."

"Try." My voice was icy—he was making me feel ignorant again, and after my recent triumphs I almost resented the fact that he had worked this figure out by himself.

"I first began to wonder when we fell down into Neapolis— Roman Naples. Rome, if you like, lay *below* San Lorenzo. Then I thought again of the *cartone* and realized that Venus is standing below a very definite 'arch' described by the leaves of the bower, almost a Romanesque arch."

I curled my lip. "A bit far-fetched."

He was undeterred. "Yes. But do you recognize the leaves? Green, glossy, and tear shaped. Not the leaves you would find in a rustic forest. The leaves of a cultivated garden shrub—you see them in every palazzo grounds in Florence."

"Laurel!" I knew the variety well, I had hidden from Bembo's bitch of a wife many a time and knew the bitter smell of the shining leaves which had offered me sanctuary.

"Precisely. Laurel—'Lawrence' in English, 'Laurent' in French, 'Lorenzo' in our tongue—the plant of the Medici family."

"All right. But Neapolis is still in Naples. What pointed you to Rome in particular?"

"A number of factors. Rome is a city built on seven hills, and as we discovered, the number seven, and the alliance of seven people, is central to the whole puzzle."

"I always meant to say," I interrupted, "why seven and not eight or nine?"

"What do you mean?"

"Well," I began, "there are actually *nine* figures in the *Primavera,* if you count the cupid. And *eight* adult figures. So why are there only *seven* in this plot, or alliance, or whatever it is, not eight or nine?"

Brother Guido drew his traveling hood over his head, against the wind. "I confess, I don't know. Perhaps one of the figures is a decoy or has been discounted for some reason."

"Perhaps me—I mean Flora. Florence," I suggested, hoping that we wouldn't have to go back there.

"Not with your face. She's impossible to ignore." I bridled with pleasure, but there was no compliment there, just a thoughtful musing and a far-off look in the monk's eyes. "It's possible, I suppose, that one figure has been left out, or is there to trick us. But it's unlikely to be Florence, home of the artist and his patron." He sighed with puzzlement. "In any event, seven is the number mentioned by Don Ferrente, and the number seven—the seventh station of the cross—opened the door to Neapolis in San Lorenzo's church. And as I said, Rome just happens to be built on seven hills."

I nodded. "What else?"

"Well, Venus is wearing a Roman costume. See? She is quite differently dressed from every other lady. All the other figures are in flowing, white spring gowns, like pastoral, bucolic goddesses."

I didn't know what "bucolic" meant; it sounded like a stomach complaint. "But those gowns are the height of fashion," I protested, trying to regain ground. "The dress I wore, with the flowers actually *painted* on the fabric, is the latest thing in Florence just now." I sighed for the days when all I thought about was my next prick and the color of my gown.

"Yes," he agreed, "the height of *modern Tuscan* fashion. But look at Venus. She looks totally different. She's wearing clothes of an age *long past:* drapes and fabrics of antiquity. She wears *strong* colors; no white, diaphanous veils but rich, classical colors—red, blue, and gold. No flowers for her; she has a headdress straight out of the Roman period, jewelry too."

I looked carefully. Venus was relatively unadorned—no pearls here. "You mean this pendant?" I pointed, and the fine gold pendant nestling at Venus's breast seemed to glow in the friendly moonlight. It seemed very plain—a round gold disk with a smaller disk or amber jewel set within—and was hard to see, for the *cartone* was on so small a scale.

"Yes."

"What's Roman about it?"

"Well, I'd have to see the actual panel painting to be sure, but it looks like a medal of the cult of Sol Invictus."

I didn't have to ask him to explain, a look was enough.

"Before men worshipped God, they lived in the rhythm of the seasons, and nature and the light that gave them life. They worshipped the very sun itself. I know this seems absurd to us now."

Actually, I didn't think so—worshipping the fiery orb that

gave life to every living thing seemed a lot more sensible than revering a man that walked on water and died for two days and lived again on the third. But I knew more than most the depth of Brother Guido's devotion and kept my peace.

"The cult of Sol Invictus, the unconquerable sun, was the major religion in Rome for centuries. Even after the coming of Christ, those who followed him were persecuted and had to meet in secret, in underground tombs around the city." He crossed himself.

I felt he was drifting from our course somewhat. "So, she's dressed as a great Roman lady."

"Better than that. She's a bride."

I boggled at the *cartone*. "How do you know?"

"As a boy I attended many a noble wedding," he said almost apologetically, knowing fine well I had never been to a single one. "And it is the custom in Tuscany for the bride to raise her hand, just as Venus is doing here, in a gesture of welcome to her guests. And her headdress and veil is one of a Roman bride." Brother Guido slid his eyes to me sidelong. "Furthermore, she will be wed on a Friday."

I let forth a swine-grunt of scorn. "Come *on*. How on earth d'you figure that? No one's married on Friday. It's unlucky."

"Ah, possibly you're thinking of the verse:

Nè di Vener, nè di Marte
Non si sposa, non si parte
Nè si dà principio all'arte

That is to say: do not marry, start traveling or begin a job either on a Friday or a Tuesday.'"

I most certainly was not, but I had had long practice in gulling Brother Guido into thinking I was cleverer than I was, so I was too smart to chase *that* coney. I might have added, though,

213

that I met *him* on a Friday and that's the day this whole shine began. "I merely meant, what leads you up that alley?"

"Look closely. The bride's cloak is covered in tiny crosses."

I peered obediently and could not gainsay him.

"Why, you might ask, when the rest of the image—a Roman bride, a heathen medallion—is so determinedly pagan? The answer is, Good Friday is the day of the Crucifixion. And if it were not, the figure's name leads us to the light, for we have identified her as Venus, and Friday—*Venerdi*—is Venus's day."

"So who is she? Are we to trail round the eternal city looking for another dead dame?"

He shook his head. "On the contrary. *This* maid is very much alive. Look at the colors she wears. Livid, vibrant, vital. No ghostly white fabrics and pale skin for her. She lives, I am sure of it. The color of her cloak is the greatest clue. Look hard— where is it matched in this very painting?"

I peered. "Mercury's cloak!"

"Exactly. There is a visual, *color* link to the *only* other figure in the painting that we *know* with any certainty to be alive."

"The artist himself, Botticelli!"

"Yes."

"So, where should we begin?" My blood was up once more and I began to pace the ramparts, keen, like a greyhound, to begin the hunt.

"Begin?"

"To identify this maiden?"

"No need. If I were truly the heir of Pisa and not a humble monk, I would wager the whole of my city that this lady is the image of the bride we go to see wed. Her name is even the same as the road that we have just traversed, the very road that leads to Rome, the Appian Way. This lady is Lorenzo di Pierfrancesco de' Medici's betrothed, and Don Ferrente's niece, Semiramide Appiani."

The name echoed in my head, and footsteps sounded with them. A figure emerged from the castle, tiny across the battlements but getting larger with every step—the form of the King of Naples, Don Ferrente, come to seek us. "Hide the *cartone*," I hissed to the brother, "and look as if you mean love."

I clasped him about his neck and pressed our cheeks together, for I knew he would protest this time if I kissed him as I would have dearly wished. But he played his part in the pantomime.

"Love, indeed," he murmured, and my heart leaped in hope, but like an attorney-at-law he had merely saved his best argument to the last. "Venus is the goddess of love. 'Love' in Latin is *amor*, A-M-O-R. Turn the word around and what do you get?" He knew letters were not my strong suit so he did not wait for a reply. "R-O-M-A."

Then Don Ferrente was upon us, but I still had time to smile and send a nod of appreciation to Sandro Botticelli wherever he was. The clever bugger had put the answer there for all to see. *Amor; Roma.* I was chuckling as the king greeted us.

"My lord Niccolò. My lady 'Fiammetta.'" 'Twas said with great gallantry, but I was pretty sure that he named me so because he had forgotten what I was actually called.

"It grieves me to disturb your amorous sojourn, as there are so few nights of such freedoms left to you." I was not sure what the king meant by this last ominous hint, and was pretty sure Brother Guido didn't either, but my friend, in character, nodded sagely.

"But there is a spectacle tonight that I knew that you, my lord, as a man of learning like myself, would not wish to miss."

"Yes, Majesty?" said Brother Guido, all questioning politeness.

24

A ring of bells later and we stood before an enormous building, silver and squat in the moonlight. Brother Guido and I had
stopped in our tracks together, our mouths agape like twin
baby birds. Don Ferrente stood watching us and not the building, a small smile playing at his lips as if he had built the
thing himself. At the king's elbow I felt the constant presence
of his majordomo Santiago, smooth and silent as ever. This giant place—not a house nor yet a church—seemed to be a relic
of the city's ancient past; even I knew it to be Roman by reason of its many columns.

Above the columns an inscription was hewn into the time-
less rock, and as I knew he would, Brother Guido read it out.
"'M· AGRIPPA· L· F · COS ·TERTIUM ·FECIT.'" He turned to Don Ferrente. "Marcus Agrippa made me."

Don Ferrente, who was to be our guide it seemed, nodded,
and named the place. "The Pantheon."

Brother Guido's eyes shone. "But this is incredible. I have
longed to see this wonder since a child."

Don Ferrente smiled, gratified that he might please his
guest and show his knowledge of a place "Lord Niccolò" had
never been. "Come inside," he invited. "I have arranged for
our party to visit privily, so we will have the run of the place
for the spectacle to come."

We entered the huge dark maw of the church and I saw two
of Don Ferrente's heavies posted at the portico, pikes in hand,
and wondered what we were to witness. I turned at the door
and looked back to the square outside—unusually busy, even
for a great city. I had thought at first that the populace had
gathered to see the grandeur of our carriages arriving from the

Castel Sant'Angelo, but the crowd remained, milling and mumbling. Some of the goodwives crossed themselves and the gentlemen talked loudly as men do in braggadocio. It must be long past Compline as we had already dined—what did they all do there? There was a buzz of anticipation and an underbelly of something else.

Fear.

As we crossed the square, Don Ferrente's guards elbowing the burghers of Rome from our path, I pulled at Brother Guido's sleeve.

"What is this place?" I had no doubt that although he had never set foot inside it, Brother Guido would know all.

"The Pantheon, means temple to 'all the gods' from the Greek *pan*—every—and *theon*—God. It was originally part of Augustus Caesar's plan to rebuild Rome in his image."

"I thought you said it was built by Marcus somebody."

"Marcus Agrippa was friend and general to Augustus; it seems likely that he designed the first Pantheon, since his inscription still fills the architrave above the portico."

I figured that he meant "above the front door." "So it's a temple," I summarized.

"Not anymore. After Rome became Christianized, the Pantheon became the Church of Santa Maria dei Martiri consecrated by command of the Byzantine emperor Phocas many centuries ago."

"All right, so now it's a *church*." I accepted his tedious corrections. "But why are *we* here?"

"That I know not."

This was typical of Brother Guido, as I now knew—he would tell you about a hundred things you did *not* want to know, but anything you *actually* wanted to know was missing from his armory of knowledge. I found the Pantheon creepy, and my neck prickled as I followed the gentlemen inside, there to recognize others of the Aragonese court, milling around the great space like flies in a bottle. The queen and the trio of royal mistresses were already within, and all nodded to me. Giovanna of Aragon was serene as ever, but the concubines were in a twitter of excitement, chattering like jays. A great ring of hissing torches was set within the walls, to illuminate the interior. And I had to admit that the place was truly a wonder. I noted at once three things.

Cosa Uno: by some strange alchemy of architecture it seemed more massive inside than it even seemed from without, and

Cosa Due: the interior was an immense circular space with a marble floor. A huge dome arched above, and

Cosa Tre: in the center of the dome sat the greatest peculiarity of the place, a huge hole, open to the skies, through which the full moon could clearly be seen.

Brother Guido turned about below this false firmament, neck cricked to the ceiling, marveling at the hole.

"The oculus," Don Ferrente supplied. "Which serves as a mirror of the round heavens." He raised his voice for poetic effect, and those gathered stopped to heed him. "Dio Cassius said: 'Thanks to its dome the Pantheon resembles the vault of heaven itself.'"

I was unimpressed; he was clearly parroting knowledge that he had learned not one hour ago, in order to impress his court, and my lip curled a little in contempt.

"Indeed," rejoined Brother Guido enthusiastically. "The Pantheon still exemplifies the Roman aim for perfection in structural integrity and philosophical harmony." His statement, unstudied and unrehearsed (and to me incomprehensible), made me as proud of his learning as if he were my eldest son, but Don Ferrente's countenance soured.

"To be sure."

Brother Guido did not heed the king's tone but continued to marvel, turning this way and that as if calculating the volume of the space above his head. "So, the hemisphere of roof actually becomes a full sphere in the space between roof and marble floor! It is miraculous."

Don Ferrente was forced to agree or betray his ignorance. He nodded sagely. "The sacred geometry of the cosmos."

This was a little too pagan for Brother Guido's palate. "Created by *God*."

The king let this pass. "And note, too, my lord, the *pavimentum*." Don Ferrente used a phrase that had clearly never passed his lips before tonight.

But he was outclassed. "Ah, yes, the *pavimentum*—in the *opus sectile* style, I see."

Here Brother Guido flummoxed both myself and the king.

"Circles within squares," he instructed, "as in the geography of Ptolemy. The Romans have succeeded in squaring the circle!" He laughed and I saw the king laugh along and then mentally retain the phrase, while at the same time shooting a look of ice at the ever-present Santiago. I knew then who had been sent to garner the knowledge to brief the king for his tour, and that the majordomo would be held responsible for the yawning gaps in His Majesty's knowledge. I could not feel sorry for him.

Don Ferrente was soon to gain the ascendancy, with a mind-numbingly dull inventory of every type of marble the blasted Romans had used for the floor. A slab resembling a slice of salami was named as purple imperial porphyry from Egypt. Pavings as pink as *porco grasso* pâté were called docimian pavonazzetto from Asia Minor, and the flagstones so yellow it seemed as if someone had vomited on the floor were described by the king as giallo numidiana marble from Carthage. Granito grigio pavings that resembled nothing so much as dirty snow were pronounced to come from the northwest, Gaul or the Alps. I stopped listening at about this point but I knew that Brother Guido would respond fittingly.

"Incredible," he said. "A statement of *imperium* writ in marble."

My proud smile slipped a little as Brother Guido's pronouncements began to annoy me. I wished he could speak plain Tuscan. I saved the king the shame of asking for a translation. "What?"

"I meant only that the Romans have here built a pavement that exemplifies, sorry, *shows* every part of their empire set into one floor from edge to edge. From all four corners of the Roman Mediterranean they have brought these marble spoils expressing conquest of Egypt, Asia, Carthage, and Gaul. It is a political statement—propaganda in porphyry."

Jesu.

Don't get me wrong, I was well pleased with this intellectual pissing contest, and thought it clever of him to have instigated it back in Naples, but I wished Brother Guido would use his game of bones to produce more about the plot of the Seven. I drew him aside and whispered some of this, as if I were prettily leaning in for a caress.

Brother Guido drew back, surprised. "But it is *all* about that. Every word was significant, every syllable relevant to our quest."

"Even all that cant about the marble?" I hissed.

"Especially that." His breath tickled my ear. "Were you not listening closely?"

He had me there. "Just try and find out something, *anything*, actually *related* to this pickle of ours." I mouthed into his neck, *"Please."*

Brother Guido pushed me gently away and turned to our host with the utmost courtesy. "And what do we do here, Majesty? Are we to celebrate an evening mass?"

The king smiled. "After a fashion—not of God but of nature. The old gods hold sway tonight. Look. It begins. Watch the moon carefully through the oculus, for truly there is no better place in Rome to see such a spectacle." His courtiers gathered around us, and his servants began to extinguish the torches. We were clearly at the appointed hour for whatever we had come to see.

I looked up, and the moon, bright and perfectly full, sat serenely in the heavens as it always did. It looked perfectly ordinary, except—wait. "The moon is . . . sort of yellow," I noticed.

"Yes, Doña," agreed the king. "The moon is in a sickly humor, for we are now in the ides of July."

"Ides?" I hissed to Brother Guido.

"The middle of the month. It will soon be full summer."

"Good." My favorite season. I used to love lolling by the Arno with the other harlots or drinking a cup of wine under a loggia. Even in this gloomy place I could almost feel the fierce heat of the Florentine sun and smell a whiff of the Arno at its lowest ebb. Rank in the noses of others, the scent of the river and all its evils—shit, waste, and even corpses—was the smell of summer to me, as beautiful to my senses as the scent of evening jasmine. Homesickness struck me in the gut, with an even dose of terror at what we must return to.

Don Ferrente echoed my divided feelings. "Summer, yes. But then the winter will follow, as it always does, a challenging one for all of us this year."

Once again his words seemed to ring with some chime of significance. I could feel Brother Guido hesitate beside me, then steel himself to take a chance.

"But then, sure as the sun will rise, *spring* comes again. *La primavera.*"

I heard the word with a shock—so long spoken between us

to refer to Botticelli's painting, I had forgot its other usage. We both looked to Don Ferrente to seek his reaction.

He looked my friend in the eyes, straight and true. "Exactly," he said, with the same weight to his words. "A new beginning."

Well, this was enigmatic, to be sure, but told us nothing. As I craned my head to see the moon, even brighter now the torches were doused, I saw the saffron disk begin to disappear before my eyes, as if someone had taken a bite out of it! The bite became bigger and bigger as we watched, aghast. What could this mean? Was the world ending? Had a huge dark celestial beast come to devour the moon like a ravening wolf? *Madonna.*

Brother Guido felt my consternation, for I gripped his arm fit to stop the blood.

"Be comforted," he said. "It is an eclipse of the moon—the earth is coming between the sun's rays and the moon, and as we live on a flat disk, the impression is given that the moon is vanishing. But it is still there and will shine again within the hour."

I gulped. "But the sun does not shine at night!"

"The sun shines perpetually, my dear. Whether we see it or not," said the king in significant tones, once again pregnant with meaning.

"Although," put in my friend tentatively, "such an event can happen to the sun too."

I felt the king go still.

"For sometimes, very rarely indeed, the sun will move behind the moon in the same way. For all heavenly bodies revolve around the earth, and sometimes the moon blocks our view of the sun too."

"You are mistaken. I fancy it is only the moon which is covered so," asserted Don Ferrente stiffly.

"No, indeed," went on Brother Guido, not sensing the danger, "for such phenomena have been occurring since biblical times. ' "And on that day," said the Lord God, "I will make the Sun go down at noon, and darken the earth in broad daylight." ' 'Tis written in the Old Testament, the Book of Amos," he supplied.

"Clouds," said Don Ferrente. "The sun can never be vanquished, else we would all perish." A memory nagged me—where had I heard such sentiments before? " 'Tis the most powerful entity in the heavens," he went on.

"More powerful than *God*?" Brother Guido's dark brows shot heavenward.

Don Ferrente quickly retreated from his position—he was clearly not *quite* ready to set himself up in opposition to the Almighty. "I meant only that the sun governs all in *nature*—the hours of day, the *seasons* . . ." He looked hard at his adversary, but Brother Guido missed the glance, so lively was he with argument.

"But the *earth* is not ruled by it," said he carefully. "Nor the moon—tonight is proof enough."

Don Ferrente had his answer ready. "Ah! But there are some who say that the *sun* is the center of all, and that all the heavenly bodies revolve around *it*. Some of those believers are great men whom *we* know well."

Brother Guido, once again, missed the hint. "Heretics, sire!"

I closed my eyes briefly, for Brother Guido had become bullish in his argument, and now had, if my ears did not deceive me, just pretty much called the King of Aragon and Naples a heretic. The little knot of people gathered around us below the oculus began to hush their own discourse to listen to ours.

I had to nudge my friend to help him to remain in character. "Some would say," I amended hastily, "but not I. I feel that the Romans had the right of it: Sol Invictus, the Unconquerable

Sun. For did not the poet say," I struggled to remember, "'The Sun makes clear all your inventions by its light.'"

Brother Guido looked at me amazed—but *you* shouldn't be, for one of a working girl's greatest talents is the ability to remember a phrase or tidbit and quote it back to a client. It is one of the cornerstones of flattery, and every man likes it, monarch or monk.

And it worked on both; Don Ferrente thawed, nodding his approval. "Look, the celestial spectacle gathers pace."

We looked skyward, relieved, and felt that the storm had passed. The moon was disappearing rapidly, now a half moon, now a mere crescent.

Don Ferrente leaned close to Brother Guido as he watched, and lowered his voice till I could hardly hear what he said. "When the eclipse is over, I fear I must leave you, to meet with my officers. Our royal carriages and litters are at your disposal to return to the Castel Sant'Angelo for a couple of hours, or would you prefer to remain in the city until our meeting?"

This was news. "Our meeting?"

"At midnight. At the appointed place."

Now we were stuck, and Brother Guido was forced to ask, "The appointed place?" I froze, afeared he had given his ignorance away. If he were truly one of the Seven, he would know the meeting place, but what choice did he have but to inquire?

The king bent close. "I cannot name it for other ears but ours are listening. But your father will have told you. I will say only this to recall it to your mind." He spoke a phrase in another tongue—I thought it English. "I will meet you there."

It seemed to me that we were sunk, but we could hold no conference till the king had gone. We all fell silent to watch the night devour the rest of the moon, now a tiny shaving like a thumb's nail. I found, by some odd humor, that I could not watch the last of that friendly planet disappear, for the moon had oft been my companion on my journeys to and fro in Florence, most of my labor being done at night. Whatever Brother Guido said, my irrational fear told me that it would not come back. I looked down, and the look saved my life.

The Pantheon was almost dark, but in the very last seconds of moonlight I saw a figure, tall and dark, at the very edge of our party, swathed and cowled in leper's robes. I was not the only one not to be watching the skies. There was another. This specter was looking straight at me, with eyes as bright silver as the ferryman's coins.

My blood froze in my arteries.

Madonna.

The leper of Naples was *here.*

In the next heartbeat the entire temple was black, and as Don Ferrente called for torches I yanked at Brother Guido's sleeve, pulling him with strength I did not know I had. My eyes were blind, but my memory knew that the portico was behind us and I shoved the brother out into the night as the guards gave us pass. He followed obediently, quickly and quietly, knowing that something was wrong. I hushed his inquiries and kept going. I looked back constantly as we passed through unknown streets, my eyes telling me that we were not pursued—that the moment of darkness was enough to shed our pursuer, but my hammering heart told me that the leper was a ghost or a deadly phantom, for none other than a wraith or warlock could have walked alive from the ruins of San Lorenzo Maggiore in Naples. The silver eyes burned me still and the impression of the ferryman would not leave me. I felt that the leper would not stop until he had taken us across the river of the dead.

We had gained the edge of the city, and memory told me we were almost back at the Appian Way. We must stop soon else we would flee back to Naples. In a green place stood ancient pillars and a dark doorway, I pulled us through it, twisting down and down to an underground chamber, with more passages than a cunny-warren. Once in the underworld—clearly some sort of shrine, for votive candles lit the stuffy caverns and twisted passages—we stopped to catch our breath, and I knew I must explain what I'd seen.

25

For a few moments I heard nothing but the drip of water and the hiss of the candles that burned in the niches, in this strange underground shrine. Brother Guido was silent, digesting what I'd told him—that the leper who had followed us since we started this thing, followed us still; that we were in greater danger now than we'd ever been.

"And you're sure? You're *sure* this was the same man? The leper you saw in the Via Nilo, the 'priest' in San Lorenzo Maggiore? For I have to tell you, Luciana, that church was almost destroyed in the earth's quake."

I set my jaw, stubbornly. "*We* escaped."

This he had to concede. He sighed. "Very well, suppose we accept your position that the leper *is* the assassin. There is no inconsistency in *my* position. I said then, as I say now, that our best chance of safety is to discover the secret of the painting, and then we have a bargaining tool. But if this fellow is *not* our assassin why would he assist us in our charade by concealing our true identities from our powerful hosts?"

I had a revelation. "Maybe he's following *me*, not you. Perhaps he thought that when he murdered Brother Remigio he *had* dispatched you. If he picked up the trail at Fiesole, he may have thought you were a monkish escort that Abbot Giles sent with me to Pisa to guard my way."

"Then how are we to explain what happened to my uncle?" He choked a little as he named him.

"Perhaps he died of the bad oysters in sooth." But I knew it was not so.

"Then why did he tell me, with his dying breath, to follow the light to the Muda?"

"Because he was dying. Whether of the oysters or of a poisoner's draught, he would have given you the same instructions."

"Why did Tok pursue us?"

I thought fast. "Because once your uncle was dead, your cousin wished to remove you as a rival. Perhaps Niccolò's motivations had nothing to do with the painting."

"And yet we know that my uncle was one of the Seven, and that Niccolò would have inherited his place in the conspiracy."

"It does not follow. Perhaps the real Niccolò knows nothing about the Seven. You 'inherited' your part in the plot when your uncle passed his ring to you and told you to follow the light to the Muda. Niccolò may have been thought unfit to join the alliance. You said yourself he was a good-for-nothing *finocchio* who thinks more of fucking small boys than studying his books. My words, not yours," I added hurriedly.

"But in essentials, you are correct," he said wryly.

"Well, then. Perhaps the leper does not know your identity. If he has followed us from Florence, you look a much different creature than the scruffy monk in Pisa who had spent two weeks on the road in his own filth. *Now*"—I looked at him, noble and beautiful in the candlelight—"you are a prince."

"All right. So you think that he will not move against you at present because he believes you are under the protection of Niccolò della Torre, one of the very seven lords for whom he works?"

"Why not? A clever working girl would change sides in a heartbeat and cling like a limpet. You could protect me, give me every comfort, buy my silence. Perhaps he thinks I am no longer dangerous. I may know the secret of the *Primavera*, but I am now in the company of one of the plotters, and it would harm your wealth and position to reveal what I know. Why would I do such a thing, if you are now my patron? Perhaps he thinks he need only watch me, for now, to follow my steps. For if I were truly your concubine, to harm me would anger you, perhaps even threaten the enterprise. Perhaps I am safe until you marry and I am then an expendable mistress."

"Very well. Let's say he followed you to Santa Croce, murdered Brother Remigio in my stead. He then follows you to Pisa by reason of my name—"

"And the stone tower carved over your door . . ."

"Of course. So then he knows I sent you to Pisa to my uncle before I died. My uncle then dies, however this was wrought, possibly because he thought that he had told me too much of the Seven."

"And, he was going to introduce us to Lorenzo de' Medici!" I cried, struck with a revelation as if I traveled the road to Damascus. "The leper thought that we were set to reveal all, that your uncle regretted his involvement and was set to warn Lorenzo that the Seven were plotting against him, that he would reveal to Lorenzo his nephew's treachery!"

"As you say. Then we escape to the Muda. As far as the leper knows, your monkish escort goes down on the boat. He cannot have reached Naples before us, for we came on the flagship, and the rest of the fleet arrived at least half a day later . . ."

"The next time he sees me," I took up the tale, "at court, I am now with Lord Silvio's son, Niccolò, a man magnificently dressed, clean shaven, and a million leagues away from a penniless monk. 'Lord Niccolò' wears the thumb ring and closely resembles Lord Silvio. The leper believes that you are loyal to the alliance, and that now your father, the rotten apple, is gone—forgive me—he may merely observe our progress. He was *not* pursuing us when we ran from the Pantheon," I admitted, "and he has not *revealed* your true identity because he does not *know* it!"

Brother Guido concluded. "The leper thinks you have changed sides and are in the pockets of the Seven. He follows you but does not act." He fell silent for a time, a silence which told me he thought my theory possible. Then he abruptly changed his theme. "Yet all this conjecture wastes time. Whether or not another party gives us away, we will give ourselves away if we do not meet the king tonight."

"At midnight?"

"Yes. We must change our tack from this discourse and apply our faculties to the more immediate problem. We cannot know for sure the leper's business. But we, *we* have very pressing business of our own, namely that, in less than two hours, we must meet Don Ferrente at a place that we do not know the location of, and my only plan to discover the whereabouts of our tryst has been wrested from me."

"Speak Tuscan."

"I meant only that since Don Ferrente must himself go to that place at the hour of midnight, my notion was to follow him there."

"But he was meeting with his officers first."

"Yes. We could have waited and followed him again to the appointed place. But now, since we fled the Pantheon in error, there is no way of knowing for sure where the meeting of the Seven will be."

Ah. "Could we not find some likely places where a king might meet his officers?" I knew I spoke nonsense even as I uttered the words.

"It could be a private house, a palace, even a well-appointed tavern. There are a hundred, a thousand of such places in Rome, and our time is short. No, our best chance of success is to apply ourselves to the only clue we were given as to the whereabouts of the meeting, for that was dropped from the lips of the king himself."

"You mean whatever he muttered in English."

"He said 'under the seventh sun.'"

"Clear as cow shit."

"It seems impossible, I know, but we are well versed in such deductions now, Luciana. We have followed the trail from Florence all the way here, with nothing but our wits and the *cartone*."

"Better get the painting out, then," I said, sighing.

He wagged his index finger at me, as if I were in the schoolroom. "Not this time; for this was a *supplementary* riddle, provided by the king himself. I'm sure that the answer this time will not be found on the parchment, although the larger themes of the painting will still, doubtless, be at work here. No, we need to think only of the king's riddle and the city itself."

"Maybe we're going about this wrong. In Naples, we found what we sought at the church of San Lorenzo Maggiore. Perhaps there is a San Lorenzo in Rome, must be!"

He raised his head quickly. "I can say that with absolute certainty, for the city of Rome is the very site of San Lorenzo's martyrdom."

"He died here? In Rome?" I was surprised—for when the nuns who had taught me Scripture spoke of the saints, I always vaguely reckoned that they had lived in far-off parts of the Holy Land, not in the cities where my own grubby sandals trod.

Brother Guido's eyes shone blue fire. "Yes. Near the Villa Borghese, not far from the Pantheon. There's even a shrine containing the gridiron on which he roasted to death."

"They *roasted* him?" I always thought martyrdom a noble, if stupid, act, but I never thought that a saint would be cooked like a Yuletide dinner.

"Yes, you do not know the tale?" His face took on a beatific look; Brother Guido was a monk once again. "He was placed on a hot gridiron by the vengeful Romans till his flesh began to sizzle. Then, with great bravery and fortitude, he said, 'Turn me over, I am done on this side.'"

I began to laugh. "I'm sorry," I apologized. "But it is funny."

He conceded a smile. "Yes. It shows that the servants of Christ cannot be easily vanquished."

"All right." I sprang to my feet. "Then what are we waiting for? Let's leave here and seek that place—Villa Borghese."

"No."

"What now?"

"It's a good notion, Luciana, but it's just not *right*. San Lorenzo has nothing to do with the words 'the seventh sun.' We are thinking too much of God and sanctity, but here in Rome everything is different. Did you not hear Don Ferrente? 'The old gods hold sway tonight.' These are the old days and the old ways. Unpalatable as it is, we must turn our thoughts to the pagan, even the heathen, not the Christian."

I saw what he meant. "For even the king is different here."

"What mean you?" But he looked like he thought so too.

"Well, in Naples, he was almost preaching the Gospel at his feast, talking of Christ, and the dayspring, and his model of the Nativity; almost as pious and pope-holy as you. Then, when we'd just left the city—do you remember, just after the earthquake—he said it was the old gods who shook the earth'? And here in Rome it's all Romans and pagans and the power of the sun."

"You are absolutely right. Could it not be," he said slowly, "that in those Christian pronouncements in Naples he was dissembling—his preachings were merely clues to lead us to the church to view the fleet? He mentioned Christ on Calvary—"

"Showing us the way!" I cried.

"And *that's* how we found the door to the underground fleet—the *seventh* station of the cross, Christ's last journey to Calvary, on the wall of the church of San Lorenzo Maggiore."

"But here, he is more concerned with the sun, the moon, the seasons . . ."

"He takes us to witness an eclipse . . ."

"Even his riddle speaks of the sun . . ."

"Sol Invictus!" Brother Guido crowed triumphantly. "The pendant that Venus wears in the *Primavera*. The *sun*. And," he went on, "that Marsilio Ficino letter that you recalled in the Pantheon. The entire extract runs, 'The Sun makes clear all your inventions by its light. Finally Venus, with her very pleasing beauty, always adorns whatever has been found.'"

It all fitted. Venus was the figure of Rome, she wore a sun pendant. We were on the right course. "Let's think this through," said I. "The king took us to a church—"

"Which was once a pagan temple . . ." Our words tumbled out so fast that they almost crossed each other.

"And told us to meet him under the seventh sun . . ."

But then we stopped, graveled for lack of matter, and could go no further.

Madonna. 'Twas a tough cipher this time. The seventh sun. The seventh sun. There was but one sun in the *Primavera*, on Venus's breast. But one sun in the heavens. What were the others?

We sat in silence then, puzzling, speaking only to begin sentences then dispose of these fragments of ideas as quickly as they had come to us. "Would there be . . . is there a temple, or palace, with seven suns painted on the ceiling? Like a fresco?" I ended weakly.

"Mayhap there is. But we would never find such a place in time." More silence.

"Perhaps . . ." he suggested in turn, "it has something to do with months of the year? The *primavera* is, after all, a season, the season of spring."

"So?" I was bullish, for my arse hurt on the cold damp stone and I was mad that my fresco idea had been dumped out of hand.

"Maybe the seventh sun is the seventh *month*. *Sept*-ember."

"Brilliant," I scoffed. "It's July, but I'll meet you at midnight in September."

He dropped his head, chastened, and we fell again to silence.

Then it was my turn. "You said that Rome was built on seven hills. What about under the seventh?"

He brightened a little. "The *seventh hill*. It could be so. And yet a hill has nothing to do with the sun."

"A sun rises over it?" I was reaching now.

He shrugged. "Perhaps. It's the best notion we have had thus far."

"So which is the seventh?" My voice was bright with hope.

"I could *name* the seven for you—but there would be no way of really determining which hill is the 'seventh,' for God made all the lands on the same day." His hand reached up to rub his chin. "I could tell you with some confidence of the name of the one which would be considered the *first* hill, for tradition has it Rome was founded on the Palatine hill by Romulus. But as to the 'last,' I could not say. The others are named—let me see—Aventine, Capitoline, Quirinal, Viminal, Esquiline, and Caelian."

Once again I could not help but admire his knowledge, unhelpful though it was in the present case. "But we're looking for one that you can get *underneath*," I reminded him. "That cannot be true of them all, surely?"

He shook his head. "Sadly, your assertion is not true—all the hills could well have subterranea—this very place where we now shelter is only one of the myriad underground tunnels in Rome. In fact"—the blue eyes blazed again—"we are under a hill now! Did you not see the ancient mound, when we entered through a dark door?"

"So you are saying that *this* might be one of the hills?" I gestured above my head, looking about me properly for the first time. I'd been so caught up in our desperate discourse that I had not noticed what was before my very eyes. I got to my feet. "What is this place?"

He stood, too, his posture giving weight to his words, like an actor. "A labyrinth of the dead. The Catacombs."

I licked suddenly dry lips. "A labyrinth of . . . of the . . . dead?" I gave a shiver despite myself.

"To be sure," he replied breezily. "All these cavities"—he pointed to the rectangular holes in the walls, set at regular intervals—"are graves. Observe, you can see the bones within, and the winding sheets too."

I backed away from the charnel.

"And they are clearly respected still in this modern day—see, the devotional candles still burn."

I cared not if the candles burned, I wanted out of this bone house and my fear showed in my face.

"Don't be afeared. Death holds no horrors for those who believe in the afterlife."

But I wasn't sure I was one of those people.

"Think once more of San Lorenzo in his agony. There are many tombs here in the Catacombs, it's true; yet there is peace and hope also."

I had to disagree. "It's pretty sinister, if you ask me."

"You find it so? I feel only serenity, for this was a place of great faith."

"How do you mean?"

"The first Christians used to worship in such places in the days when the Romans worshipped their false pagan deities and to name God or his Son could spell death. But the true faith is evident in these inscriptions—look . . . perhaps there is somewhat here that will instruct us."

"You think?"

"It cannot hurt to look for clues." He read for me the Latin characters scratched on the wall, spidery characters hewn into the stone, yet surprisingly neat and regular after the wear of centuries—a labor of love. "Here's a reference to seven!"

"Soothly?" I came to see. "Anything about suns?"

"No . . . I was mistaken. They are family names . . . a deacon named Severus, and here"—his voice grew soft—"his daughter who died while he still lived, another seven as I thought, but now I see she was named Severa after her father." He read as if he intoned a prayer. " 'The mortal body is buried here until He makes it rise again. And the Lord who has taken from Severa her chaste, pure, and forever inviolable soul with her saintly spirit will give it back adorned with spiritual glory. She lived nine years, eleven months, and fifteen days. Thus she passed from this earthly life.' "

I was touched by the fate of the little girl even so long ago, touched by the father who loved her enough to stand in this dark place weeping and carving by the light of a guttering flame till his fingers bled, to think of her all the days of his life, and to die, many years later, and be buried with her in this place, their bones collapsing into an embrace at last. I wished that I had a parent to love me so. *I'll find you one day,* Vero Madre, *and you will hold me to you and call me dear.* I could not speak for a moment, so lost was I in this little human tragedy. I remembered, too, that Brother Guido had just lost the only parent known to him, and I'm pretty sure that we both forgot our quest for a moment. I shot a look of sympathy at my friend, but it was not heeded or needed, for Brother Guido was off on a more spiritual bent.

"Do you see now? Do you hear their voices across the ages? You are hearing, directly, what early Christians thought of the last realities of death and the fate of the soul in eternity, in the days when faith must be hidden. They truly believed, even then, that the soul would rise again, like Saint Lazarus, like our Lord Jesus himself. *Now* you see what I mean, that this is a cemetery where everything speaks of life more than death. And now we are truly blessed, for in the modern age we need not fear, need not bury our faith underground." He stroked the inscriptions tenderly with his long sensitive fingers. "Indeed, His Holiness Pope Sixtus—whom God willing we will meet on the morrow—has built a wondrous chapel for all to see, to the glory of the Lord, and plans a dome for Peter's church even greater than the one that crowns the Duomo in your native Florence."

The bells of the nearby basilica struck a warning chime, telling me that time was short, and recalling me to the quest. I tried to return to the matter at hand. "So if we are in a meeting place where those who had to meet in *secret* once hid, might we not be in the right place? Under the right hill? By *chance*?"

"It's possible. But nothing I have read so far fits the riddle."

I looked about me, desperate for an idea. Saw, in the warm glow of the candles, images which I had not seen before stand forth on the walls. "Mayhap we must look to their *paintings* as well as their words—for it was a painting that began all this!"

Brother Guido squinted at the walls of our cavern. "Perhaps— for look, here and there are frescoes to witness their faith. This is a veritable jewel casket of ancient evidences."

I looked, and saw. There were loaves and fishes, angels, and a benevolent shepherd Christ carrying a lost sheep across his shoulders to safety.

Then one image made my heart stop.

And begin to thump again.

"Here," I hissed. "I think we are in the right place. Look!"

I pointed to where seven crudely drawn figures, ages old, sat about a round table waiting to break their fast. *Seven.*

"I don't know." Brother Guido rubbed the back of his neck.

"What don't you know? There are seven figures gathered here in this fresco. The Seven were meant to meet *here*—I am sure of it. The candles are lit and all is ready! To think that we came here by chance, running from the leper!" (Whom I had almost forgot.)

Brother Guido looked unconvinced. "It cannot be. For one thing, this image is common enough as a representation of the miracle of the loaves and fishes—seven figures are often depicted at the feast. For another, this place is too Christian for the Seven's gathering—as I said, it was a Christian sanctuary, and yet we have already agreed that the riddle itself and everything in the king's discourse and demeanor points to a pagan, Roman, *imperial* meeting place."

I deflated as he spoke, but he had not done.

"And lastly, what are the chances that, be we never so blessed by the true God, we would have stumbled, unaided, into the very place we were struggling to find? No, no, Luciana, it will not do."

I kicked a stone underfoot in frustration and succeeded in nothing more than stubbing my toe in its fancy pointed boot. I knew Brother Guido spoke sooth, for it was all too neat if this had been the place and Don Ferrente had walked right in after us. And even one as green in the body politic as I, felt that this barbarian bone house would not satisfy Don Ferrente's puffed-up pride—he would need somewhere grander for his meeting. Damn the King of Aragon! "Why can't he just fucking *say* where we were to meet him in plain Tuscan? And in

Naples too—all that cowshit about Christ on Calvary, and Fiammetta. Why could he not just *tell* us where to look?"

"Because he is overheard by his court at every hour—that night and this. Recall, if you will, that he had just put down a rebellion by his barons. Perhaps those at his court would not approve of his alliance with the Seven, and their scheme, whatever it may be. Powerful enemies could make things difficult for him, particularly if his barons warn those that he moves against. Tonight he spoke in English, knowing, as he must, that I was schooled by an English tutor. Remember, if you will, that the only time he spoke directly of the Seven, without any of his oblique misdirections, was the day we happened upon him and Santiago alone in the marquetry chamber. Only then did he name *me* as one of the Seven, or talk of the business with any directness."

I stared fixedly at the seven figures on the wall, gathered for a meal a thousand years ago, as he continued.

"And that's another thing. Don Ferrente gave us the clue 'under the seventh sun,' but never did he hint that *all* the Seven would attend the meeting. In fact, how could it be so, when *one* at least, as we believe, will be absent."

"One?"

"For Lorenzo di Pierfrancesco de' Medici, nephew to Lorenzo the Magnificent, surely rests in Florence, preparing for his nuptials."

I sighed gustily. I felt the sense of my friend's words but somehow could not let the coincidence pass.

"So you're saying that this is just chance? That this fresco shows an average Christian family breaking bread together?"

"Most likely. For here are family tombs set into the very wall where the image appears—see . . . many chambers for many dead of the same name. Count them—yes . . . there are seven."

Jesu. "Pretty unlucky to lose seven sons!"

"Alas, these were dangerous times for the faithful—" He broke off. *"What did you say?"*

I thought him angered at my flippant tone. But I meant no disrespect for, soothly, after the tale of Severa I cared more for those who had become dust so many centuries ago than I would have thought. "I only meant . . . seven sons was a lot to—" I did not get to finish.

"May the Lord damn me for a fool!" he cried, his tones ringing round the Catacombs. It was the closest I had ever heard him come to profanity. "Of course! The seventh son!"

"Eh?"

"Seventh son! Not seventh sun!"

I was confounded, for to me the English words sound exactly the same.

"They *sound* the same, yes, but they are *spelled* differently! Don Ferrente meant *sons,* as in *figlio,* not *suns* as in *sol!*"

I think I had the right of it. "You mean he wants us to meet him under the seventh *son,* like in a family?" I pondered. "That makes even *less* sense than before."

He paced like an opium feeder seeking a poppy. "Not so. Now it is all clear. He was even named in these very inscriptions! The name of the seventh son, underneath, the concept of *imperium,* the worship of Sol Invictus, it *all fits.*"

"Christ knows what you're talking of, but I don't. Who was named in these inscriptions? Who is 'he'?"

"Never mind. We have little enough time, for the bells of the basilica have already struck once as we talked. We have a little under an hour left, and that is all. Follow me." He made for the exit.

"Where?"

"Whence," he countered. There was always time to correct

me, I noticed. "We're going back to the center of the city. The Forum, the center of pagan, imperial Rome."

I pulled at his sleeve just before he plunged recklessly into the night. "And what about the leper with the silver eyes?" I implored. "Have we fully considered what he might do? Can we be certain that he does not know your true identity? Can we risk the chance that he may get to Don Ferrente and unmask you?"

Brother Guido turned and took me by the shoulders, the goodness in his blue eyes so different from the memory of those malign silver ones. "Luciana. We have no choice. For if I attend the meeting, he may well give me away. But if I don't, I will certainly give *myself* away."

We sped through the night like phantoms, our black attire aiding us in our secret passage. We were shadows this night, just like the ones that hid in each doorway or reached from the arches of every loggia on our way.

At every turn I looked about me for the leper, expecting to see his silver eyes, to hear the whisper of his robes. But he was nowhere to be seen. Only late revelers bumped us good-naturedly, exclaimed at my beauty, and let us pass. As we gained the ancient center of the city once more, we quickened our steps with the chime of the quarter hours, for midnight was nigh. Presently we came to a great ruined place, silver in the light of the moon that was now whole again. Like a lost world, it lay like a silver lake, a crumbling elfin city, a resting place of emperors. Before Brother Guido could whisper "The Forum," I knew this was the place—so right for Don Ferrente, a playground of kings. "It's a big place," I murmured. "We might miss them."

"No," came the reply. "The king was very specific. Under the *seventh son*. The seventh son of a Roman family was named Septimius. Sixtus, Septimius, Octavius, and so on. In the very center of the Forum, there—see—is a great triumphal arch."

I saw it: huge and massy, a great stone rainbow. But I didn't see what such a structure had to do with a Roman family. "And?"

"*And,*" he mimicked me, "it is the triumphal arch of one of Rome's greatest emperors, and empire builders. He established the concept of *imperium* that we saw exemplified in the *pavimentum* floor of the Pantheon. He also championed the worship of Sol Invictus, the unconquerable sun; the symbology of the cult even appeared on his coinage. And his name?"

Finally.

"Septimius Severus," he finished in triumph. "The Seven are to meet under his arch. Under the *seventh son*. And furthermore, a fabled carving of the goddess Venus appears upon the arch. Remember? 'Venus, with her very pleasing beauty, always adorns whatever has been found.' This is the place, depend upon it."

I had my doubts, but as we descended, I saw a clear sign that he was right, for before us stood a fearsome soldier, garbed most strangely. He wore a cloak that in the day must have been bright red, but in the moonlight was the wine-dark scarlet of blood. On his breast was the cognizance of a moon and a star— there was no escaping the heavenly bodies tonight, it seemed. And on his head rode a helmet with an arc of bristles standing forth like a currier's brush. *Madonna.*

I looked left and right as we trod the ancient pavings, saw that there were such soldiers guarding all entrances and exits, in a watchful ring. "What do we do?"

"Announce ourselves, I suppose," whispered my companion, sounding much less assured.

"Who *are* they?"

"It's incredible, but it is as if we have stepped back in time. The moon and star on the breast, the scarlet cloak, the centurion's helmet. They are the *Praetorian guard*."

"The *what* guard?"

"They used to guard the Roman emperor. They were disbanded in the third century, but someone, it seems, has reformed them."

"*Jesu,*" I breathed. "Don Ferrente must have a greater opinion of himself than I thought."

He ignored my sally, for we were upon the first guard, who lifted his pike to his side as we approached. At ease. He had been told of our coming.

"Lord della Torre," he said. "Go forth, they await you."

I moved to follow, but the pike came out again, to the full extent of his muscular arm. "No further, *domina.*"

I was not about to argue, and knew at once that this was one occasion that my feminine wiles would fall on deaf ears. In the moonlight the guard looked as if he were hewn from stone—he did not even look at me but stared at a fixed point in the middle distance. Brother Guido turned, and I wondered once more if I was seeing him for the last time.

He stepped forward as if to embrace me, then whispered, "If I do not return, go back to the Castel Sant'Angelo, and thence to the Vatican. Seek the protection of His Holiness. No one can hurt you then."

Tears bunched in my throat and I gave a tiny nod, fearing that if I bowed my head further they would spill forth. I watched Brother Guido walk forth to the arch and disappear into the shadow beneath, then I retired to the stone arena to wait.

It seemed an age that I watched the still stones and the circle of soldiers who did not flinch, however long I stared at them. But it cannot have been more than half of one hour, for I heard the bell of the nearby basilica strike twice. I could see the sense of having a conference in such a place, for under the arch of Septimius Severus where the members of the Seven met, no one could overhear them and any spies could be seen coming for a good half league, even if they got past the guards.

At last, with great relief, I watched Brother Guido return alone, and come to me. He looked vexed, but not frightened.

"What happened?"

"Not here," said he. "A litter awaits us to return to the Castel Sant'Angelo, we will talk there."

Once back at the *castello*, we did not retire to our rooms at once, but sought by silent agreement a place where we could speak unseen and unheard. I followed Brother Guido until we came to a hall full of statuary; a long passage flanked on either side by the busts of long-dead emperors. White and blank-eyed, they observed us blindly, heard us silently, but we knew that no one else could approach, as great double doors sealed the place at either end. No one could come upon us without us seeing them coming from a good way off. Brother Guido had learned well from the Seven, the secrets of *remaining* secret.

"Well?" I was all impatience.

He wasted no time. "There were but three of us there, all cloaked and hooded like myself. We used no names, but I knew one of the others to be Don Ferrente—by our arrangement and his voice—but the third I have never met before, I am sure."

"*Could* it have been Lorenzo di Pierfrancesco de' Medici then?"

He did not hesitate. "No. I would say by his voice that he was old; Lorenzo is of an age with myself. This man was statesmanlike—not Neapolitan nor yet Tuscan. And besides, as we agreed, Lorenzo *must* be in Florence now."

"Not necessarily. We are here, and yet we will be in Florence, too, in time for the nuptials."

He shrugged. "And another thing . . ."

"Yes?"

"He seemed to be the superior to all. To lead the discourse, and to be the greatest man there."

"Greater than a *king*?"

"I know."

"And what did you speak of?"

"It is evident that war is planned. There was talk of the fleets, the number of ships, and the 'date of attack.' And a *map*. The map, the map, the map, was on everyone's lips."

"But nothing was spoke of where or when, exactly?"

"No."

"No mention of the painting?"

"Not directly, no. But spring—*la primavera*—was mentioned thrice; that *must* be when they plan to move. And if Lorenzo di Pierfrancesco is the mastermind of all, then that would make sense, for spring is the Florentine New Year." He rubbed his neck as he always did when puzzled. "And flowers. Flowers were mentioned many times. In fact, it was specifically stated that the flowers hold the secret."

Madonna. "So we don't actually know the secret even now, only that the flowers hold it. The whole painting is lousy with flowers; it's one of the first things I noticed about the original panel." I sighed gustily. "That's all, really? A map which we don't have, a date that we don't know, and flowers which we don't understand?"

"Yes."

"*Christus.* If it was all so confusing, there was no point going."

"Not so. At the very least I am assured of my place among them. Let us retire and think on all this, for we have our papal audience in the morning before we leave for Florence. And in Florence, I think, more must be revealed, for there lives one that may help us—a brother of my order. For matters touching botany, we cannot do better than consult Nicodemus of Padua, the herbalist at Santa Croce. There is no flower in the field, nor herb in the hedgerow, that he does not know by name. And," he added, with gravity, "there is the wedding to attend."

I felt frustrated and annoyed, my relief at the return of my dear friend now replaced by the familiar feeling of groping in the dark without a candle. "How will *that* help?" I asked waspishly.

"Because I suspect that the painting is a gift for the groom. We may see the real thing at last."

There was so much to trouble me in this statement that I slept ill, with strange dreams of flowers and maps and a hundred thousand ships sailing up the Tiber and into my chamber. I was wrecked aboard and rose from boiling seas to regard the *Primavera* floating on the waves, massive and vivid with color. I climbed aboard and pressed my face to its image, as if I regarded myself in a mirror.

And woke.

The city from my window was tiled with dawn gold, the towers rocked by bellsong. The kites rose above the cacophony and bent their wings in the warm breeze that stole through my shutters. A pocky dark Roman woman entered the room bringing eggs and herring and fruit to my bedside, with a jug of wine and water mixed. I sat, hollow eyed, for it seemed I was to eat in bed, a new experience for me, for I had always thought it a place for other pastimes. I broke my fast and immediately felt better. The Roman maid returned to dress me, and in my austere Aragonese black I left my chamber to meet Brother Guido hovering outside, like a husband at a midwife's, anxious for news of his firstborn.

"Come, Luciana," he chided, "we must not be late. The others wait upon us."

He led me once again through endless passages of the Castel Sant'Angelo, where I recognized the hall of statues from yestereve. Soon we greeted the king and his party. Don Ferrente met us looking smooth faced and well rested, and did not betray by a look or a gesture that he had spoken of secrets with Brother Guido at midnight in the Forum. We mutely followed his train into a dark, paneled chamber.

I plucked my friend's sleeve. "Are we meeting the pope?"

"Yes." He licked his lips, his eyes darted—he was in a ferment of excitement.

"Must we not enter the city of the Vatican?"

"Yes," he said again, "but the business is secret—we must go another way."

Once again I entered a land of fantasy, as I watched two scarlet priests wrest open a heavy oaken door. Beckoned forward, I followed the king and his company into a dark mouth leading to a tunnel studded by torches to light the way.

"The *passetto del borgo*," Brother Guido murmured, "an ancient tunnel linking the *castello* and the Vatican. This audience between our party and His Holiness must be secret indeed."

After long moments of walking in the dark, I began to feel a little frightened and my throat tightened at the enclosed space. All were silent, for there was something about the place and the solemnity of the acolytes that oppressed speech; there was naught to be heard but the creak of shoe leather and the whisper of velvet on the stones. When we emerged, I blinked, molelike, and by the time my poor eyes had become accustomed to daylight again our situation could not have been more different—for we had passed from our dark subterranean underworld into a bright spacious heaven. This, of course, was the Sistine Chapel, built by Pope Sixtus for the glory of God. My jaw fell open. Brother Guido was right: Jesus was not worshipped in a corner anymore, nor in a damp hole underground; God's glory on Earth was here for all to see. Angels soared to the ceiling, gilded to the pillars with great skill. Biblical scenes adorned the wide walls as if Mary and her company lived in front of our eyes. Such colors were to be seen—such lapis, such tourmaline, such gold. For the first time I understood: painting was alchemy. Artists like Botticelli, with their glues, gessos, and varnishes, their pigments shimmering in jars and bottles and alembics, were brothers to those hopeful apothecaries who created gold from naught. I was aghast, but was not too bedazzled to miss the familiarity of the women's faces and their dress, their positions, their ways of standing, the set of the head upon the neck, and the attitudes of the hands. All these ladies before me stood with their beauteous heads inclined to their right feet while their bodies leaned and rested their weight on their left. "Contrapposto" Brother Guido had once called this attitude, and I had stood that way myself, once, in an airy studio in far-off Florence.

The king confirmed my memory. "I see you admire the frescoes, Doña," he said kindly. "Little wonder, for they were created for His Holiness very recently by a true magician among painters: one Sandro Botticelli."

I knew then the blood drained from my face and I could not speak. Botticelli *here*? The author of all this trouble? The puzzlemaster himself? I remembered how I had angered him; pictured him now as vengeful Mercury with a curved sword ready to smite me down.

"Is the artist still in residence?" I croaked, as casually as possible.

"No"—I breathed relief—"he is just lately gone home to Florence. Sadly we just missed the fellow or I would have had you meet him."

Brother Guido and I exchanged a glance.

"He is shortly to be replaced by another of your Florentine compatriots, Michelangelo Buonarroti, who comes to adorn the pediments and the ceiling."

I craned my head skeptically to the ceiling. The space was vast, with huge planes and panels to be covered, and awkward triangular spaces where the cross ribs met the ceiling. *Madonna*, what a task.

"You are thinking it cannot be done?" The king cocked a single eyebrow at me.

I knew not what to say.

"I am of your mind. But we shall see."

I looked at Brother Guido, happy in our escape, but I could see that he was cuckoo struck and staring before him. He had hardly noted our exchange. I looked where he did and knew that it was not the vastness of the space or the beauty of the decoration that bewitched him, but instead the personage we had come to meet.

For half a league away, before the great altar, sat the pope himself, ready to receive us.

As the cardinals ushered the king forward and we followed in his wake, I stole a glance at my friend. At that moment he was no longer Prince of Pisa but was once again a humble novitiate of the Franciscan order, ready to meet the greatest man of the church. He looked like he was meeting God. I began to smile, then a notion stopped me, for Brother Guido, monk and orphan, was going to greet the pope, his spiritual father and parent in the church. The pope was the only parent he had left, the church his only family. If I ever got the chance to meet *my* only parent, my *Vero Madre* (which I will, one day, mark you), I would be just as moonfazed to be sure.

The cardinals paused at the golden altar rail and the king and Brother Guido bowed for their audience, while the court and myself knelt as one at the pews directly behind. I bent my head as the others did, but through my steepled fingers I stole a glance at His Holiness, Pope Sixtus IV.

He sat on a throne of gold, adorned by fluttering cherubs and twisting beasts, the gilt so bright I could hardly look at it. His robes were so crusted with jewels and worked with golden thread that I could not tell you the color of their original fabric. His papal hat was red and white velvet, rimed with seed pearls and rising above a circlet of gold.

But below the crown, His Holiness's face was aged, the skin as thin and wrinkled as parchment, the blue eyes pale and rheumy, the papery cheeks webbed with tiny red veins. He was a man after all, and an old one at that. Yet his mien was holy and noble, he stood with vigor and spoke with great energy in ringing tones of authority.

He moved to Don Ferrente first and placed his hand, blue veined and beringed, on the king's head. The two great men shared a glance and a complicit nod. Then came the blessing. "May God and his Holy Mother bless you and keep you, now and all the days of your life."

He moved then to Brother Guido, and I smiled proudly at the joy my friend must feel. I could see his face, ashen, and white as a nun's arse-cheeks and hoped he would not faint with religious ecstasy when the holy hand touched him. I felt pride tinged with great sadness, for I knew then he was lost to me—the church was his one love, now and forever; he was wedded to his faith, now and forever. The blessing chimed in my head, and I knew he would take no other bride.

When the pope had blessed his two noble guests, he intoned three prayers with his hand on a golden psalter, then turned to go, followed by his cardinals, disappearing through a side door into the body of his palace. Thus, in a few short moments, our audience was apparently over. I marveled at a man so powerful that he could afford to give even a king so little of the time of his day.

But the king seemed genuinely moved, and we all filed out

into the great piazza of Saint Peter's in silence. I breathed the morning air and watched the pigeons peck at the golden stones, watched the faithful gather before the great palace. We were dwarfed by the great gold buildings and the experience we had just had. Brother Guido was still white, his lips pinched, his eyes glossy with tears, more moved than even I had thought. I myself was morose, thinking of the day when he would reenter his order, surely soon after today's events. Don Ferrente fetched him a clap on the shoulder, which nearly dropped my friend to the ground—I had to steady him. "Let's away. The carriages are ready. Back to your native Tuscany and the wedding in Florence. Your heart must sing at the thought of it, heh?"

Brother Guido did not reply, but his rudeness went unnoticed as the king and his retinue swept away across Saint Peter's Square, to where the carriages waited in a glittering line. I, however, knew that this humor went deeper than a devotional daze.

We quickly fell behind and I tugged Brother Guido's elbow. "What's wrong?"

No answer.

I tried again, making light of it. "*Jesu.* I know you looked forward to meeting the pope, but I had not known you could be so affected!"

He turned his stricken countenance upon me. "Not so much as you might think. For I have met him once before."

Madonna. He had run mad. "What do you mean?"

He took my face in his hands, his palms and fingers icy on my warm cheeks.

"Oh, Luciana. My faith is ended, my world is over. I recognized the voice before I even saw the ring on his thumb."

The pigeons fluttered at my feet and in my brain. "Who?"

"His Holiness. He was there—last night." Brother Guido's eyes burned into mine. "Pope Sixtus IV is one of the Seven."

· 5 ·

Florence II

26

I celebrated my return to Florence by leaning over the Ponte Vecchio and puking into the Arno.

My terror had sat hunched in the pit of my stomach like an ugly little troll ever since we had begun to descend into the valley, but as soon as we crossed the river into my home city I had to beg the king to stop the carriage, and let my fear leap from my mouth to freedom. As I leaned against the balustrade, weak and empty, I noticed three things.

Cosa Uno: everything was still beautiful here, but now it made me afraid. The old bridge was glorious amber in the evening sun, but now I saw only assassins lurking beneath the arches. The copper cup of the Duomo still arched above the city, but now I saw that it was a poisoned chalice, upended to spill its venom and soak every stone in the place with evil. We had been on a grail quest to many lands and had come home to find the vessel tainted. The innocent swallows and gulls that wheeled around the cupola were now kites and daws, searching for carrion.

Cosa Due: the Arno smelled the same, but now I saw that amid the sapphire stream floated the bloated corpses of criminals fresh from the gallows, pitched into the river upstream at Rubaconte, where the guilty were dangled and flayed. One dead fellow rolled in the current, turning his eyeless white face to me as he slipped past. I wondered if I would swim there soon too. Sickened, I turned from the river and noticed:

Cosa Tre: Brother Guido, who had descended from the royal carriage also, in a pantomime of sympathy, was hunched over the next arch along, vomiting too.

We were home.

Spent and hollow-eyed, we regarded each other and turned back to the carriage. Brother Guido handed me in and we endured the kindly, concerned tones of our royal hosts, heard a list of cures for the ague, and politely declined to have a feather burned under our noses. Brother Guido they knew to be ill, of course, for he had not spoken a word or eaten a morsel since we left Rome. The king and queen were sorry to learn that I had caught his complaint, and expressed a hope that I would be better for the wedding tomorrow. At which I almost puked again.

'Twas fear, plain fear, that gripped my belly; for there was no catching the ague that afflicted my companion. He was suffering the torment of having given his life to the church, given up his worldly life and even his inheritance, only to realize that that body was corrupt, sick and rotting from the head like a stinking fish. Only I knew what ailed him, that when he breathed that sigh in Peter's Square in Rome, he had breathed out his faith all in one long breath. He had not prayed since Rome, a marked contrast to the constant chatter of catechism on the way into the Eternal City. On the way out he was mum as an oyster and said no more litanies than I did myself. Although I could almost have prayed for him. For God, if there was one, to heal his heart and tell him that the Father of all still sat in his heaven, even if the father of the church had joined this heinous plot.

Once again we were restricted as to speech on our journey by virtue of being forever stuck with the royal couple. On the occasions that we were alone Brother Guido rejected all comfort and barely spoke. He drank little and ate less. The hair grew on his face to give him an unkempt look, but this time he resembled more of a varlet than a hermit, for his aura of sanctity had quite gone. I grieved for his faith but more for ourselves, for without his intelligence and guidance we were well and truly fucked. What chance could I have, alone, of deciphering the rest of the puzzle?

As we crossed the remainder of the bridge and the Piazza della Signoria closed around us, I looked up at the toothsome tower of the Medici palace and felt we were entering the lion's den. The arch leading into Florence's most ancient square was an open mouth waiting hungrily to receive us, the wrestling statues stilled to watch us be devoured.

We knew that the king and queen were to lodge with their newly reconciled friend Lorenzo de' Medici, but the invitation had not been extended to "Lord Niccolò"; it was assumed that as a Tuscan prince, he would have lodgings in Florence with a retinue waiting—Christ only knew where we were to conjure these. I looked to Brother Guido, sitting slumped at the window, watching the streets he knew so well with a baleful stare.

"I am a Daniel," he muttered—his first words since Rome.

I realized what he had said with a shock—our minds trod in step with each other, despite the fact we had not spoken for days. He knew we were entering the lion's den too.

I stood as the carriage stopped, preparing to descend again, but the queen put out her hand.

"Stay, my dear. Take the carriage to the prince's lodgings, with our compliments. He is not well enough to change horses. Do you know where his palace stands?"

My heart warmed to the queen with her kindness and nobility. I wished for one crazy moment that she were my *Vero Madre* and I could press my face into her powdered bosom. I knew not what to say, so, as ever in these situations, I lied.

"Very well, Your Majesty. His house is a little up the hill, toward San Miniato." I had no time to think, so as they waved farewell with a promise to see us on the morrow at the wedding, I gave directions to Bembo's house, where, a little above a month ago, I had watched my best client die.

As the carriage pulled away I shrank back in my seat but could still see the King and Queen of Naples sweep up the steps of the Palazzo Vecchio, accompanied by their retinue, to be greeted by two servants in the black and gold livery of the Medici. My stomach lurched again, with dual horrors—both personal and political. The first, the fact that Brother Guido and I had been hunted for our lives here, and may still be in grave danger. The second—that the young sprig of the Medici family and groom-to-be, Lorenzo di Pierfrancesco de' Medici, was plotting a treacherous coup against his uncle, Lorenzo the Magnificent. A coup expressed in paint—writ in riddles and encoded in the figures of the *Primavera,* a wedding present from Botticelli to his young, soon-to-be-married patron. And now I had to shake my friend from his malaise so that we may save our sorry skins and, perhaps, the city. But, as it happened, I had no need to prise speech from him—for as soon as we were alone he spoke.

"There," he said, "there it all began." With no thought for his safety he was craning from the window looking up at the tall blank walls of the palazzo. I saw only the square bitemarks of scaffolding and the pockmarks of the stucco, and one high, high window below the lantern tower.

"What am I looking at?" I was relieved he spoke yet reluctant to emerge from the shadows to look too, lest I was seen by those who knew me.

"There," he repeated, his voice gravelly from lack of use. "There hung Jacopo de' Pazzi, head of the Pazzi family, with two of his brethren, for the offense of murdering Giuliano de'

Medici. They slaughtered him, in front of his brother Lorenzo the Magnificent, in the cathedral here."

Everyone in Florence knew that story, so I waited for the point.

"And beside him swung Francesco Salviati, Archbishop of Pisa—a man I knew well, for he gave me my First Communion. Lorenzo the Magnificent escaped that day, but he signed his own death warrant when he hung an archbishop, in full ceremonial robes, for his part in the plot."

Really, Brother Guido's mind made some astonishing and frankly irrelevant leaps sometimes. Ironic that he'd just begun to speak again and was already annoying me a bit. "What the blue bollocks have the Pazzis got to do with this?"

Now he turned on me as if he hated me. "Didn't you hear me? Not the *Pazzis*. The *archbishop*."

Day dawned. In my mind's eye the guilty prelate bounced on his rope, his guts and gristle streaming to the floor in scarlet cords that matched his holy vestments, his face pulped and bloody as he turned and bashed against the windowless gray walls that were blind to his plight. "So you think the pope is conspiring with Lorenzo di Pierfrancesco against his uncle because his uncle had his archbishop hanged?"

"I do."

Surely this could not be all—I had never heard him answer so briefly. He relented. "Lorenzo the Magnificent and the whole of Florence were excommunicated for the offense. Pope Sixtus's own nephew Girolamo Riario, Lord of Imola, was dispatched to arrest and charge Lorenzo the Magnificent, but the Florentine Signoria were loyal and wouldn't hand over Lorenzo. Recourse to the law was unsuccessful, so it is my belief that Sixtus has gathered the Seven, with Lorenzo di Pierfrancesco's connivance, to make an alliance to overturn Lorenzo and place his nephew, a willing tool of the papacy, in his stead. Depend upon it," he said decidedly, "the pope is at the root of this. The clues are writ in stone."

I was doubtful. "You sound awfully sure."

"I am. When I said that the clues are writ in stone, I meant that literally, not metaphorically."

I was silent. He had lost me. Luckily he continued un-prompted.

"Every clue that has led us forth so far has been *literally* written in stone. The leaning tower above my door in Santa Croce. The newly carved ship on the Tower of Pisa, depicting the Muda's flagship. The rood screen in San Lorenzo in Naples, showing the stations of the cross. *I am Petrus.* The very church itself was writ in stone too, the papacy, the Vatican, the whole holy, catholic, and apostolic church."

I showed him a blank countenance.

"Peter," he said simply. "Saint Peter. Petrus. The symbol and saint of the papacy. The gatekeeper, the keyholder. *I am the rock.*"

"All right," I said slowly. "Then how does Botticelli come into it? If it was the Pazzis and the pope that kicked this all off?"

Brother Guido's eyes burned like the damned. "There." He pointed across the square to the customs house. "There on that very wall, Botticelli was charged by his Medici paymasters to paint the conspirators where they hung, as a warning to others."

I narrowed my eyes—there on the rough and sun-bleached stones, four faint figures could still be seen; long slashing lines above, straight as Sunday, described the ropes that hung them all.

"So when this plot was engendered, who would they choose to depict this deadly scheme but the favored artist of the Medici court?"

"And the *Primavera* reveals all?" I questioned. "All the cities that have agreed to join with the pope, make war on Lorenzo the Magnificent and remove him from power?"

"Yes."

I bought it. "So we know *why*. But we don't know *when* and *how* the attack will come. Our knowledge has no power unless we know the details. So the question is, what do we do next?"

His lips curled cruelly into a smile that was not a smile. "Nothing. Let them blast each other into hellfire—they are all of them murderers, all of them worthless. They are damned and so are we."

Now this was not helpful. We had switched places, the monk and I—he had given up on the quest and I thirsted for more. I knew that if we knew everything that the painting hid we might just have enough to bargain for our lives.

We were drawing away from the square and the site of that grisly scene—we had to think of something fast, before we were taken all the way out of the city on the fool's errand to San Miniato. Then I saw the great frontage and round eye of Santa Croce, and Brother Guido's words from two nights ago echoed in my brain. *For matters touching botany, we cannot do better than consult Nicodemus of Padua, the herbalist at Santa Croce. There is no flower in the field, nor herb in the hedgerow, that he does not know by name.*

"Might we alight here?" I called, hoping that was the right word for "get down." "My lord knows an herbalist within, and we must get a draught for his ague."

The driver slowed the horses. "Shall I wait, Doña?" he called, in his thick accent. I already had the door open and heaved Brother Guido to the ground, without waiting for the driver or footman to help us.

"No, do not trouble," I replied breezily. "The good brothers will send a runner for our own carriage to fetch us."

The driver exchanged a look with the footman, shrugged in his Spanish fashion, and touched his hand to his hat and his whip to his horse. Our last connection to the Neapolitan court drew away in a cloud of dust. And there we stood, Luciana Vetra and Brother Guido della Torre, a calendar month after we had last been here, at the gates of Santa Croce. There slumped the postern monk Brother Malachi, as ever, in his cups and asleep on the wrought-iron gate.

"Why are we here?" He spoke through tight lips; his clenched jaw white with anger, he looked on the place he had once loved, this tranquil holy haven, with hatred.

"To see Brother Nicodemus, the herbalist, as you yourself suggested." I hoped the flattery would work. It didn't.

"I will not go in."

I had expected this. "But this was your *home*. These men were your *brothers*." I indicated Brother Malachi, who damaged my case by farting noisily. "It is the *pope* that has betrayed you, not the Franciscan order."

He set his jaw. "If the pope is corrupt, then so is all the church. My life, theirs"—he pointed to the sleeping monk— "and all this"—his sweeping gesture took in the grand edifice of the monastery—"is a lie."

This was going to be harder than I thought. I remembered wryly how a sennight ago I would have done anything to prise him from the church like a barnacle from a rock. Now I would give the pearl in my belly to get him inside this monastery so we could talk with its herbalist. "All right. Suppose what you say is true. Why don't you *stop* him?"

"Who?"

I sighed. "His Holi-arse the Pope. What he's doing is wrong, er . . . right?"

He did not answer—we both noted it. "It's not our war, nor our problem. I care not what happens to the Seven."

I grabbed the front of his surcoat—it was loose and I noticed how much weight he had lost in the last week. "It *is* our problem, for our lives will be in danger again the moment your true identity is discovered. Which it will be one day. You cannot live as Niccolò forever—nor would you want to, unless you're planning a lifetime of shafting catamites." He winced. "But you must run *forever* once you are discovered, and I must too. And what of the treacherous Lorenzo di Pierfrancesco? He's plotting against the father of our great city. We could bring him down, cut out the church's canker, restore some . . . some *purity* to the church." I was laying it on thick, but he didn't seem to notice. I had seen a gleam in his eye for the first time since we left Rome at the prospect of spoiling the pope's scheme. I followed up my advantage. "Let's figure this thing out and crack the riddle, then somehow present the whole thing to Lorenzo the Magnificent himself, just as your uncle said; then we'd have his gratitude, and his protection, and you'd save your skin."

"I don't care about my skin."

"*My* skin then."

He was silent, but not from torment this time; he was thinking. He looked at me as if for the first time, and I knew then that he cared about me enough to try to save me. It was a warm night but I suddenly felt hot, as if the sun had waked. And there was something else in his eyes too; he didn't *want* to quit and I think I knew why. His brain. The fire of his faith may have died but the flame of his intellect could never be extinguished. I hit him with my best shot.

"Besides, can you really walk away not knowing what it all means? Can you really sleep at night not knowing what secret lies in the flowers? What calamities will come with the spring? Why there are seven conspirators, not eight, as there are in the picture? That you couldn't work it out, that you let the riddle beat you?"

I had him then, but I couldn't resist one more, completely practical point. We didn't actually *have* a palace to house us, nor a retinue to tend to our needs. I couldn't go back to my little cot by the Arno, flooded with Enna's blood. He couldn't go back to Pisa and his murderous cousin. "After all," I finished, "where else can we go?"

He knew I was right. He had no choice but to return to the monastery he had once called home. I glanced at the sky— night was falling, the Florentine day was beginning. We moved to the gate and I woke Brother Malachi, as I had done more than a month ago, by shoving my tits in his face.

27

Nicodemus of Padua was silent.

He had heard the entire incredible tale and now sat, stroking the white stubble at his chin and occasionally grunting faintly, as if he were digesting a meal. He was digesting our story.

I had begun by looking around me, when we had entered the herbarium at Brother Malachi's direction. It was an intriguing place—a candlelit room with a colonnade of pillars and cross-rib vaults holding up the low roof. My eyes followed the pillars upward.

Madonna.

Two thirds of the way to the ceiling the ribs disappeared into an inverted meadow. Hanging from the ceiling were flowers and herbs and bulbs of every sort, drying in the firelight, turning gently on their twines as our breath or the door draft stirred them. The scent of the flowers and herbs, all jumbled together and releasing their heady fumes as the fire warmed them, was almost overpowering in its cloying, choking sweetness. We sat at a trestle bench for our conference, the fire burning merrily at the hearth at our side. Every other niche of the place was crammed with fat-bellied pots, corked bottles, or clay crucibles, labeled in Latin and stacked to the ceiling. A long scrubbed table ran along one wall, crowded with flints and burners, copper pipes and alembics, all crazily connected with tubes of pigs' gut. Most bizarre of all was the herbalist himself, smaller than any living man I had seen yet with the wisest eyes. His age was numberless; he could have been on this earth since the Crusades, as his ancient cheeks carried more lines than a Saracen's map. His hairs were as scarce as his wrinkles were plentiful, for they sprouted in white whiskers just above his ears and round his head in a snowy frill.

I let Brother Guido tell the story, without interruption, for I realized early on that the old monk had a difficulty—he had, as all the brothers had, seen me at the postern in the old days and knew that I brought corruption within his walls. He did not meet my eye once, but I took no offense—I had had plenty of insults in my life and I could well stand a monk's disapproval, if only he would help us.

When he spoke at last, his voice was unexpectedly deep, and with a strong Paduan accent. If he felt surprise at seeing a Franciscan novice who had disappeared more than a month ago reappear dressed as a prince, with a well-known tart on his arm and with an incredible story to tell, he did not show it. And of all the things he may have said, he struck right at the heart of Brother Guido's anguish. "And you are certain, my brother, that His Holiness is involved with these seven conspirators?"

"I am, for he wore the ring they all wear on their thumbs; my uncle, Don Ferrente of Naples, the pope, and now myself as you see."

The herbalist peered at the gold band gleaming in the firelight. "And presumably, should you see such a band on Lorenzo di Pierfrancesco at his wedding tomorrow, you may be sure he plots against his uncle."

"Yes."

Brother Nicodemus was silent, and when he next spoke I realized that he had the trick of Brother Guido's—his mind, much quicker than other men's, had sieved our information and filtered from it a point of interest that others might miss.

"Seven not eight?" he asked. "And yet there are eight adult figures in the scene?"

"Yes."

The herbalist nodded. " 'Tis an evil business," he said, now shaking his wizened head.

Brother Guido took his cue. As if to a confessor he began at last to speak of his hurt. "Brother, I am in the wilderness. My faith and trust in him that we serve has left me utterly. It pains me to speak of this to you. I know that as a brother of this order, you must be as grievously shocked as I am by our father pope's involvement."

Brother Nicodemus raised his head abruptly. "Shocked? I? I could not be less so." He laughed a dry chuckle, half cough, half mirth. "Son, I am sorry for your disillusionment. But I must tell you, the man you idolized has dipped his hands in blood before this pass; yes, many times."

My companion leaned forward and the flare of the fire lit his face amber. "What?"

"Indeed," replied the herbalist gently. "You spoke of the Pazzi conspiracy. Who was it that encouraged the Pazzis forward in their murderous plot, gave them papal sanction? Who was it who excommunicated the whole of Florence for the deed, just so he could force the Medici bank to cease trading, thus writing off ten thousand florins of papal debt in a single stroke? The pope only reconciled with Lorenzo because our lands were under threat from Turkish attack when the infidels occupied Otranto. But that was above six months ago; now that the sultan is dead and the threat is gone, the pope is free to move against his old enemy once more." Brother Nicodemus shook his head once more. "Brother, you are young in the world, and innocent—you have no notion of what a man may do, be he never so holy."

Brother Guido was still, white lipped and shocked to the core. I myself was less so, for had I not been tumbling monks, and yes, priests too, for years?

The herbalist could sense the destruction of Brother Guido's world and spoke more kindly. "Son. You must learn to differentiate between man and God. Man is fallible, the church corrupt. But God is true and he will never betray you. You must find your way back to faith, as a conversation between yourself and God. Popes and prelates come and go, but God is eternal. Those of us who are true to our Rule must guide others as best we can to the light." The old man, as if tired by his pronouncements, took a sip from a wooden cup. "As to your present predicament, I think we may absolve the Holy Father from the role of the originator of the plot. The mastermind comes not from the Vatican but from the House of Medici."

"What makes you say that?"

"The ring you wear bears nine gold balls upon the band. The *palle*."

"The *palle*!" repeated Brother Guido, holding his thumb before our eyes, where the ring glinted gold in the firelight. "Why did I not see this before?"

I could clearly see the ring of nine little golden balls, circling the band. I had to ask. "The what now?"

"The *palle*, or Medici balls, appear in a circle, in differing numbers, on all their heraldic adornments," Brother Guido explained.

Of course I knew the emblem well, for apart from its appearing above every gateway and every palace wall in Florence, I had about a hundred jokes from the street about Medici balls. In fact, I think I had drained a few pairs of minor Medici balls in my time; younger sons and cousins only, unfortunately. I'd never had a crack at the Lorenzos—neither one—who I think led fairly pious lives.

Except for murder of course.

Such musings died on my lips, though—now wasn't the time—for the herbalist spoke again.

"I have not yet seen the painting, but by the three Marys, I would warrant that the *palle* will appear there too."

Brother Guido stood. "It is time," he said, and he helped the old monk to his feet, where he came up to around the younger man's navel. The two brothers moved to the long table and Brother Guido removed the *cartone* from his pouch. Brother Nicodemus weighted the corners with stones that gleamed red in the firelight—carnelians, I guessed, for use in his healing work. Uninvited, I moved behind them to watch. I had not seen the *Primavera* for some time, for it had been bound to the chest of my silent companion since Rome, and each time I saw it after long absence I was struck by the beauty of the thing—never more so than now, gilded by firelight and cornered with carnelians. Two heads, one white, one black, bent over the picture and I must wait my turn. I did not have to wait long.

"There," announced the herbalist, standing back. "The apples of the Hesperides; they represent the *palle,* the emblem of the Medici."

I stepped forth, my eyes following his gnarled finger to the trees above the figures, where above a hundred round golden fruits dangled from the leaves.

"Look more like oranges to me," I muttered.

"The apples of the Hesperides *are* oranges in classical literature, Luciana." Brother Guido did not even look at me as he put me straight. "And these oranges appear on every Medici coat of arms nine times."

"Look here too," exclaimed the old monk abruptly. He pointed to the natural arch of leaves above Venus's head.

"Laurels," said Brother Guido. "Yes, we noted them in Rome. We thought then that they identify the victim of the plot—Lorenzo the Magnificent."

"Or the mastermind himself, Lorenzo di Pierfrancesco de' Medici," put in Brother Nicodemus.

I felt a little chill despite the fire—what we were looking at here was the map of a murder. A murder that we must prevent.

Brother Nicodemus echoed my thoughts. "Then your way forward is obvious." He turned to Brother Guido. "Leaving aside your faith for a moment, your *moral* imperative is clear. Whether or not you are a monk, you are a good man. By the grace of God you have been given the chance to attend this wedding under an assumed identity. You *must* use this chance to gain audience with Lorenzo the Magnificent, and lay all this before him, and save his life. For how else will you petition him, now that your uncle, God rest his soul, is dead? He would not see a humble Franciscan novice, and"—he gestured to me—"a young lady with no credentials, but a prince of Pisa and his escort, well . . ." He had no need to finish. "And his protection, if you saved him from such a conspiracy, is assured."

"But Brother Nicodemus, our knowledge of the plot is, at present, merely conjecture," protested Brother Guido. "We know the identity of just *three* of the seven—no more. We need your help—if we can discover the 'secret that the flowers hold,' we may be able to know more details, and detail will give our information credibility."

"I understand you well. Let us take another look, and this time we shall consider only the lilies of the field."

Now as I craned to see, I was dismayed by the sheer number of flowers in the painting.

Madonna.

There were more blooms than cow shits in a midden.

As you'd expect for a painting named after the spring, there were numerous plants dotting the sward. Above the figure's heads there were orange blossoms. There were blooms all over Flora's dress, as I well remembered from that unforgettable day modeling for Botticelli. Well, too, I remembered the heavy chaplet of flowers I was charged to wear on my brow that day. There were the roses filling my skirt too, and flowers falling from the mouth of the nymph standing to my right, whom Brother Guido had identified as Chloris. No figure went ungarlanded—even warlike Mercury had tiny starlike blossoms wreathed around his boots.

"Holy fuck!" I breathed, earning myself my first direct look from Nicodemus of Padua. I was back in the schoolroom for a moment, and held my tongue thereafter, for I did not wish to receive such a glance again. Brother Guido, in his new pessimism, clearly felt the same despair as I did, but used language of less color.

" 'Tis impossible," he said. "Forgive me, Brother. We are on a fool's errand. There are too many. Even if we had days or months to contemplate the scene, we could never know which flowers hold the secret to which the pope referred."

But the herbalist was rubbing his knuckles together till his old bones cracked like flints. "Now, Brother," he chided. "God gave us our intellects to be challenged. Nothing is impossible. It is likely," he went on, "that if this picture hides a code, and if a secret is to be found within the flowers, not *all* the flowers we see here are relevant. Some will be mere decoration or decoy. I think that to interrogate *all* the flowers would be an exercise in futility."

"Maybe we could count the flowers on each character," I ventured. "That would give you eight numbers, not counting Cupid. Perhaps the 'secret' is a date, or something." I thought this a pretty good idea.

Brother Nicodemus showed no signs of having heard me but Brother Guido replied. "Such a scheme is problematic—for how are we to assign the flowers to each character? For instance, when Flora scatters flowers, do we count the flowers that she scatters or only the ones *touching* her person. And in the case of Chloris the nymph, do we note the flowers that fall from her mouth, or no?" He noted my crestfallen face. "But the idea of a *number* is a strong one. Perhaps—"

The herbalist held up his ancient hand. "Such debate may not be necessary. There may be other ways to discover which blooms are truly relevant. Think, my brother," he urged, "what *exactly* was said that night beneath the arch of Septimius Severus in Rome?"

I was impressed with the old monk's recall, for I could barely remember the name of the arch myself.

Brother Guido thought hard. "They were speaking in Latin, which fitted well with the whole tenor of the evening—the arch, the guards, the city. Pope Sixtus said these exact words: *Flora manus secretum.*"

"Then 'flowers hold the secret,'" translated the herbalist. "Very well. Then we have our answer." We both turned to him. "If you were to look at this painting for the first time, which figure would you say has the most to do with flowers?"

"Flora," we both answered as one.

"Exactly. She is *covered* in flowers from head to foot, and scatters flowers too. Her name, of course, is the most suggestive—Flora—Latin for 'flowers.'"

He folded his hands like an attorney and paced as he addressed us.

"Your problem, as I see it, is that the riddle *'Flora manus secretum*—Flora holds the secret' can mean one of four things. One: the answer is in 'flora'—as in 'flora and fauna'—the Latin collective name for all plants, so meaning *all* the flowers, *all* the herbs, and *all* the trees and fruits in the picture. We have already discussed how protracted it would be to investigate every bloom we see here. Two: that the answer lies somewhere in Flora *the figure*. Three: that the answer lies in Florence *the city*. As you have identified that each figure represents a city, this is very plausible, since Florence is the home of the *Primavera* panel itself. Or four, and most incredible, that the answer lies"—he looked at me for the second time—"with *you*."

I looked about me, in case someone had entered the room behind us. *"Me?"* It was the bray of an ass.

Brother Guido turned his blue gaze on me.

"You," repeated the herbalist. "You are the model for Flora, are you not?"

"Well, yes, but—"

"Then you may hold the secret; you may have been chosen for a reason."

"I think we may discount that," put in Brother Guido quickly. "Signorina Vetra was chosen through her . . . association with a wealthy friend of Botticelli's."

"Ah, yes. Signor Benvolio, God rest his soul." The herbalist's benediction was not entirely sincere, and I suspected that somewhat of Bembo's reputation had penetrated even these hallowed walls.

"Very well," continued Brother Nicodemus. "I think, then, we may concentrate our efforts on the figure of Flora. She is clearly the most floral of characters. Chloris is perhaps the next most adorned, as flowers drop like truths from her mouth. She reaches for Flora's sleeve—see? I think we may assume that Chloris and Flora are intimately connected."

"Perhaps Chloris is a city very close to Florence?" suggested Brother Guido.

"I think so—perhaps Prato, maybe Imola."

I had no opinion on this, since before last month, I had never been outside the city, unless you count coming from Venice as a baby in a bottle.

"But to Flora," urged the herbalist. "What can we say of the figure, aside from the flowers? For they are her major feature, but before we focus on them, perhaps we should consider her other characteristics."

I shared a look with Brother Guido—our two half-smiles made a whole, for this was exactly how we were used to proceeding.

"She is the *primum mobile* of the whole scene." Typical of my learned companion to begin with something Latin which left me behind completely. Luckily he knew me well enough to translate without prompting. "She is the 'first to move.' "

I saw what he meant. "She is the farthest forward of all the figures in the scene—she leads the way."

"Which fits my hypothesis that Lorenzo di Pierfrancesco, of Flora's city Florence, is the originator of the plot—the root of all," put in the herbalist. "Also, she looks directly at the viewer."

"Her dress flares like angel wings." This devotional last from Brother Guido.

"She has fishy sleeves." This was me.

Both brothers shot me a look.

I explained. "I mean—her foresleeves are covered in, well, fish skin."

This they could not deny, nonsensical though it sounded, for it was plain for all to see.

"Hmmm. Perhaps this indicates a maritime connection, possibly to the three Graces," mused my friend.

"She wears their color too," noted Brother Nicodemus. "Or rather, their *lack* of color. The body of her gown is white, like theirs."

"But I am not dead!" I blurted, referring to our conversation on the Muda's flagship, when we deduced that the Graces were *dead* ladies: Simonetta Cattaneo and Maria d'Aquino, "Fiammetta."

"I think the presence of the flowers, such living, *vital* things, mark you out from their number, as a living, breathing . . . person."

I knew the herbalist wanted to say "lady" but could not quite bring himself to use that word in connection with me.

"Let us begin by identifying the blossoms that adorn Flora," he went on hurriedly, "and see what we may find."

He then reached for an interesting contraption: two twin circles of glass within lead circles, which he clipped to his nose. When he turned back to Brother Guido his eyes seemed enormous behind the glass, as if magnified by the bottoms of twin bottles. I almost laughed, but my mirth died when I soon realized that he could see with such aids much better than Brother Guido or I, even though we had a good fifty years on him.

"Shall we begin with the headdress? In the center, on the brow"—he peered close with his eyeglasses—"the humble violet, *Viola odorata*. Let us have some method to this," added the old monk. He stood on a stool, for only with such assistance could he reach high enough, and pulled at a purple bloom from the flowery field above our heads. He held it at our eyes and noses. "There: a violet," he said of the fragrant bloom. Then he turned back to us and said one word more. "Next."

And so we worked as the sky clotted into night outside. Working first around Flora's headdress, down to the garland around her neck. The names fell from the herbalist's lips like the blooms from Chloris and echoed from the walls of the crypt: a pagan, not a Christian, litany. Cornflower, daisy, hellebore, lily of the valley, *myosotis,* myrtle, *occhiocento,* pomegranate. Violet again.

I looked on and helped take the flowers down when they proved too high for the herbalist, the smells and sights mingling to take me back to that fateful day in Botticelli's studio; remembering the chaplet that had pricked at my forehead, the wreath that had scratched my throat. The treacherous bell of the Pazzi Chapel—cast by murderers and giving tongue to their memorial—rang twice before we had all the flowers taken down, and Brother Nicodemus marked time with a floral clock of his own. All the blooms were found and identified and fore long a veritable garden sat before us.

At last we were done with the head and neck, but there could be no respite.

"The gown," commanded Brother Guido.

"Much easier," said the herbalist. He pulled just two blooms from their twines. "Cornflower and carnation. All over. And round her waist a girdle of roses." He pulled down a pliant branch, black thorned and beautiful, with a dozen pink roses riding the glossy green leaves. I remembered this detail—the thorns piercing the fabric of my dress to prick my skin.

"And in her hands?"

"Well, *I* can tell you that," said I. I remembered well the fragrant flower heads that were poured into my skirts that day, for me to cradle and cast upon the ground. "I was holding roses."

Brother Guido's head snapped up. "Say it again."

Puzzled, I repeated myself. "I was holding roses."

"Flora was holding roses." He almost whispered the words, like a man in a dream. Then he began to smile, and with a sudden action swept all other carefully collected blooms aside to fall to the floor in a fragrant mass.

We regarded him as if he'd become a lunatic.

"We've been wasting our time," he crowed. "Naming all the flowers, classifying them, taking them down." He capered about the room, playing a pantomime of our actions for the last hour. He hooted with laughter for the first time since Rome. "We are asses all! Flora *holds* the secret! Roses! That is *all* we needed to know! *She is holding them in her hands!* She is the *only* figure holding flowers! Such humble blooms that grow in every garden and hedgerow! We could have named them ourselves!"

Brother Nicodemus sank down onto the milking stool, took off his eyeglasses, and passed his hand before his eyes; when he took the hand away he revealed a toothless smile.

"You are right," he said, "and had we been true scholars the Latin would have told us; the riddle was *'Flora manus secretum.'* *Manus* means to hold *in the hand,* from the root *mano*—hand. If Flora had held the secret in a *metaphorical* sense, like a guardian, Pope Sixtus would have used the verb *custodia,* '*Flora custodia secretum.'*" He turned to me. "Child, you *did* hold the secret after all, in the most literal sense, when you modeled for Botticelli that day." The dust-dry chuckle came again.

I began to feel a little annoyed. I didn't see what there was to smile about. We'd just spent from Vespers till Compline naming flowers, and yet finding the *actual* answer was the work of a moment. I felt rather disappointed. We did not need to be here at all. *Roses.* We could have named *that* frigging flower in the carriage on the way up from Rome in the time it takes to fart, if Brother Guido had not been sulking in the seventh circle of his personal hell. A child could have done it; we didn't need the old monk after all. I began to think about dinner, while Brother Guido apologized to the herbalist.

"I'm sorry, Brother. We did not need to trouble you after all."

"You did, my son. For you still do not know the *meaning* of the roses. Or how they may conceal anything."

This was true; we were no further forward.

"Since we are here, then," said Brother Guido, "we must use the resource we have for this night—namely, Brother Nicodemus's extraordinary knowledge of botany. Besides, I think the codes of the *Primavera* are too clever to have a direct appearance. Botticelli has been cleverer than that so far—all the puzzles have been oblique, and have clarity only to the Seven. We must look for something clever. I think the type of flower is important; perhaps its properties too. Let us spend a little time in colloquy and consider all we know of the queen of flowers, the rose."

Brother Nicodemus then took a rose from his collection, the pale pink of a shell, and another of blushing coral, exactly the two hues that were bundled into my arms in the painting. We all sat at the table now, gazing at the two perfect flowers as if we expected them to speak.

"Rose; *Rosa centifolia*," mused Brother Nicodemus. "As you have well said, she is known as the queen of flowers. Roman brides and bridegrooms were crowned with roses, so too were the images of Cupid and Venus and Bacchus. Such a headdress was much favored by poets too—Anacreon's odes speak of poets sporting rose crowns at their feasts of Flora and Hymen."

I didn't see what a bunch of fey poets could have to do with this—the bridal theme seemed much more relevant—but Brother Guido pounced on the poetic thread.

"I think that is significant. Poliziano, the Medici court poet and the very man who wrote the *Stanze,* the verses upon which the *Primavera* is based, has written many times on the beauties of the rose. In fact"—he brought his hand down on the table with a crash—"the *Stanze* themselves, if memory serves, contain a very specific couplet on flowers, *'Ma vie più lieta, più ridente a bella / ardisce aprire il seno al sol la rosa . . .'* which expresses that the rose is more daring than the humble violet!"

Brother Nicodemus sat a little straighter. "Violet is the flower that crowns Flora's headdress—it sits full in the center, at the forehead!"

"Perhaps the poet, and thus the painting, is saying that we must not use our heads to find the secret, but our—"

"Our what? Our stomachs?" I began to laugh at the downcast faces of the monks, as their theory fell flat.

"Wait, though—isn't Flora with child? Did not Signor Benvolio say as much to you when he urged you to model for his friend?" Brother Guido demanded of me. "That she bears the fruits of the coming season?"

"That's true!" I confirmed eagerly. "I *was* supposed to be up the stick." The elderly monk winced a little at my indelicacy but I didn't care—we were on to something. "Maybe the 'secret' has something to do with a baby or a child? Perhaps someone *is* with child? Perhaps Semiramide Appiani is pregnant, and the brat will be heir to the Medici fortune when Lorenzo the Magnificent is dead!"

"Signorina!" thundered Brother Nicodemus. "I will grant you that the Medici family are not without sin, but Signorina Appiani is reputed to be a virtuous maid, chaste as the first snow."

"All right." I sat back on the bench with a skeptical look. "But you must admit, it would suit Don Ferrente to have his niece the mother of the Medici heir. And Lorenzo di Pierfrancesco too—that's two of the Seven happy."

"And it is true that roses have many connections to Venus," added Brother Guido in my defense. "It is her own flower, and she wore a chaplet of roses at the Judgment of Paris—according to the rhetor Libanis—the very contest that is represented in the *Primavera* by the appearance of the three Graces."

"And Greek legend dictates that the rose originated at the birth of Venus, according to Anacreon," agreed the herbalist. "'A tender rosebush sprang up from the earth when Venus rose from the sea, and a sprinkling of nectar from the gods made the bush burst into flower.'"

"I think we have strayed from the theme somewhat," asserted Brother Guido gently.

I agreed—all the fucking poetry was holding things up, is how I'd express it.

"After all, in the *Primavera* it is *Flora* not Venus who holds the secret. *Flora* who is pregnant, not Venus." Shyly he looked askance at me.

I answered his unasked question. "Not likely." I was too smart to be caught that way; for a working girl it could be the end of your career—a baby was worse than the pox. I thought of the waxed cotton squares where they sat snug and useless at the neck of my womb, replaced after each monthly bleeding. As for the last month—chance would be a fine thing, for I had not had a jump since Bembo. Venus, though—Miss Appiani— was a different matter. Many a Florentine maid had been tumbled by her betrothed—and if a baby was born a few months early, where's the harm? "Look at her dress," I urged. "You could easily hide your bump under there if you were graveled with a brat."

"Hmmm. I think that is the, er . . . Romanesque style," suggested Brother Guido. I snorted through my nose for I knew more of the world than these two, that's for damn sure. "It's a thought," he conceded "and this theorem would certainly be given credence by the fact that tomorrow's wedding date—July

19—is the eve of the feast of Saint Margaret, patron saint of pregnant women; but perhaps we are missing something more obvious."

This I agreed with. "All this cant about Venus and yet you're missing the main point—it's a as clear as the cock on the *David*. The obvious to *me* is that roses are given to women by men who want to fuck them," I blurted, irritated by the whole debate and not caring if I shocked the old booby. But he surprised me.

"She is right, 'tis true," said the herbalist calmly. "They are gifts of love. And the poet Boiardo said that roses were scattered to celebrate joy in love."

Datime a piena mano rose e zigli
spargete intorno a me viole e fiori . . .
Di mia leticia meco il frutto pigli!

"Flora is *scattering* roses in this picture—in Roman times roses were scattered at feasts of Flora and Hymen, in the paths of victors, or beneath their chariot wheels, or adorned the prows of their war vessels."

Brother Guido's attention was caught on a baited hook. "In the paths of victors," he repeated. "This *must* be relevant. For this whole conspiracy revolves around the waging of war and hundreds upon thousands of warships which we have seen with our own eyes."

"Perhaps," agreed Brother Nicodemus. "But I would not at once think of this rose in connection with war, but with healing. I use it again and again in my work here."

"For which maladies?" questioned Brother Guido quickly.

"It strengtheneth the heart, the stomach, the liver, and the retentive faculty; is good against all kinds of fluxes, prevents vomiting, stops tickling coughs, and is of service in consumption. Of course, I use many classes of the rose here in the herbarium, usually in the distillation of rose water for these treatments—the properties I mention are not specific to this type, the *Rosa centifolia*."

"*Rosa centifolia*," Brother Guido mused. "'The rose of a hundred leaves.'" He translated for my benefit. "Perhaps the *name* of the rose is telling us to look for a *number*. Codes and cryptograms are oft writ in numbers, perhaps that is the answer that lies within the roses. If we find a number, we may find a date, or some such."

"But, Brother, the classification *centifolia* is not to be taken *literally*," warned the herbalist. "These roses have any number of leaves, varying each time from bloom to bloom."

"So much for the leaves—how many *petals* does the rose have?"

We looked at the two flowers before us—even those two seemed to differ in the number of petals. "Again," confirmed the herbalist, "different in every case. Perhaps it is the number Flora *holds* which has some significance."

"And the number she casts away," added Brother Guido.

I could swear I had said something like this about two hours ago, but I held my tongue as we crowded round to count the roses in Flora's arms. The task was nigh on impossible, even when Brother Nicodemus donned his eyeglasses once more.

We argued hotly about whether to count whole blooms or partial petals, and whether there would be more blossoms lying in layers underneath. But at the end we came to a number of thirty-one. Our greatest debate sprang from the rose *between* Flora and Venus. It was exactly the same type as the ones in Flora's arms, but it was impossible to tell from the *cartone* whether it grew from the ground, and thus could not be counted as part of the bundle, or whether it fell from Flora's arms, and as such was one of "her" roses. We could not see whether the stalk of the flower was above the petals, indicating a fall, or below, growing from the ground.

"Does it matter?" I asked helpfully.

Brother Guido stroked his chin. "I think yes. Botticelli does nothing by accident."

We both turned to the herbalist, where he bent almost double above the painting. We held our breath, hoping that he would have an answer. He did, but not the one we wished. Brother Nicodemus rubbed the white frill of his hair where it cleared his cowl at the back of his neck. "Well, and now we have an obstacle. I cannot tell because the *cartone* is too small to see the detail. The code is designed to be read from the real panel painting of the *Primavera,* which is a hundred times bigger than this parchment, which has, if I am not mistaken, seen some adventures of its own."

He was right. Shipwrecked and sweated upon for longer than a month, the *cartone* had seen better days, and the paint between Flora and Venus, where the crucial rose grew or fell, was beginning to crack and fade.

Brother Guido seemed to lose a couple of inches in height. "Then it is hopeless. The painting is probably installed at the Medici villa at Castello by now, which has a hundred guards. We must just hope that this final rose is not significant."

"But wait—did you not say the *Primavera* was a *wedding gift*?" asked Brother Nicodemus urgently.

"I am sure of it."

"Then there is no problem. The painting *will be at the wedding.*"

"I beg your pardon?"

"Eh?" Brother Guido and I spoke together, in our different styles.

"It is Tuscan tradition that the gifts await the happy couple at the narthex of the church," the herbalist explained. "Depend upon it, the painting will be there—presented or displayed with grand gesture. 'Tis the Medici way. And this in itself suggests to me the last rose *is* significant."

"How so?"

"From what you have told me, *all* of the Seven will be at this wedding. And the painting too. They may *all* read what lies in Flora's arms. I think it's a fail-safe."

I was lost, and my face showed it.

"An insurance," explained the herbalist. "You place a code in a picture. You want the picture to be read by certain exalted persons and *not others*. So you take the picture to a place where they will *all* be, and the painting is in full sight. The last rose is the insurance. Suppose someone steals a copy of the picture—the *cartone*."

I saw where he was going. "Someone *did* steal a copy."

"Exactly. Botticelli has built in a detail that *can only be seen on the real panel*. He has insured the code as one might underwrite a fleet at sea—only those noble enough to see the real painting at close quarters, only those lofty enough to be invited to a Medici wedding—the conspirators—will be looking for the fail-safe and be able to interpret what they see. That rose is significant, I am now sure of it."

"And if anyone knows about insurance it is the Medicis, the richest banking family in the world," added Brother Guido.

"More significant still is the fact that since Roman times, the rose has been associated with secrets. It was then the custom to suspend a rose over the dinner table as a sign that all confidences shared there—*sub rosa,* or 'under the rose'—were to be held sacred."

This intriguing thought clearly made my companion's heart beat with the chase like a hunter's hound's. But *my* heart was steady—we were curs on a dead scent. For even if we could tell if the rose grew or fell, we still had not discovered the secret that lay "sub rosa." We had nothing to tell il Magnifico. "Are we *actually* going to march up to Lorenzo de' Medici and say, "The secret is thirty-two roses'? Or 'thirty-one roses, becauses we're not sure which'? Brilliant."

Brother Guido slumped again. "I know. But what choice do we have?"

"Perhaps it's a password, and he will know the significance at once?" offered Brother Nicodemus.

I snorted through my nose. "So let's sum up: we are to tell the father of all Florence that his cousin and ward is plotting against him, with six other conspirators, four of whom we don't know. We have a password, 'thirty-two roses,' or 'thirty-one.' All this we got from a painting which is one of the wedding presents. Wonderful."

The sky lightened outside—the wedding neared. And I couldn't help adding a very feminine concern. "And the wedding is in two hours and I have nothing to wear."

Brother Guido stood abruptly. "You are right. If we are to attend the ceremony, and petition Lorenzo, with whatever little we have, there are certain practicalities we must turn our minds to. You need an outfit, and I need a retinue, fit for a prince."

"May *la signorina* not just attend in what she wears now?" Brother Nicodemus, silent through this exchange, piped up now to quash my sinful vanity. I looked down at the crumpled black velvet gown I had worn for a trinity of steamy days on the road since my audience with the pope, and back to the herbalist with a crushing look. I could not, as the consort of the Prince of Pisa, wear a dress travel stained and caked in sweat to the wedding of the year; nor did Tuscan protocol allow that black should be worn at a wedding. Added to this, the thick nap of the velvet was suffocating—well enough for a dank herbarium at midnight, but in the Florentine midday I would expire. I did not deign to say all this aloud, for Brother Guido at least had enough knowledge of the world to know it would not do.

"I need other weeds myself, but the retinue would seem to be the greater problem."

At this the herbalist spoke again. "Not a problem, Brother. For here before me I see a monk in layman's weeds; other monks could dress so too. I have four novices, so not yet tonsured, who can be roused from their beds and dressed to accompany you."

"Dressed in what?" I asked, curious.

"We are given precious garments from time to time, as tithes or donations, or even bequests from the dead. I will have the coffer brought here—for there may be somewhat to help you too, signorina."

It was kindly meant, but I could not imagine myself going to the Medici wedding in fusty old clothes fit for monasteries' coffers, left by dead debtors.

I could not have been more wrong—nothing could have prepared me for the treasure I was soon to see. Four sleepy novices soon entered the herbarium, buckling under an inlaid walnut chest that they carried. As the youths were greeted and briefed by the two older monks, I opened the lid onto Solomon's treasure. I did not heed their planning as I plunged my hands into the softest rainbow silk, silver tissue as light as gossamer, spun cloth of gold flimsy as a spider's web, and bales of samite. Most of the clothing was for gentlemen, but there lay, too, three ladies' gowns, folded and waiting like shed snakeskin. While the menfolk fitted themselves out—the herbalist's quartet of novices bubbling with excitement that they were to attend a wedding in the outside world—I took the three gowns behind the firescreen and emerged in one of spring green threaded with gold. I had no mirror today but knew I resembled Spring herself. The notion reminded me what my apparel lacked; I rolled the *cartone* once more and placed it in my bodice. Now my costume was complete and I turned to face the company. The silk lay cool against my body even before the fire, but the gaze of the novices and Brother Guido—although he tried to conceal his admiration—heated my skin once again.

The herbalist circled me. "Should she be disguised though?" he said, as if I could not hear him. "For if the painting is there, it will be clear to all that Flora is also present in person. Unless her hair is covered."

Brother Guido regarded me. "There will be those present who know her as my consort, and will recognize her in the picture," he considered, "but to the general populace—well, it would be better if her presence does not attract too much attention."

I thought for a moment. My vanity usually dictated that my hair be worn loose in a golden fall, but as the hour of the wedding drew near, my stomach was full of moths and my nervous, bubbling humors prompted me to be as hidden as I could be.

"Here then," I said, pouncing on the cloth of gold. "I'll bind my hair in the Turkish style—all the fashion at present." It occurred to me then how fickle a goddess fashion was; from the herbalist's tale, we were all in fear of the savage Turks six months ago, and now the ladies of Florence paraded forth in infidel headgear.

I wrapped the cloth around my hair till it was all hidden, feeling strangely naked without my curls to frame my face. I presented myself to Brother Guido for an opinion and saw in his expression that he was admiring but intrigued. "Well?" I demanded.

"It's amazing," he said. "You look no less beautiful, but without your hair you are a different person. Among the guests no one will know you for Flora save Don Ferrente, his queen, and—"

He stopped short.

"And?"

" 'Tis nothing," he faltered. I knew he was dissembling, but before I could ask what he hid, he turned abruptly to his brother herbalist.

"One thing more, Brother. Do you know aught of a man, a Florentine, who goes about in leper's robes?"

"I know many such, sadly."

"He differs from the common herd of the unclean. He is immensely tall with a wasted right hand, and a strange appearance of silver in his gaze."

Even hearing the creature described gave me a shiver. And I was not alone in that; Brother Nicodemus visibly started. "You've *seen* him?"

"Three times now. You know him?"

"Not well. I have met him but once, many years ago, when he came here for help—for my skill as an herbalist and healer." It was said without boast. "I had to send him away, for his malady was too far gone for help. I have never seen him since. I thought him now a legend, a story to scare children. His name is Cyriax Melanchthon."

The name repelled.

"Who . . . what is he?"

"Cyriax was a babe born of a Florentine mother and a Flemish father. He entered the Dominican order as an youth, and took a very hard line there—he was involved for some years with the Holy Office."

I saw Brother Guido swallow.

"Who are they?" I asked.

"The Inquisition," answered the herbalist briefly. Even I had heard of the Inquisition, with their hideous tortures and burnings of infidels.

"He became the Medici family confessor—"

"And now works for Lorenzo di Pierfrancesco!" I finished. Brother Guido quelled me with a look, for the herbalist was not done.

"He went once on their business to the Holy Land, traveling with a Florentine delegation after the peace of Constantinople. It was there that this thing landed upon him—he caught the leprosy and began to waste. It was said that at the church of the Holy Sepulcher in Jerusalem he stripped off his Dominican robes and cursed God. His wasted flesh, naked and rotting, was such a horror to all that saw it that it was said the sky darkened that day. He burned his robes on the sepulcher, took leper's weeds, and has been an instrument of the Devil ever since."

"But the Medici still maintain his services?" asked Brother Guido, incredulous. Even a man who had fallen out of love with the church could not but be shocked at the offense of cursing God at the holiest church in Christendom.

"Not officially," replied the herbalist. "It is certain that he returned here to Florence, for it was then that I saw him and sent him away. I have not heard his name for many years, and thought him dead—that his malady had eaten him. But there have been sightings of him, again in Florence, as I said, instances that have passed into legend to scare the children. But there are rumors, too, that he is the most efficient assassin the world holds. He cannot speak, for the leprosy pulled the jaw from his face like a wishbone. To look upon his countenance, his half-face of horror, is to look on death, for if he takes off his face cloth, his victims die of fright, or he cuts their throats like swine."

Enna. Bembo. Brother Remigio.

"How is he the best, if he is so afflicted?" I breathed, dreading the answer.

The herbalist turned his calm eyes upon me. "Because, child, he is already dead."

My blood froze. I had been right in Rome when I thought the leper a phantom. "He's . . . a . . . ghost?"

The dry chuckle again, this time the humor of a graveyard. "Not quite. I meant only that he will die, sooner or later; there is no saving him. So he does not care anymore—he feels that God has turned his back on him, so he carries out his contracts with absolute dispatch. He is the perfect killer; silent, for he cannot speak or betray those who hire him, and he may go anywhere untouched and untroubled because of his malady and his leper's weeds. For who will challenge one of the unclean? Who will pluck him by the sleeve or wrap their arms about him to detain him?"

I felt sick with terror. "Then, we are surely done for."

"Not so. I think you are safe, for now at least."

Easy for him to say. "How do you figure that?"

The answer was brief. "Because if Cyriax Melanchthon *wanted* to kill you, you'd already be dead."

The word echoed from the walls like a knell. Brother Guido piped up for the first time in this exchange.

"Then what does he want with us?"

"He is following you, it seems. Why, I cannot tell. But it is to be hoped that your alias protects you—when that is gone, who knows?"

To herald this cheerful thought the bells of the Pazzi Chapel gave tongue again, calling us to the wedding of their ancient enemy, and now a new chime added to theirs. The church of San Lorenzo, the Medici family church in the distant quarter of Santa Maria Novella, began to sing in counterpoint with their old enemy, the two rivals finding peace in the harmony of their intervals. Time marched, and there was not a moment to do aught more but offer our hands to Nicodemus of Padua in thanks.

"Come home to us soon, my son," said the old man, who had followed us to the cloister door and stood blinking in the sunlight at the gate of his kingdom.

Brother Guido shook his head. "This is no longer my home. I will never return here." There was great resolve in the words but great sadness too. I felt my lips twitch downward in sympathy for what he'd lost. The bright eyes of the herbalist searched those of the younger man.

"You will, one day," he said, and took Brother Guido's hand. I had expected him to take the outstretched hand of his friend. I did not expect him to then turn and take mine.

But he did.

28

Florence was a world of color.

After the black and white of the Neapolitan court, I was dazzled by my gaudy city. We processed through the streets with as much pomp as our makeshift retinue allowed us, and everywhere I saw the hues that I had missed in the black-and-white world we had left. By our sides the four novices marched in liveries of rose and amber; we had no Pisan pennants so Brother Guido had bade them carry scarves of orange and red, the colors of the della Torre Cockerel party, which flowed behind us like flags. We passed under the massive looming shadow of the Duomo, and even this holy building seemed a patterned palace today, the strong sun picking up the triple marbles of green, red, and gold. My eyes were dizzy with color, my ears deaf with the bawling of the bells. I saw from the corner of my eye three shabby harlots lounging on the Baptistery steps, yawning and scratching in the sun, legs lolling apart for the passing gentry. I raised my chin an inch, feeling how far I had left them behind. Today I felt as noble as I was pretending to be.

But as we turned into the Mercato Lorenzini and I glimpsed the rough brown frontage of the Medici church, my courage left me and my bowels turned to water—I felt they would drop from my stomach like the guts of Francesco Pazzi as he dangled from his noose.

My mouth dried as we entered the square and were assailed by more carnival and color and chaos. Truly, here I felt my senses deserted me. Petals fell from the sky as cheering citizens cast them from high windows, a multicolored snowstorm. This was a city of flowers, last night and this day. The church of San Lorenzo itself, a rough brown treasure casket, was today elevated from its workaday appearance; it was garlanded at the door with festoons and bouquets. The portal swallowed a steady stream of guests, nobles and dignitaries, bright as Barbary parrots in their wedding-day finery and screeching like them too.

I felt that I had left the common world and entered a world of fairy tale. I knew it to be so when the Medici giraffe—the same creature I had once seen wandering through the blue dusk on the hillside of Fiesole—strode across the square. Its neck was hung about with flowers, its long black tongue snaking out to snatch the laurel branches that hung from each window.

After a night of dark and quiet in the old stones of Santa Croce I felt overcome, and would have stumbled but for Brother Guido's strong grip on my arm. He looked at me once, did not smile but nodded. I felt a little strengthened, and then we were at the church, and the dark doors swallowed us.

In the cool of the interior, I began to feel better—the colors were not so bright here, the shrieking voices of nobility likewise muted. We were shown to the garlanded pews behind the royal House of Naples and gratefully sank from view behind the king and queen, canary bright in blue and yellow—so different from their native black. I hoped that the eyes of the casual observer would travel to them and no farther. My turban began to itch.

Seated and safe for the moment, I was free to look about me as the drums and timbrels played a wedding hymn to the arriving guests. I looked at every haughty figure, every noble face, for the remaining members of the Seven. There was Don Ferrente, there the Judas-pope himself in a cloak of cinnabar red. Where were the others, that quartet of unknown conspirators? Were they here, ready for their instruction? Three things clamored for my attention above all the wonder before me.

Cosa Uno: across the aisle from us sat a strange creature, so exotic that even in such company she attracted the eye. She was clad in a gown of green and gold like my own, but with her face entirely covered with a golden mask. The workmanship of the mask was exquisite—it was the face of a lioness, studded with seed pearls and chased with curlicues of gilt, while a filigree veil of finest gold mail hung from chin to throat. I was fascinated by the strange lady, almost Eastern in her mystery. She sat silently next to an elderly man in white and scarlet robes wearing a white velvet hat shaped like a penis. My eye soon left him, bizarre though his weeds were, to stray back to the lady, for she invited my gaze like a fisherman draws a catch within his net. I gawped openly at the lion mask, almost forgetting there was a person within, until I saw that, from behind her disguise, she regarded me, too, with eyes as green as my own. I turned away, flushed, but as I did so I realized—she was the dogaressa.

The doge's courtesan—a woman so fair she did not remove her mask.

So the man in the cock hat she escorted must be the doge of Venice.

And if it were so, she was the mother of the girl intended for Niccolò della Torre—Brother Guido's cousin and the man he now pretended to be.

Madonna.

My thoughts did not tend this way for long, for it was then I noticed:

Cosa Due: a figure, grander and greater than all before me, seated in an elaborate carved chair, at the left of the chancel steps. This man I knew, as all Florentines knew him. Though we had never met, I had seen his image a dozen times—the noble nose, the darkly curling hair, the elongated face. But never before had I seen him in the flesh. This, I knew, was the father of our city, banker to barons, politician without peer. The man they called "the Magnificent"—Lorenzo de' Medici.

Never had I seen a man so vital, nor one who wore the mantle of his power with such confidence. He was simply dressed in purple velvet, the color of dark grapes, a hue that I knew was written in law to be worn only by Medici men or Tornabuoni women. He wore a matching *berretta* hat with a twisted fall of velvet folds to the left of his face. His fingers were ringless—his one embellishment a heavy chain of office around his neck. Now I had, in the last crazy months, been in the presence of princes and popes, not something I had ever expected in my humble lot. The man before me wore perhaps one tenth of the value of the clothes that adorned Don Ferrente. And yet, he was a man to be reckoned with, a crouching tiger. At once I saw the ridiculous hopelessness of our plan. He did not look like a man who would ever be vanquished or in danger. He was not a man whom a monk and a whore could approach and prattle of riddles and plots. He looked like the king of the world. And yet, as I turned to whisper to Brother

Guido that we should go quietly away and let this great man shift for himself, I suddenly caught sight of:

Cosa Tre: the greatest and most heart-stopping of these three unusual sights. For there, garlanded with flowers and grass-green ribbons, and propped on a great oaken easel, awaiting the happy couple, was the *Primavera*.

Finished.

Madonna.

It was glorious.

The figures had such color and vitality that they seemed more alive than any in the company here. Larger than life, they were gods and goddesses come to Earth. There was Fiammetta as Naples, Venus bidding us welcome, Botticelli dressed as Mercury, and—strangest of all—Flora.

Me.

I had been so used to seeing the *cartone* for this past month, so used to the faceless figure, that I had not remembered that Botticelli had captured me so accurately, so completely. My face was beautiful but worldly—my lips curling and my green eyes knowing, exactly the face I make when I conceal something, or when I tease my clients, or when they have entrusted me with a secret never to be told. A good working girl knows when to keep her trap shut, and I know better than most.

The Flora of the Primavera *had a secret.*

I may not know what the roses meant, but I knew in that instant that I was wrong about Lorenzo de' Medici. Right about this. He *was* in danger. There *was* something hidden here. I recalled at once our purpose here; what Nicodemus of Padua had said of the one flower, one single rose among the others that we must note. That we'd have to see it here, in the painting, for real, to know if it fell or grew, whether it was to be counted in the number of Flora's secret bouquet or discounted as one of the innocent blooms that dotted the sward.

The secret was hidden sub rosa. It was the key to all, a touch-stone, fail-safe—a way to know that only those at the wedding, those seven conspirators who would see the thing up close, would know the meaning.

Annoyingly, from my seated position I could see the bunched roses in Flora's skirt but not the single rose that stood or fell between her and Venus. I did not dare to stand and draw attention to myself as the subject of the painting. Already Don Ferrente and his queen were turning to smile and nod in their appreciation of the likeness.

I smiled back and craned and twisted, wriggling my bottom on the pew as if I had cunny crabs, but it was no good; the vital bloom was just lost to sight in a sea of bobbing heads.

My escort turned to admonish me. "Be still!" hissed Brother Guido. "A lady sits like a statue, in a seemly fashion. Do you have an itch?"

I looked poniards at him "No, I am *trying* to see Flora's rose—can you see from where you are?"

He looked, shook his head. "We will have to peruse the thing closely when we file out at the end. Until then, keep your head down."

"Did you see il Magnifico?"

This time he nodded. "Yes. He is well placed for our purposes, for all the guests will file past him at the end of the ceremony to be presented. See? His gentlemen-in-waiting hold baskets of laurel branches for Lorenzo to distribute to the guests at the end, as a sign of peace."

I saw the two liveried attendants with their meaningless leaves—I pictured again Lorenzo's own pet giraffe munching happily on the laurel leaves outside; the family pet happily devouring the family emblem. I snorted through my nose. Peace indeed. The Medici will eat itself, for the family plotted against its own head.

"Look, Luciana," continued Brother Guido, instantly forgetting his own decorum. I followed his pointing finger, pleased that his voice held the first note of worship I had detected since his audience with the pope. But I saw no one but a quiet, astonishingly ugly man, with a robe of dun gray, writing on a tablet. The only spot of brightness in his costume was a crown of roses he wore on his brow, making him look faintly ridiculous. Even his companions found him dull, it seemed; for the two young peacocks that flanked him had both turned around to converse with their friends in the pew behind. Yet to look at Brother Guido's moonstruck expression was to recall when he had first laid eyes on the pope.

"Who is it?" I whispered.

"*That* is Angelo Poliziano. The Medici court poet. Remember, he wrote the *Stanze*, upon which the *Primavera* is based, and the verses on the rose which we heard this very night?"

"Oh, yes. They were quite pretty." I looked at the man with new respect, and was pleased that Brother Guido had not lost all his idols—for him, seeing the man whose verses he had copied so oft and so painstakingly in the scriptorium of Santa Croce was clearly a cause for joy.

My own pleasure in his ceased in an instant when one of the poet's companions turned back around. I had seen him before that day, of course, but then he had been in two dimensions, harmless, rendered on the poplar panel of the *Primavera,* clad as Mercury. Here he was in the flesh.

Sandro Botticelli.

And by some ill chance he met my horrified eyes and, in that instant, recognized me.

Three things happened at once.

Cosa Uno: he stood, but so did the whole congregation.

Cosa Due: he cried out, but his voice was drowned by a fanfare of crumhorns.

Cosa Tre: The bride and bridegroom entered.

They came through the open doors as black shapes against the bright day, then resolved into creatures of fable, living and walking before us. They walked down the nave arm in arm, in the Tuscan tradition.

The bride was, as Brother Guido had guessed in Rome, Venus to the life. She even wore the clothes from the painting to the last detail, the oyster silk dress with embroidered flames at the neck flaring to burn her lily throat, the vivid ocher and azure cloak with the beaded hem, and the gold filigree pattens on her dainty feet, the veil on her red hair as light as mist on a spring morning. Bright at her breast was fastened the amber and gold roundel of the medal of Sol Invictus. I studied her face—delicate and white as a magnolia petal with the merest hint of pink high on each cheek, her eyes glassy and calm. I felt drawn to this quiet maiden and sorry for her at once—she was an innocent pawn in this. I studied the swell of her belly with a practiced eye but could not tell if she had tasted the sweets of the marriage bed as yet. I had to concede that my companion was right—the Romanesque style of the dress covered every sin in that quarter. Yet having seen her, I now thought her pure; she did have the countenance and bearing of a maiden. I am indifferent usually to the charms of my own sex, but I had to admit that her beauty and purity were striking, as far from my own earthy beauty as the moon floats high, cold fathoms above the warm terra. She was worthy to be Venus, queen of love, and her resemblance to her twin in the *Primavera* was complete when she turned at the head of the aisle and raised her hand to the congregation, in a gesture of welcome and greeting exactly matched in the painting.

The groom, on the other hand, was a jackal. He had eyes for everyone but his lady as he walked up the aisle, laughing, japing, and greeting his friends as he went, with no heed for decorum or rite. His teeth were bright white and plentiful, his caper-green eyes roving. He bore a physical resemblance to his powerful cousin and guardian, but wore none of the authority and power with the name he bore. I felt him unworthy to be heir to this, my city. My nostrils flared as he passed and I caught a whiff of male musk—*he* had not kept his chastity for the wedding night. His scent and his character soured together in my nose. God knows, I have few moral boundaries, but this I knew. He was a treacherous conspirator and he had to be stopped.

The couple turned from us and a priest in a splendid chasuble walked to the center of the chancel steps to meet them, and began to intone the mass over them. Having, as I said, little Latin despite my convent education, I would have slept in my seat but for the strong impression of Botticelli's eyes burning into the back of my neck, the skin naked to his gaze without my usual tumble of hair. I knew now that we had little time after the service, to reach il Magnifico before Botticelli reached me—to say what, I dared not contemplate. I alternated for the rest of the service between nervously dreading the end of the mass and impatiently willing the priest to be done. I did not pray, for I never did; but I noticed that Brother Guido kept his full lips clamped tight shut through the proceedings—not a prayer did he offer, not a psalm did he sing, not a response passed his lips.

At length the priest began the handfasting, winding the couple's hands together in the Florentine tradition. As the spring-green ribbon passed over and above one brown hand and one white, I craned to see the groom's left thumb and knew that Brother Guido did likewise. For the longest time we could see nothing as the ribbon blocked our sight, but at the final binding all was clear.

No ring.

It was as plain as day. The groom's thumb lay over his lady's, naked as a new babe.

Brother Guido and I exchanged a look, as my heart thumped. What could this mean?

"Perhaps if he's the leader, he doesn't have to wear a ring?" I suggested hopefully.

"Except it bears the Medici symbol. Perhaps he left it off to keep his hand naked for the handfasting?"

But neither his theory nor mine rang true. *Fuck.* Could we be wrong?

There was no time to think, as the ceremony was drawing to a close with the final prayers. The bride and groom married, passed back down the aisle, and I could see once again at close quarters that the groom's thumb was definitely bare. But, packed in as we were by leaving guests, we had no chance to see the painting properly, no time to peruse the rose. "What do we do?" I hissed, as the tide of silk and satin swept us ever forward to il Magnifico, where he sat in state in his carved chair. His servants handed him the laurel boughs, which he gave to each departing guest. Saying little, but smiling and bowing with true nobility. "Let's appeal to him," said I, suddenly finding kindness in the noble face. "Throw ourselves on his mercy, beg for sanctuary. We have no choice." Through the press of the crowd I saw Botticelli pushing his way down the aisle toward me.

We were next.

Brother Guido gave his false title to the manservant nearest us. The powerful scent of laurel was in my nose, the powerful hand of Lorenzo de' Medici was at Brother Guido's lips, accepting the kiss of greeting.

I saw the flash of gold too late.

Il Magnifico's fingers were ringless, but his thumb was not.

At the same instant that Brother Guido's lips touched the

ring hand, and his blue eyes flew wide in realization, a black shadow peeled from the wall behind Lorenzo, inclined its cowled head to its master, and extended a diseased hand from the robes of the unclean to point to me.

My numbed brain trotted out a trinity of panicked thoughts, like the litany we had just heard.

Credo Uno: Lorenzo il Magnifico was one of the Seven. Not his cousin the groom.

Credo Due: he was in no danger—he was the *source* of it.

And most terrifying of all,

Credo Tre: Cyriax Melanchthon was *his* creature.

I turned to hush the servant before he announced us, but it was too late—he intoned in his loud Tuscan: "Lord Niccolò della Torre of the city of Pisa."

A voice from the doorway, calling back, just as loud, as in answer to catechism:

"No man has a right to that name but *me*." The accent was Pisan. We all turned as one to the door.

Like the happy couple at their entrance, the figure in the door was black gainst the sun. Yet I would know his foppish stance anywhere, for all that I had met him only once. And there was no mistaking his retinue, wearing the colors and holding the streaming yellow-orange pennants of the Cockerel party.

It was Niccolò della Torre.

Many, many times between that day and this I have asked myself why it never occurred to Brother Guido or me that the *real* Niccolò della Torre might have been there at the Medici wedding. Was it that he had, for us, disappeared from the earth's disk once his cousin had taken his name? Was it that we were so absorbed in the riddle of the *Primavera* that we had forgotten that he existed, had been invited? Or was it that we assumed a fellow who would not attend his father's feast when he lived in the same city would not cross Tuscany for a wedding, however exalted?

In the end it mattered not why we had not considered this pass—I looked into Brother Guido's anguished eyes and knew we were done for. The eyes of all were upon us—my companion and I were silent, knowing this to be the end.

The crowd parted as if before Moses to let Niccolò through. Although he was gloriously dressed in cloth of gold, his weak face and mean eyes were unimproved, and his voice dripped evil as he spoke the dreaded syllables. "This is my cousin, a Franciscan novice, *Guido* della Torre."

He ignored the gasps and raised his voice over them. I had to drop my eyes as the furious gaze of Don Ferrente raked us from the crowds. "And this is his doxy. You will know her as the *goddess* Flora"—his voice dripped irony—"but she is no deity, merely a common whore."

Before I could prevent him, he yanked at the turban that covered my hair; I spun around like a top as the cloth unraveled and my wheaten curls fell around my shoulders to my waist. The sunlight streaming in at the door snatched greedily at the gilded filaments, turning my tresses to spun gold. The staring faces about me seemed to wheel and spin around me in dizzying circles, and as I tried to steady myself before my accuser, I was powerless. My painted twin gazed from her spring scene, smiling her mischievous smile, offering no help, for all the world enjoying my disgrace. I knew not what would happen now, but I could never have expected what did.

The dogaressa rose from her seat and spoke in clear tones. "That is no whore, Prince. She is my daughter, and your betrothed." Then she took off her mask.

Now, I cannot tell you much of what happened next, for I was beyond all sense and reason. I will have to refer you to what my husband told me afterward, for yes, he was in the church that day. He said that when the dogaressa took off her mask, there were three of me in that room, myself, Flora, and she. Mother and daughter, he said, were so alike it was as if a Venetian mirror stood between us. I saw the resemblance for a mere heartbeat, an instant impression that we had the same green eyes and gold hair, that we were even wearing the same hue of green gown. But as she came toward me and I slipped from consciousness, I could even see that her expression held the same half-smile of Flora; she found amusement in this predicament.

As I fell to the ground, insensible, I knew three things.

Cosa Uno: Brother Guido was wrestled to the floor by two Medici men-at-arms with pikes; there could be no escape for him.

Cosa Due: the crowd parted to allow the dogaressa to come to me, and I could see through to the *Primavera* with a straight and uninterrupted view of Flora's last rose. It had a green stem and a glossy leaf, and it was falling to the ground. I fell with it. And as I fell, I thought,

Cosa Tre: I had found my *Vero Madre.*

· 6 ·

Venice

29

Water, light.

I was a babe again, rocked in the watery sac of *Vero Madre*'s womb. I was a child, rocking in her arms. I was a woman, rocking in a boat. Water beneath me. Light above. I opened my eyes and the world spun around me like a top. Light below me, water above. I was propped against velvet cushions in a golden boat. The prow of the boat was curved and slatted like an executioner's axe. Behind, a servant pushed us along with a pole, betraying the fact that the water was no more than waist deep; there were no countless fathoms below, just a shallow ditch. As I was to learn, many things in this place were not what they seemed.

The sky above was dull silver, the sun a white lunar orb, hanging low trying and failing to burn through the thick gray arras. Around and about me was a city made of glass. On both sides of this channel of water were great crumbling silver palaces rising directly out of the water. Hundreds and thousands of skinny windows were crowned with roundels of glazed panes that watched me like eyes. The houses dissolved into the lagoon and their reflections carried on with no interruption— they were one continuous mirror image broken into mercury by the wake of our boat. In my altered state I knew not what was real and what was not. There was no horizon where the water met the sky, and fine white mist swirled around us to further befuddle the senses. After the hot Tuscan sun 'twas quite a sea change. I was in a looking-glass land, an isle of smoke and mirrors.

I was in Venice.

And the sovereign of this waterland sat before me in the boat, her masked face turned to the prow like a ship's figurehead, her sumptuous form still as an effigy. I felt sick and closed my eyes again. I knew from the bitter gritty taste in my mouth that I'd been drugged, for however many days it had taken to get me here.

I was not ready to wake. Not yet.

And now, before I wake, while I am in limbo for a few moments, a babe waiting to be born, while I am suspended in glass once again, it is time. I must tell you at last the story of how I came from Venice as a baby in a bottle.

Most of it I got from the nuns who took me in, for I was too young to be sensible of my fate. I have thought of my journey many times, though, as if seeing it through my own infant eyes: a tiny babe is wrapped in swaddling bands and placed gently into a bottle—a huge green jar, a fishbowl of a thing with a thick-lipped rim. The baby lies still at the bottom, soothed by the swaddle, looking calmly at the light scattered by the glass, with little eyes as green as the bottle. Then soft, white bread is packed around the baby, the sweetest warmest dough, pulled from the center of the loaf by dexterous hands as white as the flour. The baby is packed comfortably now in the white bread, like a cherub on a cloud. The woman that does all this opens her robe, and pulls at her milky breasts till the bread is soaked in her juices. She squeezes her dun nipples as if she milks kine, the full breasts giving forth milk the pale blue of the veins that map the rounded flesh. The baby smells the milk and puts out her little tongue and wriggles around to suck the milk from the soaked bread, as she will have to do for the entire journey. Slim white hands caress the baby's forehead once. The bottle is corked with a flat round porous stopper, tight enough to stifle sound, loose enough to allow the passage of vital air.

The bottle is carried gently to the boat by the woman who does all this. She herself puts the bottle with its fellows, twelve in all to make a tun. The others contain the finest Veneto wine, a Valpolicella that will be a most welcome gift to the sisters. The boat leaves its mooring with a jolt and the baby in the bottle is on her way, the infant sleeping as the waters of her native lagoon rock her. In the port of Mestre the bottle and its fellows are transferred to a cart and the long round south to Florence. The baby wakes, screams, suckles the sour milk, and sleeps again, and at long last the wine reaches its destination.

The Ospedale della Innocenta in the Santa Croce district of Florence is used to receiving foundlings. Most of them are left on the great cartwheel that is set into the wall, one side within the convent, one half outside. Hapless deformed or unwanted infants can be left, with no question or censure, on the half of the wheel that protrudes from the wall. The wheel is rotated and the babe is taken by kindly hands within. But the sisters were not used to their foundlings arriving in a gift of a tun of Venetian wine. Only the abbess knew to follow her exalted instructions and look in the twelfth bottle. There, against all expectation, but in answer to her prayers, she lifted out the babe alive. Passive, floppy, so thin her swaddles had fallen from her body and the bread she had suckled covered in evil-smelling, mustard-colored shit. The abbess cared not for this—a truly good woman, she warmed the filthy baby in her own habit and wiped the feces away with her own vestments. Until, from the warmth and smell of female flesh, and the touch of feminine lips on my forehead, I awoke.

So, now that you know, I was ready to come out of my bottle, like a djinn, to return to myself and the present. I stirred, and the woman in the prow turned to look at me. My mother wore her half-lion mask again. I could see her eyes only: serene, green glass. Unconcerned, as if she knew I would wake, that this day and this moment would come when we were together again. I knew what my first question would be, and I'm sure that she did too.

"Are you my *Vero Madre*?"

"I am."

There was a small smile in her voice. She found the phrase, the childish name I had given her, the fantasy that had been my spine, held me upright through the years of whoring, been my bread to sustain me, nothing more than a joke. "And you sent me from Venice as a baby in a bottle?"

"I did. For your own safety."

I narrowed my eyes. I was afraid of her but not afraid to ask the question. "Did you send me from you because I was a bastard?"

She did not flinch. "No. I sent you from me because you weren't. You were and are the true-born daughter and heir of Giovanni Mocenigo, the present Doge of Venice."

I was silent, taking in this amazing statement.

Madonna.

I *was the dogaressa's daughter!*

She took my silence as a question and was coaxed into explanations. "When you were born there was a crucial maritime law to be passed in the council. The ruling party needed my husband's connivance, but he would not support them. Your life was threatened as a bargaining tool so I sent you away, said you'd died and we had overlaid you."

"Why did you not come for me?" It was little more than a whisper.

"This city was a caldron of poison. As well as the threat to you, there were alliances to be made with those whom we did not wish to adjoin. But we had already promised you to the Prince of Pisa for his son, forming a critical maritime alliance. You were safe with the nuns—they taught you Scripture and kept you chaste. We thought it best to leave you be for the time being."

The time being. Twelve *years* I was at the Ospedale. My mother blithely removed me from her life and missed all of the landmarks of my youth. She was absent while I began to walk and talk, take my First Communion. Best for whom? For *her.* My heart began to harden—to mirror hers.

"Then, at twelve, you disappeared."

And did she know why? Because I fell in with Enna, whom I met on the way back from mass when I'd dawdled behind the others; the sisters' white wimples disappeared round the corner as I admired Ennas's pretty dress. Because I'd thought her a beautiful vision, perhaps my *Vero Madre* come for me—for then at thirty Enna was already old enough to be my dam. Because she'd told me I could earn five florins for an act that would take a moment, that if I could suck on a man's cock and pretend it was a honey teat, I'd have three coins for myself and two for her, and I could buy a pretty dress of my own. Because I'd gone with her to a palazzo in Tornabuoni and sucked off one of those minor Medicis, got my three florins as promised. Because

I'd gone into business at the age of twelve and never looked back. Because I'd whored for four years till I stole a painting and met a monk who changed my life.

"We kept your disappearance secret from the Pisans; spread tales of your great beauty, your convent education. I told everyone you were the image of me, and you are. I prayed that you would be found, and you were. Benvolio Malatesta, the pearl merchant, told our spies of a girl he was . . . seeing."

Bembo gave me away? Huh.

"He knew her to be the right age and the image of myself." The masked head inclined graciously. "So we took steps to verify your identity."

"You got Botticelli to paint me so you could see if it was really me?" It sounded incredible.

"No, not that. We knew who you were by then, that is *why* you were asked to be in the painting. It was no accident. But before we could claim you, you were gone. You led us quite a dance, and we were not able to recover you until now. Granted, it was not done in the best way, thanks to your betrothed—you collapsed from the shock of the events of the wedding and have been insensible ever since. We gathered you up and brought you here."

Betrothed. She uttered the word oddly, in the present sense, as if Niccolò della Torre and I were still intended. Lord Silvio had betrothed me to Niccolò in the cradle. He had known of me before Brother Guido and I had even met.

Brother Guido. I asked now the question that should have been my first, but I had been afraid of the answer. "What happened to Guido della Torre?"

"Who?" The faceless voice was impatient.

"My . . . companion. The Pisan lord."

"Ah, yes, the monk who would be nobleman. Cousin to

308

Lord Niccolò. He was taken away by the Medici guards. He will no doubt be dispatched for his insolence."

I near fainted again. "Executed?" The fly-blown Pazzis dangled from their nooses in my mind's eye. The hanged man turned in the Arno, holding his eyeless face above the current.

"Of course. He impersonated his liege lord, a matter of treason in Tuscany. And moreover he disrupted a ceremony of the Florentine state. He is in many kinds of trouble." She waved at a passing barge, and the company that rose there bowed to her reverently. "Lord Niccolò may decide to be clement, if he is in a merciful mood."

My heart thumped in my throat as I remembered Niccolò's corrosive, competitive hatred for my friend. If Brother Guido's fate was in his cousin's hands, he was as good as dead.

"But he will be tried first?"

She shrugged, delicately. "Perhaps. Here—yes. Our system of justice is well regulated. But in the barbaric middle lands? I think in Tuscany you are used to more . . . summary justice?"

Prickles of sweat broke from my skin despite the killing cold. My heart raced in a panic. "Then I must return. I must seek him—help him!" I stood and the golden barge lurched, my head spun, and I lurched with it. I fell back on the cushions, but not before my mother's white hand closed on my arm in an iron grip.

"*If* you stay and do my bidding as my dutiful daughter, I shall do all I can to hear news of him. Perhaps I could use my connections to mitigate his fate. My *considerable* influence could certainly ease his path to the gallows, at the very least." I began to protest, but she held up her hand. "If you disobey me, I will do nothing; so choose."

I shut my trap and we both sat down again as one—I had

no choice and she knew it. I had handed her the shackles with which she could bind me to her and keep me here.

"There can be no question of you returning to Florence just now," she continued, more calmly. "You, also, have angered il Magnifico."

Il Magnifico. I remembered, sharply, the ring I'd seen on Lorenzo de' Medici's thumb at his ward's wedding, and with it, the realization that this great man, with the aid of his leprous henchman, was cooking something up with the rest of the Seven. I could not resist the chance to have the riddle solved once and for all, if only my mother would give up the answer.

"Signora?" I began meekly.

"You can call me 'Dogaressa.'"

I thought she would have said "mother," but clearly we were not at such a pass just yet. "The *Primavera*—the painting—do you know what it means? The purpose of it all, the riddle it contains? Do you know what il Magnifico intends? The war that he hopes to wage?"

The eyes were now hard as chips of jade, but a merry laugh trilled from behind the mask. It was a musical, charming sound, like a carillon of golden bells. It was also entirely false.

"What can you mean? What riddle? What war? The *Primavera* is naught but a fine gift that the groom made to his lady, by his favorite artist. It serves no purpose beyond a celebration of the greatest beauties that our land has borne, with the bride the queen of them all. You should count yourself lucky to be among them, as do I."

"You, Dogaressa?"

The noble head inclined again. "I am depicted as the nymph Chloris."

Of *course*. I thought back to the night in Santa Croce's herbarium, which now seemed worlds away, when we had concluded that Flora and Chloris were cities close to each other. Flora and Chloris *were* connected, not by distance but blood. They shared the same features and the same lineage. And I *did* "hold the secret" after all. We had been right, too, when we thought that the secret was to do with the bearing of a babe or a child; now I knew *I* was that child. My forearms were clothed in fish scales to connect me to the sea; I was a child of the sea, the greatest sea republic ever—Venice.

But as to the rest—the cities, the Seven, the alliance—could my friend and I have been wrong all along? Was there no more to the painting than a celebration of beauty—myself, my mother, Fiammetta, Simonetta, Semiramide—and Botticelli's presence as Mercury as an artist's joke? I looked at my mother's hands. She wore a huge beryl ring carved with arms, presumably of the Mocenigo family, but there was no golden ring bearing the golden balls of the Medici *palle*—or otherwise—on her thumb. Doubt doused my flesh like the salt spray. "But . . ." I began, and was frozen by a stare as green as a frozen sea.

"Ask no more of that, it is a request, a warning, and my command as your mother."

And my doubts vanished—there was something hidden here, else she would not threaten me so. The dogaressa leaned forward in a sudden fluid motion which upset the boat not at all, as if she were at one with the craft and the sea itself. "Let me be rightly understood. Your father and I will require your *complete* cooperation if we are to help you in the matter of your . . . unfortunate friend. Your actions have already embarrassed our family in the eyes of the Florentine court, perhaps worse. And that is why we thought it expedient to leave *before* the celebrations at Castello—my Lord Doge, of course, stayed for the feast to appease our exalted friend and smooth the diplomatic waves, and will return soon."

My heart plummeted in my throat at the notion of meeting

my father—that dour, colorless man I had seen in his bizarre ceremonial weeds. Odd that during all these years of missing my mother, I had never contemplated the identity of my father. My impression of Venetians was formed from the ones I had screwed, so naturally I had assumed I was some brat got by a sailor in a quick shoreside jump, only for my father to leave the next day for some distant port. If I had ever pictured him, his image could not have been further from the reality. I could not believe that my father ruled all this.

I sullenly stared at a fantastical city emerging fleetingly from the mists, at once grandiose and crumbling into dust. To illustrate this dual identity, we passed a smaller tributary, a little canal leading off between two palaces, where on the bridge over every inch of the balustrade dangled dozens of pairs of breasts belonging to the working girls that were showing their wares to passing trade. The sign above the bridge was clearly visible before the mist swallowed it and them—*PONTE DELLE TETTE*—Bridge of the Tits. As in Florence I looked upon those girls remembering that I had once been like them, but this time I felt not pity but envy. To have such a life again, to think only of your next jump and your next crust, such a life seemed simple and beautiful to me now. I was so lost in the notion that it took me some time to realize that my mother was speaking again.

". . . must lie low and winter here," she finished.

Madonna.

I looked at the glass city with dismay—winter, here? It was barely August; I could not spend a year's half here in this place!

She missed nothing. Noting my expression, she went on. "My dear, great things are at stake, things that I—*we*—must be a part of. Your wedding *will* take place next summer when you turn seventeen, as ratified in our treaty with the Pisans. And by God, you will be a very different creature before you meet Niccolò again. I know how you spent your teenage years, and it is . . . regrettable. We have some history to rewrite, 'tis true. But it can be achieved. When spring comes, you will be a princess of the *Serenissima,* not some little Florentine trollop."

The words dropped from the mouth of her mask like blocks of ice.

For the last hour on this floating blade I had been struggling to find something to like about my mother—to forgive her desertion, to transform her coldness into warmth, to mitigate her complete lack of interest in the fate of my one love and the only person who had ever looked after me. When she poured her scorn on my profession—the one *she* had forced me to by her desertion—I gave up trying abruptly. I remembered what Don Ferrente had said at his Neapolitan court—that she was an upstart courtesan—and found all this talk of transformation a little rich for my palate. She was no more noble than I; I was one of a succession of worthless whores.

I spat neatly on her golden-masked cheek. "*Fuck* you, you evil *bitch.* Don't think I don't know how *you* rewrote *your* history—you're no better than an upstart courtesan." I repeated the phrase with pleasure. "I'll bet you were dangling *your* tits over that bridge a few years ago, back when they were nice and firm and juicy, like mine." I leaned in and whispered my last shot. "You *fucked* your way to my father's side and everyone knows it."

I was tingling, alive again with the scent of blood, and waited, not caring, for her response.

"Ah, yes. Undoubtedly the language of a Torcicoda tart. No matter. We have a number of months to correct your tongue, among other things."

I could tell that the impossible woman was now smiling behind her mask, and that she liked me more, not less, for my outburst. She liked a fight too, and I was ready for one. "I don't give a *shit* what you say; I'm *not* marrying that Pisano toad. And I *am* going back to Florence as soon as your back is turned."

"How?" she asked simply. "Venice is a hundred islands surrounded by water, and all waterways are controlled by your father. His eyes look from every window. And if you did leave here, what welcome could you expect from Lorenzo's city? We spoke of summary justice just now. Let me tell you a tale of Lorenzo's revenge in action. You have heard, I suppose, of the Pazzi conspiracy?"

Madonna. Not the fucking Pazzis *again*. They were ever at the root of all of this. I was sulky and silent.

"All the Pazzis paid for their crimes, but none more so than Signor Jacopo de' Pazzi, the head of that unfortunate family. After he betrayed il Magnifico he fled the city, but was soon found and dragged back by Lorenzo's men, thrown in the Bargello jail and tortured. Only then, when he could take no more and still live, was he brought to the Palazzo della Signoria, and stripped and bundled out of the window to hang, writhing with his fellow conspirators . . ."

The archbishop, as Brother Guido had said.

"His remains were cut down to be buried in the Pazzi Chapel in Santa Croce . . ."

The very place Brother Guido and I had hidden the night I first asked for his help. Why did every sentence recall him to mind!

"But angry crowds broke open his tomb and the good friars exhumed his body and buried it near the gallows, in unconsecrated ground, to appease the people. But even there Signor Jacopo was not allowed to rest—he was dug up and a great throng of boys dragged the naked cadaver around the city, by the noose by which he was hanged. At the Palazzo Pazzi, the mob bashed the cadaver's head against his own doors, shouting, 'Open up! The Great Knight is here!'" She was enjoying herself—her voice was thickened with bloodlust. I could see her searching for my reaction, so I gave her none, but in reality I could have shit my stockings. What kind of man had I angered? The people loved him and hated those who crossed him.

Madonna.

Evidently *Vero Madre* had finished her grisly tale. I reflected that not once had she told me a fairy tale, as she dandled me on her lap at bedtime. But this monstrous story of blood and torture she was happy to recount. I shivered, not for the dull day and the cool breeze, and not for fear of my own skin, though I would not be returning to Florence anytime soon. I shivered instead for my one true friend, who was a prisoner still in that viper's nest, perhaps even now in the notorious Bargello, where the unfortunate Jacopo had lain.

"Do you see, now, the power and influence of the man your friend has insulted? For Lorenzo is light and dark, he is a great friend but a powerful enemy. He himself wrote a couplet to describe his dual character. 'Orange blossom seen at dawn is bright, / Yet seen at dusk it holds the first of night.' Our best hope for your future, and all of ours," she went on, "is to remove you from that sin, from the offense committed—the disrespect to him and his family by the disruption of the wedding. To re-create you as a noblewoman, heir to the *Serenissima* and the bride of Pisa. Then we may once more join the greater plan, count ourselves in that number at the command of il Magnifico. Luciana."

The word sounded strange from her lips, from the lips of the woman who had given me that name. "*This* is your home now, until you marry. But it may not be so bad. There is much I can teach you."

"So my name *is* Luciana then." I ignored the rest.

"It is. But your family name is not Vetra—you were given that alias by virtue of your . . . mode of travel to Florence."

The light in the glass. Some of the first words *he* had ever said to me.

"Your family name is Mocenigo, that of your lord and father."

Mocenigo. It would take some getting used to. "And are there any more in this happy family? Any doting brothers or sisters I don't know about?"

There was a tiny pause, perhaps half a heartbeat. "No. You are our only heir. You had a younger brother, Francesco, but he . . . died." She did not invite sympathy.

There was a sunburst of comprehension in my brain, as if that hapless orb had broken through the gray lid of the sky. I narrowed my eyes against the truth, as if against the light. "When?"

My mother was silent.

"*When* did he die?" Louder now.

"When you were twelve."

I met her guilty eyes, hating her. I understood it all now. My loving mother had shipped me off to Florence, then clambered back into my father's bed before my cot was cold and got herself another brat on his ducal bones—my brother. Rejoicing in their new male heir, my doting parents had forgotten me. A Florentine convent was quite good enough for me, a girl child, no more use than a marriage prize, a tool of alliance. They left me to rot till their beloved boy died and they suddenly needed an heir again.

My mother's agate gaze bored into mine, defiant, but our journey was ending and the subject changed with the landscape, to her visible relief. The canal had spilled into an open sea and a great domed church marked the end of the channel.

Now we bobbed on the open tide, skirting the shore till our boat drew alongside a great square with pigeons and colonnades and twin pillars reaching high into the mist. A great campanile, coral tipped, reached out of the lake like a sword, the blade red with gore. As a backdrop to the glory, a range of far-off mountains draped behind the city like a silver shawl.

"And here"—a sweep of the green and gold sleeve—"is your new home."

I looked on the enormous white palace, huge and yet delicate, its snowy walls and slim pillars iced with pearly pinnacles and filigree traceries. The façade changed with the water like a very opal. How arrogant, thought I, how confident to build a palace of lace with your duke within, right on the lip of the sea. This was no castle or citadel; the doge's power was such that he had no need to hide behind curtain walls and arrow slits.

Crouching next to this snowy palazzo was an Eastern basilica like a guardian dragon of the Orient, hunched in golden domes and with a hide of jeweled frescoes, with golden spires reaching to the sky like Turkish pikes. I might as well have been in Constantinople.

Home, my arse.

The dogaressa's servant moored the boat and handed her ashore, and my mother herself turned to do the same for me. For one mad moment I thought to sever the golden rope that held us with the neckrim knife of my green bottle, the piece of glass the sisters had saved for me, and take the boat wherever I could, to escape this watery prison. But I knew I could not get far, and I suspected that to pole and steer such a vessel was harder than it looked. Reluctantly I took my mother's hand and stepped ashore, looking her full in her masked face as I did so, matching her defiance. Behind my mother the white frontage of the palace was a blank face and staring eyes, just like her.

"Do you always wear that thing?" I asked, as we moved forward to the palace doors. "That lion mask?"

"Outdoors, yes. The lion is the symbol of our great city, and the she-lion the head of her family."

I did not expect such honesty from her, such openness about how she stood with my father, an admission that she was the ruler of all. "You can hear her balls clang together like a ring o' bells," Don Ferrente had said.

As if she had given too much away, she hurriedly continued. "It is expected. As my people see me, so they esteem me."

And I knew her then for what she was, a cold beautiful surface, deadly beneath, like this city that was once my home and was now again.

30

In the next few months I grew a mask too—I was given the veneer of nobility but my insides were frozen with misery; I had everything and I had nothing. I was pampered and preened and gentrified, yet I was unhappier than I had ever been.

I spent my mornings a caged bird—in the beautiful apartments of the doge inside the white snow palace of the Palazzo Ducale. I never forgot that I was a prisoner—for I was soon assigned a guard. A plain woman named Marta was sent to attend me. She was a sullen creature with a small hairy wart riding her lip and eyes that looked in different directions but nevertheless both seemed to be watching me. The wench was introduced to me as my lady's maid and certainly she did as I bid her, albeit with a grudging, sulky air that made me itch to slap her. I would have been within my rights to beat my servant, but I dared not, for lady's maid she may have been though in truth she was my jailer and we both knew it. I had no doubt that every detail of my behavior reached the open ears of my mother.

My days proceeded, each one, thus in a regimen of sameness: in the mid-morning I was bathed and combed and scrubbed daily by a gaggle of attendants. I was dressed in the richest cloths of green or gold or sapphire or ruby—silks and satins from the East and velvets and taffetas from the North. These glowing colors were always covered with a long black surcoat, to accentuate the whiteness of my noble skin. This coat gave me no comfort, for it was as thin as parchment, and the palace whistled with draft; I shivered from dawn till dusk. I was made up as was fitting for a young noblewoman, with wine must and red ocher to give blush to my pale cheeks, charcoal pencil to line my eyes, and pulverized malachite to color my eyelids. I was not used to such artifice. Of course, we whores had our tricks and I had been known, on feast days back in Florence, to use oxblood to color my lips and cheeks, but for the most part I left such things alone. I wondered how much my mother depended on such arts for her youthful perfection.

My hair was dressed by a Moorish girl named Yassermin, who spoke no Tuscan but knew how to curry my hair all right— her black fingers fairly flew as she braided, pinning priceless gems in my locks which cost more to buy than she did. After all this elaborate dressing, my hair was then covered with a black veil called a *zendado*—a light drape of black silk, attached to my hair with a small golden crown, designed to keep my skin pale. Golden bracelets were loaded onto my arms and a gold-handled fan of white feathers dangled from my wrist. The bells rang four quarters before I was even dressed.

I was brought my breakfast in my chamber on a silver dish and would dolefully eat while staring out of my window onto the lagoon, watching the curracles and spiceboats and wishing

I were traveling far like they. Then I was taken to one of the fresco-clad presence chambers—a great room with sea charts and maps covering every wall—for my schooling. A procession of tutors came to me so that I might learn the business of being noble.

A stern Dominican monk, Fra Girolamo, taught me to read. I worked hard at his lessons, not for fear of his dour person but for a vow I had taken in the herbarium of Santa Croce that I would never again be graveled by the lack of letters (besides, I had plans of my own, which would rely upon this art—more of this later). A Flemish goodwife taught me needlepoint—daily I pricked my poor fingers and flung my frame across the room, much to the mouselike dame's shock. A young and fancy Frenchman, Signor Albert, taught me how to dance the latest pavanes from the Continent, and this I enjoyed the most. I was privately surprised that my mother, in her determination to re-create my history, would leave me unchaperoned with the dancing master, who was frisky as a marionette and sleek as an otter, but soon realized he was as much of a *finocchio* as my dear intended. In fact, the only person that might have been a threat to my chastity was Signor Cristoforo, a young Genoese who had been engaged to teach me map reading, seacraft, and all the maritime arts that one could learn without going aboard ship. "Essential," my mother said, for a young noblewoman from Venice to know all this, for the city, and indeed my father's wealth, was built on the seafaring trade. Now, I knew naught of the Genoese as a people, but if all that city's citizens were as ugly as Signor Cristoforo, I was in no hurry to see the place. I remembered then, of course, that there was a time once when I *may* have gone there, with he who filled my thoughts and preoccupied my mind, for all my waking and sleeping hours, as the conclusion to a quest that now seemed as far away as fairy tale.

In the afternoons I would sometimes walk out into the city with my retinue, or take a gondola (for now I had learned the name of the blade-shaped boats), or even the doge's personal craft, the *Bucintoro*. This last was a fantastical ship straight from the tales of fable, a great golden barge with a figurehead of gold and gilded waves and curlicues skirting the helm. I always felt uncomfortable in this floating crown, for there was no question of being able to travel about the city quietly—everywhere we went the vessel announced my presence and the people of Venice goggled to see the dogaressa's daughter, back from her convent education to prepare for marriage. On my afternoon excursions my mother would always accompany me, talking constantly, but always of the city, never of us. I heard one phrase again and again—"*Stato del Mar,*" "*Stato del Mar.*" The phrase was forever on the dame's lips, a musical phrase washing in and out upon her breath like the tide itself. She wanted me, it seemed, above all to grasp the concept of Venice as a State of the Sea, and to know that the sea gave everything to the city. We went everywhere in the city together, dressed almost alike in our fine gowns, cloaks of coney to keep out the freezing winds, and chopines, shoes built up from the sole to elevate the feet above the inevitable floodwaters. All that separated us was my mother's gold mask. I learned that she had above a hundred masks in her chamber, made by the finest craftsmen in Venice. All different, but all gold, and all depicting the face of a lioness, with no mane. Though many of the citizens went about masked in the winter, I never saw another lioness and I wondered if it was my mother's special privilege. The She-lion, rampant, showed me her city.

She taught me first of our home, the Palazzo Ducale. I half listened to her description of this center of government, of the privileges and restrictions due to the doge for his short term of office, an office strictly rotated to deter corruption. Instead, I looked up at the white lace palace and was interested to note that when you took a closer look, the brickwork was not white but patterned with ornate diamonds of pale rose, inset with sapphire blue. Studded as if with the looted jewels on which the *Stato del Mar* was built. Like everything in Venice, if you look closer, nothing is as it seems. My gaze continued upward. Set in the middle of the loggia were two pillars that differed in color from their snowy neighbors, like wine-darkened teeth after a glass of good red. My mother followed my eye and explained that these twin pillars had been stained with years of blood as traitors to the republic were drawn and quartered between them. I understood her well, and the whisper of a threat built into such a beautiful façade.

Obediently I learned the names of the *sestieri*, or "sixths," that divided the city and repeated them as a child does her catechism—San Marco, Castello, Cannaregio, Dorsodoro, San Polo, and painfully, Santa Croce, a district named after a demolished church that shared the name of Brother Guido's former home. In a few short weeks I began to know every *calle*, or canal, every palace on the Grand Canal, the great S-shaped waterway that cleaved through the city.

S for *Serenissima*, *S* for *Stato del Mar*, said my mother.

S for She-lion, thought I.

At each great house I had to name its owners and their antecedents, following their families back to the Crusades, learning by rote as my mother instructed me. I knew every church spire and every bell that gave tongue. I could name the boats that crowded the mouth of the canal, their wares and whence they hailed from. I learned of trade routes as we visited the Arsenale and watched the ships under construction, each with a proud lion poised on the prow. My mother talked endlessly, as if she perversely enjoyed my company. As if she were cramming sixteen years of lost conversations into these first weeks together. Yet her discourse never strayed into the personal. She would speak of a particular painting or fresco that we were going to see, or the mass we would attend, or of the pointed shoes we were to buy in the best leather *botteghe* of the Rialto district. Once she got me up early to take me to the fish market, a place of strange dead shoals with staring glass eyes, and a stench like a rabbit warren. She showed me the Jewish quarter, where the infidels were sequestered for their protection and, she said, the city's. She took me to the island of Murano, where Venice's foremost export is made—glassware. There I watched leather-clad craftsmen working at their furnaces, and making miracles from hot amber globs of molten sand. With their long iron poles they blew bubbles of saffron glass that cooled to rose, to be pinched and pulled this way and that till a beauteous vase appeared as if by miracle. Coughing at the sulfurous fumes of that merry little hell, I was warm for the first time since I had come to this freezing city. We traveled thence to the island of Burano, where identical old ladies sat black clad in every doorway, catching the last warmth of a dying winter sun, tatting delicate froths of thread in their laps, not even looking at their hands as they created lace as delicate as the snowflakes that would soon come to these islands. Autumn bleached to winter and my mother continued relentlessly to teach me of my home. It was she who told me that in the winter months it is best to go about masked, with a posy of dried flowers and herbs stuffed beneath my nose, for the contagion of plague and lung fever swept in from the lagoon. It was she who taught me to keep hot rocks in my pocket, to warm my freezing hands as the days drew in. It was she who taught me that there is only one piazza in Venice, that of Saint Mark where our palace was placed, and that all other squares were known as *campi,* or "fields." It was she who showed me round the great Basilica, numbered and named all the saints, explained every fresco, showed me the priceless treasures within. It was she who told me that this gold-lined church was not the city's cathedral but my father's private chapel, and bade me then to understand the power of my family, the power of the Mocenigos. Marveling at the rich booty of this place, the golden Pala d'Oro altar screen, the richly jeweled icon of Saint Mark, the quartet of bronze horses stolen from the East, a growing impression of the last months clotted into certainty. I had heard every word of my mother's instruction but, ignorant as I was, I could still draw my own conclusions. I knew this place for what it was—Venice was a city of booty. This pirate people had stolen everything that distinguished it from somewhere else. The treasures in the Basilica, the style and design of the windows on every palazzo, even the words in the Venetian dialect, were looted from the East.

I learned, too, from my mother, what happened to enemies of my father's rule—I walked with her through the sumptuous rooms of the palace, through a tiny doorway and down narrow darkwood stairs to the chambers of torture and imprisonment known as the wells, or *pozzi,* for they are so sunken and cold, set as they are below the waterline of the canal. One room will stay with me always, a gloomy paneled square, three stairs in the dead center of the room leading nowhere but to a cruel noose hanging above. I walked, too, around the damp cells of the notorious jail, where the imprisoned are watched every moment, for if a guard lets his charge escape, he finishes his prisoner's sentence. No one had broken free yet, my mother told me with cruel pride and a warning. Petty criminals were kept at the roof of the palace, the *piombi,* or leads, where the heat of the roof tiles made their lives unbearable. In summer months their blood would boil, their flesh sizzle in preparation for hellfires. Hotter than coal or colder than ice was the choice for the unruly in Venice—I hardly knew which extreme of misery was worse. As I heard the drip of the walls and the cries

324

of the inmates, I keened for Brother Guido, in his similar fate. Yet I could not share such thoughts. And still, in all this time, my mother would never refer to our relationship, nor our pasts, nor our meeting. She was tolerable company, accomplished, funny even—witty enough to make my frozen belly laugh, but never did I once feel that we were mother and daughter. I watched her, though, with reluctant admiration; she had a soft low voice which I tried to emulate. I began to curb my filthy tongue at her command. I watched her walk into a room and began to imitate her seamless glide—even on the awkward platforms of the chopines she had a graceful stride, while I lurched and stumbled like a newborn foal. I watched her stand as if a golden thread passed through her body and out the top of her head, holding herself as erect as a queen. I ate my food as daintily as she—watched her white hands pick at morsels or daintily cut with her trencher knife. I began to wipe my mouth on my sleeve as she did, not the back of my hand. I began to carry a silken kerchief to wipe my nose when I had the ague, rather than blowing it directly into my skirt or my hair as I'd been used. I admired her as a woman and her easy way of conversing with everyone with charm—from the man who rowed our gondola to the princes of the Orient who came to dine. I admired her, yes, but she was not a mother to me. She took her desire to reconstruct my past to its logical conclusion. She instructed me, in great detail, how a dollop of pig's-trotter jelly inserted into my woman's part the night before the wedding would form a skin o'ernight to be broken the next eve, and make me once again a virgin. I did not have to ask how she knew this jade's trick—clearly she had gulled my father with such arts. This was the closest that we ever came to an intimate conversation. Even on the days when the sun shone near as hot as Tuscany, and we repaired to the roof with our sewing, we never spoke of what lay within our hearts, even though we were totally alone. At such times we wore wide-brimmed hats with holes at the crown, and spread our identical golden locks out in the sun's rays, to bake to an even lighter gold. I would look at my mother, dignified even in this garb, from under the safety of the wide, wide brim and search her face while she did not see me. We were alike. But we could not have been more different.

I met my father officially shortly after my arrival—on the day of his return to Venice I was allowed to watch him in audience with some of his citizens. After three moot sessions on various shipping rights, and one neighborly dispute about right-of-way on the canal, he beckoned me to him. I kissed his hand as expected, looked into his pale blue eyes and felt nothing. His skin had a waxy pallor, and his dignified stillness added to the impression that he was not, in fact, real.

"I am glad to see you back, Luciana," he said, kindly enough. "You may kiss us." I had no time to press my lips to his tallow cheek before I was ushered from the room. And that was the closest I ever got to him. I saw him little, for he even ate apart from us except for formal occasions, and then he sat at the head of the great dining board, as distant from me as the moon. Faraway he may have been, but he was still close enough for me to observe one important detail. On the thumb of his left hand, he wore a golden ring, adorned with nine golden balls—the Medici *palle*.

My father was one of the Seven.

My intended groom, Niccolò della Torre, was not mentioned, but I knew that my marriage treaty held with the city of Pisa. I even toyed with swallowing my pride and begging Niccolò to intercede for his cousin. *Madonna, I would* even marry the wight if he could save Brother Guido—but I was kept from his sight until the spring when my instruction was complete. If he visited my father's house I did not know it, and I was kept from all negotiations. From snippets of gossip from my washerwoman I knew that the dowry was settled and the wedding set for summer, but I could not think of this now. I would never wed him, and knew in my heart that there could be no use in pleading for Brother Guido; I recalled Niccolò's venomous person and knew such pleas would fall on deaf ears.

But as I settled into my new life I thought of Brother Guido constantly. I was a three-legged dog or a bird with one wing—so used was I to his companionship for those sweet months. And now I knew not whether he lived or died. My mother, pleased with my obedience during her instruction, kept her word and made inquiries as to his whereabouts from the Florentine commune. I paced my room waiting for an answer, and when the runner finally returned, the news was good: Guido della Torre had been released from Bargello but nothing further was known. I felt a huge rush of joy at the news, but soon began to fret once again; I knew that if he'd been released into the hands of his cousin, he may have been safer in jail. I pestered my mother to find out more, and in the space of time that was only a sennight but seemed a year, she reported to me. In a voice filled with truth (I must admit), she informed me that my monkish friend had been released into the arms of the brothers at Santa Croce there to continue his calling on the condition that he did not try to leave their precincts. Relief filled my chestspoon, although a note of doubt sounded—I knew he did not want to reclaim his monkish life, but supposed that, if faced with death, he might have made his peace with his Lord. With that, I had to be content, until I could find a way to quit this place. For I was now trapped indeed. Not just by the city but by the winter, the cruel winds, mountain snows to the north, and freezing tides. However, nothing less than this news could have made me stay. My mother watched my reaction to the news carefully, in some ways as relieved as I. She suspected, I knew, that had I known Brother

Guido to be in true danger I would have found a way, some-how, to leave that night.

Yet I was not content for long with my precious snippet of information, and my doubt at Brother Guido's religious about-face swelled on the horizon like a cloud fattened with rain. I needed some contact, some more news of how he did. Was he well? Had he truly found the church again? I worked as hard as I could with my stern Dominican tutor and one day after a lesson I scratched out a laborious, blotted, short note—an ink-stained plea for information, with pain and hope in every word. After long deliberation I decided to send the missive to Brother Nicodemus, the herbalist, as I did not wish to invite suspicion or draw attention to my friend by having him receive strange messages from Venice. I felt sure the Medicis would be keeping a close eye upon him. I wrote the direction myself and sent a runner to Florence on my own account; these little free-doms were small compensation for my watery prison.

When the reply came, all hope died. Brother Nicodemus of Padua had, of his great kindness, written a reply so simple that I could read it.

"You are mistook. Brother Guido not at Santa Croce; in Bargello awaiting trial. Courage."

Black hate filled my heart against my mother. That lying *bitch*. How could I have ever thought her noble, found her com-paniable? I, *even* I, had been seduced by her company, after sixteen years of desertion. And she had repaid me with this. How she must have laughed at her little deception. I spent the afternoon in my room, alternating my humors between rage at my mother and anguish at Brother Guido's fate. How long would he wait for trial before facing the inevitable noose? Had they tortured him, damaged him in mind or body? How long did I have to save him?

I toyed with the idea of confronting my mother with her

fraud but knew it would avail me nothing. I was in the She-lion's den and she would do anything, say anything, to keep me there. It would not do to show her all I knew. I was learning the Venetian way.

Betimes I thought of Lorenzo de' Medici and his hellish assassin, and allowed myself to speculate on their future plans—for it was certain now that the father of Florence was one of the Seven and had some deadly plot in mind. But such thoughts never occupied me for more than a heartbeat; I forgot all about the thirty-two roses, whatever they may mean, and the rest of the clues we had unearthed in our month-long odyssey. I hid the *cartone* in an inlaid chest in my room, but never took it out to look—the pain was too great, for I had pored over it so often with him that was gone. I cared not for any plot nor painting anymore—just for my lost companion. I would not rest easy till I saw him again, but as the winter closed in I knew I must wait. Unbearable though it was, I must contemplate a winter here in this freezing city, without the warmth that knowledge of my friend's fate would give me. I knew, too, that the commune of Florence did not keep miscreants alive for long—there were enough thieves and varmints to fill the Bargello twice over, and the turnover was fast—my friend would soon be dispatched.

From the day the herbalist's letter reached me, I began to plan my escape.

31

In this cause I began to pay more attention to the lessons of Signor Cristoforo. I wanted to learn all I could of the *Stato del Mar*—for I knew the only way off this rock was by sea. And I had to admit that the Genoan's tuition interested me. I was more a child of the sea than I thought, for his stories of great voyages and far-off lands held me bewitched. Only at these times could I almost forget the gaping hole Brother Guido's loss had blown in my life, like a cannon's ball through the fo'c'sle. I was a blasted ship limping to shore; I was a doomed siren drowning a little more every day. *Hold tight, my love,* I vowed. *I'll sail away and rescue you, as soon as the spring tides turn.*

At least there was no chance that my Genoese tutor could ever replace my lost friend in my affections. My mother, knowing my history, had chosen a tutor ugly enough that even *I* would not want to fuck him. Actually, there was never a chance of a jump with Signor Cristoforo, for my interest in getting laid had waned to naught. Even if it had not, there were three major objections to his person.

Obiezione Uno: a flat mat of red hair sat on his head.

Obiezione Due: his nose was bulbous.

Obiezione Tre: his cod was plump to the point of grossness.

But from the first time I met him, I knew that he was cleverer than any man I had ever met, save one.

We had our daily lesson always in the same place—the Sala delle Mappe—a great salon in the upper reaches of my father's palace, where the walls were covered in maps and charts rendered by Venice's greatest artists. Voyages were expressed in great sweeping lines, winds were depicted as bearded gods cracking their cheeks and blowing from every corner, spiked compasses sat at each cornice like alien fruit, and fabulous monsters peeped from the curling seas while ornate ships with full-bellied sails dodged their jaws.

Signor Cristoforo, despite his ill-favored appearance, was extremely friendly and—once I had penetrated his thick sailor's accent—an amusing and gentle man, very good company, and had an absorbing passion for his subject. Once again I could see that a man's carnal appetites could be suppressed by another genuine passion. Botticelli, a genius in his own time as I suppose I must own, had thought of me no more as a woman than as a bowl of fruit he must paint. And here was this strange little man, not much older than I, who stared into the eyes of the wind rather than my own, would rather gaze on a compass's face than my countenance, and stared more intently at latitude lines than the faint blue veins that mapped my bosom.

For now I knew a little of the mystery of the place where I lived; the city herself, in a unique trick of geography, was the gatekeeper of the Black Sea and all the trade routes from here to Constantinople. From Signor Cristoforo I heard of the rivalry between Venice and Genoa for these routes, for it seemed that his own city was the only port to approach Venice in her maritime supremacy. He explained to me the intense competition in chartmaking, the race to map the world, the contest to build bigger and better ships, all of which meant that our peninsula ruled the seas from both west and east. I learned from him the great units of measurement—of fathoms and leagues and latitudes; here he made me laugh, claiming that the curvature of the horizons at sea suggested strongly to him that the world was round like an apple, not flat like a *frittata* (I told you he had good humor). From him, too, I learned that one of the earliest and most accomplished maps was made right here in Venice, by a priest called Fra Mauro. Signor Cristoforo took me across the lagoon to the island of San Michele, for we had special permission to enter the monastery to see the thing. As I gazed upon the crazy lines and divisions, the countries of our world marked out in gold upon an immense azure disk, I marveled at how small our own peninsula was, and yet how powerful. As we crossed back over the lagoon, choppy angry jade waters that day, I noted at firsthand how skillful Signor Cristoforo was at sea. I sat in my cushions, tasting the spray that flecked my lips salty as a man's seed, and relaxed. Not for me the heaving and retching over the side that poor Marta, my constant chaperone, was experiencing. I watched the treacherous witch heave her guts up, with no small pleasure. For I had been in a worse pass than this in the straits of Naples, shipwrecked and near drowned. I looked at my tutor, competent at the tiller, his pale eyes narrowed at the sky, seeing to the horizon and beyond, and wondered what he would say if he knew I had more practical experience of seagoing than he thought. But my tutor was busy warning me of the high tide, or *acqua alta,* that flooded the city each autumn and spring, And it was Signor Cristoforo who told me, when we were safe in San Marco's basin, with my white prison looming above, the most valuable piece of information he had ever imparted to me. As he cursed the ignorant tourists clogging the waterways, he complained that in a sennight things would be ten times worse, for every gondola and *traghetto* the city owned would be abroad on the Grand Canal for Carnevale. At this time the city held a great celebration before the privations of Lent began; fourteen days and nights of drinking and debauchery and daily regattas on the Grand Canal. Twenty times worse, said he, for at Carnevale everyone went about masked and costumed and jug-bitten, so the inexperienced sailors were further handicapped by being drunk and having their vision obscured by masks and their limbs impeded by heavy costumes. Several revelers drowned each year, said he, but, he finished with typical dry humor, not nearly enough. I pictured these unfortunates falling from their perch to be dragged below by heavy velvets and brocades. I thought fleetingly of those well-dressed skeletons dancing below us, weighed down by their fancy shoes, upright and dancing for eternity in an eerie measure, their own underwater Carnevale of the dead.

By that time I had made up my mind.

I dismissed Marta as soon as I reached my room. Tool and

spy of my mother's she may have been, but she was also lazy, and went quickly enough, knowing that I was once more safe in my cell. I had to be alone to think. I calculated—I had been here some months; the long winter was passing. My heart had turned to ice in this snow palace but was beginning to thaw again; a little of the beating matter remained, a small ruby of flesh within me that burned like a tiny coal. That tiny kernel blossomed and grew together with the beginnings of an idea that spread the warmth all the way through my body and burned in my cheeks. I knew at once that that time of Carnevale—of masks and confusion, of dissembling and deceit, of constant, unnoticed leisure voyages—must be the time that I quit this place. I planned to leave the city as I had done sixteen years ago—by boat to Mestre and then by horse cart to Florence, there to seek the one I could not bear to be without.

I knew that I needed help, and knew I must look to my tutor for it, because he was the nearest to a friend that I had—all the other servants of this place, and even my father, were bewitched by my mother and utterly in her thrall. I knew also that I put Signor Cristoforo at great risk if I told him what I intended; yet I could not think of anyone's safety but that of Brother Guido. I needed a boatman to take me from Venice, February was already upon us, and I was certain that Signor Cristoforo knew every seagoing wight in the city. I decided to broach my problem at our next lesson. On the appointed day I could not break my fast but sent my kitchen girl back with the tray untouched. I could barely stand still to be dressed— appropriately, in a gown and shift as blue as the sea, with snowy sleeves peeping through the surcoat as white as the horses that crowned the waves. I twitched and bitched and moaned while Marta, the toad, laced my bodice. I fidgeted when the Moorish maid smoothed my hair with olive oil and turned it round a hot poker to make glossy ringlets, into which she fastened sapphires and moonstones. I scarcely glanced in the mirror to note my mermaid beauty, for I could almost taste my freedom—I was now twitching to be gone and could almost not bear another day in this place. For all these cold winter months I had been hibernating, stupid as a bear—now I felt an unbearable urgency, as if Brother Guido's trial were tomorrow. I had written ten, twenty times for more news from Brother Nicodemus, but had had just one more reply, that Brother Guido was still languishing in the Bargello to be tried on Ash Wednesday.

Ash Wednesday was in February, just after Carnevale.

What if I were too late?

I nearly ran down the passages to the Sala delle Mappe. Signor Cristoforo was waiting for me, for my toilet had been frustratingly long that day. He rose as I entered, but as usual, he took not a jot of notice of my finery.

"Signorina Mocenigo," he said with a courteous nod of the head. He sat as I did at the great oaken table and unrolled a yellowing parchment, and weighted it at either side with an astrolabe and calipers. A needle of memory pricked my belly as I remembered the numerous times Brother Guido and I had unrolled the *Primavera cartone,* as a prelude to a heated discussion of one of the figures.

"Today's lesson will treat upon perhaps the most important tool at the sailor's disposal," began the seaman in his thick Genoese accent.

I was twitching with impatience, did not even look at the paper before me. "Signor Cristoforo—"

"The compass rose."

I stopped. This sounded useful.

"Thanks to this device, designed by the finest men of science, it is possible to know exactly where we are when at sea, even in storm, even in dark."

Even in dark. Tomorrow, with Mary's blessing, I would be leaving this city, in a boat, by dark. I began to listen and to look. Before me, inscribed neatly on the paper, was a compass of many points, with a direction writ beneath each point. It looked like a wicked flower, and in fact, a rose sat at the center of all, like the axis of a ship's wheel.

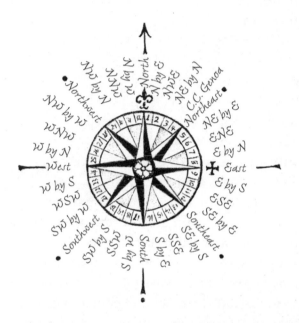

"Here"—Signor Cristoforo pointed with a rough blunt finger—"this figure is known as the compass *rose,* so called because the many-petaled appearance of the cardinal directions gives a floral impression. We may see the well-known directions of the four winds—north at the top, south at the bottom, west to our right, and east to our left."

So far so good. "But what of all the others in between?"

"These finer directions denote the divisions *between* the winds—for example, between 'north' and 'east' are the following directions."

North
North by east
Northwest east
Northeast by north
Northeast
Northeast by east
East northeast
East by north
East.

"You see?"

No. "Yes."

"Between east and south the same, and on around the wheel, back to north. In ancient times the Romans made do with just twelve *divisio* at thirty degrees each, a perilous practice indeed. Now we have the full thirty-two divisions, and by reference to the *gradians*—the subdivisions between each point—we may know with great accuracy our position at sea, a method known as 'dead reckoning.' This very compass," he went on with a bashful countenance, "was transcribed by myself and my brother at our map shop in Genoa, down by the old harbor." He had left the room and gone home; I could see his eyes were wistful for his city, and his voice was full of pride and homesickness.

I softened toward him, now that I knew he missed a part of his heart too. "Did your brother teach you to love the sea?"

"Him, and my father-in-law too."

"You're married?" I was too shocked to hide the surprise from my voice. Ugly men were married aplenty, but usually with a fortune to soften their looks. But ill-favored young tutors with little wealth and fewer prospects? Surprising. Perhaps things were handled differently in Genoa.

"Yes—to a lady named Filipa, who lives in the Azores." (I did not know where this is and still don't.) "With a son, just lately born, whom I have not yet seen. He is named Diego." His eyes turned to glass briefly, wet with tears, and I was mortified: I had been so busy musing on my own personal tragedy that I had not thought to ask what a young man did so far away from his family. "Now," he said, recollecting himself swiftly, and carrying forth with the task in hand. "Shall we see if you can remember the directions between north and east?"

Shit. My mind was anywhere but on my lessons, but my tutor did not notice anything amiss. He lifted the astrolabe and the compass drawing rolled up with a snap, leaving me blind. I just about remembered north and then was stuck, but by gently prompting me, the sailor gently led me through all the directions. 'Twas easy when you had completed one quarter, for the rest followed by rote, and I finished my catechism, returning north with triumph.

"North northwest, north by west north!"

"Very good." He clapped his dry paws together. "You have boxed the compass."

"What's that I did?"

"You have named all thirty-two points of the compass rose—we call it 'boxing the compass,' an essential part of a sailor's education." He looked at me like a proud father, and I remembered another, too, who had looked at me that way.

"And now for the other piece of the puzzle—the winds themselves," he said, unrolling another chart and anchoring the corners.

"This is the *wind* rose, much older than the compass rose, and in use since ancient times. Where the compass uses the latest in science, the wind rose has a more classical provenance, relying on ancient myth and legend, and seafaring superstition. Curiously, both are equally reliable, and relied upon. The wind horses, as they are known, are the four steeds of the ether, north, south, east, and west. Classically they were known as Boreas to the north, Eurus to the east, Notus to the south, and Zephyrus to the west. The wind rose is still in use in the Mediterranean, and because we dominate these waters sailors have named the directions in our modern dialect. Thus north becomes *tramontana*, meaning over the mountains, and is usually denoted, as here, by a fleur-de-lys. East, the Levante direction, is usually denoted by a Maltese cross, since that way the holy city of Jerusalem lies. You will see here that the other seven directions, or 'rhumbs' as they are known, are also named in modern tongue, Tramontana, then we have Greco, Levante, Syroco, Ostro for the south, Africus, Ponente for the west, Maestro, and back to Tramontana."

I had stopped listening and hoped he would not test me on this. I was sure whomever we found to ferry me to Mestre had a handle on all this and would not be asking his noble passenger for help.

"Using the winds *and* the compass points as our guides, modern sailors have succeeded in discovering the unknown. The wind rose and the compass rose, these two simple figures here, have enabled Venice to become the *Stato del Mar* par excellence. You have heard, I suppose, of Marco Polo?"

I knew a little, from my travels with my mother, but did not want to hear more, so nodded. But Signor Cristoforo, like Brother Guido, knew when I was lying.

"He came home after a quarter of a century traveling in the East, as far as Peking. His family did not know him, dressed as he was in the garb of a rough Tartar. Then he sliced open his tunic, and diamonds and precious stones poured forth. He wrote painstakingly of all his travels for the rest of his days, but even on his deathbed complained that he had written not even *half* of what he saw."

I stifled a yawn, for I had not slept as you will recall. Although I liked the idea of limitless jewels.

"He made a beginning. And yet there is more out there, that other states may claim. Much more," he said with a faraway look. "I myself am here in your city to raise money for such an expedition."

"Really?" I felt I was nearer to divining why he had accepted this humble post in my father's house, teaching a green girl far away from all who loved him.

"Oh, yes. I'm hoping to petition your father for funds. One day, men will travel beyond the edge of the map."

I would be happy to sail to Mestre and no farther. I would be done with travel if I could but see Brother Guido again. I thought I better ask a question, for my tutor's sake, but I made it pertinent to my journey, for my own. "And which wind prevails at present?"

"Zephyrus, the west wind." He smiled. "Here is where mythology reigns over science. The ancients believed that the wind Zephyrus, brother to the north wind Boreas, fell in love with Chloris. This nymph transformed into Flora, the nymph that is associated with spring flowers."

I said naught for I had not the energy to explain that I knew more of Flora and Chloris than I ever wished to. "Zephyrus forced himself upon Chloris, and their issue, Xantus and Brutus, were horses, later to belong to Achilles. Hence the term 'horses' used for the winds."

I recalled suddenly that Brother Guido had once named the blue figure in the *Primavera* "Zephyrus," and I now knew why. He was in the process of raping Chloris, my darling mother, who then turned to Flora—me—for help. I snorted softly through my nose. I'd die before I helped her. The four winds could all rape my mother, in turn, right up the arse for all I cared. And I would hold her down for them.

"But I stray from my course."

(As did I.)

"Essentially the prevailing wind at present, mid-February, is Zephyrus. He heralds the spring, which will be here in one full month."

I could listen no more; I calculated later that it must have been the mention of February—the month of Ash Wednesday and his trial—that brought Brother Guido so sharply and painfully to my mind that my heart ached. Now, I know that you, having witnessed the whole of my lesson with Signor Cristoforo, will judge me. Stupid little tart, you will scoff. She was given so many answers that day. Why did she not listen, why could she not see? But you must understand that at that time, I had but one thought in my head. I did not see that my questions had been answered, that a door had been opened, that a code had been broken. I gripped Signor Cristoforo by the arm, the first time I had touched him and 'twas no gentle caress. He stopped in surprise.

"I need you to help me," I begged, putting all that I had into one beseeching glance. "Someone I love is in trouble. Someone I'd do anything to help." I took a breath, gave my next words as much emphasis as I could. "*My* Filipa. *My* Diego."

He looked at me for a long moment. Then sighed. "What do you need?"

32

This was a castle of lions, a harbor guarded by ravening beasts. I had been to the Arsenale before, on one of my mother's little educational trips, but never before had I defied the creature that ruled this city. Now that I planned to leave I saw its countenance everywhere; only now that I wanted to wrest myself from its bloody jaws did I know that the lion of Saint Mark guarded this citadel jealously, was a constant presence and nowhere more than here. The great stone beasts guarded the iron gates of this place, a fortress of bloodred stone, capped with white crenellations of sharp teeth. They were creatures of my mother—spawn of the she-lion that suckled them. If I passed through these gates, I was entering the circus. She could raise her hand like a Roman empress, to have me ripped limb from limb, for the gladiators to follow and battle on my blood-soaked sand. Signor Cristoforo was let pass through the gates and I followed. Even at the doors the beast was guardian—the first thing I saw was a great stone face of a lion, set into one wall, paying out rope through his mouth for the sailors to pull and cut to size. I stared at the gaping mouth, mesmerized. I was once again a Daniel.

I knew from my mother's instruction that security here was as tight as a cur's arse (my words not hers), but the doors were opened without delay to Signor Cristoforo and myself. We used the same deception which had taken us out of the ducal palace without challenge. I had simply run to my mother's room for one of her trademark masks (I say "simply"—in truth I was more terrified while entering my mother's chamber than the gates of the Arsenale). Our similarity meant that I had only to put this on and I was she. I blessed the times I had aped her speech and bearing while trying to improve my own. Chin high, I swept down the passages, heart thumping lest I should meet the real thing. I did see Marta, carrying coals, but nodded and swept by, and even that bitch did not know me. I glided down the Giants' staircase to the foot where Signor Cristoforo awaited me, and we left the place without question. If the dogaressa wished to visit the Arsenale with her daughter's tutor, it was clearly no one's business but hers. We hurried down the Riva degli Schiavoni toward the docks, aided in our deception by a pissing drizzle which kept every passing wight huddled into his hood.

Inside the citadel of the Arsenale I was reminded, now as before, of the night when Brother Guido and I had stumbled upon the shipwrights working in the old castle at Pisa; the smells of tar and wood and linen were the same. I followed my tutor to the side of the covered harbor where smiths, caulkers, and sawyers ran about and weaved around each other, fetching and carrying in an ever-flowing stream of people. These, I knew, were the *arsenalotti,* a buzzing hive of drones with my mother as their queen. This was the *Stato del Mar* in action.

Signor Cristoforo fixed the mass with his weather eyes and shot out a hand to grab the arm of a passing man. The fellow was small and slight, with gray hair and a young face, albeit with skin tanned to leather by seagoing. His eyes turned down at the edges and gave him a sad expression, but when he recognized his captor he smiled a smile of great charm—surprising, for as far as I could see he had absolutely no teeth at all. The two men clapped hands and hugged—slapping each other on the back in a brother's embrace. And when the stranger spoke I knew him for a Genoese, for he had the same thick vowels as my tutor. Perhaps this *was* his brother.

"Cristoforo, you old cunt! How come they let you out of Genoa?"

"They let you go, didn't they?" replied my tutor in the same spirit. "I hear that they're getting rid of all the ugly sailors."

"Must be quiet back there then."

It was an acknowledged joke and I smiled politely, before I realized that no one could actually see what I was doing behind my mask and under my hood.

"How is Lisabetta?"

The stranger spat neatly. "A pain in my arse and my pocket."

"The children?"

"The same." But it was said with love and gave me a jolt—I realized I envied this toothless sailor; he was married with children whom he loved, just like my tutor. I had a moment of misgiving—I was about to put him in danger.

"And how about you? You still teaching? Taught the dogaressa anything in the sack yet? Christ, she's a tasty piece—makes my prick pain me."

Now I chuckled, and the seaman looked beneath my hood and noticed my mask for the first time. Fell to his knees.

"Jesus shat! The dogaressa!" His tan face blanched. "My lady, forgive me," he babbled. "I knew not . . . that is, I meant nothing—"

"Get up, you old pisspot," exclaimed Signor Cristoforo, "before the whole place sees you. This is not the dogaressa, but her daughter. Signorina Luciana Mocenigo, meet Bonaccorso Nivola, the best sailor on these shores or any other."

I gave the man my hand, as it seemed the right thing to do,

and he kissed it, like a man who had just been hit round the head with a *frittata* pan. Signor Cristoforo drew our little trio behind a stack of pine planks twice as tall as we. The sweet sap filled my nostrils.

"She's minded to go on a trip and wants you to take her."

"A *trip*."

"Yes. You still running the rope boats to Mestre?"

"Of course. Only way I can pay for all the *bambini* my Lisabetta pops out. 'Nother one on the way."

"All right then. One trip. And you can feed them for a year."

"Gold?"

"Gold."

"How much?"

"Fifty ducats."

The seaman gave a toothless whistle, and I swallowed. Fifty ducats was a fortune! Where the hell was I supposed to get that money? Signor Cristoforo must be mad! Then, in a horrid instant, I knew; but the thought bathed me in a sweat of terror. My mother had a coffer of gold ducats in her chamber—I had seen it only this morning as I had searched for her masks. *Madonna*. Then I straightened up. Only one thing could make me go back in that room, and that was Brother Guido. I'd do it if I must. The sailors continued their bargaining, as if I wasn't there.

"When?"

"Tomorrow night. First night of Carnevale."

Bonaccorso Nivola considered, then jerked his head in my direction. "Her mum know she's going?"

A tiny pause from Signor Cristoforo. "No. It's a matter of the heart."

This was true enough—I'd laid all before my tutor and he knew that I fled for love.

Bonaccorso caught on quick. "One way then?"

"Yes."

The sailor was silent.

"It's risky, I won't lie to you," admitted my tutor. "But then you can retire."

Bonaccorso sucked in his gums, the air whistling through his lack of teeth.

"What the hell," he said, then addressed me directly for the first time. "Be on the San Zaccharia pier at midnight tomorrow. Bring the gold in a lace kerchief. I'll be on the rope barge. I'll stop for a moment, no more. You ask me if I've ever been to Burano to see the lacemakers. Got it?"

I nodded, mute with terror and triumph.

"Till tomorrow then." And he was gone into the crowd as quickly as he had come. I felt faint and elated at once. It was done. I was committed. Tomorrow, I would be gone.

My tutor and I hurried back to the palace as fast as we could and parted at the staircase without a word. Both too frightened and agitated to give note to the fact this would be our last meeting. I knew I would not see him again, and I could not speak lest I give myself away, but I hoped that as I hurried away he might know that I would not forget him, and that he knew how much I owed Signor Cristoforo of Genoa.

33

I did not sleep that night, and would have spent the next day in a jitter but was informed at breakfast by the witch Marta that my mother had a particular excursion to take me on today. I steeled myself for a day of polite chatter as we circled the canals of Venice in the *Bucintoro* and wondered how I could bear the burden of my guilty secret without breaking down under her green eye and admitting all. But when I met my mother in the presence chamber she was wearing no mask and had left off her platformed clogs. She wore a cream lace shift and a sleeveless surcoat of her favorite green, with tiny gold lions embroidered at the hem. She wore no jewels or ornaments, but as ever with my mother her costume was not less than priceless. I don't know much, but I do know clothes; the workmanship of the lace had clearly demanded that the old ladies of Burano worked their ancient fingers to the quick, and the embroidery of the tiny lions at the hem of her gown was worth hundreds of ducats alone. Yet her hair was unbound and rippled to her waist. She had left her face unpainted, had merely rubbed her lips with a shiny salve so they glowed full and natural rose, and touched her eyelids with the same gloss so her eyes were left to speak for themselves, the green of deep, deep water. She looked about fifteen. I knew then that all my finery, the primping and preening of my ladies, was worth naught—my mother in her most natural state was the Venus of this sea. Yet when she smiled I thought she looked more mortal and friendly than I had ever seen her. For one instant I felt a pang that I was about to lose her again, my *Vero Madre,* the woman I had obsessed about finding for all these years.

She took my hand. "Come," she said. "Today we are to learn the most valuable lesson of all. We are to learn about justice—Venetian justice."

The words were strangely at odds with her innocent appearance.

Somewhere, a distant chime of foreboding sounded in my head.

She led me through numerous passages to the inner sanctum of the palace—a warren of offices and passageways that interlocked with the public rooms of the building. Such was her power and presence that her servants melted away as we approached; rooms emptied when we entered, as everyone ceased their business and gave us privacy for our progress. At length we fetched up at a quartet of darkwood offices I had never seen before. Set within the walls of one such chamber was a lion's head with a gaping mouth, leading God knew where. It was a terrible thing, and I tasted fear in my mouth—I now faced the beast that I so feared.

"La Bocca del Leone," announced my mother. "The Lion's Mouth. Political traitors are denounced here, in writing—the accusation writ down and passed through the mouth to the offices within. Our judicial system relies on such information for the wheels to turn aright."

My heart plummeted, as I realized that those that filled the prisons below and above us began their journeys here, damned by their friends, rivals, or jealous associates.

I had to clear my throat twice before I could speak. "Is not such a system . . . open to abuse?" I stammered. "I mean . . . is it not used for . . . vengeance?"

She shrugged. "Betimes. But what matter? In each case we exact punishment to fit the crime, in case there is a kernel of truth in the matter."

I swallowed.

"You will forgive me, my dear Luciana," she went on, "if we now repeat a little of your former tour—I believe that the best tutors believe in the revision of earlier learned lessons, do they not?" She flashed a green glance at me and I had to drop my eyes—suddenly stone-cold certain she was talking about Signor Cristoforo. "So I will not apologize, but merely assure you that you will not find it dull."

We went once again through the gloomy paneled chambers to the little door in the wall; I knew now—at the back of my mind I had always known—where we were going. Once again, we descended the darkwood stairs to the prisons—the underbelly of the Venetian state. The chime of terror grew stronger and my skin started to prickle. Once again light turned to dark as we left the airy palace for the dark passages of the *pozzi*—once again the shrieks of prisoners reached my ears, the pleas of the sane and the babblings of the ones who had run mad. Once again the biting cold turned my skin to plucked chicken, and the killing damp entered my chestspoon. I saw scratches above the doors indicating the numbers of the cells—once names, the prisoners were now numbers, waiting for torture or death, for release would never come.

"Here," said my mother lightly. She nodded to the burly guard who uncrossed his beefy arms and stood aside.

I looked questioningly at my mother, who nodded. I stepped inside, half expecting the clang of the door behind me. For I was certain, now, that my mother knew something. Instead I was assailed by the smell of shit and vomit, overlaid by a sweet alien smell. My nose recognized the odor before my brain did—I was back in my old house by the Arno, the floor a carmine pool, my feet wet from the gore, my eyes looking down on Enna, her throat slit and gushing.

Blood.

In the corner a creature of darkness was curled like a babe, keening and crying, his tears dripping in time with the water from the walls. I recoiled from the thing before me and looked at my mother's dispassionate face. Conversationally, as if she were introducing guests at a gathering, she said the horrible words.

"Of course, you know Signor Bonaccorso Nivola."

At the sound of his name, like a child or a dog that is sensible of no more than what he is called, the thing in the corner uncurled and turned his face to mine. I could not look upon what I saw there, so dropped my eyes to worse—his hose had been slashed at his groin, and a single bloody appendage dangled there, unnatural, two essential orbs missing in a gruesome mirroring of what had happened to his face. The knife, newly wet from the deed, lay guiltily by on a wooden stool, and my mother picked it up, laid both edges against her tongue in turn and tasted the man's blood. The stain rouged her unpainted lips and her eyes glittered in the dark like jade. I fled the cell then, and as I vomited I comprehended what I had seen.

His eyes and balls were gone.

As I heaved I was conscious of someone rubbing my back, an action any normal mother would employ with a sickly child.

"Your tutor has gone back to Genoa," she said. "We did not harm him. But your father and I would like you to stay."

Again it was said with kindness and affection, as if to a guest who wished to take leave too soon.

The guard, used to such scenes, looked on with dispassion. He pulled a filthy cloth from his belt, dropped it over my leavings, and scuffed the mess back and forth with his foot, leaving a wet smear on the flags. My mother flipped him a ducat, payment for removing the dogaressina's vomit. And I stumbled back up the stairs, back along the passages, back to my room.

34

Bonaccorso Nivola, Bonaccorso Nivola.

I had heard the fear in his voice. I remembered he had said, "Does her *mum* know?" Not her *dad*. I remembered how he had paled when he thought the dogaressa stood before him. I realized he knew what I had divined when I first came here—the She-lion was beautiful but deadly. I ached for his family—suffered agonies of guilt about the unknown, unseen Lisabetta. If she had loved her man as I loved mine, what agonies must rack her now? Her man lay in jail as did mine; we shared a fate but hers was a hundred times more dire—she was a widow in truth, with fatherless babes and no money, an empty bed and an empty cupboard and an empty heart and no wealth to ease her days. *Dead reckoning*—Signor Cristoforo's phrase came back to me, and suddenly seemed to have enormous significance to the fate of the poor sailor who had agreed to navigate me out of here. I vowed one day to send succor to Bonaccorso's wife and children, for God only knew if he would ever quit the *pozzi*. At least Signor Cristoforo had, if my mother spoke truth, been merely banished—allowed to return to his brother and his beloved map shop by the sea, and thence to his wife and the son he had never seen but could bring tears to his eyes at a word. For that I was glad.

But my own cause was hopeless. I knew that I would now not be able to escape; that I would languish here until, by a cruel twist of fortune, I would be taken over the mountains to Pisa where I would be wed to the cousin of the man I loved. To be reminded every day by the similarities of blood that I had bought a counterfeit, a poor copy of the man I wanted. Worse still, Brother Guido was still in the Bargello, a jail at least as bad as the one I had just fled.

In despair I went to the inlaid chest at my window—had she searched my room? No, the gold I had stolen from her room the night before was all there. I took it out and tied it in the kerchief I had meant to give to Bonaccorso Nivola for my passage. I strapped the packet of coins tightly to my upper thigh. If it could not buy me freedom, I could at least send it to his family as I had pledged. There was something else in the bottom of the chest lying forgotten and crumpled. I drew it out. The *cartone*.

I opened the casement to cast the thing out into the lagoon, for it had destroyed Enna, Bembo, Brother Remigio, Bonnacorso, Brother Guido. And me. But it was the one thing that still connected me to Brother Guido. The one thing left to me that we had both touched. My fingers would not give the parchment up, however hard the west wind snatched at it. In the howl and moan of the warm current, Signor Cristoforo's words ebbed back to me, as if the spring tide carried them.

The west wind. The west wind heralds the spring. *Zephyrus*.

I closed the window abruptly. Lit a candle. I unrolled the painting carefully, tenderly, weighted the corners as we always used to do. Looked once more on the picture that my lost love and I had gazed on so oft together. My eyes were drawn to the figure of Chloris—my mother, who had tasted a man's blood today—looking innocent, frightened, running from the blue-winged wraith at her right shoulder.

Zephyrus.

Her hands reached toward the figure of Flora—toward *me*—for help. I noted the shift Chloris wore was so close to that which my mother wore today. Then I noted again the flowers that issued from her mouth. And the herbalist's words came to me once again.

Flowers drop like truths from her mouth.

Suddenly I *knew* that they must mean something and I set my jaw. Very well. If I could not escape, I could at least foil whatever deadly plan my mother was cooking up with Lorenzo de' Medici. I concentrated hard—checking the flowers that fell from her mouth against the ones that we had identified on Flora's garb, racking my pained memory to recall all that was said in the herbarium, forcing myself to recall *his* sweet face, *his* sweet voice, *his* long hands writing down the names of the flowers. I looked hard at each bloom. There seemed to be ten in all, although I could see at once that a number of them were duplicates; there was more than one of each type of flower. I counted four different types in all, and after a great deal of thought I believed that I had identified them. The two flowers almost lodged between Chloris's teeth were *occhiocento,* or "hundred eyes," a common flower of the hedgerow. Then I knew the little white flower with the yellow center to be the anemone, by recalling the herbalist's teachings. Next fell two coral roses, of exactly the type I had held in my skirts, the roses which we had been at such pains to number in vain, for we had never reached any useful conclusions about the number thirty-two. Finally, a twin-headed cornflower, blue as the twilight lagoon. A *fiordaliso.* Ten flower heads and four types of flower. *Occhiocento,* anemone, rose, and *fiordaliso.* I could not divine further for try as I might I could not recall the Latin for any flower but the rose, even if I ever knew it. So all I had to work with was the number four, the number ten, or the letters *R, F, O,* and *A.*

I sighed. I sensed it would be useless to try to construct a word from this quartet—for one thing, the flower names I knew were in Tuscan not Latin, and for another, I could barely read at this point, and barely set down letters in the right order, let alone construct a word from a jumble of letters. Still, there were only four, and I resolved to try. I knew what I was about—I was taking refuge in the puzzle. If my brain were busy doing this, that poor member could not dwell on the real horrors of the day, nor the imagined horrors that could befall another man, in another jail, in another city-state. Well, then.

R for rose
A for anemone
F for *fiordaliso*
O for *occhiocento*

The exercise was short. Eventually, painstakingly, I came up with:

RAFO

ROFA

OFAR

ORAF

FARO

FORA

AFRO

ARFO

None of these seemed to me to make a word, at least, not one that I knew. I wished heartily for another flower with another convenient letter. If only I had an *L*, for instance, I could make FLORA, which would seem suggestive (of what I did not know). But my desires could not add what was not there—I must stick with what I had. Perhaps if I added one letter for each bloom—two *F*'s as two *fiordalisi* were shown? And so on. But this didn't work either—I was left with a crazy collection of letters, none of them useful to me.

Presently I turned from letters to numbers. Perhaps the number four, the number of flower *types*, or the number ten, the number of *blooms*, was suggestive—but here I was graveled even sooner. There were four seasons and four winds and four apostles, but I could not think of any tens save commandments and only because I had broken most of those.

I gave up and stared from the window, seeing nothing. From habit I rolled the *cartone* and placed it in my bodice. It was no good. Like a moth frighted from the candle when he scorches his wing, like a wasp frighted from a ripe peach by the angry diner's hand, I returned again and again to the place that spelled my doom. I could not help but think of him that I had lost. I recalled another evening in another place, where I had stared once before over another sea. That evening it was the Bay of Naples the day I had come upon Brother Guido lying in his bed, back scourged till it ran with blood for the sin of kissing me. Now, hundreds of leagues into the north, my heart bled out too, and I grew colder and stiller. Perhaps it were best that we should part, that he should die, for I could never have been with him again and not touched him, not kissed him. Better that he should die, and me too.

I stayed in my room all day, refusing all food and drink and company. The sun drowned in the lagoon and the gondoliers and whores competed for evening trade. Exhausted, defeated by the sleeplessness of the night before and the day's exertions, I fell fully clothed onto my bed, asleep at once.

Only to wake as my mother entered my room. I knew it was she even before I could see her—my back was to the open door, but I knew her from the swish of her skirts and the sounds of her breath. I knew from the thrill of fear in my chestspoon and the thin film of sweat on my upper lip. I fought to keep my own breathing steady, to feign sleep. But opened my eyes a tiny degree and peered through my lashes. She walked into my view, an angel of midnight, her face lit from below by a rush dip candle, her hair a gold halo. She went first to the window and her breath misted the quarrel panes of the glass, for it was a wild night outside with the rain coming down in stripes. It would have been a torrid voyage to Mestre, rain soaked and rough seaed, but I had rather been there than here under the eyes of this woman. She turned and I closed my eyes again, breathed steady to belie my wakefulness. I heard her search the room, quickly and quietly. I heard her open the inlaid chest where the gold and the *cartone* had lain till this very night, but there was nothing now within. The gold I had stolen was safe in my makeshift money belt under my skirts, and the painting now nestled in its accustomed home in my bodice. I silently thanked the Virgin that I had not changed to my nightshift this eve and that both secrets were upon my person. There was naught for her to find, and realizing this she turned to go. Gliding so smoothly across the rush mats that I wondered if she slept still. Then she stopped and I felt her eyes on me, heard her approach. The bed sagged as she sat beside me and I waited for the cold slice of the knife that had unmanned Bonaccorso Nivola. Still I did not let her see me wake; if she wished me dead I would die now, for all that I lived for was lost to me. I felt a touch, but it was a gentle hand that brushed a golden curl from my eye, tucked it tenderly behind my ear. Then she bent close, kissed me sweetly on the cheek as if I were still the babe that she had bottled and sent away. I felt her breath warm on my cheek, misting my skin as it had misted the glass; I felt the touch of her lips, the lips that hid the tongue that tasted the knife. Then she was gone.

It rained all night, outside my window and on my pillow.

35

I woke as if from a nightmare, queasy and hopeful. Sun gilded my window and the horrors of yesterday retreated for an instant, till memory called them to hand. I rose and stretched, my treacherous body hungry and thirsty, wanting succor, wanting to live. Marta came with my breakfast and I ate hungrily, not knowing what else to do. She brought me a magnificent gown, covered in its entirety in peacock feathers, with a mask to match. I stared at the crazy outfit, not comprehending.

"Carnevale" she said briefly.

Madonna. I had forgot.

Mutely I dressed, dumb as a puppet with no strength or will. I would be my mother's creature, for I could no longer see a way to escape, no longer hope to see Brother Guido again. It mattered not what I did.

At Prime I was summoned to my mother who kissed me on the same cheek as the night before, and eyed me fondly in my finery. She was dressed all in white feathers and had changed her lion's mask for a swan's countenance which she donned as we passed outside. My father met us at the foot of the Giants' staircase, where I had taken leave of Signor Cristoforo, in his *corno* hat and ceremonial gown. He did not greet me; I would have guessed that he had been told of my planned escape but for the fact that he *never* greeted me. I wondered how much he knew as he held out his hand to my mother and she placed her hand upon his.

As we progressed with the ducal retinue across Saint Mark's Square the pigeons rose before us in a cloud of smoke. Venice was a menagerie—citizens dressed as parrots and lions cavorted with tigers and monkeys, courtesans covered their faces but exposed their breasts. Vendors sold masks and cups of wine; circus wights danced on stilts or juggled fire. Actors screeched their bawdy lines in grotesque leering masks. The sun shone relentlessly, but the air was freezing. My breath smoked, yet the crown of my head burned. I did not know where we tended— I did not care. I walked behind my mother and she talked constantly to me over her shoulder of the sights we were to see, in such a kind and interesting manner that I wondered if my poor brain had invented the events of yesterday. She was a weathercock, altering with the climate. Yesterday storm and darkness, today burning sun.

Apparently we were to progress through the square, so the people may see us, then embark on the *Bucintoro* at the San

Zaccharia pier, to begin one of the most important rites of the festival—the Marriage of the Sea. My father was to take his barge to the center of the lagoon, and throw a priceless ring into the sea, to bring her favor on the city for the next twelve-month. I almost laughed—the San Zaccharia pier was the place I was to meet Bonaccorso Nivola.

The weather had another notion. Perhaps God, if there was one, was angered at the poor sailor's fate, for the sky darkened quick as a frown and thunder rolled in from the mountains. Rain beat down from the heavens and the crowd scattered under the colonnades—forks of lightning jabbed silver and blue from the clouds. The courtesans screamed and fled, hiking their skirts to reveal their hairy legs, breasts bobbing as they ran. Feathers and fur flattened, costumes bled their cheap dye onto the paving in a dirty rainbow stream. Everyone sheltered under the loggias around the square, chattering and laughing in fear. I was briefly alone, blinded by rain, a small smile curling my lip—a pox on the Venetians and their Carnevale! I opened my eyes to the heavens, willing the lightning to strike me, hoping my sodden hair was still gold enough to tempt its bolts. As if in answer to my prayer I was blinded once more as the sky split—but the lightning did not strike me; it served to illuminate a sight I had looked at every day but never really seen.

Before the great dome of the basilica, high, high on a gilded platform above the great door, stood four bronze horses, bathed in fire, noble, necks arched, mouths frothing and forelegs pawing the ground. They stood over the city, a threatening quartet. Many years in the future my husband would tell me that they were in fact thieved from the Hippodrome in Constantinople, the only remaining quadriga of the Roman world, and a symbol of Venice's secular might. But I am getting ahead of myself—that was long in the future, when I was married; at this point I had not even been reacquainted with my husband (I had met him, of course, more than once by this point in my history). That day, however, I thought I knew what the horses meant without any instruction. They meant the Apocalypse was coming to Venice. And I didn't give a shit.

And yet at this very second of the world ending and my not caring, for some strange reason, my brain decided to make amends for my thickheadedness of yesterday. The pieces suddenly resolved themselves—as the four winds battered me from every point of the compass, as my shoes filled and the great square began to flood, as I alone held forth like a doomed ship at sea, I finally realized what I had been taught. The rain beat down on my head, and as if they arrived with the raindrops, three thoughts suddenly plopped into my head.

Credo Uno: Flora had thirty-two roses in her skirts. There were thirty-two points of the compass rose.

Credo Due: there were four winds of the wind rose and four horses before me.

Credo Tre: Zephyrus, the west wind, raped Chloris. Chloris, the lover of the wind. Chloris my mother. Chloris who was Venice.

I knew, as if the lightning bolt had finally lit the dark corners of my mind in an illuminating flash, that whatever secret this city held was in the horse that stood at the extreme left, the west horse, the *ponente* horse.

The Zephyrus horse.

Then I felt a great tug of my sleeve. Marta, my millstone, had come for me and took me into the porch of the great basilica, where the ducal party dripped and steamed. Outside, the storm raged, the rain battered the great square till an inch of water stood on the ground. *Acqua alta*—high water had come; the sea made a bid to claim her city. My mother noted my presence with obvious relief—once again I realized that she cared for me and that she was pleased that I was safe. But I wasn't safe yet; none of us were. God was not afeared to strike his own house. With the herald of a great thunderclap, a boom and crack sounded from above and masonry began to fall. My father shouted above the screams:

"The gold of the roof attracts the lightning; we must repair to the palazzo."

It was the longest sentence I had ever heard him say.

He and my mother left first, followed by the crowd of ducal retainers. Marta was swept along with them, and I knew she could not yet miss me. I ducked into a niche and hid. I had no clear plan but to be as far away from my sorceress mother for as long as I possibly could. I needed space to think, space to act. As the atrium emptied I looked up, as if for inspiration, and saw before me a fantastic Roman mosaic of the four seasons. The figure of Spring, wreathed in flowers and mythical beasts coupling to reproduce—pairing off in this Noah's ark against the flood—sheltered by verdant leaves, looked straight at me and pointed skyward with her hand. I knew then that I was right.

I crept into the great dark space of the basilica, the floor already glazed with an inch of rain. The ark was taking on water. The incense was choking, and the voices of my father's priests were raised in supplication. They had failed to keep the plague from Venice, even to save my father's first wife from the pestilence. But with touching faith they tried once again to keep this most biblical of disasters at bay. I hung around the narthex, looking for a door which I knew must be there, for the goddess of Spring had told me so. I found the little portal and climbed the stair, higher and higher into the gallery. As I wound upward into the cupola, Byzantine faces regarded me with interest from their great almond eyes, unmoved as the lightning snaked into the arched windows, attracted to the golden tiles that paved their haloes.

As I stepped out onto the balcony the rain hit me like a blow, lightning struck the dome above, once and again, and I thought I would be sizzled like a scallop. I ducked behind the nearest horse to shelter—ironic, really, that these steeds of the wind should now shield me from a tempest. Only a few moments ago I would have happily jumped from here to my death; now I clung to the beast that sheltered me, hiding under his belly as a foal would suck milk. I knew I was at the wrong extreme—the eastern horse—so I inched past eight long hind legs and eight massive copper balls. At the westernmost horse I crept round to the front, clinging for life, and glanced up, dashing rain from my eyes. I looked into the huge, noble copper face of the Zephyrus horse, but his wild eyes told me nothing. He did, however, proffer his right foreleg, raised as a friendly cur would ask you to shake his foot. It felt natural to take the limb and I wrapped my frozen hand around the hoof, looking for an inscription, a clue, anything. The copper limb rang as the lightning struck the cupola again, humming faintly like a coin on a bell. The leg I held shook more, creaked, and fell into my hand. I barely caught the thing, and looked down, appalled at what I'd done—but it was hollow. Hollow, not heavy.

Madonna.

There was something within. I drew out a wooden roll, as long as my forearm, like a pin that pastry cooks use for flattening their *pasticcio*. Excited, I knew there must be something inside, a folded document, coins, a painting. I expected the roll to be hollow, a kind of cylinder, but it was solid wood. To be sure, there were markings upon it, but the grooves and curves, and crazy inscriptions, were meaningless to me. For all I knew it was merely a support that the copperwright had used to construct the beast, a skeleton to form the cast bronze, never meant to be seen by the eyes of admirers. I dropped the wood on the floor with a clatter, covered my face with my hands. When I took them away I knew that there would be someone standing before me, Marta or one of my father's guards.

And there was.

"I am ready," I said, "you can take me now."

But the presence before me was neither of those I expected, nor was it a creature of this world. A great lion stood there on his hind legs, with a face made of wrought gold and the body of a man. The mask resembled my mother's, save that it was a full-face mask not a half, a burning sun, a mane around the circumference like rays of fire, eyes and mouth open like the *Bocca del Leone*. Now I knew I was finished—the Apocalypse had come for me. The lion of Saint Mark—the creature I had feared since I had entered the Arsenale and sealed Bonaccorso's fate—the ruler of this city, had come to devour me.

I am a Daniel.

"I am ready," I repeated, "you can take me now." I thought I was already dead, for the creature looked on me with eyes that I'd dreamed of, spoke with a voice that I knew.

"Luciana. It is I."

I ripped the mask from his face, flung my arms around him fit to squeeze the life away, cried and laughed, would have kissed him a thousand times, but he held me away.

"No time," he said. He picked up the wooden roll and pressed it into my hands. "Keep the map safe. Have courage. I will meet you in Milan."

He looked straight at me once, as if memorizing my face, then he was gone in another flash of lightning as blue as his eyes, and Marta was upon me almost before I could hide the wooden roll in my sleeve.

Brother Guido must have passed her on the stairs.

By the time we left the basilica, the storm had passed and the sun shone again. The square was filled with water—the whole city stood on a mirror. I had never seen such a beautiful place. Marta, taking no chances, had an iron grip on my upper arm, a bruise tomorrow for certain. We waded in water up to our knees till we met the ducal litter coming for us, but I cared not.

He was alive.

36

I knew Marta would say nothing about my disappearance, the cowardly bitch. Luckily for her we had been parted so few minutes that no one in my father's house had noticed that we were not together. On our return I said we had been praying together for salvation. I saw my mother's swift glance, for she knew me not for a devout, but Marta agreed so swiftly that the matter was dropped. The girl knew what was good for her—my mother would have had her roundly whipped for losing sight of me even for a heartbeat, probably done the job herself, vicious witch that she was.

But I gave Marta no more trouble after that, oh, no. I was as nice as pie, as obedient as the good convent girl I once was. I attended all the Carnevale celebrations, talked politely to my father's allies, sewed at my mother's side, and took my lessons with obedience and diligence. It was enough for me that Brother Guido was alive, that he was not damaged by torture as Bonaccorso had been, and that he had pledged to see me again. I did not know or care how he had followed me here—that he had been here was enough. I dwelled on our brief meeting hundreds and thousand of times, every look and every word. I could not divine the meaning of any of it. I knew not how the wooden roll that I kept on my person at all times could be a map. I knew not how or when we would meet next, nor how the city he had mentioned fitted into the plan of the Seven. But I did not tax my poor brain—I accepted my fate. I had never been to Milan but I damn well would go now, no matter how long it took me to figure out how. My best chance for the present was to lie low and do exactly what the witch expected of me, until she relaxed her watch upon me.

And it was to prove easier than I thought. As soon as Carnevale was over, my mother announced that I was to ready myself for a long voyage. Now the thaw was coming we were to make our progress to Pisa to meet my betrothed and ready the marriage contracts in time for my summer wedding. I didn't care about any of this, but when my mother spoke of our itinerary I pricked up my ears—our route would take us first into the mountains to a place called Bolzano on some business of my father's, thence across the Dolomite range down into Lombardy where we would break our journey in Milan before passing through Genoa to Pisa. Better and better, I learned that even though we were to carry out some political mission in the doge's name upon the way, my father was not to be actually traveling with us. This was good news for me—although my mother was traveling as the doge's ambassador, she would only have such protection as was due to the Mocenigo family. The guards that attended my father—watchful, efficient, violent men—were attached to the ducal office and stayed with the doge at all times.

At last the day came—we were packed and prepared, the Carnevale was over. I took a chilly leave of my father, and my mother and I were back on the Grand Canal again, a full six months after we'd arrived.

Water, light.

I was a babe again, rocked in the watery sac of *Vero Madre's* womb. I was a child, rocking in her arms. I was a woman, rocking in a boat. Water beneath me. Light above. Light below me, water above. I was propped against velvet cushions in a golden boat. The prow of the boat was curved and slatted like an executioner's axe. Behind, a servant pushed us along with a pole, betraying the fact that the water was no more than waist deep; there were no countless fathoms below, just a shallow ditch. Many things in this place were not what they seemed.

But I cared no more for any of that, for the shifting deceptions, the appearance and reality of my birth city. Our possessions followed in flat barges behind us—we were headed to Marghera and the mainland—"Tramontana" to the mountains and beyond, and then—then—to Milan and a longed-for reunion. Farewell, cold, cold silver city. Good-bye, glass sea, glass houses, glass canals.

I cared not if I ever saw Venice again.

· 7 ·

Bolzano

37

I discovered just three things in the winter kingdom of Bolzano.

Scoperta Uno: that Zephyrus, the blue-green winged tree goblin of the *Primavera,* represents Bolzano.

Scoperta Due: my mother's name.

Scoperta Tre: the fact that it was possible for me to be colder than I was in Venice.

I jest of course.

That is, I suppose that won't do. I should tell you a little more of my stay in the mountains, but I do it reluctantly and I'll explain why. From the time I arrived to the time I left I was eaten up with impatience—I wanted to be nowhere else but Milan, and I wanted to get there as quickly as possible. I wanted to be with no one else but Brother Guido, and desired no other company. If my mother and I had stayed in Bolzano no longer than the time it takes to puff away the stamens of a dandelion clock, 'twould have been too long, too agonizingly long.

All right, here goes. Only do not expect me to be quite as thorough in this section of my history, as I was in the other cities we have visited. In the *Primavera,* Zephyrus does not have his feet on the ground. He is high and floating, above the other characters. Let this be my excuse: I suspected, perhaps I wanted to believe, that this city, of all, did not play such a vital part in the measure as the other cities did—that it was perhaps a little to the side, a little left out, perhaps not part of the grand scheme. Necessary, yes, but not (to use one of my husband's words) *integral*.

(He was right.)

In fact, I would have gone so far as to guess that Bolzano would not prove to be one of the Seven. For there were eight adult figures in the painting and a conspiracy of just seven—I guessed that Genoa and Milan would be the remaining members, that Bolzano would lift right out.

(I was wrong.)

It was certainly true that I felt my own feet did not touch the ground while I was there; I was suspended in limbo but elevated on a cloud of happiness and expectation, looking down on the world below, gulping the thin cold air, and wishing my time away, breathing away the hours like the dandelion clock.

My mother's business here was with Archduke Sigismund of Austria, a sprig of the Hapsburg family tree and cousin to some emperor. The name Hapsburg meant nothing to me, but it seemed to drop everyone else's mouth open like a market-day fish, so I guessed they were a family on a par with the Medici but from Austria, or was it Hungary? Or Germany? Anyway. Someplace in the frozen north, beyond the mountains. My mother and her retinue were in a constant babble about the Hapsburgs, and the Holy Roman Emperor, and the mountain routes, and mines, and something called the "Old Swiss Confederacy." But I closed my ears to all their cant as our covered carriages rose high into the mountains, white peaks turned amber and rose by the cold northern sun. Beautiful certainly. But chillier than Christmastide.

I just huddled down into my furs and thought of Brother Guido.

Presently, a sennight after we had left Venice, with Castelfranco and Trento behind us, climbing all the time, we entered a place of fable. I thought I had left the capital of deception behind us, but Bolzano had as many facets as a rose diamond. I would see a mountain transformed into a city, then a city transformed into mountain, each face and angle presenting a different view of the place. An enchanted sorcerer's eyrie, now here, now gone. And the whole thing bathed crimson by the sunrise, like a monstrance under stained glass.

We entered the town at a prettyish kind of square, huddled around with quaint wooden houses with boxes of winter blooms crammed at every window. There, too, stood a pattern-tiled duomo with a great spike for a spire, a sharp summit to rival those that ranged around. We drove through the square ever northward and just outside the town climbed to a great castle that seemed not built by man but hewn out of the rock. And pink. I thought at once that the impression of color was given, again, by the sun, but I was to learn as the day brightened to morning that 'twas no trick of the light, but merely the nature of the crop of porphyry rock from which this fortress, Castello Roncolo, was built. This fact was explained to me not by my mother but by one of the many Venetian strangers who traveled with us. A man whose name I never bothered to learn but who always rubbed his knuckles against my breasts when he handed me from the carriage. My mother, I noted with relief and regret, seemed to have given up my education entirely since my attempt to escape from Venice. She treated me with kindness and courtesy but largely let me be, which suited me fine. I had much daydreaming to do . . .

We wound through the castle gates and up to the massive battlements and gatehouse. After a series of endless ramps we entered a courtyard where we were met by the ducal retinue, who came to hand us down from the carriages, not fast enough, unfortunately, to stop what's-his-name jumping me down first in order to get his hands on my *tette*.

We swept through to the great hall amid any number of pleasantries, but as we entered the huge chamber I could not at once locate the archduke. For one thing there was such a press of people crowding his court, and for another, much more interesting scenes adorned the walls. The entire place was painted with coats of arms, scenes of games and jousting, gorgeous nobles and ladies, and grotesque giants and dwarves. I was so absorbed in the frescoes, rendered more real than if I watched players act before my eyes, I nearly missed a most interesting piece of information. The crowd parted like the Red Sea, and Ramses and Moses eyed each other. One of my mother's cronies announced in ringing Venetian:

"The Dogaressa Taddia Michiel Mocenigo!"

(This, if you can believe it, was the first time I had heard my mother's given name)

I turned my attention to the archduke, who rose to take my mother's hand. Archduke Sigismund was yet another in a series of powerful old men that I had met on this odyssey. Perhaps a little over fifty, he was unremarkable, save that he had silver curling hair that waved to his shoulders, was rail thin, and spoke with a thick guttural accent that I had to strain to understand. My poor ears were only just getting used to the Venetian dialect, and here I was battling with yet another strange tongue, as he greeted my mother and myself. Wearily I began to realize that this entire peninsula was run by powerful old men. Don Ferrente, the pope, Lorenzo de' Medici, and now this archduke. For a short and insane moment I felt a touch of pride in my mother—at least the crazy bitch wore the breeches in the city of Venice and ruled her man while letting him think he ruled her. I wondered how often such men were ruled by the women they'd married, or not married, but before I could speculate on this further, my questions were answered by my mother consoling the archduke on the loss of his wife, and in the same breath inquiring politely about the archduke's upcoming nuptials—apparently he was to be married when I was, to a maid called Katherine of Saxony. Their union promised to be at least as happy as mine, for I learned later that the Princess of Saxony was but sixteen and would have to endure that old lizard creeping over her young flesh at night. *Madonna.* I hoped he was rich.

Apparently he was. In a very short conference between him and my mother, I learned that he was being petitioned to finance some enterprise, in some sort of partnership with Venice. Here I pricked up my ears—did the archduke refer to the business my mother had come to transact in the name of the doge, or was there a larger scheme at stake—in fact, the unknown ultimate design of the Seven? I had to strain to decipher his accent, for his Venetian sputtered forth from him as if he were choking on thick soup.

"We have agreed on the larger principles and will use your sojourn here to establish the details. In fine, the matter of metals—"

My mother cut across him swiftly.

"Archduke, Archduke." She was at her most charming. "Such conference is not pleasing to the ears of young maids, and I have brought the finest maid in all of Venice to meet you. May I present my dearly beloved daughter, Luciana Mocenigo."

Marta gave me a vicious little shove and I stumbled forward so that all the eyes of the court were on me, including the twin gimlets of their overlord. You would think that I might be outfaced by such scrutiny, but I can tell you that when you have halted a Medici wedding, and your intended groom unwraps your hair in front of the congregation, to point to your own likeness in a painting, pretty much nothing will disconcert you again.

The archduke looked me over as if he were appraising horseflesh.

"She is exquisite. Not unlike yourself sixteen years ago. I remember well, a time when you were as young and untried." A look of great significance passed between them.

Now I divined three things from this statement.

Cosa Uno: my mother had been successful in keeping my history quiet. "Untried," indeed—little did the archduke know that I'd been ridden more times than a packhorse.

Cosa Due: the archduke and my mother had some sort of history—in fact, the words and the way in which they were spoke seemed to suggest that the old goat had taken her virginity. Wonder how she squared *that* with my father.

Cosa Tre: whatever had taken place in the past, I'm not sure he liked her now. There was an unmistakable barb in his voice, amid all the flowery pleasantry, as if a needle had been left in a finished tapestry to prick the fingers of the unwary.

The archduke spoke again. "She is betrothed to Pisa, I hear."

"She is. To be wed in July."

"Pity," remarked the archduke with a sniff, clearly already forgetting his own betrothed. I guess I was about the right age for him, being not seventeen myself. "I suppose she is full young to suffer our business. Do you, my dear, repair to your room, where I hope you will find all possible comfort."

I was betrothed to another and of no further interest.

Our audience concluded with a promise to meet this evening at the feast to be held in our honor. I sighed inwardly, wishing we could just be gone, but we were to stay until the morrow and I had to tolerate the delay as best I could. We both bent to kiss the archduke's hand. I was half expecting what I saw there, so you will certainly not be surprised when I tell you that there was the golden Medici ring, complete with *palle*, glinting upon his thumb.

Thus dismissed, I followed Marta and a servant from the room, while my mother remained behind to unburden her business to the archduke. I was at once vexed and relieved; my mother had demonstrated once again how little she now trusted me, and had gone to great lengths to prevent the archduke from spilling any of their dealings in my presence. Ah, well. At least I did not have to be troubled with her instruction, for I had no head for politics. I just wanted to see my friend again.

I was conducted up a cramped stone spiral to yet another grand chamber in another alien palace, this time a painted one with incredible scenes rampaging across the stones. This time the frescoes told a story that seemed to pertain to a knight, a king, and his lady love. It was evident that the maiden was having her fun with both the king and his dragon-slaying champion. I sighed wistfully. But one man would do for me, if only he were the right one.

The chamber was gloomy; indeed I could hardly follow the story of the doomed lovers in the low light, so I flung open the casements. The view from my window was so dizzying it made my breath short, for a sheer drop greeted my curious glance down, and wicked mountain peaks closed all around. I shut the windows swiftly but was instantly plunged back into gloom— the quarrels of the panes were round and crude, as if someone had hacked off a dozen bottle bottoms and cobbled them together with more lead than pane. Clearly the glassmaking genius of Venice had not reached the barbarous north. I snorted contemptuously down my nose. An odd trick of distance made me proud of my home city. Now that I didn't have to live in it.

I opened the window again. We were so high that the clouds hung directly outside my window, and kites and buzzards landed on my windowsill to eye me curiously with their glass-bead eyes, before taking a stomach-lurching dive into the abyss below. I wondered if my mother had chosen my chamber deliberately, that I might not escape. I did not even bother to try the iron ring on the door. I had clearly heard the key turn behind me. It was so; my mother was taking no chances. Well, at least I was alone—better to be locked in than to be allowed to promenade under the eyes of the ever-present Marta.

I heard the bells ring Nones with the dull clop of a cowbell. With nothing to do till Vespers and dinnertime I took out the *cartone* again, brought it as close to the window as I dared, sitting precariously on a wooden bench by the sill. The wind whistled through the casement, but the lack of glazing left me with an unwelcome choice to be freezing cold or be in pitch-darkness. I kept my fur on and the shutters open, for I needed the light.

I wanted to learn as much as I could of Bolzano, one, I now knew, of the Seven. To make Brother Guido proud. To do, as I was here, what he couldn't do at his distance, to divine the role of this place in the great plan. Would north be true?

First I looked at the entire *cartone* once again. We now, I thought, knew all of the Seven. Pisa, Naples, Rome, Florence of course, Venice, Bolzano, and obviously Milan, as Brother Guido said we would meet there, and my mother agreed that we would break our journey in that city. And the conspirators too: Lord Silvio della Torre of Pisa; Don Ferrente, the King of Naples and Aragon; His Holiness the Pope of Rome; Doge Giovanni Mocenigo of Venice; Archduke Sigismund of Bolzano; and someone or other in Milan, a name I supposed Brother Guido would supply.

We had built up a better picture of the players involved, but we still did not know what they intended. We knew who, but not what or when or *why*.

And what role did Genoa play? That seagoing city, home of my faithful friend Signor Cristoforo? Why was Genoa in the painting if not in the Seven?

I thought on this till my head began to hurt, then gave up and focused my attention on the Zephyrus figure. Now I imagined Brother Guido beside me, guiding me. *What may we observe? Just begin with whatever comes to mind.*

In a very little time I had quite a list:

He had wings.

His hair was blue.

His wings were blue.

His gown was blue, and curled like the sea.

His flesh, now I came to look at it, was more silver than blue.

His feet were not visible.

His cheeks puffed out.

A silver stream of wind issued from his lips.

His eyes looked into Chloris's and nowhere else.

He grabbed at Chloris, intent on ravishment.

He was behind some laurel branches.

He was before some orange trees.

He was higher than Chloris, or any other figure in the picture save Cupid.

Behind his left knee, and the trunks of the oranges and laurels, was a silver-blue mountain range.

Even without my educated friend I was able to draw some conclusions from what I saw. Zephyrus was higher than Venice—Bolzano was in the mountains, a fact supported by the silver-blue mountain range at Zephyrus's knee, and by the wings to lift him high. Bolzano was northwest of Venice (I blessed Signor Cristoforo's instruction) and possibly represented some sort of threat, for Zephyrus was swooping down from the mountains. Perhaps to attack? And the color blue? That was easy—I only had to look at my poor fingers where they held the *cartone*. Blue as Boreas, or rather, Zephyrus. The meaning of the laurels and oranges was also clear; he was between the laurel, Lorenzo di Pierfrancesco's emblem, and the orange, Lorenzo the Magnificent's emblem. Zephyrus was girdled all around with Medici foliage, buried deep in a Medici plot.

I could not guess why his skin was silver, unless 'twere some reference to water. The wings, too, puzzled me. Did they indicate a certain bird, or was Zephyrus just depicted so because he was a wind and traveled on the ether? I began counting feathers, mindful that Flora's thirty-two roses had led me, finally, to the compass rose. But that had been hard enough; this was impossible. I gave up quickly and instead spent some little time trying to interpret the expression that the West Wind wore, and the nymph Chloris too. The legend, according to Signor Cristoforo, went that Zephyrus ravished Chloris, got her with child, and the nymph gave birth to the wind horses. But although his posture to her was very threatening— swooping down from on high—and although, to be sure, she seemed to be running and reaching for the protection of Flora, there was, on second look, more tenderness in the eyes of the couple than you might think. Chloris looked almost mesmerized, both desiring and fearing all at once—like a virgin, touched for the very first time. Zephyrus, too, though serious in his mien, inclined his head to his lady. And the hand he placed upon her was relaxed and soft, not grabbing, for the thumb was not visible—in a *violent* act surely it would have appeared to help the fingers grab gown and flesh. No, this was more of a . . . a caress. I wondered if this was a union of mutual benefit, much like the puzzling conference I had heard downstairs. I think my mother needed Sigismund *and* feared him. And the archduke needed Venice's connivance for some reason, but meant the city no harm. Rather he wished for the relationship to have an issue, to bear fruit. We knew my mother was Chloris—'twas plain from the likeness and from her own admission—and now I knew we must cast Archduke Sigismund as the actor who would represent Zephyrus in our play. If only I had been able to divine what their joint venture might be! But my mother had couched her words so carefully and caged their meanings—as I had guessed, she did not trust me an inch since I had planned my flight. I almost crumpled the *cartone* in frustration. Not for the first time I cursed my impulse to escape from Venice—I had bought a whole heap of trouble for more than just myself. I should have trusted Brother Guido to come for me. And now here I was in prison, shut out of the conference that was taking place downstairs, ignorant of what connected Bolzano and Venice, two members of the Seven.

'Twas lucky I had almost balled the *cartone* in my fist for the key turned in the lock and I was obliged to shove the painting down my front. A rosy apple of a goodwife entered, wearing a gray house robe and a linen wimple. She was almost hid behind a huge soft mass of white fur—had she brought a bear to share my cell? Her smile had more charm than teeth, and she handed me the bundle, so heavy it made me stagger.

"For you. The archduke—he wants," she choked in her weird voice, bowed and left.

I examined what I held. Was it a coverlet to keep me warm at night? No, it had sleeves and a hood—it was a *coat,* of white fur, the like of which I had never seen. Thankfully I snuggled into it and felt the difference at once. I *blessed* whatever monstrous mountain creature had shed its skin for me.

I danced a little twirling jig so the pelts swung around my legs, and I was warm at last. The scenes of the faithless maid and her two lovers wheeled around me in a colored mass. Then I stopped at once, as if stunned.

I had not heard the key turn back again.

Heart thumping, I turned the iron ring of the door handle. It turned silently, the latch lifted. I could have kissed the goodwife who had brought the coat. I was free.

I drew up the hood of my new gift. Since no one had seen me wearing it, perhaps it would give me a little anonymity, although it certainly would not conceal me from the eye, as it was white as milk. I descended down the passages and steps I remembered, to the hall of the Giants, by virtue of the paintings I had remembered on the walls. The door was guarded by two surly soldiers.

Shit.

So I turned on my heel and climbed up the stairs again. I made a few turns to find the chamber I thought would be above the great hall, and here my luck improved. A chamber, empty, with candles burning. Painted, as the rest of the place, but this time with scenes of devotion. It was a chapel.

I closed the oaken doors and looked about me. Here once again I was assisted by the ancient building. Drafts whistled up through boards along with snatches of conversation. I knelt as if in prayer and applied my ear to a crack in the planks as long as an oar. Voices were raised—my mother's and the archduke's too—which helped me hear all.

My mother first. "And yet you market through Venice to Alexandria, to Tunis, to India . . ."

The archduke: "Precisely, Dogaressa. We market *through* *Venice*. Our treaty states that we will use your port and your port only, your ships. I see no reason for such niceties to cease . . . afterward. Then, too, you have the treaty ratified by my cousin Hapsburg, the guarantee of safe passage through these mountains, the emperor's own seal upon it that there will be no attack on the Seven from the Hapsburg lands. We have repaid our debt many times over. Yet this matter of the angel is another issue."

"The golden angel has been circulating in England for more than twenty years, with great benefits to commerce. Regulation can only strengthen trade." My mother's voice, lively with argument.

"That is so; I don't think we have ever been in dispute over the matter. Is he entirely decided upon the weights and measures?"

"Our understanding is that the fineness would be that of his own florin. Or our own Mocenigo."

"Ah, yes, the Mocenigo. Your family stamp. I am sure that is what *you* would prefer. Yet I was thinking back a little further, to the fourth Crusade. To your forebear, Doge Enrico Dandolo. For did he not set the standard for the *grosso*? War costs, and peace is even dearer. This enterprise upon which we embark will be dearly bought. Now that we crusade again, shall we not strike an equivalent?"

My mother's voice, raised now. "A *grosso*? Surely you jest. The standard of the *grosso* was 124 *soldi*. Are you seriously suggesting an angel of this weight? Venice does not have the seam!"

The archduke's voice, calm, quiet, assured, infinitely powerful. "Venice does not. *I* do."

A pause. "In truth?" My mother, a little awed.

"I have my *own* standard here, you know."

"I do know, not for nothing are you known as *der Münzreiche*." My mother, flattering now.

"Indeed. Then you should know that I can underwrite that side of the bargain, for these mountains are richer than even

379

Solomon could ask. Yet our request from you, ratified by our mutual friend, is that, as you know, we will borrow your own expertise in this area. For the overheads are considerable. Assaying, casting, cutting blanks, stamping. Will you use the Zecca?"

My mother again. "Not the Zecca. All operations must be outside the city. This enterprise is to be kept secret, on *his* orders. And since you cannot come to the Zecca, I have brought the Zecca to you."

"Here?"

"Here. In my train are the finest craftsmen our city can provide, the heads of their divisions at the Zecca. I thought to leave them here, so that they may instruct your own men in your own seam. Or *our* own seam."

"It will belong to the Seven, as *he* has agreed. So *neither* of ours."

"Or *both* of ours." They were sparring again, and my mother had won the bout. "We leave tomorrow, for we must meet my lord the doge in Milan presently."

"He brings the map?"

"He does. It is safe under his own roof."

Now this, as you can imagine, made my ears prick and my bowels loosen. *My father was to bring the map.* If they meant the wooden roll I now held in my sleeve, when he went to seek it in the Zephyrus horse, he would find it gone. But I still could not see how the wooden roll could *be* a map—perhaps there was another map that my father would bring from "under his own roof"—in another location, signposted in the painting, hid somewhere in the palazzo maybe. And yet, the basilica was his "own roof" too; my mother had ofttimes told me that the great church was my father's private chapel and part of his palace. I stilled my pattering thoughts lest I miss some tidbit from below.

"Then tonight it must be. After the feast my sappers will lead your men down."

"My men *and* myself."

A pause from the archduke. "Dogaressa, it is a perilous place."

"No matter. I am accustomed to peril."

"Then if I may address you on a matter of some delicacy, may I recommend that you . . . ah . . . wear some . . . breeches." A snuffly laugh, like a pig truffling, issued from the archduke and I got the idea that he rarely gave way to mirth. I knew from the jest that Archduke Sigismund had heard the same rumors about my mother and father's relationship that had reached the ears of Don Ferrente, namely that she wore the breeches in the marriage.

"Very well." My mother was cold as the climate. "But let it be understood that I will need to take a blank with me, so that it may be properly and independently assayed."

"Independently assayed by your own inspectors." The archduke scoffing now.

"No." My mother was all steel. "By *his*."

A pause from the archduke. "Then of course. In fact, let me have one stamped. Then *he* may admire the design. I assume you have brought the cast?"

A silence. I guessed there had been a nod from my mother.

"Well. I will be interested to see it for myself. Perhaps I will join you tonight, if you will permit me."

"So be it."

At least one party left the room at this point, and as I heard the doors I raised myself up on stiff knees, rubbed my sore ear, and scampered back to my room as quick as I could, lest my mother be coming up the stair to me. Back in my freezing eyrie I tried to make sense of what I'd heard.

The repeated reference to an angel explained Zephyrus's

wings, but a *golden* angel? Zephyrus was more *silver* if anything. At least I knew for sure that my mother and the archduke were involved with the Seven, that it wasn't some invention. *Madonna,* my mother could lie like the devil! All her cant about the *Primavera* being an innocent wedding gift, a celebration of beauty. My arse.

I did not know what the Zecca was, for if it was someplace in Venice, my mother had, deliberately or no, left it off our itinerary. Talk of treaties and trading had largely gone over my head, and I wished I'd paid more attention to my mother's tuition back when she was willing to give it to me. I was a little nearer to knowing why she had brought a carriage of strange men with us—they were experts of some sort. I sighed. Eavesdropping had made me no wiser, but I knew one thing. I had to follow my mother and the archduke tonight, wherever their "perilous" destination might be.

I knew this would be difficult, for no sooner had I returned to my room than Marta entered with the goodwife that had brought the coat. This time, the little woman had her arms full of rose silk—a gown from my own coffers cunningly chosen to match the stones of the castle—and some rare pink diamonds set in ivory combs for my hair. Together, mutely, they began to prepare me for dinner. Marta's clumsy hands, which stuck me once and again in my tender scalp with the combs, made me wish for my own Yassermin, but I must have looked nice when they had done, for the goodwife exclaimed in her strange tongue and clapped her hands together. I shivered without my coat from cold and nervous excitement about what the night would bring, and put it back on as soon as they were done.

Then we proceeded down to another grand hall, girdled around with scenes of jousting, and sat at one side of four tables set end to end in a great square. I greeted the archduke and thanked him for my coat. He coughed something polite at me in his dialect, presumably a compliment for he was smiling his wolf's grin. Then he said something which sounded like *"Ursus maritimus."* I had a little more Latin these days, from my association with Brother Guido, but my translation here cannot have been accurate—did he really think that my coat had come from some great white bear that swam in the cold northern seas? I smiled and nodded, and backed away. Left him to my mother's considerable charms.

I had no high hopes of the meal, for everything in Castello Roncolo seemed to take us back in time, at least a hundred years to the time of knights of old. Already I could see the open fires burning in the vast castle hearths, with the room so smoky it was hard to see your hand in front of your face. Castle curs crouched below the boards slavering at the meat smells and hoping to catch a few morsels. I half expected a jester to appear, and someone not far off did, a foolish fellow dressed in motley, wailing out local folk songs in a howling voice so discordant that the curs joined in. Then, as another fellow blew an enormously long mountain horn, our entertainment began to leap and dance like a lunatic, slapping his short leather hose and other parts of his body in a bizarre percussion. I wondered if he was jug-bitten, and his antics gave me an idea.

As was customary, Marta and I ate from the same plate, lest someone should try to poison the doge's heir. This was a strange feast indeed—the backward nature of the place was reflected in the fare, and we dined on peasants' food of smoked ham called speck, foul-smelling local cheese chestnuts, and strange little dumplings that seemed to be called *Knödel*. I longed for my father's table and the fine fish and pasta that we dined on nightly. But the food was not my concern this night—crucially, Marta and I drank from the same jug of wine. The meal may have been rough and rustic, but the wine was plentiful—yellow as piss and set before us in clay jugs packed in mountain ice. One long pull made me feel colder inside than out. *Good.* It helped that I did not like the wine, for I needed a clear head. I pushed the jug aside and filled up Marta's cup, watched her drink, then filled it again. The greedy wench drank again.

Now, usually I will match my servant at the table. But I did not care for white wine, and besides, my plan was to let Marta have the lion's share of the jug. She drained it. I called for more. By her second jug the dour, plain wench was flush-faced and chattering, lolling on my shoulder like a soul mate, and confiding in me about a kitchen lad of my father's, called Alvise, who had once tumbled her in the *calle.* I almost felt sorry that I might be buying her a whipping by dawn.

My scheme worked almost too well. Marta was in such a state that we almost had to leave the table sooner than was polite. My mother's eye was upon me, but since Marta was with me, she could see naught amiss and turned back to the archduke.

Outside, plenty was amiss—as we hit the fresh air Marta vomited copiously in the courtyard. I had to help her to my room, and since she could not even put one foot in front of another, it was child's play to help her with the key and then pocket it. In the painted chamber she slumped upon her truckle bed at the foot of mine, her snores sounding before her head even hit the pillow. I slipped out and turned the key on her, the captor captive.

I crept back down to the courtyard and loitered in shadow till the feast ended, at once blessing my new coat and cursing its color. I damned the *Ursus maritimus,* wherever he may live. I knew it would be difficult to follow my mother so dressed, for I was a walking snowdrift.

Finally, finally, my mother's party emerged with the archduke and my mother dressed as if for hunting, with her half-dozen Venetian strangers in tow. I loitered by the gatehouse and joined the party fluidly as the guards let them pass, then hid in the undergrowth again as soon as they were clear of the walls, heart thudding in my throat. Now the *Ursus maritimus* was my friend once more, for in his white pelt I was invisible in the snowy landscape. I let the party get ahead, in no fear of losing them for they all carried burning brands, and the torchlight glowed down the mountain leading me like the Bethlehem star.

I followed the amber comet down the mountain a little way, till the party stopped. Then the streaming tail of the comet disappeared to leave a burning circle, and all of a sudden the light was gone.

Pulses pounding, I rushed to the spot where the light had disappeared. A small clearing offered me no cover, but the party had vanished and I recklessly rushed into the open, looking about me, everywhere but down. Presently I came to a halt and fell to my knees, looking down at last in despair. Then I learned that 'twas fortunate, indeed, that I had stopped when I did, for I was on the lip of a gaping hole, open like the mouth of a well, descending to inky black. I shivered inside my coat, for I could easily have run straight over it and broken my neck as I crashed into the fathomless depths. Now I understood why the torchglow had become a circle then gone, for all the party had climbed down here, the light pouring from the mouth of the cavern, only to fade as the group moved down into the shaft. I got on my belly and inched to the lip of the thing—yes, there was a deep saffron glow from within, and I knew now that 'twas not a well but some sort of entrance to an underground tunnel. There was silence from below and I knew them to be some way down. I felt in the soft earth for handholds and found a greasy rope tied to a stake. I took a deep breath, as if I were about to swim, and lowered myself over.

There were footholds in the walls, great gobs of bites taken out of the stone, and my fancy pointed shoes refused to be stuffed into them. My feet scrabbled and the tendons in my arms cracked. The coat was heavier than a millstone—I should have left it in the spinney. I longed to kick off my shoes but dared not, lest they fall on some fellow below and give me away. I half slid, half kicked my way to the ground, my ungloved hands burning on the rope, my legs flailing. I hoped the shaft were none too deep, and a morbid thought visited me of the head of Brother Remigio, severed and bouncing down Santa Croce's well. I swallowed my rising fear and thought of a happier time underground—when Brother Guido and I had been together in the Roman Catacombs. With his face in my mind's eye I found courage, and at the same moment my feet found the ground.

And now—a fresh problem. There were six tunnels radiating out from the main shaft, and since the atrium itself was studded with torches set into wall sconces, I could not guess which one the archduke and my mother might have taken. I listened, trying to quiet my breathing and still my heart, then I heard a ringing sound—a blow, like metal upon metal. Surely no one fought here? Was there treachery afoot? Had the archduke brought my mother down here to murder her? With mixed feelings about the fate of my mother—did I care or not?—I hurried in the direction of the sound upon silent feet.

The passage took me down and down, the stone underfoot becoming more and more slimy and slippery with moisture with every step I took. Presently the narrow tunnel ballooned into a cave, and the amber glow grew stronger. I knew the party were in the great rocky chamber I approached, for I could hear the voices of the archduke and my mother, booming through the cave. I clambered high upon an outcrop of stones, peeped over the lip of the rocks, and could see everything; all the players were there, in a circle of torchlight having a conference. I felt as if I watched a play. My mother, alive and well, was speaking, and her voice echoed from the stones.

"Archduke. May I present the best that the Zecca can offer. Signor da Mosto, our assayer." A dour fellow in a black-and-white cloak, with a soft square black felt four-cornered hat, stepped forward. "Signor Mantovano, our ironsmith." A squat fellow with the filthiest hands I've ever seen. "Signor Contino, our silversmith." Ah! The lecherous fellow from the carriage train. "And Signor Sarpi, our moneyer." Signor Sarpi was a giant of a man, wearing naught but breeches and a wide wrestler's belt, and brandishing a hammer. I no longer feared for my mother with such a fellow at her command. "And when I say that they are the best that the Zecca can offer, then you know I am telling you that they are the best anywhere, for you do not need me to tell you that the Zecca of Venice is the finest mint to be found anywhere on this earth." I heard the civic pride in her voice but was no nearer divining her meaning. What did this strange collection of men *do*? Why were they so important that they traveled with her in the Mocenigo carriage? Two of them had a noble stamp, but the other two looked like peasants.

"Signor Mantovano, the cast, please." My mother held out her hand and the fellow named as an ironsmith dropped a heavy object into her hand—heavy by the way that her palm dropped. The thing divided into two. "The seal," she commanded.

"May I see?" The archduke stepped into the light. After a moment he said, "A very striking design. A trifle aggrandizing, but we know the tastes of our friend. And the themes are most apt. Let us see the blank." The silversmith stepped forth with a round silver disk that winked in the torchlight.

Then it was the assayer's turn. He stepped forth with a pair of delicate scales, two little brass pans suspended from a copper bar, all on a fine golden chain. He neatly dropped a lead ingot into one pan, the disk into another. "One hundred and twenty-four," he announced. "I declare this a silver angel."

"Well, then," said the archduke, rubbing his hands like a child at Christmastide. "Let us strike one. Signor?" he addressed the moneyer. The silversmith took the cast and placed the blank disk upon it, put the other half of the die on top, and stood back. "We are witnessing history," pronounced the archduke, just as the moneyer swung his hammer and fetched the top of the die an almighty thwack.

History was not quite ready to be witnessed, for the burly moneyer, clearly put off his stroke by the archduke's awesome pronouncement, misstruck; the disk sheared off into the dark, whistling past my ear. They all looked in my direction and I ducked as fast as I could. As I hid, the truth was revealed; for at my feet was a silver coin, lying where it had fallen. The angel had flown to me. I had time to put the thing in my sleeve before I stood once more.

There was an uncomfortable shuffling of feet when I looked back, and the archduke had raised an eyebrow at my mother.

"I'm sorry, Dogaressa," mumbled the giant. "'Tis the light. I do not habitually strike by torch."

"Do it *better*," spat my mother, and I know she would have slapped him had he not been so large. "Your guild's reputation is at stake, and Venice's too."

This time the strike was true, and the sound rang out like a bell. The first angel had been struck, and was lifted from the stamp and handed to the archduke.

He turned it in his hand. "Very fine," he said. "I will keep this upon account, to show to the emperor." He handed it to his servant before my mother could protest.

As this could only be the conclusion of their business, I slid to the ground as swiftly as I could.

But my luck had ended. My descent began a small avalanche of pebbles, and the party beyond the rocks fell silent at the sound.

"Spies!" hissed Archduke Sigismund from the cavern. *"Move."*

As if he addressed me, I ran back to the atrium for my very life. Not the coat or my shoes could hinder me as I shinned up the rope and into the clearing, and tore into the woods to hide behind the thickest trunk I could see. I almost ran for the *castello* in my panic till I realized I could not gain entry without the party. The next few heartbeats, waiting for them, were agonizing—my body screamed at me to run but my mind knew I must not. Two guards, my mother, the archduke, and the Venetians emerged from the shaft in turn.

"No one," said the archduke. He looked directly at my mother. "A rat, I suppose." There it was again, that half-taunting, half-joking cadence to his voice—I could still not divine whether he hated her or loved her. They were Zephyrus and Chloris indeed. "You do not fear rats, Dogaressa?"

"Not of the animal kingdom, no," she replied, but she had a watchful air. "I suggest we return to the castle—there is a little matter of which I need to make certain."

With a cold rush that had naught to do with the midnight chill, I knew she was talking about me. I trailed them back to the *castello,* more silently than before. Their conference continued, but I could not hear for the blood that rushed in my head. I could think of nothing other than returning to my room before my mother knew I was gone. I could not believe, now, that I had risked so much, when I could have stayed safe in my room, slept soundly, and just waited for tomorrow's carriage to take me to Milan and Brother Guido. I hoped the coin I held was worth the risk. I could not believe I would be able to gain entry with the party without discovery, for surely anyone may leave a castle; getting in may be another issue. But the sleepy guards merely counted our number back in, and as the tally was the same as those who had left, I was given pass with the others. Fortunately my mother was obliged to offer her good-nights to the archduke as was his due, so I was able to slip up the gatehouse stairs. I fled to my room, fumbling for the key I had stolen from Marta. It fairly rattled in the wards as my feverish hand trembled. Would I wake Marta? The door swung open and I saw my drunken sot of a maid in the exact same position I had left her. I turned the key behind me and kicked off my shoes and slithered out of my dress. I leaped upon the bed and dragged the white bear pelt over my naked body, now no longer goosefleshed but incandescent with heat. I knew my cheeks would be hectic and my hair damp from the cold night air so I turned my face from the door and tried to still my breathing, for I knew *she* would come.

And she did. There was a furious rap upon the door. "Marta! Marta!"

A hellish groan from my side.

"Marta!" The rapping grew louder. And my maid lumbered to her feet, stumbled to the door, fumbled with the key. The door flew wide and my mother strode in. She must have seen me at once, for she lowered her voice to a whisper—but her tone was clearly no less frightening to the terrified Marta.

"Foolish girl, did you not hear me call?"

Marta slurred something. Then I heard two stinging blows as my mother slapped her twice across the cheeks forward and back. "Yes, you will hear me now. Listen to me well. Has Signorina Luciana left the room this night? Has she left the room?"

"No, Dogaressa!" protested my hapless maid. "We feasted and returned here, and we have been asleep ever since."

I heard my mother breathe relief, then seek to justify her hasty entry. "Look alive, you stupid, drunken chit. You are to look after my daughter at *all* times, do you hear? I did not give you permission to sleep! You may sleep in the carriages tomorrow, when *la signorina* is in *my* safekeeping. Do you hear?"

"Yes, Dogaressa."

I feigned sleep through this but was also listening carefully, as you may imagine. Once again I got the puzzling sense that my mother really did love me, and that she was in equal parts concerned that I had spied upon her and worried for my safety if I had left this room. She was an odd mixture indeed—but what I most feared now was that she would come over to me and sit beside my "sleeping" form as she had done once before. If she should smooth my hair, or even kiss my heated cheek as she had done in Venice, I was done for. But I thought I knew my mother well enough to know that she would not show the weakness of affection in front of a servant, and I was right. She withdrew, and my maid sat at the hard bench at the window groaning and wakeful, to watch me as the night paled to dawn. As my heart slowed and I drifted to sleep at last, I almost felt sorry for her. Almost.

In the rosy morning we left the city. As our carriages wound away from the gates, I noted that the archduke had not risen to bid us good-bye and I didn't blame him—for I had only had a couple of hours' sleep myself. The strange Venetians were no longer with us. I knew now they would stay and train Sigismund's miners and moneyers. My mother, it seemed, felt comfortable that their business had been successfully concluded, for even she felt able to lower her guard long enough to sleep. It was a sight I had never seen before, and it was an arresting one—she slept quietly and tidily across from me. Not for her the grunting snores or drool that assailed me from Marta at my left shoulder. In rest, my mother's face relaxed from its haughty expression and she looked younger than ever. Her long lashes lay on her cheeks, the dawn sun gilded the tiny hairs on her skin like the warm fuzz of an apricot. Her lips slightly parted, full and pink, her pearl teeth peeping from within, and her yards of precious hair loose on her shoulders like a new bride, gold in the sun like the first barley harvest. I had to admit, the bitch was beautiful.

I shifted in my seat, ready to sleep myself, and the silver coin in my sleeve cut into my side. I pulled it out to take a look, safe in the sleeping company. On one side, a man's head stamped with a profile I knew well, for I had seen and admired it in his family church of San Lorenzo in Florence, watching his cousin wed.

It was the noble Medici profile of Lorenzo il Magnifico.

Lorenzo was the "he" that the archduke and my mother constantly mentioned but never named.

Something strange, though—he was wearing his own laurel leaves in the sunray arrangement of the garland of Sol Invictus I had seen in Rome. And on the other side stamped into the silver was a single word—whose letters I spelled out laboriously: I-T-A-L-I-A.

Italia. I turned the coin over and over again in my hand, the morning sun glinting on the newly marked silver, the flashes crossing the face of my sleeping mother. What was she *up* to, she and Lorenzo and the others? *Italia.* The word meant nothing to me but was not wholly unfamiliar, and I knew I'd heard it before. I was too tired to rack my poor brain. It would come to me. *Italia. Italia.* The word became one with the rumble and rhythm of the carriage wheels. *I-tal-ia, I-tal-ia, I-tal-ia.*

I slept.

· 8 ·

Milan

38

My mother watched me lazily as we traveled, through eyes that were mere glittering crescents.

I felt the *cartone* in my bodice, the wooden roll in one sleeve, and the silver coin in the other every time I shifted position, and felt as if her gaze saw through my clothing. I determined not to sleep at all on the journey, fought hard to keep awake after the night I'd had, for I trusted my mother no more than she trusted me. I knew she suspected me, knew she thought there had been foul play in Bolzano—that I'd given Marta the slip. I knew she searched my chamber routinely, wondered that she hadn't yet searched my person. I even had the bitch's mask in the hood of my cloak. I met her eyes and dropped mine, wary lest she guess at my thoughts. My treacherous lids closed and sleep took me.

A tinkle of falling metal awoke me moments or hours later. Marta was gone from my side but my mother still regarded me lazily, a lioness watching her prey. But outside the carriage the world had changed again: I looked from the window to see enormous glassy lakes lying at the foot of emerald mountains. Still and serene, they invited the eye with their loveliness.

"The water is poisoned," said my mother, following my gaze. It was the single thing she uttered to me on the journey. We had shifted once again, like the breath of the breeze ruffling the waters of the lake, disturbing and repainting the sky in its image. The wind had changed and the weathercock had turned. We were once again, for some unspoken reason, at war.

In another day we were passing through the massy city gates of Milan, a closed place, ringed with a rosary of walls and gates. I was once again in a ferment of impatience and excitement, and the moment the guards on the postern let us pass and closed their pikes behind us I began to look for Brother Guido in every doorway, to listen for his voice over the beat of hooves and the hollers of traders, to seek his features in the face of every noble and peasant we passed. I barely noticed long, wide roads with brand-new silver-stone buildings; nor the elegant Roman pillars of the colonnades that showed the new marched side by side with the old. Even the miraculous Duomo, with its forest of silver spires tipped with gold like a diadem, left me unmoved. It was not a place but a person that I sought.

At every moment I willed him to come to me, to snatch me from the carriage to press me to him and carry me away— even though I knew such things were not his monkish way. I tried to sit still and trust, but my heart sank as we approached a vast bloodred fortress with battlements like the wards of a thousand keys that would serve to keep me in and Brother Guido out. We passed through the great gates of a clock tower beneath the baleful eye of a coiled serpent carved in stone upon the castle arms. Poised to strike.

Inside, the stone walls were the brutal red of battle-gore, but the castle itself was beautiful; a fortress with a moated palace within. The round towers reached high into the orange sky, where strange shredded clouds the color of oxblood flew like pennants. Had Brother Guido penetrated these precincts, this barracks of a place? For a massive square of grass had become a parade ground—ranks upon ranks of soldiers were drilled through their paces. Hundreds of lean, tall young men all had cropped hair, curved swords, and cloaks of the same shade of ocher, a shade that was familiar to me but wouldn't be pinned down by memory. The men reacted as one to the shouts of a man in armor mounted on a huge black brute of a horse. We descended from the carriage amid the maneuvers, my mother and I, but the soldiers were so well trained that not one of them spared two such visions a glance. The *capitano*, however, trotted over, and his steed pranced and reared like a statue, the huge black shadow near blocking the sun.

"Dogaressa!" he yelled, as if he still continued the drill. "This is delightful. And your daughter?" He jumped from the beast, and a single soldier broke rank to dangle from the stallion's reins. The *capitano* threw his helmet onto the turf where it landed with a clank. A neat curtain of smooth black hair fell about his ears, cut like a pageboy's, as if his man had placed a trencher on his head and sliced around it with the shears. Even more familiar now, he took off his iron gauntlets and offered us both a vast sweaty paw. The three words that he uttered—"Ludovico Maria Sforza"—were enough to make my mother drop to her knees. Thus I learned three things from this tiny encounter.

Cosa Uno: he was overlord of the whole place.

Cosa Due: my mother was much more in awe of this friendly, bluff soldier than she had been of that cold fish Sigismund.

Cosa Tre: he wore the golden ring of the *palle* on his left thumb. Such sights had long since ceased to shock me.

I waited for my instructions as my mother and the lord of Milan exchanged pleasantries. I thought I knew my own drill by now: lovely to meet you, here are your rooms, see you at the feast tonight.

But this time it was different. I was not taken to the residence across the moat, which clearly housed the court, but up

the battlements to one of the towers. The room had no furni-
ture, save a faldstool. There was no bed save a straw pallet in the
corner. There was no window, just a drafty arrow slit, and the
only comforts afforded me were a tinderbox and a bundle of
candles.

It was a cell.

I turned back, sure there was some mistake, met the heavy
oak door as it slammed in my face, and heard the key turn.
There was no mistake. I was a prisoner.

Shit.

Well. This was far from the glorious court I had heard about
from my various Milanese clients over the years. Why had my
fortunes changed so, in a heartbeat? In Bolzano my lodgings
were sparse, but at least they were comfortable and befit my
new rank. Had my mother, in her short conference with the
Milanese lord, shared her suspicions of me? How was she so
sure I had betrayed her somehow? Why had she placed me in
this empty cell? I even began to miss Marta, Marta who had
left the carriage abruptly somewhere in Lombardy, there one
day, gone the next. I thought of the deep and deadly glass
lakes and their poisoned waters. I wondered if she had been
dumped there, weighted down to dance on the bottom, like
the figures in the lagoon. A Venetian death. Or perhaps she
had been taken back to Venice and would once again rut with
her kitchen-boy love. Despite her actions to me, I rather hoped
that this last would be her fate. I knew my mother's capability
for revenge—she had been let down, and did not forgive. She
had guessed, in the carriage that day, that Marta had failed to
watch me closely, and now she was leaving it to the profes-
sionals. An armed soldier—doubtless one of the multitudes I
had seen in the courtyard—paced outside. I heard his sword
tip scrape my door as he switched back and forth. The watch
changed, it seemed, every two hours. I was out of the world

with frustration. How would Brother Guido contact me now, with a locked door and an armed guard between myself and the world? I heard the watch change once, twice, and no one else came near. I had not food nor drink, and my growling stomach soon served to remind me of the tale of Brother Guido's ancestors, imprisoned in the Muda tower, driven to starvation so extreme they devoured each other. Nor did I have any diversions save the view from my window. I dared not take the picture from my bodice, the wooden roll from my sleeve, or my mother's mask from my hood, lest someone burst in upon me. I had to content myself with watching a small sliver of a city through the long arrow slit that was my only light and air. The wind perished my eye and whistled and moaned in counterpoint to the percussion of the soldiers marching outside. I was trapped in an organ pipe.

On the third watch there was a knock and a burly soldier entered, with a cadet at his shoulder.

"Signorina," he said, as if such pleasantries were alien to him. "I regret to disturb you, but you are to be searched on the orders of il Moro."

Madonna.

I assumed il Moro was his name for his lord, but I knew the orders came from my mother and I invoked her name now, in desperation. "But sir, I am the dogaressa's daughter!"

He blinked once. "Indeed, and I regret the necessity. But these are sensitive times and all guests must be searched, including your exalted mother."

He lied and we both knew it. There was no way a duke would offend his noble guests with such mistrust. My heart stopped beating. They would find the painting, and the roll, and the coin, and the fifty gold ducats and mask I'd stolen from my mother. I was as good as dead. Fleetingly, I toyed with the idea of offering them a fuck apiece if they'd let me be, but I knew that the notion was hopeless—sex was my currency when I worked the streets, but for a noble maiden to lose her "reputation," she may as well lose her life. *Shit.*

Mutely, frozen by the certainty of doom, I stood as the cadet searched me with surprisingly gentle hands. I stared the sergeant at arms full in the eye, defiant as I waited for the hidden things to come to light, the objects that would damn me and cost me my life. Yet incredibly, the cadet felt the roll in my sleeves and passed on to my shoulder. He felt the parchment in my bodice and passed on to my waist. He bypassed the mask in my hood. I was at once flabbergasted by my good luck and amazed by the stupidity of the soldier who searched me. If he was an example of the army outside, then they were destined to lose whatever war they waged, hands down.

Search over, the sergeant at arms thanked me, apologized again. I inclined my head, borrowing one of my mother's gestures, not sure what to do now. I had been used to the feel of strange men's hands on my body and was too relieved to feign insult.

" 'Twas a mere formality, my lady, as I said. I was asked to remain with you throughout, to make sure your honor remained intact, and the fellow here that searched you was chosen especially for his chastity, for he was once in Holy Orders."

Then I knew. I didn't even have to look closely at the cadet—the gentle hands, the way he passed over what was hidden without giving me away, should have told me. I didn't have to look but I'm glad I did, for he turned at the door with his sunburst smile.

Brother Guido.

39

I knew then that he would come, and I knew how. I ate my frugal dinner when it arrived on a trencher of hard bread; there were to be no more feasts for me, it seemed. I cared not. I did not wait to hear the watch change—I knew Brother Guido would be one of my door guards, and knew that he would have contrived to have been given one of the night watches. Darkness fell over Milan; I lay down on my straw and actually slept.

A knock woke me and I was up and into his arms holding tight to his wiry body for a second before he pushed me away in haste, as he had done in Venice. I did not care—I had him back.

"Have you a candle?"

A fine hello—but I struck the tinderbox and lit the rush dip by my pallet.

"I have left my torch in the bracket outside. I thought that if the tower were dark, they would know I had left my watch." Even before the flame flared and lit his face I knew I would see a different man. His appearance in my room earlier, the thinness of his body when I briefly held him, told its own story. I looked carefully at him, joyfully, sadly. For he had suffered a trial. His face was thinner, older, with hollows under the eyes and in the cheeks. Soldier's stubble sanded his cheeks. There were flecks of silver there and in the hair too, which was cropped short in the military style. His hands, always long and elegant, were almost skeletal. Only the eyes were unchanged—sadder perhaps, wary certainly, but still the startling blue of the enameled roundels in Santa Croce. Still, I need not worry that my mother would know him again, for I scarcely did myself. I swallowed. "Did they hurt you?" There was no need to explain who I meant.

"A little. They asked about the *cartone,* for days and weeks—always I gave the same answer. I knew it would be futile to deny that we had it—I said it had been lost at sea, when the Muda was wrecked, and in the end they had to believe me, for I would not change the tale. They did not dare to damage me much, for they needed to keep me alive; for the moment." He did not explain further. "I was starved, though, and kept with no light and little water. I was awaiting trial, for months, many months."

"So long!"

His lips twisted without mirth. "Things change quickly in Tuscan politics. Alliances shift. The worm at the bottom of the dungheap can next day be king of the castle. My guess is that Lorenzo kept me alive to be some kind of bargaining tool with my cousin. To threaten Niccolò with deposition—to keep another heir alive so he would be an obedient member of the Seven and follow in Lord Silvio's footsteps to bring Pisa to the alliance. They took my uncle's ring." He held out his left thumb, bare except for a white band where the skin had escaped the sun's stain. "I imagine Niccolò now wears it obediently upon his hand."

I considered. I thought that Brother Guido had neared the truth, but I knew there to be another twist in the tale. Lord Niccolò had had to be coerced into accepting *me* back as his betrothed—after all, an ex-harlot who had been racketing around the peninsula with his cousin was no great wifely prospect, be she never so fair. But as the dogaressa's daughter I was a vital link in the Seven's chain of power. And while I was being feted around Venice and taught how to be a proper wife, Brother Guido was living on fetid water and darkness.

"Were you alone? In the prison, I mean?"

"Not at first. I was in the general cell with all manner of

unsavory characters—the Bargello's finest. Oh, it was not so bad, not unlike the monastery, for the church, too, is full of thieves and pederasts and criminals, so I was right at home. The only difference is that these varlets were honest men, honest in their criminality; they do not deal in dissemblance and hypocrisy. They do not pretend to be devout while they break every commandment in the calendar."

I realized that prison had not robbed Brother Guido of his words, for the length of his sentences seemed to match the length of his sentence. Nor had it, seemingly, given him back his God. I had thought that in a time of such trial he would once again turn to the Lord, but he seemed to hold the church in as much contempt as ever. "How can you condemn your foundation? For there is one there who has been a friend to you, and to me too, for he wrote to tell me of your fate."

"Aye. Brother Nicodemus. Yes, yes, I must absolve the good herbalist. He has been a better friend to me than you know. And a worse one. For he gave me my freedom and made me a murderer." He fixed me with tortured eyes.

"What do you mean?"

"When you were choosing your gown at Santa Croce, in the herbarium . . ." I remembered, but it seemed years ago.

"Brother Nicodemus took an herb from his bunches and folded it in my hand. It was belladonna. In case something should go awry."

I knew the plant. Everyone did. A deadly poison indeed. I shivered. "You never told me!"

"Of course not. I placed it in my shoe, and the guards never looked there." He rubbed the back of his neck in his accustomed gesture. "Every day I took it out and looked at it. Every day I said, if I can but live through this day, I will take it tomorrow. And then the next day I said the same. I deferred my suicide for near on six months."

My flesh chilled. I had thought many times that he might die, but never by his own hand. I realized with a shock how far he had strayed from his God. "How did you live?" I whispered.

"I thought about the *Primavera*. I remembered every detail that I could. I could see it in my mind's eye. Every day I escaped my surroundings into that grove, walked around the figures, conversed with them about Dante or Boccaccio. I could remember every detail that we had discussed, interrogate every leaf and flower, every stroke of the brush. But some of the figures were mere shadows, the ones we had not yet examined, and some details were blurred or misty, insubstantial, flitting from my eye like fishes, the net of my memory not swift enough to claim them. But others"—he paused—"such as yourself were clear as day."

My heart flamed; I knew not what to say. "And they tried you, in the end?"

"No." He seemed relieved by the change of subject. "I was told by a guard I had befriended that something *had* changed, that Lorenzo had to move fast and needed me dead. I was to be executed the next day without trial. Summary justice," he said, his lips curving with irony.

I remembered my mother using the same words in Venice, and I knew her handprint was upon this. Niccolò della Torre had no doubt signed the marriage contracts, for I remembered he had visited my father. He had made any undertakings that the Seven had demanded, and once they were assured of Pisa's connivance, Brother Guido was as good as dead. My blood froze, at how close I had come to losing him.

"I was given a last request. I asked for a Chianti of the Pisan region, and two cups, that my friend might share it with me through the bars. Even as I poured I questioned whether I should put the belladonna in his cup or my own. I had not forgot, you see, that I was once a man of God."

"And God spoke to you?" I breathed.

"Not he. He has been quiet in my ear since Rome. Even in my cell he did not visit. I spent time with the old gods of the *Primavera.*"

"Then who?"

"I spoke to myself. I decided one man's life had to be weighed in the scales with the nameless evils that the Seven have planned. I put the belladonna in his cup, and he died instantly." Brother Guido looked at his hands, as if he expected to find blood on them. "He had a wife and children. He spoke of them often."

As did Bonaccorso Nivola. So Brother Guido was guilty, had taken a life. I knew now that this, not his ordeal, was what had aged his countenance and darkened his eyes. I wondered if, guilty thing that I was, I wore the same expression, wondered if I could ever tell him what I had done to an innocent sailor in his name.

"Then?"

"It took me three hours to wrest the keys from beneath his body—I lived in fear for every moment as the sky lightened that the watch would change and I would be taken to my death. But before dawn I was free and made it back to Santa Croce just as they were beginning their day. Malachi let me in. I went straight to the herbarium, and Brother Nicodemus hid me for some weeks. He said he'd been in contact with you—I commend you, incidentally, for your newfound abilities as a scribe." He smiled properly this time, once again the old Brother Guido for whom reading and letters were everything. I blushed—not something I'm in a habit of doing—but was helpless in the face of a compliment from the only man whose opinion has ever meant anything to me.

"I then knew of your whereabouts. Brother Nicodemus took me out of the city as one of his assistants on a medical mission to the city of Mantua. There I joined a train of Franciscans who were heading to Trento for a colloquy. I peeled off at the foot of the mountains—the good brothers lent me the mule I rode. I found a boat at Mestre and came to the city of Venice. Once there I stayed on the island of Giudecca with a company of Jesuits who were building a foundation there. In exchange for my labor I was able to board with them, and upon my rest days I was able to follow you."

My flesh heated. "You saw me?"

"Many times. Always going about with your mother, never alone. I guessed that Carnevale was to be my best opportunity to make contact, in the confusion and lawlessness of the festivities."

In that, his thoughts and my own had marched as one. My flesh now chilled to think that I had planned to take advantage of the Carnevale to escape—on the eve of the very day he had planned to come for me! Oh, Bonaccorso, your sacrifice was in vain! I was unable to speak, and my friend continued unchecked.

"I saw you that day in the Piazza San Marco. The storm came and I followed you into the basilica. When I saw you examining the horses I knew you must have found something. I remembered what the Seven spoke of in Rome—that Flora held the secret and that a map was mentioned many times. I thought you must have found the map of which they spoke, but I had time to do no more than tell you to keep it safe and that I would meet you in Milan. For by then, through all my days of musing in prison, I knew that the Botticelli figure represented Milan (the clues to which I will explain in good time), but I could not divine the meaning of the Zephyrus figure. I take it, then, that you had similar epiphanies in Venice?"

It was my turn. I told him of my time in Venice, of my mother's story, of my own tale of the baby in the bottle. I told him of my father, of Signor Cristoforo, of my Venetian education and all I had learned there. The one detail I did not share was the episode of my escape and the fate of Bonaccorso Nivola—I did not feel ready to share that hideous truth. I did, however, recount with pride the meaning of the thirty-two roses indicating the compass rose, and the wind rose which led me to the Zephyrus horse.

He smote himself a couple of times on the forehead, when all was revealed, exclaiming, "Of course!" and he even smiled again. "All satisfactorily maritime solutions, appropriate for the city of Venice. I was following the wrong course, in prison and at the herbarium too; I was looking only at the Venice figure, the figure of Chloris—your . . . mother. I did not recognize then that the other figures would hold clues to the *following* cities—for *all* the Naples clues were contained in the figure of Fiammetta, if you recall, and *all* the Roman clues in the figure of Semiramide, Venus. It did not occur to me that the clues held in the figure of Flora would read in *Venice*."

"Botticelli is getting cleverer as we get closer." My statement made no sense, but he took my meaning.

"Yes. Myself and Brother Nicodemus were attempting to recall the flowers that issued from Chloris's mouth—without the *cartone* before us it was no mean feat."

"I had a look at them too," said I, and took out the *cartone* and unrolled it, weighted the corners, joyful as we leaned over the painting as we always used to do, as I thought we'd never do again. Our heads were almost touching. I pointed to the blooms dropping from Chloris's mouth as I spoke. "*Fiordaliso,* anenome, *occhiocento,* and rose, but I did not know the Latin names, just the Tuscan common ones, and could not make any words or meanings from them."

"Ah, then we *were* right. The good brother and I guessed at rose—*Rosa centifolia*—cornflower, or *fiordaliso,* as you say, which is *Centaurea cyanus* in Latin, and anemone, which is *Anemone nemorosa.* And *occhiocento,* also known as centocchio, or periwinkle, which is *vinca* or *Vinca minor* in Latin."

"*Madonna.* That's an even worse collection of letters. *R-C-C-C-A-N-V.* Or *V-M.*" I showed off my new skill.

"Or perhaps the true divination of the meaning is as simple as this—that there were four classifications of flowers and that there are four winds. 'Twas perhaps another signpost to guide you to the wind rose and the four wind horses that crown the basilica of Venice."

I wasn't sure—it all seemed a bit simple for Botticelli, who had proved himself to be clever as the Devil.

But Brother Guido wasn't finished.

"Brother Nicodemus did add, moreover, that *occhiocento* is known colloquially as the 'flower of death.' It might be interpreted, therefore, that Chloris may have an evil intent, and her enterprise might end in one death, or many."

I shivered, remembering, once again, the unfortunate Bonaccorso Nivola. It would certainly not surprise me if my mother came out of this with more blood on her hands, the evil bitch.

"Maybe the meaning will become clear later, like with the compass thing."

"Indeed. But even without decoding these flowers, we are now two cities past Venice. And even without reading the flowers, we now have the map!" he finished in triumph. "Let's see it, for we do not have long."

"Yesss," I said slowly. "I don't want to piss in your polenta, but this wooden roll isn't what you think. You keep saying a *map.* But it isn't a map, at least not like any I've ever seen. And in Venice, I saw quite a few, believe me, studied them too." Thanks to Signor Cristoforo.

"Nonsense," he said swiftly. "Let *me* see the thing."

I shrugged "All right." I pulled out the wooden roll and laid it in his hand. He examined the strange marks and squiggles all the way round the thing, frowned, then his face cleared. "Oh, but of course. It must be hollow. Documents are often carried in such things."

As if that wouldn't have occurred to me. I felt the old familiar irritation rising, and felt almost comforted to know that the traits that annoyed me about my friend were as alive and well as he was. He looked closely at the ends and I said naught—let him find out for himself.

"Hmm. No. Not hollow." I was smug and silent. As if there could be anything about that roll that I didn't know, after I'd carried it around like a third arm for twice sennights.

"Yes—just a marking—here."

"Where!"

"Look."

Now I had to give him credit, for I'd not noticed a tiny marking on one of the flat ends—a little squiggle carved into the wood. "It looks like a snake."

"Or an *S*."

"*S* for what?"

"Seven? Sforza?"

"Sigismund?" I added.

"Who?"

Now the pupil became the schoolmaster as I explained about my trip to Bolzano, and Sigismund, white-haired king of the Alps who had such an odd love-hate relationship with my mother, a mountain full of silver, and a ring on his thumb.

"Of course. I suspected we should look to the mountains for the figure of Zephyrus, but I must admit I had in my mind the city of Trento, which has enormous political significance for the peninsula, as the location for many religious councils. I thought, as you did, that the blue color was suggestive of cold, and the height may denote great altitude." That's not exactly how I'd have put it, but I graciously accepted the compliment. "Well done. And you learned of the archduke's part in all this?"

I explained about the conversation I'd overheard and my midnight trip to the mine. He did not comment on my ill-thought-out adventure but went straight to the meat of the matter.

"Well, that's all clear enough. The Seven are clearly minting their own currency, using the template of the English angel coin, which is gold, but making a version of silver. Silver being the metal that is most plentiful in Sigismund's region and all the Hapsburg lands. That must be why Zephyrus has silver wings; he *is* a silver angel."

I let him take credit for something I'd already divined, for he was in full flood as he explained all that I had heard on my mountain sojourn.

"The Zecca is the famous Venetian mint, as you now know—your home city, among its many superiorities, happens to boast the best money strikers in the world. *Münzreiche*, the archduke's nickname, means 'rich in coin,' and a seam is a natural store of silver in the earth—it sounds like you entered one of the mine shafts yourself."

"I did, and I also found a coin that they had struck." I could not help but sound a note of pride.

"Show me."

I reached into one sleeve, then the other. But the coin was gone. *"Fuck!"* I exclaimed, then looked at him through my lashes, waiting for the usual censure, which this time didn't come. I expect he was used to worse in the ranks of il Moro's army. "It was *here*. Shitting fucking mother of *Christ* and all the saints. I must've dropped it." I was genuinely furious with myself—not only was it an important piece in our puzzle, but

I'd retained my whore's care of the coin and was looking forward to spending the thing when this was all over.

"Do not distress yourself. Can you remember what it was like? The design?"

"Yes. It had a profile portrait of Lorenzo il Magnifico, with his laurels in a sunburst, just like the symbol of Sol Invictus."

He nodded. "So far so consistent. And on the other?"

"One word. It . . . I—" My mind was a blank.

"Well?" he barked.

"Don't *yell* at me, you're making it harder to remember," I whined. But it was no good. The word, read once and lost in the sound of the carriage wheels as I drifted into sleep, was gone.

Brother Guido leaped to his feet and paced the room, eyes blazing. Angry, but not at me. "Evil, pernicious alliance! What must they be plotting? Could the Seven be planning to march into the mountains, north and east to the direction of Zephyrus, to overrun the Hapsburg lands? Perhaps they plot to overthrow the emperor, overrun the Holy Roman Empire, build an empire of their own?"

It sounded likely but for one thing. "But the emperor is *in* on it. Don't you remember? When I overheard Sigismund and my mother talking in the great hall, Sigismund said his cousin the emperor had given my mother safe passage in the mountains and guaranteed protection from attack from the Hapsburg lands. And another thing too—when the coin was struck in the mine that night, Sigismund took it to *give* to the emperor. So the emperor clearly knows all about the Seven and has given his blessing. So that dog won't bite."

"You speak truly. But certain it is that there is war coming to *someone*'s door. For let me continue my own tale—I traveled with a Milanese merchant back to Milan as his chaplain, and left him at the city gate. There I saw a bill calling on all the youth of the city to enlist at the Castello Sforzesco for a new model army. I came to the gates to join up and was asked no questions, even though I was wearing the robes of a Franciscan novice. I was given this ocher cloak and sword, and this helmet with a pointed visor." He flourished his arms and armor. "I was asked no questions of birth or experience, given pass for all that I wear the prisoner's brand of the Bargello. See." He held out the inside of his wrist, stamped with an ornamental *B*, the flesh healed but angry. "And I am not alone. Branded men, lunatics, men of the cloth, all have lined up to fight for il Moro and God knows what. They take the pay of a *paghe vive* soldier gladly, and every hour from that day to this we have been training to fight hard and dirty. I have been here a month and Ludovico has honed us all from a ragbag of villains to an efficient fighting infantry, ready to fight whatever war the Seven have planned." He took my arm, hard, hurting. "And by God, or Venus, or whoever rules this earth, we're going to stop them. Come. Let's use the time that we have and interrogate the figure of Milan until we can divine what their purpose is."

40

"Let us begin, as we always used to do—with the obvious," said Brother Guido as we leaned into the painting once more. "The figure is, as we know, Botticelli, the artist himself. He wears an ocher cloak, as he did that day when he painted you. He wears a curved sword in the Turkish style, as I do now. He wears Roman sandals, as do I. He wears a pointed helmet, as do I. In short, Ludovico has modeled his army on *this* figure."

"Or Botticelli has painted Mercury as one of Ludovico's infantry."

"Indeed. Either way, a nice little piece of military propaganda. What do we divine from this?"

I didn't understand what he just said, so I thought it safest to recap. "That Ludovico Sforza is building himself an army with a new uniform, new weaponry, new armor—"

"And that's not all," Brother Guido interrupted. "He has a Tuscan engineer, some fellow from Vinci, making war machines for him—they are all here, in a huge secret chamber below the castle. Great mechanical monsters to wreak destruction. God knows upon whom."

"All right. He's building himself an army of men and machines."

"Not *himself* an army, the Seven's army. Just as the Seven now have new coinage, they have a navy—the fleet of the Muda from Pisa and their sister fleet in Naples. Naples also provided the meat and drink of alliance, a marriage. Semiramide Appiani not only unites the houses of Naples and Florence, but she brings her father's lead mines as a marriage prize, a metal crucial for the waging of a war. The Seven also have papal blessing—the backing of the church for their enterprise. Each city represented in the painting we have visited has contributed something. Venice has given her expertise in coinage, and Bolzano has the silver to make those coins."

"Doesn't seem like Venice brought much to the party."

"No. But they also gave a priceless treasure."

"What's that?"

"Not what. Who. *You.*" He smiled. "We should not forget there is another marriage alliance in the case. With the doge's daughter allied to Pisa and the Seven, trade—the lifeblood of a city-state—is assured. Venice is the gateway to the Black Sea and all points east, and the Mocenigo family, even when the doge's office is ended, is crucial to Venice's shipping monopolies and trade routes. You, and you alone, secure them."

My mind boggled. I could not yet think of myself in these terms. It didn't help, of course, that I was currently sitting in a cold cell no bigger than a privy, which smelled like one too. "What about Florence?"

"Lorenzo de' Medici is the mastermind of all—'tis his head upon the coin. And crucially—he has the Medici bank. He will underwrite the whole operation, whatever it is; he will move money between branches using his new *giro* system. And now, as we know, Milan is to provide an army."

"All right. So, now that we're *here,* and we see all the soldiers dressed like Mercury, it's obvious that Mercury is Milan. But you must have known before, for you asked me when we met in Venice to meet you here. How did you know *then* that Mercury was Milan?"

"Simple. The snakes."

"Snakes?"

"On his caduceus."

"His what-eus?"

He pointed to Mercury's right arm, extended up to the sky. "What's he doing *here.*"

"He's stirring the clouds with a stick."

"Look closer. At the rod he's *using* to stir the clouds and bring the spring. Look, two snakes entwined upon the rod, poised to strike."

"So?"

"Snakes are the symbol of the Sforza family—the rulers of Milan. Snakes are everywhere—on our armor, look"—he pointed to his breastplate—"walls, banners, tapestries. Even the seal of il Moro, which all those in his service carry so we may do his bidding without stay or prevention, depicts the Sforza serpent. See." He held out a little plaque, fashioned from red clay, with the snake squirming atop. "Everywhere."

The snake above the gatehouse as I'd entered the castle. "So the snake tells us *which* city. But there must be more. How about this map that we still haven't found? There must be a clue here if only we could see it. So what else?"

"Well, how about the details now. He has got tiny flames on his cloak . . ."

"And tiny white flowers growing around his boot . . ." We were back in our old rhythm.

"Cress, *crescione* or *Cardamine hirsuta*. I saw some in the herbarium."

"We're missing something. What's he trying to tell us?"

"Pisa is looking at him," I ventured.

"That's it!" he exclaimed.

"Really?"

"Not who is looking at *him*," he clarified. "Where is *he* looking?"

"Up at the whatd'ye call it."

"Caduceus. Exactly."

"So we're back to the snakes again. Milan. Well, we're in Milan. The map's in Milan. Great. It's hopeless." I slumped back on my straw.

There was a silence. Then, "Not hopeless," began Brother Guido slowly. "Look. Botticelli is the *model* for this figure. Why? He *must* hold the key; he *must* be an important figure; he *must* hold the answer. And," he added with sudden vigor, "we are so busy identifying this figure with Botticelli that we are forgetting who he *represents*. Mercury. The *messenger* of the gods. He has a message for us; we just need to divine what it is." He scrutinized the figure again. "I think he is telling us to do what he does, see what he sees. He's even using a pointer. He could not be clearer."

"So we're to look up at the clouds." I was skeptical.

"Perhaps. No, no, wait. We are not being told to look up at the clouds. We are being told to look up at a *snake*. Where may we do that?" he mused.

I sat up abruptly, for I had the answer. "The gatehouse."

"I beg your pardon?"

"The clock tower. Of this very castle. As you come into the castle, there's a huge stone snake, just like that"—I pointed to the caduceus—"above the gates."

"The Torre del Filarete. You are right! I have marched beneath it every day now for a month! I have been blind!" He leaped to his feet once more, full of pent excitement, as I knew him of old.

I got up too. "Never mind all that. If we're to look up at a snake, let's go and do it."

"Now?"

"The guards change every two hours. Believe me, I know. You've been here, what, an hour, say? Compline has just rung. We have another hour—let's go and look!"

His blue eyes burned. "Very well. Get your cloak, and bring that mask too."

41

The air was warmer here and I was back in the mink I had worn in Venice. The color was cousin to the night, much closer to dark than the ridiculous white bear coat I'd worn in Bolzano. I drew up the hood and followed Brother Guido, who for the sake of appearance frog-marched me with a tight grip on my upper arm, as if he were taking me prisoner, lest we be challenged. We snuck out of the tower door onto the battlements and crept along the stone walkway to the clock tower—I'd already forgotten how Brother Guido had named it. He drew me close.

"There are two guards on the gate," he whispered. "So we cannot go down the stairs to look up, so to speak. But if we look down from above, there may still be something to see. Let us take turns. I'll look first, for if I am seen, at least I am one of their company." He leaned out between the battlements.

And was back in an instant. "Well. It is the same snake all right. Six coils—not seven as we might expect—north facing, I think, directly above the gate. Take a look."

I looked down from the same spot. 'Twas a difficult angle, and there was little light save that from the guards' torches. To be honest, I'd gotten a clearer impression of the carving in the heartbeat I'd passed under it in my mother's carriage, for at least that was by day. I could see the curves of the coils, the evil fangs, the yawning jaws stretched wide to devour. But the serpent was giving no other secrets away. I stared so hard I began to feel dizzy and feared I would fall. I jumped back down to the battlement, shrugged.

Brother Guido shook his head. "We are being blind," he said.

"Perhaps it's something you can only see from *below*," I suggested.

"Or perhaps the snake just represents the Sforzas—and *this* castle as the headquarters of the new army—and nothing else."

"That doesn't help us find the map," I snapped. "Let me try again." I jumped and craned over, the stones of the battlements crushing my ribs once more. But this time I saw something else. Another panel, another carving, beside the snake. "There's something here!" I hissed, snakelike myself. "A figure of a man. No—he has a halo. A *saint*."

"Let me see." Brother Guido almost shoved me from my position. "You are right." His head reappeared.

"Could you see who it was?"

"I do not need to see. I know. It's Sant'Ambrogio, patron

saint of Lombardy. The people here invoke him for everything from a dying horse to a lost cat; they name their children after him, call on him when they stub their toe. It is he, for certain."

He jumped down to crouch in the shadows by my side.

"And what was his story?" I demanded. "What was he famous for?"

"Nothing. Except—" He stopped, turned his extraordinary eyes upon me.

"Except?"

"He made a blind man see!" he breathed.

"Really?" My voice was heavy with irony, for I had no truck with miracles. They were just another way for the church to make money.

"That's it!" He forgot to whisper and I had to shush him. "The saint is going to make us see!"

Despite my doubts, I felt the old familiar excitement build in my chestspoon. "How's he going to do that? And where?"

"Easy. Let us go and ask him."

"He's still here, in Milan?"

"Never left."

"Explain, please."

"Il Moro himself worships at the monastery church of Santa Maria delle Grazie, and he requires his soldiers to be devout—a sop to *His Holiness* the Pope, no doubt." His voice dripped with irony like the serpent's fangs. "They say he built Milan on a sword and a crucifix."

"So?"

"So we worship at the larger church—needs must for our numbers—of Sant'Ambrogio, Saint Ambrose, hard by Santa Maria delle Grazie, not far from here. The saint is still there— his mummified body is there, in a tomb with two lesser saints— and can be visited in the crypt! Everyone in Milan knows the legend. A blind man was restored to sight by looking on the mummified body of Sant'Ambrogio. 'By virtue of these remains the darkness of that blind man was scattered, and he saw the light of day,'" he finished in triumph.

"Well, when do you next attend?" I asked impatiently. "Sunday is . . ." I began to count on my fingers.

"Six days away," he finished. "Too long. And I would have a regiment around me. We must move faster than that."

He leaned over the battlement again, and before I could ask him what he did, he hailed one of the guards below.

"Hey, Luca!"

A jovial voice from below. "What ho? Oh, Guido, it's you. Thought you were watching that pretty Venetian piece."

"Locked in and snoring." Brother Guido was doing a good job of mimicking the bluff, curt tones of a soldier—curbing his words and blunting his pretty speech. "Are you watching her next?"

"Yes, Vespers to Terce. 'Tis no trouble, I'd still be watching her in my dreams even if I were abed." I could picture him grabbing his crotch. The other guard laughed.

"Look. Let me do your shift. Then tomorrow, go double for me?" Brother Guido wheedled. "There's this girl in Porta Ticinese."

"Didn't you used to be a monk?"

"*Used* to be. Why d'you think I gave it up?"

More laughter. "All right then, *Brother*, you're on. I'll be glad of the rest."

"*Dio benice.*" Brother Guido sketched an ironic blessing and sang in plainsong, making them laugh again, then he was back down below the battlements and at my side.

"Let's go. We still only have two more hours before someone relieves Luca's watch."

"Where?"

"The church of Sant'Ambrogio, of course."

"Now?"

"Yes."

"How?"

"There is a way."

Back we ran, across the battlements and down the spiral stairs in the tower, across the deserted parade ground hugging the shadows of the keep. In the curtain wall, a low door led to a short stair and a dark passage that smelled of new-cut stone.

"Come," he said. "Let us hope they have finished it."

"Where are we?" I breathed.

"In a passage that leads from the castle to the Dominican monastery of Santa Maria delle Grazie. Il Moro is constructing it so that he may freely reach his place of worship, and also freely escape if there should ever be the need."

"Madonna."

"Such things are commonplace."

I knew that much—I well recalled our secret walk between Castel Sant'Angelo and the Vatican in Rome, but I thought it better not to remind Brother Guido of the day his faith died. As we ran I mused that it did seem quite gone. I had not known how much I had connected him with his faith, and it had been a shock to hear him addressed as Guido, to hear him talk of women, to mock his God even in jest. I gave myself a little shake. What was wrong with me? If he was entering the worldly world, might there not be a chance for me, for us?

We ran on, swift and silent, until a greenish hue told us of light above. We were up another stair and through an arras, and emerged into a vast cavern of the monastery church. Gothic vaults colored in powdery blues, reds, and ochers were still illuminated by the full-moon light flooding through the arched windows of a high dome. There were a company of monks near the high altar, intoning one of their midnight prayers, and we scuttled swiftly to the exit and into the dark night. Once outside, Brother Guido grabbed my hand with more urgency than tenderness and turned left and right through the silvered streets. I could see our destination the moment the clouds cleared the moon, a huge pile of a place with two high towers: the basilica of Saint Ambrogio.

"Put your mask on," urged the brother, as we reached the great doors. "Slow your breaths. And follow my lead."

We waited in the portico for a moment to compose ourselves then Brother Guido swung the heavy doors. "Unlocked?" I asked.

"The house of God is always open," said Brother Guido, with a sneer I didn't like. Inside, I could see that the brothers here kept time with their brethren at Santa Maria delle Grazie, for mass had just finished; the brothers had shuffled off for another pair of hours in bed before their next devotions. A single sacristan remained, as once before in a doomed church in Naples, extinguishing candles.

We proceeded noiselessly down the aisle, and Brother Guido cleared his throat. The old man turned and smiled sweetly, as if he'd been expecting us.

"Your pardon, Brother," began Brother Guido. "I am a member of Lord Ludovico's personal guard." The old monk looked him up and down, taking in his brand-new armor, his height, his noble face. "I have the honor of escorting the Dogaressa of the Republic of Venice." He indicated me, and the old fellow's jaw dropped open.

I tried to look as haughty as I could.

"I am directed to ask you to allow the dogaressa a private visit to your famous relics, for she wishes to pray privily, at an hour when public eyes are not upon her."

The sacristan seemed to have lost the power of speech. I wore only a mink cloak and my mother's lioness mask, but it was chased in gold and gilt enamel, and I must have cut quite a figure with my golden hair in the bargain.

Brother Guido attempted to break the spell. "I carry the seal of Lord Ludovico, as you can see." He held out the clay plaque with the snake design he showed me earlier.

"Yes, that's quite, that is, that's quite in order. Except . . ." the old monk bumbled.

"Well?"

"It's just, well, *which* relics would the lady, the dogaressa I mean, wish to see? Our Blessed Saint Ambrose or"—he looked down at the seal—"Nehushtan?" He seemed to sneeze.

Brother Guido exchanged a look with me, and I could see that he didn't know what the second word, if it was a word, meant.

"The saint, to be sure."

The sacristan nodded. "This way, please."

We followed obediently to steps leading down into what could only be a crypt. I tugged at Brother Guido's sleeve urgently—we couldn't have this monk standing by as we tried to figure out the significance of our findings. He nodded briefly.

"Do not disturb yourself, Brother. Do you go about your business. I will escort the dogaressa. A *private* penance, you understand."

The monk bowed in my direction and left. I rewarded him with a fraction of a nod, such as I had seen my mother give to servants who pleased her, and swept down the stairs.

A gloomy crypt, three candles burning for three saints, all huddled together as if they shared a bed. Their forms twisted and their flesh waxen, their finery now shredded bandages around their wasted bones. Gervaise, Protease, and the Blessed Ambrose, mummified for eternity, even the splendor of their golden bed doing nothing to glorify the hollow features of carrion. Saint Ambrose was possibly the ugliest of all, his corpse misshapen, his head swollen like a bladder, and his face caved in to one cheek, giving him a lopside.

Brother Guido caught my look. "Saint Ambrose was missing one of his eyeteeth," said he. "It gave him an odd appearance in life too."

We carefully searched the crypt, silently, whispering to each other occasionally, as if the three saints were not dead but asleep.

"Well," I said at last. "There's nothing here, not to do with snakes at any rate." I looked to the lumpen head for a miracle.

" 'By virtue of these remains the darkness of that blind man was scattered, and he saw the light of day,' " intoned Brother Guido, repeating the words of Ambrose's legend once again. In these surroundings, they sounded like a prayer, save he had not prayed since Rome.

"*We* are the blind ones this night," I grumbled. Then I had an idea. "Perhaps we should look *up,* like Mercury does in the *Primavera.*" We both craned into the vaulted darkness and could see nothing beyond the friendly circle of candlelight.

"*Up*stairs then?"

My companion shrugged. "It's worth a try. This tomb seems to avail us nothing." He laid a hand on the saint's shriveled arse, not without affection, but I was again shocked at how worldly he'd become. The monk was now a soldier; he'd shed the last of his faith with his habit and had donned a different persona with his armor.

We emerged into the great church and began to look about us, the sacristan's lamp hovering distantly like a firefly. Hundreds of votive candles lit the interior, so light was not our problem. Inspiration was. We searched every inch of the place, all the while attempting to look like interested tourists. At length, the sacristan began politely extinguishing candles nearer and nearer to ourselves; the darkness crept forth and around us and threatened to engulf us till we were on an island of light in a dark cavern. Our search now seemed hopeless. At last I found a particularly fine altarpiece, with strange animals at the top of the pillars. I could see rearing horses, twisted dragons, and a great assortment of bizarre creatures. I called my escort over.

"Here," said I. "Here are some animals. Any snakes? Help me look."

"Hmm," he murmured, "very interesting, very fine work. Transmutations and transformations, animal to animus."

"Do any of those words mean snakes?" I said testily. "If not, save your syllables."

There were a great variety of strange things to behold in the carvings, but nothing that resembled the Sforza serpent.

Downcast, Brother Guido touched my sleeve. "We should go. We cannot have long before the next guard relieves me, and if I am not there, there will be a hue and cry."

"And if *I* am not there, there will be a bigger one," I agreed.

As we headed for the great doors I kept one eye on the sacristans's light. Remembered what he'd said. Stopped in my tracks.

"*Madonna*. We *are* blind!"

I put out an arm to Brother Guido's breastplate to hold him back. "Truffling about like pigs in shit, and all the time *he* gave us the answer."

"Who? The sacristan? In what way?"

"He said *which* relic, the saint or something else, that word that sounded like a sneeze."

"That's right! He did!"

"*Shush*. And he looked *down*. He said the sneeze word and looked *down at the snake,* on the seal that you showed him. So there is *another* relic here, and the *second* relic, the *N* word, has something to do with a snake."

He nodded quickly, eyes afire once more.

"Come on."

We approached the old fellow and beckoned him over. "The dogaressa has prayed to the Blessed Saint and admired your church. She wishes you to commend her to the abbot and mention that she enjoyed *all* of the basilica's wondrous features."

The old fellow beamed. I waited for Brother Guido to mention the second relic, but he did not.

"We will take our leave of you now. Please accept this for the poor."

He held out a Milanese soldo, one of his pay coins as a *paghe vive* soldier no doubt. I was briefly touched, but as the monk took the coin, I trod heavily on my friend's foot. I couldn't believe he was going to have us leave without asking the crucial question. But I need not have worried.

"The dogaressa very much enjoyed seeing *all* of your church's beauties."

"Oh, but *soldato*," broke in the sacristan, "she has not seen *all* of them. I cannot permit the dogaressa to leave without—that is, I must insist, suggest, *beg,* that she look upon Nehushtan."

There it was. That word again. I took my foot off Brother Guido's and we followed the sacristan to a remote corner of the church at the left of the nave, to an ornamental pillar standing alone, as if it belonged to another time and place.

"A Byzantine pillar, very fine," said the sacristan with pride.

Brother Guido voiced my disappointment. "And this is it? Ni-hus—"

"Nehushtan?" The sacristan smiled again. "Bless you, no. You must look *up*."

When he said that, I knew we were in the right place before I even saw what he was pointing at.

At the top of the pillar, flicked into a loop and ready to strike like the Sforza serpent, was a bronze snake. In the remaining candles it gleamed softly; exactly the copper hue of Mercury's wand in the *Primavera*.

I was dying to ask what it was but knew from many months with my mother that an exalted lady would never address a lowly monk directly. I knew, though, that I could leave the questions to Brother Guido, and so it proved.

" 'Tis wondrous strange. Pray, what is the significance of this serpent? I am sure the dogaressa would like to know."

"We are privileged indeed," replied the old man, "for this artifact came to us across many lands and seas, all the way from the Holy Lands of the Bible, and across time from those days too."

"Ah, then it is perhaps connected to Aaron's rod, which turned to a serpent?" Brother Guido gently nudged the wordy fellow to spill the story. "I thought that Aaron's serpent was to return to the valley of Josaphat at the Day of Judgment, not to rest in a church in Milan, even one as fine as this."

The monk looked at him sharply, and I gave him a small vicious kick to the shin. For certainly he knew too much Scripture for a private in Ludovico's army, be he ever so devout.

"You know your Scriptures," said the sacristan guardedly, but with approval. "I am glad il Moro keeps you devout. But for this serpent's story we must look to another chapter and verse of the Book of Books. For Nehushtan has to do with the *other* brother of that blessed family—Moses, not Aaron. The Israelites were complaining about their problems in the desert somewhere near Punon. God, angered at their lack of faith and ungratefulness, sent poisonous snakes among them as punishment. Then Moses, who had prayed in order to intercede on their behalf, was told by God to make a brass snake so that the Israelites merely had to look upon it to be cured from the snake bites. Allow me to find you the passage."

He trotted up the nave to an eagle lectern with spread wings and heaved the good book off the top. We exchanged a look as he brought it back to us and began to leaf through the yellow pages. I saw Brother Guido's hands itch to take it from him, but the sacristan found his place at last.

"Here, as I thought, 'tis the Book of Numbers which provides an origin for an archaic bronze serpent associated with Moses, with the following account."

And the Lord sent fiery serpents among the people, and they bit the people; and much people of Israel died.

Therefore the people came to Moses, and said, We have sinned, for we have spoken against the Lord, and against thee; pray unto the Lord, that he take away the serpents from us. And Moses prayed for the people.

And the Lord said unto Moses, Make thee a fiery serpent, and set it upon a pole: and it shall come to pass, that every one that is bitten, when he looketh upon it, shall live. And Moses made a serpent of brass, and put it upon a pole, and it came to pass, that if a serpent had bitten any man, when he beheld the serpent of brass, he lived.

"The thing was named Nehushtan by the boy-king Hezekiah."

As he fell silent, we all looked up at the snake, an odd trinity of harlot, soldier, and monk, collectively as sinful and as devout as any that had touched it in that cursed valley.

"Brother," breathed my friend at last, in a voice low and urgent with excitement, "are you telling us that *this* is Nehushtan, this is *actually* the snake that Moses made at the word of God? Brought *here* to Milan?"

"As the Lord is my witness."

I didn't doubt that the Lord was his witness. I looked again at the snake, in awe, and the snake looked at me.

"Then if you will permit us, the dogaressa will pray before this wonder alone. We will leave in a very few moments."

The fellow nodded and withdrew entirely; his light extinguished, he had gone to his shortened rest.

"Now," I said. "Let's crack this egg." I took the *cartone* from my bodice, unrolled it for the umpteenth time, and laid it on the open page of the Book of Numbers. "This pillar, in Ludovico's army's church, has a snake at the top, like the cad . . . cad . . . Mercury's wand."

"Caduceus. Yes."

"But there's only *one* snake here, on this pillar. Mercury's wand has *two*, look." We both craned in to peruse the warlike figure stirring the clouds with the rod of snakes. Sure enough, two serpents twisted about the haft.

Brother Guido was untroubled. "Well, I think there we must look to the *name* of the idol. In Hebrew נחש, *nachash*, means serpent, while נחשת, *nachoshet*, means brass or bronze."

"So?" I was all impatience.

"*Let me finish.* The -*an* ending of 'Nehushtan' denotes a plural—in short, it signifies that the original idol was actually of *two* snakes. Two snakes on a pole."

"All right, so the caduceus, with which Mercury stirs the clouds, is Nehushtan."

"Undoubtedly. But I was thinking of another wand in our possession. One which boasts only *one* snake."

I stared blankly. He touched my sleeve. "The 'map,'" he said briefly.

I took the wooden roll from my surcoat. We huddled to the flame to see, clearly carved, the serpent Nehushtan on the top, burned into the wood like a brand.

"So what we're holding here," I said slowly, "is a model of this pillar."

"A replica, yes. Except it is not an exact copy, for the markings on the wood are muddled scratchings and marks that mean nothing."

"Whereas this pillar," I slapped the polished stone, "has absolutely nothing on it."

"Hmmm," mused Brother Guido, stroking his soldier's stubble, "just the snake at the top. Very well. Let us consider what Nehushtan may tell us. For there must be a reason why we have been led here, to the church that made blind men see. The snake holds a secret." He craned upward and traced the snake's shape in the air with one long finger—one loop, around and back.

"One revolution . . . and the snake head resembling an arrowhead . . . go *this* way . . . yes . . . it's almost as if . . ."

"As if you might finish a sentence?" I rapped.

"Forgive me. As if we are being given a *direction*. Loop *around*. *Go once around*. Let's obey, and take a turn about the pillar."

We walked round the pillar in opposite directions, the snake balefully regarding us from the top, and fetched up exactly where we had started. The pillar was as plain as a Pentecost platter.

"Wondrous," I grumbled as we met once more. "Around the pillar and up the garden path."

"Very well. Perhaps the snake is not telling us what to do with *this* pillar, but what to do with the *replica that it adorns*."

In the candlelight we turned the wooden roll this way and that, but the markings made no more sense.

"Unless . . ." began Brother Guido slowly.

And then he seemed to run mad.

He dashed to the altar, snatched up a half-full chalice. I gaped at him, for this was no time for refreshment. Then he came back to me, took up the great Bible, and tore the page the sacristan had read us right out of the good book, leaving a ragged strip of parchment where it had been. He then heaved it back on the lectern, closed it to cover his crime. My jaw dropped further, for never would I have thought him capable of such heresy, such disrespect to his former idol. I was not sure what shocked me more—the fact that he would tear the Bible or the fact that he would wantonly destroy a book, his friend and help-meet, the delight of his youth and his greatest love. He was back, and he laid the page on the floor next to the candle. Then he dipped his hands in the chalice, bringing them out dripping and carmined like a murderer's. He rubbed the dark wine on the wooden roll, and rolled the thing over the torn page once around, as if he were making a pastry. The wine dried at once into the parchment and he took the roll away. The image was blotted and smudged, the text muddled the lines, but the nature of the design was quite clear. Here was the land, here the sea.

A map.

"But a map of what?" I murmured, in wonder.

"I don't know. But the serpent has told us all it can. Let us go, before we are discovered."

He took up the last candle and we carried it to the door, puffed it out as we left. We ran back to Santa Maria delle Grazie, and I thought for a moment that stilled my heart that the doors would be shut upon us. But no—the next cycle of prayers were in progress and we crept through the incense-heavy dark to the arras that led to the causeway. We ran through the greenish night along the moat, Brother Guido talking as we went, murmuring instructions in a low and breathless voice.

"I'll come to you tomorrow night, and we will talk further," he said. "We're getting close."

"How will you come to me? You swapped your shift," I gasped back.

"I'll swap it back. Luca won't mind. I'll say my lady denied me, and I'd rather be at my post than in my cups. I'll be at your door between Vespers and Compline."

With that we tore up the stairs to my tower till my chest felt fit to burst. We could see the torch of the next guard begin to bob along the battlement and raced it home. I hurried inside and closed the door silently behind me, heard Brother Guido snatch his torch from his bracket, long since burned out. Just as his fellow soldier came round the corner. I pressed my ear to the door.

"No light, *soldato*?"

"Double shift, sir. For Luca. It went out about an hour ago."

"Why didn't you get another torch from the sergeant at arms? At the sentry post?" The man was clearly his superior.

"They're at the Torre Serpiolle, sir. Didn't want to leave my post."

"All right." The voice seemed convinced, even a little impressed by such devotion. "You can get off now."

I heard Brother Guido's feet receding. My breathing started again.

"Oh, *soldato*?"

And stopped.

"Yes, sir?"

"Get your grappa ration from the quartermaster. Been a long one, heh?"

"Will do. *Notte*."

"*Notte*."

After that, I collapsed on my bed, spent with exertion and fear. But before I laid my head to rest I took another look at the map. It was not easy to make out, for the print made in wine rode atop the words of Scripture that covered the page—the chapters and verses of the Book of Numbers writ in crabbed, close, black Latin. I strained to see in the dawnlight. There were no place-names. Nothing to indicate which corner of the world it might mean, just what seemed to be a small star on the northwest coast of the land. I gave up and tucked the parchment back in my bodice, with the *cartone*. I tried in vain to remember if I had seen the landmass before, during my weeks of tuition in Venice with Signor Cristoforo.

As my lids grew heavy the image of that unknown country swam before my eyes. And as you cannot see what is before my eyes, I will show you.

I suppose you'd describe it, as, well, a boot.

42

I woke in my cell at dawn, dressed still and stiff with cold—
Zephyrus had taken his revenge by puffing his cool spring
winds into my organ pipe of a tower and fluted me awake
with the dawn.

I watched the sun rise over the city and strike the silver pinnacles of the cathedral. From here, too, I could see the twin
towers of Sant'Ambrogio, and only these reminded me that last
night was not a dream. I took the parchment from my bodice
to look at the map once more but had to stuff it back instantly
as the key turned and the door opened. There stood the sergeant at arms who had overseen the search yesterday. Holding
a bolt of flame-colored silk.

"Your lady mother begs an audience with you in her chambers," he said briefly.

'Twas not a suggestion.

Instantly my heart began to thump and my cheeks heated,
banishing the cold. Did she somehow know how and where
I'd spent the night, using the same sorcery she'd used to guess
I'd left my room in Bolzano?

"She bids you put this on." The sergeant tossed the silk on
the straw pallet. And I was a little cheered—I wouldn't waste
precious silk on a daughter that was for the chop, would you?

I wondered if the fellow would watch me dress—something
I was used to back in the old days—but the door closed again.
I wriggled out of my gown and into the flame-colored one. I
was glad to say good-bye to the besmattered rose silk, for it was
stiff with sweat from my long carriage ride and then my run
through the streets of Milan the night before. I sniffed under
my arms and wished I had some cloves to rub in my pits, but I

would have to do. At least my mother had not sent a maid to dress me, for then the *cartone* might have been discovered, along with the money belt, wooden map roll, and the page from the Bible. My hair was loose and a mass of tangles, whipped into a bird's nest by my windy tower, but I had no way of dressing it, no comb, no mirror. I combed it with my fingers as best I could, yanking through the worst of the knots and making one heavy braid, which I pulled over one shoulder. Not sure what to do, I knocked on my own door, and the sergeant turned the key, opened the door, and took my arm without a word.

I wrapped my mink around me and followed the soldier's broad back down the same stairs my friend and I had taken last night. I was taken across the parade ground, still rimed with frost and crunching underfoot. A division of soldiers were being drilled, their sergeant's voice echoing from the four red walls, bloodier than ever in the bright morning. I looked among the men beneath the ocher cloaks and copper helmets for Brother Guido, but he was not there. Had my mother recognized him? Had she had him arrested once more? I thought not—my mother never spoke to the little people, never looked them in the eye, she would never seek the face of a nobleman in a battalion of soldiers. But perhaps she had spied upon *me*, knew my movements of last night. My hatred of her, for imprisoning me, and starving me too, deepened to fear.

I crossed a small moat to the residence and entered a palace of such splendor I could not believe my poor prison was part of the same castle. Every wall was hung with apricot silk and cloth of gold, and the Sforza serpent was everywhere, fixing the court with a watchful single eye.

Nehushtan.

My mother's apartments were just as beauteous, painted

the pale blue of an eggshell, with silver cords sewn into the fabric of the walls. She sat at her looking glass in a gown of flame silk to match my own, to match also, I realized with a jolt, the little flames that adorned the cloak of Mercury—Milan. Was everything a key or a signpost to the conspiracy in which she was steeped? My mother was combing her own hair with a sandalwood comb, while her feet sat in a silver ewer filled with rose water. The air was sweetened with the scent but my fear soured to anger. The bitch had me locked in a tower, and she bathed in silver like the Queen of Milan.

But once again my mother surprised me. She set aside the comb, smiled graciously, as if I had just returned from a game of tennis, not a prison cell.

"Daughter," she said, spreading her arms in welcome, "I am right glad to see you. I trust your accommodation is not too uncomfortable?"

Fortunately, she did not wait for a reply, for I had some of my choicest words ready.

"I am happy to tell you that you have to endure such necessary privation for only one night more. You understand, of course, that I could not risk losing the thing dearest to me. After your *travel* plans in Venice."

Hmmm. So perhaps she *didn't* know what I had got up to in Bolzano. She certainly didn't seem to know what I had got up to last night.

"For I have good news. Your father this way comes—he will be here tomorrow."

Good news for whom? I wondered. I remained surly and silent.

"And he will of course have our own guards, so we will have to trespass on Lord Ludovico's soldiers no longer."

Madonna. At last I took her meaning. If the ducal guards were

435

coming to watch me, I would never get away again. I'd have to get a message to Brother Guido. We'd have to leave tonight.

"And there is a further surprise, which I will let our lord duke share with you. For he desires that we accompany him this morning; he has great wonders to show us. Tell me, have you yet broken your fast?"

"If you mean have I had anything to eat, then no," I said bluntly. I was not sure how to behave to this woman. In Venice I had seen a block of glass in my father's palace, seemingly crystal white but which split the light into seven colors. A prism, Signor Cristoforo named it. My mother was just such a one—she had seven colors at least, and I never knew which hue of her character would appear next. But she did not seem to heed my rudeness, merely waved a hand to her lady's maids.

"And tell them to bring me supper too, for I had fuck all last night either," I yelled after the retreating maid.

My mother's brows shot up to her hairline. "Soothly? An oversight, I'm sure."

An *oversight*. Too busy feasting on suckling pig and marchpane to spare a crust for her daughter.

"Let us talk a little, while we are alone," she said. (My mother had about three maids in the room—I told you she didn't notice the little people.) "Softer! You are not shoeing a horse!" This last to one of those maids, who was drying my mother's feet on a linen cloth. My mother kicked out and sent the poor woman sprawling on the rushes. "You know, of course," she continued without pause, "why your accommodation here is a little less . . . *commodious* than in Bolzano?"

I watched the unfortunate maid scuttle to the door. I shrugged, not wishing to give anything away.

She held up one long white hand, and between her fingers, flashing in the sun, she rolled a silver coin.

My heart thumped so loud she must hear it.

It was the angel from the mine in Bolzano. That I'd picked up. And lost.

She collected my expression. "Yes. It fell from your sleeve as you slept in the carriage."

The tinkle of metal that had woken me up, to see the lakes of Lombardy outside the window.

"I knew you had been out that night," she said. "Marta, as you will note, is no longer with us."

Whether or not Marta was back in Venice or with the Almighty was not clear, and my mother did not expand.

"Sooner or later, Luciana, you will see that you cannot win, and obedience to myself and your father, and indeed your husband, will prove the most direct path to happiness. Disobedience brings only privation, imprisonment, and despair." She rose and began to walk the room purposefully, like a lawyer giving weight to her pronouncements. "Forget whatever you think you know of the business of politics; you are in error. Seek not to know further than the things you are told, for your own safety. That said, in deference to your overweening curiosity about matters of state, you will today be taken into the confidence of the great Ludovico Sforza. Look and learn since you are so keen, and tomorrow will make a new beginning. Ah, your meal is here." She switched smoothly from politics to breakfast with no change in tone.

The repast, when it came, almost made up for the threats—salted beef, beer, fruit, and good white bread. I wolfed down the lot, as my mother watched me from under veiled lids, for all the world like Nehushtan. When I'd finished, I belched loudly for her benefit. She did not flinch nor censure but surprised me again with her next gambit.

"Your hair is a disaster," she said. "Chiara. Bring the comb and the oil. And, let me see. Yes, the moonstones, I think, will meet the case."

Her elderly lady's maid, whom I'd recognized from Venice, brought the needful things from my mother's traveling cabinets. My mother placed me before the mirror and dressed my hair herself, her touch surprisingly soft and skillful. She combed my knotted locks into smooth skeins and twisted little ripples of curls to be pinned up with the moonstones, leaving half of the mass to fall down my back. When she had done, she clasped my shoulders and looked into the mirror beside me. We met each other's eyes somewhere behind the glass. Two blond green-eyed women, dressed in flame silk, our blood relationship writ all over our faces, in the wideness of the eye, the dark wing of the brow, the small upturned nose, and the full rose lips. She did not say anything as she pressed her cheek to mine, but I got the point.

We were family.

Cloaked, booted, and masked ("for you will be among soldiers, dear"), my mother sent for the sergeant at arms again, and we were led from the residence down a flight of stone steps and past an ornamental lake stuffed with carp. The fish flicked their golden bellies to the sun as they turned in the water. I could have flipped one out, crunched his head, and eaten him whole, for I was still starving.

Into this picturesque court came the duke and his retinue, at a swift pace—I noticed il Moro always seemed to march. Not walk. His mien was military, his business war—everything about him martial. In the morning light I noted the duke's dusky skin and olive-black eyes and hair, and understood, for the first time, why I heard him everywhere dubbed il Moro— the Moor.

Again he greeted us in his soldierly way and was as bluff and friendly to me as yestereve, as if I had not spent the night in one of his cells.

"Come," he said. "I will show you great wonders, madam and miss, that we talked of at dinner."

With that, he led us down a little loggia, arched black and white in strong sun, and unlocked a low door with the hand that wore the Medici ring. He turned to his guards. "Six stay, six go," he ordered. "No Romans."

The sergeant at arms counted out the men. "You, two Milanese. You, from Maremma. You from Siena. You from Modena, and, Pisan, you." I looked up at the word, and saw that Brother Guido was the Pisan picked to guard us.

We entered the dark door and spiraled down on a left-turning stair, the soldier's sandals clattering behind. Down, down, down to a vast chamber flooded with light from arched window shafts that reached through twelve feet of solid rock to the upper courts of the castle. I was reminded again of the covered causeway where I had run till and from last night. But if the causeway had been inhabited by such creatures as I saw here, I would never have left the castle.

Madonna.

They were great beasts of wood and iron, towers of siege standing high like giants, war machines with teeth like dragons. Constructed on a grand scale with wheels and pulleys and ropes, and joists and cannon, and bristling with blades.

We moved as one down the huge hall, cavernous as a cathedral, but a place to worship war, not God. And as if intoning the Scripture, Ludovico Sforza began to speak in a tongue that I recognized as Latin. Was that why the duke had specified no Romans? Would people from Rome be more likely to know the language of the church? I, of course, understood but one word in a hundred. My mother, nodding at the duke's instruction, understood all. But I knew, with a fierce pride in my chest, that there was another here that would understand every word of il

Moro's commentary and would be able to relate it to me in time.

Each creature had its attendants, its keeper; engineers, tinkering, adjusting, experimenting, running trials, adding a bolt here or a nail there, planing wood or shaving metal. And at the hub of it all, a small ugly man, his features obscured by beard and moustaches. Who bowed low to the duke and then proceeded to gabble to him, in Latin faster and more fluid than his master; a firecracker of a man, fairly bursting with ideas and passions for these things he had made. By the twang of his Latin I knew him for a Tuscan. I knew that this must be the engineer from Vinci that Brother Guido had mentioned the night before. In another moment I knew more, for he was presented to my mother as Signor Leonardo da Vinci. As the two men talked and my mother listened, I wondered briefly why I, who had been kept in the dark deliberately by my mistrustful mother was now being shown such things. My mother played me at cards but was showing me her hand—she was as good as admitting that a war was planned and that she was a part of it, and this new war, with this new army, would be fought in a new way. Fought with machines that burgeoned from the fevered imagination of this little Tuscan engineer, whose ideas swelled and burst like birthing sacs, to spew forth blood of innocent soldiers devoured by his machines. My mother turned to me and echoed my thoughts in a low voice.

"These are engines of death. Whosoever has such things *cannot* lose a war. Do you understand me? *Cannot* lose."

Now I knew the reason for disclosure. More threats.

I met her eyes. "I understand that. What are you really telling me?" I noted the duke and his engineer had stopped their discourse to listen.

"That it is useless to resist what is coming. It is as inevitable as the seasons."

The little Tuscan added a Latin saying (which was actually destined to be the third Latin tag that I know): *"Ver fugo hiberna."*

And they all laughed together. I hated them all, traders in terror, dealers in death.

"And now, let us retreat from warlike sights and enter instead the realms of love and marriage," said my mother, wrapping one arm around my shoulder.

"Mars greets Hymen, eh?" Ludovico barked. "'Tis true. Lady, be glad." He looked fondly at me, as if he were a favorite uncle, not my jailer. "For tomorrow, we greet at court your betrothed, Lord Niccolò della Torre of Pisa."

I almost dropped to the floor. "Lord Niccolò? Here? Tomorrow?" I piped as loudly as I could, so that Brother Guido might hear.

"Yes." My mother smiled down on me, indulgently. "Is that not joyous? He comes to join our party and reacquaint himself with you, the queen of his heart."

I felt sick and could only hope that this information had reached Brother Guido at the back of the ranks. We all moved to leave; I hung back to fiddle with my shoe until my friend had caught up with me, then at the foot of the stair I stumbled and threw out an arm to Brother Guido to steady myself. It worked.

"You—help the signorina up the stair, she is faint with the news that her lover comes!" And Ludovico laughed, his booming voice ringing up the spiral.

Brother Guido and I had six turns, perhaps, to say what needed to be said. It took less.

"I'll come to you tonight, as we planned," he murmured so low I could hardly hear above the footsteps, "between Vespers and Compline."

"But did you not hear? Niccolò is expected tomorrow! He will know you at once."

He seemed startled, recovered quickly. "But I will be disguised by numbers, he will not note the footsoldiers."

There was not time to state that my mother had seen him but once at the Medici wedding, but Niccolò had grown up with him, boy and man. I went straight to the poniard's point. "Let me tell you," I hissed. "I've known fellows of your cousin's tastes before, and the one thing they like doing *best* is looking at footsoldiers." We were nearly at the door. "Moreover, from tomorrow I am to be under the watch of my father's guards this time. And they know their business."

That did it. "Very well. Then we must go tonight. Be ready."

I nodded quickly. One turn to go to the light, one more question. "What did the Tuscan engineer say in Latin?"

He looked at me once. "He said, 'Spring chases the winter.'"

The rest of the day I spent in an ague of anticipation. I recognized the symptoms well from the day before my intended flight from Venice. My appetite disappeared and I was a weathercock spinning from excitement to terror. My cheeks burned and my eyes flamed, such that on the way to mass in il Moro's litter my mother asked if I had a fever. At which Lord Ludovico slapped me on the back, as if we were sharing a grappa in the guardhouse and said, "Fever indeed. Cupid's fever, I'll warrant. For nothing else puts roses in a maid's cheeks and the sparkle in her eyes than the reunion with her true love—these symptoms are all in della Torre's cause, mark my words."

As I coughed from the blow and smiled politely, I thought that I could not fault his logic—my fevered state *was* all due to an assignation with my true love who bore the della Torre name, but he was in error as to which branch of that family tree I awaited.

And thus I found myself in the third Milanese basilica I had been in this day. I had visited church more times since I had come to the city than in the whole of the last four years. This time we worshipped in the great Duomo, the mass of spiny pinnacles without, with a vast many-pillared nave within. The light streamed in through the stained glass with a greenish hue, turning the pillars to bone—they reached above and curved about like a giant rib cage. Not Daniel in the den this time but Jonah in the whale—I was in the belly of a beast; would I ever be able to escape this city? The service went on for two hours; I fretted for both of them and never heard a word of it.

Back at the castle I fidgeted until feast time—this night I was invited but might as well not have been, for not a morsel passed my nervous lips. I had to be back in my room by Vespers, so I excused myself from the pomp, pleading that I must get my sleep to be fresh for my betrothed. My mother seemed to believe my protests but still assigned me two guards to escort me back and turn the key.

Once back in the cell I had little to prepare. *Be ready,* Brother Guido had instructed. But I had long since learned to carry all that I needed on my person at all times. I took out my warmest cloak, and bundled my mother's mask within it, and laid them across the wooden faldstool that was the one seat in the room. Then I set myself to wait for the bells. As one church, then another, then the great booming bells of the cathedral gave tongue to the hour of Vespers, I heard a shuffling outside the door and the key turn. So soon! My heart leaped to my mouth and I leaped to my feet.

The door swung wide.

'Twas my mother.

43

She smiled at once, but this did not lessen my fear—a friendly expression meant naught with my prism-mother; if she meant to end a life she would smile and smile as she pushed the knife in. I held her eyes like a frighted coney with a fox, willing her not to question why my cloak was readied on the stool. Of course, it was the first place she went, tossing the fur to the ground to sit down. I winced in case the stolen mask fell out, but the bundle remained secure, and my mother never marked it. I thought she would question why I was still dressed, but a couple of moments in that room with its whistling winds would quickly inform the casual visitor why I would not shed one garment.

She sat on my stool in her feast-day finery, looked about her. Once again, she took on a different hue. She looked distressed; her speech was hesitant as I had never known it. She seemed genuinely upset by the conditions in which I had been held. "No bed! Nor panes in the window. I did not . . . I had not guessed . . ." She turned her great green eyes on me, pleading for the first time. "I came to ask you . . ." She seemed to struggle to find words. "Let me protect you. If you try to run, if you disobey, if you try to prevent what is in train, those that I now keep at bay will pursue you again."

With a chill I knew she spoke of Cyriax Melanchthon, the murderous leper and tool of Lorenzo de' Medici, whom I had all but forgot during my sojourn in Venice. For the first time I considered how cold it might be outside the strong circle of my mother's arms.

"I wish you married," she went on, "and happy, with children growing like vines around your table. I never watched my children grow." Her voice cracked and she suddenly looked much older.

I did not go to her, did not speak, but behind the mask of my stony expression I was, despite myself, a little touched at all she had lost, for all that she had brought our separation upon herself.

She came close. "I wish the best for you. In that way, I am your *Vero Madre.*" My arms almost twitched upward. I almost wrapped them around her but did not.

She kissed me once and left.

I was still and stunned for a moment. I was astonished that she had remembered what I had once called her. I had uttered the words *Vero Madre* to her but once, when I had woken beside her in the gondola in Venice; she had all but laughed at the phrase. I had never used it again, even to myself, my dream of sixteen years shattered, the notion of my warm and loving mother smashed like the false idol that it was.

As she left I heard more footsteps and was instantly on the alert again. It was the *cambio di guardia*—the changing of the guard. I froze—for although my mother would never have picked out Brother Guido from a battalion of soldiers, surely even she would know him if she passed him, she and he alone, in a narrow passage.

But no, she must have been as affected by her little interview as I, for the guard left, she left, and Brother Guido—I even knew his tread by now—was outside my door again.

I hesitated once as I went to pick up my cloak and mask from the floor—I knew that as soon as the door had opened and I left this room, I was setting myself against my mother and all the rest of the Seven. Forever and ever, amen. Against armies, against fleets of ships, against all the silver in the mountains, against a murderous leper who wanted me dead.

But when the door opened he only had to ask me the

question and I knew I would follow him to the ends of the earth, no matter what danger we were placed in. For we would be in it together.

"Ready?"

"Ready."

We took the little stair down and down the tower as we had done the night before. I assumed we would use the covered causeway again to Santa Maria delle Grazie, and then somehow try to get out of the city gates before dawn.

"Too risky," said Brother Guido. "Fortunately, there is another way."

We doglegged left and down into a different passage, high and cavernous, an underground thoroughfare. "Why, a whole regiment could pass through here!"

"That's the idea."

"Where does it lead? Another church?"

"No. It leads behind the fortress, out into the hunting ground behind the castle."

"*Outside* the city gates?"

"Outside the city gates."

Before he could finish his confirmation I heard stamping footsteps and guttural grunts. Of course the tunnel would be guarded—I stood rooted, knew we were discovered, and hoped Brother Guido could talk fast enough to get us out of this one. From my mother's demeanor tonight I knew that even she could not protect me if I transgressed again.

"Do not distress yourself. It is only our transportation."

We rounded a corner and there, oil-black with a gilded coat of torchlight, stood the mountainous horse I had seen between il Moro's thighs yesterday.

"*Shit.*"

"Yes."

"But that's . . ."

"I know."

"And you want me to?"

"Yes. I'll mount first. You get up behind me. The Templars rode two by two for many centuries. 'Twill not harm you."

I didn't give a fuck about the Templars, whoever they may be, but I did know that I'd never ridden a proper horse in my life. The nearest I'd come was my pony ride from Fiesole to Pisa with Brother Guido, hardly the same thing. Despite my new education into the nobility, riding had not been among my list of lessons; Venetians are not horse people, since the only horses in that entire city are the four bronze ones atop the basilica.

Madonna.

Brother Guido vaulted expertly onto the black mountain and heaved me up after him. The horse stood stock-still, surprising me, as I expected him to rear and skitter.

"Do not worry," said Brother Guido, sensing my fear. "He is well used to battle and is steady as a rock. Hold on, though."

I barely had time to wrap my arms about his waist before he dug heels into the beast and it took off. I was bounced about like a sack of polenta, until I caught the rhythm, but my haunchbones would be sore for a sennight, I was sure. Brother Guido, apparently, was taught horsemanship in his noble education, for he rode fluidly, his hands light on the reins, his weight shifting expertly. We thundered along the torchlit passage, until I saw the last obstacle in our way, twin guards between us and the night sky beyond the walls. Without stopping, Brother Guido took out the snake plaque once more.

"Way in the name of il Moro! I must get the dogaressa to safety!"

The guards hesitated, then separated their pikes—they had little choice for the night-black charger had not been told to stop and would have barreled through both of them, taking them with us if need be.

We burst out into the starlit night and thundered across the *barco,* crossing the hunting plains as if we, too, were quarry.

We rode on without looking back for perhaps an hour, for the distant bells rang behind us as the ground began to climb. The horse, battle hardened and supremely fit, never slackened pace until we reached a wooded hill with a silver stream, and Brother Guido stopped to let the stallion drink. He slid expertly to the ground, lifted me down, and let the creature dip its head with a grateful whicker. I looked back on the city we'd left, still not far enough away.

"Where are we going?"

"At the moment?"

"No, I meant—"

"I know what you meant. Genoa, that's the last city."

"All right, then shouldn't we be going *west?*"

He turned to look at me properly.

"Because if you look," I babbled, "see, there's Polaris, the North Star, and in the compass rose, well, we should be heading north by northwest."

He was clearly surprised. But smiled. "You're right. But it was imperative to get away from the city, for to steal il Moro's horse alone would mean death, even without our other transgressions. Now that there seems to be no immediate danger of pursuit, we will bear west."

We sat side by side on the freezing turf, gazing back on Milan together. The city walls, silver in the moonlight, snaked around the city in a jealous coil, keeping the citizens in and the world out.

"It even looks like a serpent, doesn't it?" I ventured to my silent companion.

"Yes. Nehushtan. Or Aaron's rod, which—"

He stopped, as if struck. Drew in his breath.

"What?"

'Jesu.'

"What?"

"I know what they're up to."

"Who?"

"Who do you think? The Seven, of course. Blessed Mary and all the saints . . ." He was shocked back into old speech patterns.

"Could we hold the Scripture for a moment? *What* are they planning?"

"Aaron's rod. I was right about that at least."

"Come *on!*"

"Aaron's rod became a *serpent.* At the Day of Judgment it would crawl back to the valley of Josaphat."

"I said *hold* the Scripture."

"But that's *it.* In Joel 3, Verse 2, we read: "I will gather together all nations, and will bring them down into the valley of Josaphat." *I will gather together all nations.*"

"Sorry, you lost me."

He took me by the shoulders and fixed me with those eyes. "Do you remember, when we were in the Pantheon in Rome, just before the eclipse, and we were admiring the marble floor? The marble came from *all over* the Roman empire, set into *one* floor. I told Don Ferrente it was *a statement of* imperium *writ in marble.*"

"So?"

"So, this, *this.*" Without asking, he shoved his hand down my bodice and pulled out the *cartone* and shook it in my face. "*This,* the *Primavera,* is a statement of *imperium* writ in *paint.*"

"I still don't get you."

"Lorenzo and the Seven plan to build an *empire.* Just like the Romans did. They plan to bring back those days when our peninsula was one, and the peninsula went on to rule the world from west to east. *I will gather together all nations.* They have an army, a fleet, a bottomless bank. They plan to overrun the whole peninsula, bring their nations together and build a new *Italia*."

"That was it!" The word burst upon me like a sunbeam.

"What?" Now it was Brother Guido's turn to be confused.

I couldn't get the words out fast enough. "The silver angel. The coin I found in the mine in Bolzano. The one I dropped and my mother found in the carriage. On the reverse. Sol Invictus and Lorenzo on one side. And on the other—one word. *Italia*."

"There it is. Writ in silver. Judas's metal for seven treacherous villains." He shook his head, then, "What's the date?" he demanded urgently.

This sudden change of tack threw me, but I tried to answer as best I could. "I left Venice at the beginning of March, but then we were in Bolzano, then traveled here, so . . . middle of March, I'd say."

"The ides of March, precisely."

"But I don't know exactly."

"I think *I* do. We don't have much time left."

He took up the reins and jump-mounted the stallion, dragging me up with even less ceremony than before. He kicked the poor horse so hard it shot out of the spinney—the stars wheeled over our heads like a planisphere and the wind whistled past my ears. I had to bawl my question lest Zephyrus carry it away.

"Much time left before what?"

"The twenty-first day of March. New Year for the Florentines and a new empire for the Medici." He turned his head so that I might hear. "Before the first day of spring."

· 9 ·

Genoa

44

Our journey to Genoa was the worst yet.

My joy at being reunited with Brother Guido could not be cherished, our reunion not nurtured, for now we raced against spring herself. Brother Guido calculated less than a week till the twenty-first day of March—a day considered to be the first day of spring by Christian and pagan calendars alike—as we were now at the ides, or the fifteenth day. He was sure that the attack would take place on that day, for not only was the painting named for the season, but Poliziano's ode was firmly rooted in the subject of the coming spring, and renewal, and new world order, and other meaningful concepts. I knew nothing of poetry, but I believed my own eyes—Flora, my own figure, was so inviting, so central, to the painting, and it was she who looked the viewer in the eye, she who stepped forth in front of her fellows, she who was pregnant with promise. I could appreciate the irony—nigh on a year ago my last client and bedfellow Bembo had promised me I would be the most important figure in Botticelli's painting. Then I had thought it flattery—now I knew the truth.

Ludovico's army was at our heels every step of the way. Brother Guido told me they would mobilize as soon as it was discovered that the horse and myself were gone. Once we actually saw the vast company of infantry, insubstantial as ants, on a far mountain pass, but only a day's ride away. And as the army of the Seven gained, so did spring; soon mountains of shimmering ice turned to green hills with white villages spiraling round the top, then ever down to balmy coastline, with a brilliant lapis sea and coral caves. That warm breath of the coming spring, that first day of the year when you cast off your cloak, usually so welcome, was to us a terrifying signal of the turning season. The thaw was coming.

And there were still so many mysteries to answer, before we gained the city gates. What was Genoa's role in the whole plot? How could the city be a member of the Seven if we had seen seven gold membership rings already? "Unless 'the Seven' refers to all the *other* conspirators that have *joined* Lorenzo de' Medici, the founder."

"Then surely they would have named themselves 'the Eight,'" argued my companion. "No, I would wager that the ruler of this place does not bear a ring, but why I cannot tell you. Perhaps Genoa is innocent of all this." This I could almost believe, except for the presence of Simonetta, the pearl of Genoa, as plain as day, that famous face.

Il Moro's horse cast a shoe at the hilltop town of Torriglia, so, forced to break our journey, Brother Guido and I stopped for our first repast since we had been on the road. We shared a jug of wine and a loaf at a wayside tavern, seated at a table set outside the door of the inn, so we could see all entrances to the town square and the smith shoeing our mount across the square. Way down below, now revealed by the shifting sea fog, was a granite-gray walled city set on the lip of the sea, the rooftops and turrets silver faceted like an iceberg.

Genoa.

We unrolled the *cartone* once more, set our goblets at each edge, and stared into the beauteous features of the last figure in the scene, Simonetta Cattaneo, that famed, long-dead beauty, a portrait true as life, according to Brother Guido. "She seems so . . . so *important* to the whole thing," said I. "She is holding Naples's hand, and Pisa's too."

"Not only that but Botticelli's—I mean Mercury's—sword, the curved scimitar just like the one I bear here"—he patted his scabbard—"is pointed right at Simonetta, see? The point of it almost touches her leg—indeed, I am sure it touches the fabric of her dress at the very least. Surely that must indicate Genoa's place in this conspiracy, ring or no ring."

I peered closer. "You're right."

"And there's something else too," he went on. "Simonetta is the only *known* face in the whole painting."

"How d'you mean?"

"Well, she was a very famous beauty. The other ladies here are only really renowned in their own states. Your mother's beauty is legendary, but no one knows her features, as she goes about masked. You were a child, raised on the Florentine streets, the fairest of all"—I suppressed a secret smile—"but fully unknown. And Semiramide Appiani, a virgin bride, was protected by her family from the public gaze, and only found fame with her marriage. Only Fiammetta of Naples comes anywhere close to Simonetta's fame, and she was more of an archetype."

"A what?"

"A trope, a model—based on Maria d'Aquino, certainly, but a fictive construct of Boccaccio's. Whereas Simonetta . . ." He looked on her in a way that almost made me jealous. "I'm sure that any common man, certainly in Tuscany or Lombardy, or here in Liguria, would know her if they saw this portrait. And if they did not, she wears this pearl on her forehead," he pointed, "to identify her beyond doubt."

I fingered the pearl at my belly, which must rival Simonetta's for size. "And what of this other jewel?" I pointed to the brooch at Simonetta's bosom. "More pearls, four more, set with rubies, in a cross or star."

He shook his head. "I don't know the significance of that, but it only serves to reinforce her importance, and therefore the point. Why is she marked out so? Why is she rendered in such detail? It seems that Genoa, far from being an afterthought, is the one city that *has to be in the painting.*"

"So Genoa *must* be involved . . ."

"So it seems, and that is a great wonder to me, for Pisa and, even more so, Venice, are traditionally sworn enemies of Genoa."

". . . and if it is, what's the next move for the Seven?"

"France," said Brother Guido briefly.

France. I had heard of the place, of course, slept with a few of its residents, but thought it many thousands of leagues away, possibly across at least one ocean. I said as much.

"No. It's cheek by jowl with us now. Over yon mountains is the kingdom of Monaco, the gateway to Provence, and all France. The Hapsburg lands we know to be safe through the alliance with Sigismund of Bolzano, cousin to the emperor. Therefore, the only other target which adjoins these lands is France."

I rummaged in my bodice for the torn and printed page and smoothed the map over the *cartone.* "Would France be"—I jabbed at the star mark I had noted on the northwest coast of the map—"here?"

He peered at the little mark, obscured by the Bible text. "I know little of cartography, but I do know that France lies to the northeast of us. So my guess would be, yes."

I gave a long slow whistle. "So the Seven will gather here, and then attack France through the back gate!"

"By land and sea, yes."

"On the first day of spring. The twenty-first day of March." I calculated. "Tomorrow!"

"Yes. Tomorrow, probably at dawn for the greatest advantage of surprise, the attack will begin. And the hapless French will feel the full might of the Seven's army, innocent French men, women, and children . . . speak your thought." It was said without pause.

He had seen me squirming with doubt. "Well, that is, why do we care? I mean, they're, well . . ."

"French."

"Yes."

His lips curled in a half-smile. "All those who live are equal in . . ." He stopped.

"God's eyes?"

He looked down at his cup. "It's not *right*. These men of the Seven have a kingdom apiece, and they're willing to embark on a campaign of butchery to revive a long-dead dream of empire. Don't you want to prevent more bloodshed? You saw those war machines in the crypts of the Sforza castle. Do you want to see them bearing down on families? Children? Besides, after all they've done, after all those who have died—your friend, mine, after all the leagues we have traveled and all the puzzles we have solved, don't you *want* to stop Lorenzo and his allies?"

I thought of my mother. "Yes."

"Then we don't have much time." He drained his wine.

I nodded. "The end is near," I said soberly.

"Nigh."

"What?"

"Nigh. The end is nigh."

"I can't believe you're still correcting me when we're in this much trouble."

"It may be my last chance."

I did not question him but felt a cold wave of foreboding flow into my chestspoon. I drained my own cup to ebb the feeling away.

We paid for the smith from my money belt and set off down the pass to the walled city in the distance. I looked back once and thought my eyes deceived me, for I seemed to see a tall figure in leper's robes, standing in the dead center of the town square. Looking after us with eyes like two silver coins.

"Faster," I urged.

This last part of the journey seemed to take the longest time of all. By some trickery the city seemed to get farther and farther from us as we crossed the sea plains, like a faraway mountain long sought but never reached. Yet, at last, we were at the gates. As we joined the general throng of visitors and trades-men gathering to gain entrance to the city, Brother Guido turned in his saddle. "As I told you," he whispered, "they are no friends to Pisans or Venetians here, so we must keep our provenance and families secret. But there is a standing treaty between Genoa and Milan, so I will use the Sforza seal once again to gain entry. I am a Milanese soldier and you are my doxy; I have a letter for the doge."

"The *doge*?" I said with a jolt. How could my father have beaten us here?

"Calm yourself. The ruler of Genoa is also called the doge. There are great similarities between Genoa and Venice—for both cities, the sea is the lifeblood. Both cities vie for maritime dominance of the east-west trade routes. Both have a saint that they revere above any other—you have Saint Mark; they have John the Baptist. In fact, Giovanni Battista is said to be buried here, and they show the platter that held his severed head. The doge himself bears the name of Giovanni Battista. You see? Similarity is often at the heart of rivalry."

The gates of Genoa were twin towers, dark and high and topped with battlements like two ebony crowns. We were given pass at the gates by two scruffy guards who seemed half asleep; they barely glanced at the Sforza seal as they waved us through. If they were an example of the military might of Genoa, I didn't think they would offer much to the Seven's alliance. These gatekeepers offered a stark contrast to Brother Guido, who was tall and strong as an elm, in his new uniform and armor, which was still shining after a week on the road.

"So what's the plan?" I asked as soon as the gatehouse was behind us. "Confront the doge of this place with what we know?"

Brother Guido gave a short bark of laughter. "No. We would be inviting imprisonment or worse. We must cross the border and warn Monaco, and that quickly too."

My heart sank at the thought of more riding, and I pitied the valiant black horse who had brought us thus far. "So what are we doing here then?" I asked.

"First we must be sure of our story. We must know that this mark—this star upon our map—is Monaco; without that certain knowledge our theories are mere conjecture."

"And how, exactly, may we be sure?"

"This is a maritime city. There must be many accomplished mapmakers and mapreaders here. We must petition for help from one such."

A flash of inspiration was borne in upon me. "A map shop!"

"Well, that would certainly be a start—"

I flapped my hands to shut him up. "Signor Cristoforo!" My mother's words came back to me: *we have sent your friend back to Genoa unharmed . . .*

I explained. "I know a fellow, a friend, from Venice—he has a map shop here in Genoa, in the old port, with his brother. He may not be here—he was raising money for an overseas voyage, so he may have already sailed. But his brother may still be here!"

My companion wasted no time. "Let's go."

We wound through the maze of streets, so dark even in daylight that we could barely see the road ahead, for the houses were so tall and bent over toward each other overhead so that they nearly touched. Blinding daylight slashed down now and again into the gloom like a knifestrike, to illuminate the way. At such times when the light broke in I could see that many of the great houses and palazzi were striped in polished black-and-white marble like a polecat. And the streets stank like a polecat too, of piss and the fishlike reek of the whores hanging around at the corners; the alleys were so high and closed that the fresh sea air could not circulate to blow the stink away. Instead, hollow-eyed sailors crouching in the shadows perfumed the general stench with the heady sweet aroma of the blue clouds of smoke drifting from their opium pipes.

At length we found ourselves on the edge of a glittering bay, with the spars of clustering masts sticking up from the shoreline like a quiverful of arrows. I scanned the faint blue line of the horizon, hanging between sky and sea in the far distance, for the dark low thundercloud of a thousand ships rolling in toward unknowing France. But there was nothing to be seen, the skyline flat and uninterrupted; the whole idea seemed incredible on such a peerless blue day. Genoa showed us an innocent face; a hectic, bustling port going about its daily business. Looming over all stood a tall stone finger of a tower—one level perched above another with battlemented terraces at the middle and top. Seagulls wheeled mewing around the merlons, perched and dived off to follow the catch. We headed in that direction, guided by the tower as so many must have been before us, till we were in the huddle of houses and shops, fishermen selling their catches in strange accents that I recognized from Signor Cristoforo's tones, their wives and children knotting the nets with fingers so swift they were a blur. The fisherfolk melted away from the path of our horse; adults and children alike stood gaping, fishes themselves, at the sight of the two of us atop our black mountain. We were attracting too much attention.

"What is your friend's name?" I thought I detected a guarded tone in Brother Guido's voice, sensed that he did not like the notion of my having found an ally, not a young male one at least.

"Cristoforo."

"His *family* name," he snapped back.

I pondered. "I don't know. I never learned it." I had a flash of memory. "His brother is Bartolomeo," I said in a rush.

"Wonderful." He sighed and dismounted, leading me for a little way like a manservant until he spied a fellow sitting on a barrel baiting a hook. Brother Guido nodded to him. *"Giorno,"* he greeted the man in the worst Milanese accent I had ever heard. "Cristoforo and Bartolomeo?"

The fisherman spat a silver oyster of phlegm at Brother Guido's feet and my friend moved back a pace. But the fellow showed no enmity—as his spittle rose and crawled away I realized he was keeping baitworm warm in his mouth and must expel the creature before he spoke. I was so busy trying not to gag I did not catch his answer, but his nod was expressive, and we headed in the direction he indicated till we came upon a tiny hut with a low roof made ingeniously of barrel sides, making the whole dwelling resemble a boat. Through the open half-door came the smells I had come to love and were dam's milk to Brother Guido—parchment and ink. Even without the map scroll above the door we knew we were in the right place.

A scribe sat within, his back to us, scratching carefully at a parchment pinned upon a slanted desk. He did not look up as we entered, giving me time to dig Brother Guido in the ribs and point to a sight that lined the far wall, rows and rows of wooden map rolls, carved and marked like our own.

461

The fellow kept his eyes on his work still. "Can I help you?"

I had hoped against hope that Signor Cristoforo would, by some miracle, be here; but the voice was not his—this must be the brother.

"Might you read a map for us, sir?"

"We don't read maps," came the curt reply. "We *make* them."

I took over. "But signore, we have traveled a long way, and we have money." If only the man would look at me! My voice is not my best asset—but I thought my chest might help our case. But there was no need to use my wiles, for a voice hailed me from the back of the shop. "Luciana!"

Now we had never been close companions, but the service Signor Cristoforo had rendered me in Venice had made me his friend for life. I shot into his arms, and he kissed me on each cheek, clearly as delighted as I was.

"I never thought to find you here!" I gasped. "I thought you had gone to sail the seas and map the world!"

He rubbed his bulbous nose. "Believe me, I am trying. I came back home to petition our own doge, after Venice's doge, or rather the dogaressa . . . removed me from your city." He smiled ruefully.

"She did not harm you?"

"Not a hair on my head." He ruffled the matted red mass at his crown.

Once again I marveled at my mother's weathercock nature. She gelded the boatman that was to sail me away, but the man that planned the whole thing was sent home in safety because he was my friend.

Brother Guido was still as a sculpture beyond me, and the look with which he greeted Signor Cristoforo was as frosty as a mountain blast. He was soon disarmed as the sailor clasped his shoulder. "And this is your friend, whom you went to seek?

462

Well-a-day! I am right glad you managed to escape at last. And Nivola?"

I thought of the poor sailor, rotting without eyes or balls in my father's prison.

"He lives," I whispered, bowed down with guilt. I did not lie, could not share the truth lest Signor Cristoforo refuse to help us.

"I am glad of that too." He smiled; Brother Guido smiled. Signor Cristoforo introduced Signor Bartolomeo, a fellow as ill-favored but pleasant-natured as he, and we all smiled at each other. Then Signor Cristoforo made it even easier by repeating his brother's question. "What do you here? Can we help you?"

"We need you to read a map." I looked at Brother Guido and he gave me a tiny nod, license to share our confidence. "We think the star denotes the site of an attack which will come tomorrow."

I unraveled the silk from my bodice. He bent in to look at the landmass depicted, and I saw his smile die.

"Where did you get this?"

"In Venice. I found this." I showed him the wooden roll. "And we, well, printed it in Milan." I did not trouble him with the facts that we had used a Bible page for parchment and communion wine for ink—the story was incredible enough, and the map spoke for itself.

He took the thing from my hands, weighed it in his. "A rotogravure. A roll with the design of a map etched into it—we make them here as you can see." His gesture took in the similar rolls upon the walls. "Maps are often transported this way on long and perilous voyages; they are not damaged by wind or rain as parchment may be, nor can they be torn. And if the ship is wrecked, they bob to the surface and float with the jetsam, to inform those that come after." He turned the roll in his hands. "Let us just be sure—I'd like to make another print,

463

for you did not use the best materials"—he grinned his lop-sided grin—"and the design is as clear as a February fog. *Con permesso?*" He asked our permission, and the monk and I nodded as one.

Signor Cristoforo took us to a flat wooden block and pinned a clean square of parchment in place. He spun the rotogravure in a tray of sticky black ink and rolled it once, cleanly, across the virgin sheet. Printed expertly as this, we could now see the detail as never before, and the star that we had seen at the left upper side of the unknown country now revealed itself to be a cross, with four short arms. Signor Cristoforo seemed thunderstruck and I followed his glassy gaze to the inky roll in his hands, which stained his fingertips with ink that he seemed not to notice.

I thought I guessed the reason for his dazzlement. "Is this one of yours?"

"No." He peered closely at the top end. "Very like. But there is a snake etched into the wood. We have a cross, the cross . . ." he said, "of Genoa." He plucked one of his own rolls from the wall shelf and showed me.

"It's the cross from the map!" I said slowly.

"Four arms of even length like the Maltese design," put in Brother Guido.

"Precisely. Or the Genoese design, for it rides upon our flag.

And so I must ask you again. Where did you get this rotogravure?"

Briefly, not believing it myself, I told him: of the storm, the basilica, and the Zephyrus horse. He merely nodded once or twice, not questioning at all. I could see Brother Guido trying to read his look, and the twin expression upon Signor Bartolomeo's face.

"What is it? What is amiss?"

The two brothers looked at each other. "It's just that," began Signor Bartolomeo, "this landmass here is the peninsula known as Italia."

That word again.

"We thought so," admitted Brother Guido. "And the cross denotes Monaco? For it is at the extreme northwest of the landmass. It is so, surely? The point of attack is Monaco, the gateway to France?"

Signor Cristoforo shook his head. "No, friend. It is certain. The city is denoted not just by the latitude and positioning but also by the emblem of the city itself. The site of attack, if there is to be one, is Genoa."

45

We sat, four not two this time, all seated on faldstools around the *Primavera,* rolled out on the printing table. For it was time to share the most incredible aspect of the puzzle with them—that the strategy of the Seven was hidden in a painting. The brothers leaned in as we had been used to do for these many months, and scanned the *cartone* with their mapmaker's eyes, plucking fresh details from the design like cormorants plucking fish from the brine.

"So all these are *cities,* these figures and deities." Signor Cristoforo's voice was full of wonder.

"Yes," confirmed Brother Guido, pointing to each in turn. "Pisa, Naples, Rome, Florence, Venice, Bolzano, and Milan. We have been to every city, either by accident or design, in the last twelvemonth. And every duke, king, archduke, and the prince of the church himself we know to be determinedly guilty."

"And this is clearly Genoa," put in Signor Bartolomeo, "for it is our own Simonetta, God rest her soul."

"Yes."

"Are we saying, then, that the Seven are planning to attack the eighth figure, Genoa? That Genoa is not in the Seven, but their victim and target? That your doge is not in league with the rest?"

"I can more readily believe that than believe that the doge would join Pisa and Venice in anything. Begging your pardon, lord and lady, he would rather have his wife couple with a cur than join in any enterprise with his sworn rivals and enemies," asserted Signor Cristoforo.

I remembered then what Brother Guido had told me as we entered the gates, why he addressed the guards in a Milanese accent, anxious that we should not reveal his Pisan tones, nor my Venetian origins, to anyone.

"But, why?" I asked. "Why Genoa?"

"The answer lies in what my brother just said," answered Signor Bartolomeo. "Genoa must have refused any part in Lorenzo's plan for unification, for what could it avail them? If the Hapsburgs have a trading treaty with Venice, Genoa—on the eastern seaboard—would dwindle from being *la Superba* ('the Proud' as we call her) to a mere outpost; descend from being a maritime state with full independence, to a fishing village."

"And if Genoa would not ally with the Seven," his brother said, taking up the argument, "then the union would not be safe. For Genoa is the back door to France, Portugal, Spain, and England too. These great nations would frown upon the peninsula joining together, for such a state would be an immensely strong force set right in the middle of Europe. We would have a stranglehold upon all trading routes through the *Mare Mediterraneo,* and the *Mare Atlantico* too."

I was getting a little lost. Brother Guido joined in to clarify the discussion but, as usual, muddied it with words as long as baitworms. "You see, internecine wars and civil strife keep 'Italia' at peace with the rest of the world." He collected my look. "We are too busy fighting each other to fight anyone else."

"Ohhhh." I nodded.

"The Italian wars, and centuries of struggle between the Guelphs and Ghibellines, kept the rest of Europe safe from greedy eyes," added Signor Cristoforo.

"While at the same time our many states were open to treaties with other powers, in order to strengthen their relative positions on the peninsula—Genoa with France, Milan with the Bourbons, Venice with the Hapsburgs, the Papal States with England," continued his brother, his ugly face lively with intelligence. "But a unified Italy could be an unstoppable force. Wealthy, with soldiers who had cut their teeth on years of warfare, and with four great navies—Venice, Naples, Pisa, and, greatest of all, Genoa."

"I very much wonder, if we have battled each other for so long, that there is anything left to unite," said I.

"More, much more than the sum of its parts," Brother Guido assured me. "For our states have not just developed their military capabilities, they have made huge cultural leaps too. Men like Poliziano, who wrote of the *Primavera,* and Botticelli, who painted it, are the sons born of such competition. Each state needs a glorious court to outdo her neighbors. And to military and cultural brilliance, add the power of God himself," continued Brother Guido grimly, "for *His Holiness* the Pope is the head of the Catholic Church." He spoke of the office with contempt. "They could rule the world."

"As they did once before," I breathed, recalling Don Ferrente's hymn to the glory of the Roman empire.

Brother Guido nodded. "The pope is a crucial figure in the conspiracy. He legitimizes the scheme in the eyes of the world, and, for his connivance, I think Lorenzo has promised that Rome will be the capital of the new nation. For see how Venus stands at the *center* of the scene, the highest figure save Cupid."

"And," I added, "she is dressed as a queen and holding her hand high in greeting."

"And Lorenzo de' Medici is at the root of all. The needle in the compass!" reflected Signor Cristoforo in a voice of wonder.

I thought on his metaphor, of Lorenzo as a needle showing the others the way. My eyes strayed to Mercury's sword: sharp, pointed, metallic. *Showing the others the way.* "Now we understand why Mercury's sword is pointing toward Simonetta," I burst out. "The enemy is Genoa."

"We should consider, too, the *nature* of that sword," added Brother Guido, pulling his own weapon from its sheath. The blade sang faintly and we all looked upon the deadly curve of the steel blade. "It is a harpe scimitar in the Eastern style, a Turkish design borrowed from our vanquished enemy of the Battle of Otranto. The Turks were expelled by the Genoese."

"And Simonetta wears a cross of pearls at her throat; the emblem of her city," I finished.

"And how did you know the others for conspirators," broke in Signor Bartolomeo, "these exalted men when you met them all?"

"Some of them damned themselves with their own words," answered Brother Guido. "Some gave others away. But all of them wear a gold band, with the nine Medici *palle,* on their thumbs."

"Their *left* thumbs, yes?" It was Signor Cristoforo that spoke, suddenly and urgently, and Brother Guido turned amazed blue eyes upon him.

"Yes. How did you know?"

"Look closely. All the seven conspirator figures have their *left* thumbs hidden."

I looked at each of the figures in the scene in turn, unable to believe my eyes.

Madonna.

How had we missed it?

Flame-haired Pisa hid her left thumb as she clasped Simonetta-Genoa's hand. Fiammetta-Naples hid her left thumb behind the fingers of her sister Pisa. Semiramide-Roma hid her left thumb in the scarlet swags of her wedding cloak. I, Flora, had my left thumb hidden below my skirt of roses. Chloris-Venice's left thumb was hid behind the hand she reached forth to clasp her daughter's arm. Zephyrus-Bolzano, the blue-winged sprite, had his left thumb hid in the gown of the nymph that he ravished. Mercury-Botticelli-Milan hid his left thumb behind his hip. Only Genoa—only Simonetta—exposed her left thumb to view, holding it high and proud, inviting the eye, linked with the right thumb of Naples, one of the highest points in the scene. Even tiny Cupid, our guide through the painting, had his little left thumb hid behind his bow.

"By the rood, you're right! You are absolutely right!" Brother Guido breathed.

Now I had seen it, it was obvious. "It even *looks* wrong."

"Precisely," agreed Brother Guido. "And we know that in *this* painting, *nothing* is an accident. Botticelli is the finest artist of his generation. His understanding and execution of the human form is second to none. And yet here, some of the hands look positively awkward. The right hand of Zephyrus, in particular, looks incorrect—surely if you were to grab at someone in anger or passion one would use the thumb to grasp her gown." His cheeks heated a little and he moved on swiftly. "Even Semiramide's left hand does not grasp the scarlet cloak as it should. But Botticelli would never paint someone with an unnatural attitude or posture. He is too accomplished for that. It *must* be by design, and the inference is, *they are all hiding something,* namely, their place in the alliance."

"It *was* by design!" I burst in. "For it was Botticelli himself who arranged my hands for me when I sat for him. I remember now how he hid my thumb under a fold of the fabric which held the roses. It was no accident. But why thumbs, of all things?"

Brother Guido shrugged. "In these lands it is common to bite your thumb at someone that you challenge to a fight. I think the origin of the gesture derives from the chivalric act of removing a gauntlet with the teeth, starting with the left thumb, so that the right hand can take the left glove and use it to strike the offender's face."

The brothers could not follow above a half of this cant about thumbs and were growing understandably impatient in light of the threat to their city. "So now what?" urged Signor Cristoforo.

"We must alert the Doge of Genoa," decided Brother Guido. "We gain audience somehow, and if he doesn't wear a ring on his left thumb, I think we may be sure he knows nothing of this conspiracy."

Signor Cristoforo leaped to his feet. "Bartolomeo, alert the harbormaster and the militia. Get them to ready the cannon ships in the port. Tell them there is an attack coming. Say we have intelligence from Venice. Take this"—he ripped up the new printed map from the table—"show him the cross of Genoa. Hurry."

His brother took the map and turned at the door. "Where are you going?"

"I must away with my friends to the doge. They know me at the palace, they've been kicking me out on my arse for a month for asking for money. They would never admit a Pisano. I can speak plain Genoese to the guards."

"What about me?" I protested.

"Stay here," they thundered in unison. Looked at each other.

"I," began Brother Guido, "that is to say, *we,* all want you out of danger."

"You must be joking." I grabbed my cloak. "I've come this far. I've hardly been 'out of danger' these past months. I can help! Have I not helped, so far?" I wheedled at Brother Guido, turned him around bodily by his shoulders and forced him to meet my eyes.

He looked me full in the face. "More than that," he admitted reluctantly. "We would not be here without you."

Signor Cristoforo shrugged. "Come, then, but stay in the rearguard." He turned back to his brother.

"Get the militia to come to the *faro.* We must post a lookout at *la lanterna.*"

A flash lit my brain as if lightning had struck. "What did you just say?"

Something in my voice stopped them in their tracks.

Signor Cristoforo turned slowly. "What, *la lanterna*?"

"Before that."

"Militia? *Faro?*"

"*Faro.*"

"It means lighthouse."

"What's a lighthouse?"

"I was no tutor if I did not tell you that," he replied testily. "The stone tower, yonder, has a great lantern atop the upper terrace. At night, and in sea fog, it lights the ships safely into harbor." He pointed to the tall finger of stone, clearly visible from this and every shack in Genoa.

"And it's known as a *faro*?" My voice shook a little.

"*Yes,*" he said with great impatience. All three men were staring at me now, as if I were a lunatic to stay them from their tasks with such mindless twaddle.

"How d'you spell that?" I asked grimly.

Signor Cristoforo regarded me as if I were an idiot child. "*F-A-R-O.*"

"*Faro!*" I shouted. I ripped the painting from Signor Cristoforo's hand. "We said, didn't we, that some cities held clues for *other* cities?" I demanded of Brother Guido. "Florence, for instance, holds the thirty-two roses to point to the compass rose in Venice?"

The brothers looked nonplussed but dear Brother Guido nodded.

"Yes, I see all that."

"Well, d'you remember, we could never read the Chloris flowers?"

Now I had lost even him. "What are you talking about?"

"Chloris," I insisted. "Don't you remember? Brother Nicodemus said '*flowers drop from her mouth like truths.*' And he was right. They *are* truths. There are four botanical types issuing from her mouth. Remember? *Fiordaliso,* anemone, rose, and *occhiocento.*"

"Well, those are colloquial vernacular names, not the Latin genus terms, but yes."

I waved my hand. "Forget about that. Think about their *first letters.*"

"*F-A-R-O,*" he mouthed, eyes enormous as he turned them on me. "Lighthouse. That's where they're going to land."

"And remember," I urged, "that *occhiocento* is the flower of death. The word *faro* ends in *O; it ends with death.* We said that the enterprise would end in death, one or many. Well, it will, if we don't get a move on."

Signor Cristoforo may not have followed the reasoning, but he took the meaning. "Bartolomeo," he said, never moving his eyes from me, "when you go to the *faro,* go armed. Tell the militia."

Signor Bartolomeo nodded once and was gone. The three of us were hard on his heels. Outside, on the waterfront, twilight was already beginning to thicken. Brother Guido put a hand on the bridle of il Moro's horse without a word, gentling him, while Signor Cristoforo untied the reins. Suddenly it was all real—now we hurried to save not nameless French families in some disinterested crusade but living, breathing Genoese who were a sunset away from the fire and the sword. My skirts brushed the Genoese brat who had watched our horse for a coin. *"Scusi,"* I said absently. She looked up and smiled at me, the dying sun catching eyes as green as mine. She was beautiful. I smiled back as Signor Cristoforo hauled me up to the saddle. I put my arms round Signor Cristoforo's waist while Brother Guido mounted behind us. "Hurry," I urged.

46

Signor Cristoforo led us swiftly, unerringly, to the great piebald Palazzo Ducale, seat of the Doge of Genoa. As we approached the gatehouse the daughter of the Mocenigos and the son of the della Torres shrank into the twilight shadows, together with their mount. I stroked the velvet nose of the Duke of Milan's horse, willing him to be quiet while the lowborn son of Genoa went forth as our ambassador. From where we hid we could easily hear the exchange.

"You again," said the first of two guards. As the doge's personal retinue, they looked a much tougher breed than the hapless pair we had seen at the gates. "I thought il Doge told you to sling your hook." His fisherman's slang seemed oddly fitting.

"Hang on, Cristoforo," said the second guard, mock serious. "I think I've got a couple of soldi. Look"—coins clanked—"how far will this get you in your expedition?"

The first guard laughed. "Well, it would be churlish for me not to help too. Let me see." He dug in his leather purse. "How's this? If I give you this *grosso,* maybe you could sail as far as the edge of the world and *fuck off* over the side." They fell about laughing.

We heard Signor Cristoforo's voice, low, persuasive, dignified. "Today I do not come to ask, but to give. I'm here to warn the doge against a coming attack. An attack that will see you and your families dead if you do not heed me."

"Who's attacking?"

"How do you know of this?" They spoke as one.

Signor Cristoforo answered the second question first. "A merchant contact in Venice. Does a bit of spying on the side. You know how hard it is to raise funds for expeditions." There was an ironic weight to his voice. He had their attention and now addressed the former question. "He says there's an alliance. Venice, Pisa, and more too. Coming by sea and land." I noted that he named Genoa's traditional enemies first and admired his cunning.

The first guard spoke to the second, less sure now. "He looks serious, Salva."

"He always looks serious. Beggars always do."

"Still, I'd hate to be the fellow that knew of this and didn't tell the doge," put in Signor Cristoforo breezily. "He'd be hanging upside down within a sennight. *If* he survived the attack, that is."

That did it. The second guard pushed himself off the wall

with a sigh, opened a small, man-sized door in the bottom of the great double doors, and called within.

"Giuseppe! Cover me. I'm going upstairs."

A young and pimply guard took Salva's place—they were clearly not as well manned here as they appeared. The three stood in silence for some moments. I don't think I breathed once in all that time. Presently the second guard was back.

"You're out of luck, Cristoforo. D'you know what he said to me?" The fellow leaned in and gave our friend the benefit of a rotten grin full of teeth as brown as medlars. "Il Doge said, 'I'd rather give audience to the first whore you find on the street than Signor Cristoforo, for at least she will render me some service for my money. So being as how il Doge is not a one for jokes, you'll forgive me if I take him at his word." He pushed past Signor Cristoforo so roughly that the sailor fell to the ground. I started forward, but Brother Guido pulled me back. He knew where I was going, of course.

"No," he said.

"But . . ."

"No."

"I'm not going to *fuck* him. I just want to talk to him. He said he wanted a whore, and he's going to get one."

He held my arm hard enough to hurt. The guard was almost past us, and I didn't have time for this. "If you're worrying about my maidenhead, I said good-bye to it long ago. Or is it my soul that concerns you? I thought you were done with piety?"

He recoiled, and I recognized with shock real pain in his eyes. "I'd rather die than let you bed another man." He caught himself, too late.

I looked into his face, heart thumping, and saw all I'd ever wanted writ there, just as it was too late to do anything about it. I pulled my sleeve free. "Die then," I said, but softly. "For if I don't go, we all will."

I ran after the guard, biting my lips and pinching my cheeks as I went, and pulling my bodice right down to the raspberries. Plucked his sleeve just before the dark streets of the stews swallowed him. "Please, sir, I couldn't help overhearing. Let me go to the doge and I'll save a little sugar for you." I leaned in and gave him the full benefit of my tits, pushed up like two glorious plump partridges on a plate. Chi-Chi was back. There was little light, but it was enough. I must have been like a cup of wine in a desert for this fellow, clearly too ill-favored to get many women.

He put a filthy hand under my chin. "Very nice," he said, licking his lips. "All right. But remember, when he's pissed his noble seed, it's milking time in the guardhouse. Just ask for Salvatore."

"Salvatore," I cooed, willing myself not to flinch at his breath. "That was my father's name."

He held my arm all the way to the doors and smacked my arse to propel me through.

I was in.

47

"An attack? At dawn? An alliance of seven city-states?"

Doge Battista of Genoa didn't believe me, and I didn't blame him. I wouldn't have believed me.

He lounged on a scarlet velvet couch, in a strange bedchamber striped, as the rest of the city, in black-and-white marble. He was younger than I expected, chubby, as overstuffed as his couch, moonfaced, with a pink and white complexion so smooth it seemed he could not yet grow a beard. He had the pale blue eyes and the strawberry-blond hair of a northerner. He could have been the Cupid of the *Primavera* all grown-up. But even if he were Cupid's cousin, it was clear he knew nothing of the plan. By his naked left thumb I knew him to be innocent. I also knew him to be clever—his little eyes were penetrating and his questions searching.

"And you know this, how? Yes, tell me, how does a common jade find out these lofty matters of state?"

It wasn't going to work. I took a deep breath and threw away my alias. "Because I'm not a common jade. I'm the dogaressa's daughter."

"Of Venice?" His pale brows flicked upward into twin fishhooks. "Come closer."

The light was low in the room. I moved to the window to catch the dying day.

He looked at me lazily, considering like a cat. "You do have the look of her, 'tis true. Like a lion's daughter. Giovanni Mocenigo is your father? The Doge of Venice is your father?"

"Yes. And I have lately been, in my mother's train, to the kingdoms of Bolzano and Milano where both Archduke Sigismund and Ludovico Sforza have joined the alliance. Il Moro is even now heading through the mountains with a thousand horse and ten thousand infantry. In company with him are my mother and father, and my . . ." I choked on the words. "My intended husband, Lord Niccolò della Torre of Pisa." These names, and the extent of my knowledge, tempered his mockery a little. But not entirely.

"Prove what you say."

For a moment I was stuck, then remembered the money belt. "Here." I reached below my skirts. "Venetian ducats of the Mocenigo stamp. And here too," I said, "the dogaressa's mask." I pulled it from my sleeve.

He raised himself from his cushions by no more than a handspan. "These things tell me no more than that you have been in Venice. No more than that. In fact—not *even* that. You could have stolen these things or even earned them on your back right here in Genoa. And if you are, as you say, Venetian, why would I trust you? For we are enemies."

I closed my eyes in frustration and could almost hear the rumble of a thousand horses cresting the mountains and pouring into the sea plains, almost hear the thunder of the great siege machines rolling down behind. I toyed with the idea of getting out the painting but realized that waving the *cartone* around could only compound my lunacy in the doge's eyes.

"You *have* to believe me. I'm trying to save your city and its people."

"And why do you care for my city?"

A goodly question. Inspiration struck, as I realized why I cared. "I know one who lives here! Signor Cristoforo, who was just lately at your gates. He tutored me in Venice, at my father's house!"

"The sailor?" Now he seemed jolted.

"Yes! Did he not tell you, he was just lately in Venice?"

"He did. And petitioned me for permission to go in the first place. I gave him leave to take their money for his lunatic trips if he could get it, for it is a fool's errand and he could not have mine."

"Well, then. And you know him to be loyal?"

The specter of a smile. "I thought him so, yes. Crazy but loyal."

"Then ask him," I urged. "He waits below."

The doge sighed. "Salvatore!"

In a very few moments Signor Cristoforo was in the room. His presence was enough to make the doge sit all the way up.

"Cristoforo. You have lately been in Venice?"

"Yes, my lord."

"And you met this lady there?" I noted I had been elevated from jade to lady at least.

"I did. I was her tutor in maritime matters for a short

while, while I petitioned the Council of Ten for expeditionary funds."

"Yes, yes. And you are aware of her true identity?"

"I am. She is Luciana Mocenigo, daughter to the doge and dogaressa, and heir to the Republic of Venice."

"You have heard her story of an impending attack?"

"I have."

"And you believe her? Before you answer, answer as a good and loyal Genoese. Think for a moment of your city, for treachery will be rewarded with death."

I saw my friend swallow. "I do believe her, my lord."

The doge stroked his hairless chin. "Very well." He called to his guard. "Salvatore, close the city gates and double the guard." He turned back to us. "Satisfied?"

Signor Cristoforo and I exchanged a look. "With great respect, *no,* my lord."

The doge raised his brows once again at such insolence.

"For il Moro brings with him such siege machines as the world has never seen, invented by a Tuscan engineer."

"Very well," conceded the doge. "Then this I will do. I will send a scout into the mountains to verify your tale. You, my dear"—he waved his languid hand in my direction—"will stay with me here—let us not say as my prisoner nor hostage, for these are ugly words; but as my guest, until he returns."

I went to him then and knelt by his couch. "My lord, you might as well send me down to the shore and bid me hold back the tide. For in the time it takes for your runner to go and return, the army of the Seven will be upon you, and will beat your outrider to the gates. What you *must* do is send every available footsoldier and every cavalry knight to the mountains—*now.*"

Signor Cristoforo took up the cause. "If our forces meet them on the slopes, in a surprise attack, their superior numbers will not avail them any advantage. If you meet them in the Torriglia pass, they will be forced through the neck of a bottle."

The doge stroked his hairless chin. "One *tiny* thing, though. If I denude my city of all its soldiery, who will defend us against an attack by the sea?"

Signor Cristoforo and I swapped glances. "We're just coming to that."

"There's *more*?" The poor besieged doge gaped like a codfish.

"A fleet of Pisan and Neapolitan ships is bearing to your coastline even now, and will be here by first light, led by Don Ferrente, King of Naples."

Now the young duke blanched whiter than milk. "Then we are done for."

"Not so, my lord. Even now my brother is rousing the harbormaster and militia. Our fleet can be ready, the cannon loaded by dawn. They are planning to sail right into our harbor, but we can put up a fight they will not expect."

The doge's little eyes sparked alight and I felt glad—this corpulent fellow had some fettle. I began to like him.

"Further, my lord," Signor Cristoforo went on, "we should with all possible speed douse the *lanterna* in the *faro,* and light a beacon on the cliffs to the west at Pegli. That way if the fleet is heading for the lighthouse, we can lead them to wreck upon the westward rocks."

The doge hesitated for no more than a heart's beat. "Do it."

Signor Cristoforo and I made for the door, as Genoa's duke called for his generals and his armor, pacing now as he waited before his couch while his kingdom crumbled around him. The door closed behind us, and I heard him sink back down into the velvet cushions. I opened the door again and crept back in on silent feet. The doge was seated, with his head in his hands. "Why has God turned against me so?" he muttered.

"Not God," I said aloud. He looked up with a ruined face.

"The fault lies elsewhere." I put out my hand, sorry for him now. He seemed so young and alone. I suspected he had never been to war—that he had been trained in combat but never seen action, a noble in name but never, till now, in the breach. Like Brother Guido. "My lord, let your generals lead your armies. Why don't you come with us to the *faro*? You are needed there on a matter of politics." I knew with sudden certainty who would be waiting there. "There's someone I would very much like you to meet."

48

Brother Guido met us at the palace doors with great relief, matched only by my own—for once the plot had been revealed to the Genoese, a Pisan in soldiers' garb with a warhorse could be executed as an enemy outrider. The doge did not question Brother Guido's presence once he was identified as our friend; I think he soon realized that there were very strange alliances on both sides of this battle. The doge's grooms brought his horse, and a white charger and a black one sped us to the lighthouse. It was not until we left the tall and narrow sheltering streets that we realized quite how heavily it was raining. I pitied both armies, floundering in a muddy mountain battlefield, and for the first time thought about my mother. Would she survive the night to come? I felt no pity though—*that* I reserved for the mothers' sons that fought for their families, or the city that they loved, or even a weekly purse: all more honest motives than hers.

Now it was fully dark, and the *lanterna* burned bright at the top of the *faro*, guiding the enemy fleets close. We skidded to a stop at the harbor, and Signor Cristoforo slid off at once, bellowing for Bartolomeo, running to help with the muster. We both dismounted and Brother Guido took my arms, yelled in my ear against the hashing rain. "Take the doge into the light-house, he will be safe. It is guarded by the Genoese militia, with lookouts posted. Signor Cristoforo says there is a chamber in the first *terraza*."

"And I?"

"Go to the second *terraza*, and *douse the lantern*. It must be *completely out*, Luciana, so do this one last thing, and do not fail in it."

I clung to his sodden cloak. His hair was plastered into black slabs which fell across his blue eyes like prison bars. "Where are you going?"

"I must take the horse to the westward cliffs and kindle a fire," he bawled. "We need a beacon of gorze and heather to burn at Pegli and divert the ships." He looked to the skies. " 'Twill not be easy in this rain, but it must be done."

Still I clung like a monkey. "Cannot someone else go?"

"No." He shook his head and the raindrops flew. "Signor Cristoforo is mustering the fleet, and the duke must be kept safe within. This is the fastest horse in the city, and as I am no swimmer, I must serve on land not water. Let me go to my task and do you go to yours." He looked me straight in the eye. "You may pray for me though."

The raindrops were my tears—I felt that I was saying good-bye.

"I thought you had done with God." I choked.

"I did have done with God, but he had not done with me."

I looked back at him, and he smiled his sunburst smile, the old Brother Guido, with the light of faith in his eyes behind the blue.

"Then you'll go back? When all this is over?" I needed to look beyond this night, needed to know there may be a time when I could visit him at Santa Croce. Just to know he was alive would be enough for me now.

"To the monastery? No."

"But . . ."

He held my face in both his hands. "I could never go back. Not because I don't love God. But because I do love *you*." He kissed me once then, hard, his lips freezing without and warm within, moving across my cheek and to my ear. "Love is when you like someone so much you have to call it something else," he whispered. And was gone.

Joy and sadness rushed in upon me: joy that he loved me but tempered with an unshakable feeling that I had touched him for the last time. Stricken, both with bliss and loss, I stumbled to the lighthouse with the doge in tow. The door was guarded by two militiamen with the crosses of Genoa on their chests. Their pikes sprang apart at a nod from the doge, allowing us inside without question. My skin began to prickle with foreboding, images nudging my dull brain as I climbed—one guard had had a sleeve so long that it flapped over his hand, another so short that a white circle of wrist showed above the hand that grasped the pike. Something was wrong.

Once within, the howling wind, the driving rain, and the crashing waves ceased—the walls so thick as to block out the tempest. The only sound as we climbed was our breathing and the clanking of the doge's armor. I could see the glow of candlelight spilling down the steps even before the last turn of the stair. I knew who would be there in the chamber, unable to stay away, watching from the window as the grand scheme played out.

We entered the square room. Empty save for one figure at the window, clad in magnificent purple velvet and gold brocade, looking out to sea as the day bruised to the first of night. He turned at our steps.

Lorenzo de' Medici.

49

"Lorenzo?"

"Battista, my dear fellow." Both men registered shock and surprise, swiftly covered by their urbane courtier masks, in many ways as substantial as my mother's.

The younger man spoke first. "What do you here?"

The gray Medici eyes were wary. "My, er, ship foundered in the storm. I took shelter here to wait until I could make my way to your palace and beg for your sanctuary."

"Indeed?" The doge expressed polite surprise. "The spring tides are somewhat unpredictable."

The noble pair regarded each other like street cats, not sure whether to purr or strike.

"Where were you headed?"

"To Pisa. There's a marriage there soon, is there not, my dear?" I stepped out of the shadows of the door. "And I would so hate to miss your nuptials, child, since you were good enough to attend my nephew's."

I met his eyes steadily and saw that he knew everything. I did not know what to say, but fortunately the doge did.

"Strange. What an odd route to take, from Florence to Pisa by *sea*." His voice was dangerously soft now. "You are sadly off course, my lord."

Now it was Lorenzo that foundered and sought an answer.

The doge forestalled him. "Forgive me, my lord. Before we continue this *interesting* conversation, I must assist my guest in a small matter. Perhaps you will stay a while and admire the drama of the tempest." He was all deadly politeness.

Lorenzo caught the tone. "Oh, I think I have trespassed long enough. The winds seem to be easing."

"Indeed you are mistaken. The storm is as threatening as ever; I really couldn't let you risk a journey in such conditions. I really must insist, and to help you make up your mind, know that my men are posted downstairs."

"*Your* men? Is that so?" Lorenzo seemed amused, even though he was as good as trapped. I felt that prickle of unease again—it was all wrong for the lobster in the pot to laugh at the fisherman. "In that case, it would be churlish not to stay a while and converse a little. What shall we talk about?"

"How is your foreign policy?" The question was as pointed as a stiletto.

"Uneventful," Lorenzo answered smoothly. "On the *domestic* front, however, I have invested in an attractive alliance which I hope will soon accrue great interest."

"There is a difference between legitimate interest and usury."

Like scrapping toms they stopped, circled, waited for the next blow. Lorenzo got in first.

"Speaking of interest, how *is* your bank loan?"

"Helpful."

They broke once again, and I took my chance, aware of the urgency of my task. I plucked the doge's scarlet sleeve.

He turned to me, then back to il Magnifico. "Ah, yes. As I hinted earlier, my guest here has a little business upstairs. You will, naturally, make no attempt to stop her course."

"I would not dream of it. Away you go, my dear, *la lanterna* awaits."

Bemused, I held his granite-gray gaze as I backed out of the room, wary of some trick. Surely Lorenzo il Magnifico would not just stand idly by as I wrecked his cherished plans?

I left them to their counterfeit courtesies and climbed higher, to the second terrace. Entering the upper chamber, I noticed three things.

Cosa Uno: that the lantern stood in the middle of the room like a sunburst—a glass constructed of many-faceted crystals, cradling an enormous vat of flame burning what my nose told me was olive oil. The light burned bright, despite four great windows open to the four winds, letting the tempest howl through, snatching at my hair and clothes. The wind horses conspired to ride me over the merlons, so that I had to hang on for dear life or grim death. And still the lantern burned steady. It was a beauteous thing—a lens to catch the light and send it back a thousandfold, like the biggest diamond that the world held. A gem, bright as the Bethlehem star, to guide ships home.

Cosa Due: my feet stuck to the floor in a way that recalled my house by the Arno—for a flood of blood leached from the slashed throats of the two dead Genoese lookouts, sprawled where they had died upon the floor. A brief glance told me neither one was Bartolomeo, *grazie Madonna*. And:

Cosa Tre: I realized why the Prince of Florence had not prevented me from climbing the stair, for there, black as night and dark as death, standing sentinel over the lantern like the reaper himself, was the cowled leper, Cyriax Melanchthon.

For a heartbeat we regarded each other. He was utterly still while his tattered robes of the unclean bellied and snapped in the wind like a sail. Black bandages covered his face to leave only his silver eyes to penetrate my soul. Hunter and prey face-to-face at last. This time my terror was compounded by a further fear—that I would not be able to douse the lantern, that I would fail in the task I had been set. But there was little time to think, for he leaped for my throat.

His grip was iron around my neck—black spots danced before my eyes, fire and blood gurgled in my ears. I could not breathe, and yet he assailed me with only one of his wasted hands—the other reached for his butcher's knife. I would have begged but could not speak . . . could not speak . . . then remembered in a flash what Nicodemus of Padua had said: *he has no lower jaw, so has lost the power of speech.* I thrust a hand out to the leper's throat. Fearless of contagion, I scrabbled beneath the facecloths and met an open gizzard and twisted raw giblets of flesh. It bought me respite—he let me go—choking with a horrid gurgling sound. I fell to the floor and cracked my head upon the lantern, tried to scramble for the door, but he was upon me again, and those powerful hands lifted me like a feather, smashed me back against the lantern, the glass and the leads hot enough to brand my flesh. One powerful hand held my throat once more, and this time he managed to get his knife free—held it high to strike.

My last moment seemed to go on for hours—images flashed into my mind; time turning backward like a wheel. I saw everywhere and everything from my birth to now—I was a baby in a bottle, a girl in a convent, a whore, a noblewoman. And Brother Guido, so many images of him: every road we'd traveled, every time he'd touched me, all the way back to the time we had first met. I was back in Florence on that burning day, before I'd met Botticelli, before all this had begun.

The hand of my killer tightened, the lantern burned at my back, and the crystals cracked under my skull. I shut my eyes to the present. I wanted to die in Florence, with Brother Guido beside me. I remembered what he'd first said to me: *Luciana Vetra, it means the light in the glass; let the light out. Let the light out . . . I was a baby in a bottle, let the light out, let it out.*

With the last of my strength, I smashed out at the crystals of the lantern and we both fell back into the fire. As if we danced, I turned the leper beneath me, and the flaming oil soaked us both. But the fire in the glass protected its namesake; my sodden cloak and hair did not burn, but the bone-dry leper caught like a beacon. Like a human torch, he ran about the little room; turned about and about in unnaturally silent agony as I watched, appalled. The oil had set the floor aflame and I beat at the fire with my saturated cloak, dousing the pockets that threatened to engulf me. The leper fell at last, his superhuman strength at an end, his silver eyes dull and dead. The fire had burned his bandages away and I could not look at what was revealed. I had not expected to feel pity for him, but if God had cursed me with such a disease, then I, too, may have become what he had become.

Now in near dark and alone with three corpses, one of the dead as hideous as hell, I busied myself with dousing the last of the flames, wondering all the time how Brother Guido did on the westward cliffs. I peered from the west window but against the battering rain could see no light on the cliffs. I was just praying that one day I would see him again, when God answered and, incredibly, I heard Brother Guido's voice, bawling from below.

"Luciana! Luciana!"

"Here!" I shouted and waved, gladness filling me.

There he was, waving from below. He carried a small bark upturned above his head against the rain. Like a *corno* in his shell.

"Luciana, is the lantern out?"

"Nearly—I'll be down soon. I'm dousing the last of it now." I turned back, happy now to finish my task.

"No!" he yelled, with such desperation that I stopped at once.

"Listen to me carefully," Brother Guido shouted from the rocks below. "Take the map and douse it with the olive oil. Set it alight and throw it from the window. Do it *now*."

"What, why—"

"Just do it." There was such urgency in his voice I did not question further. I took the map roll from my sleeve and rolled it in the spilled oil on the floor. I found the last tiny pocket of flame in the very heart of the lantern and willed the roll to light. My will was answered more than I desired for the roll went up with a whoosh which threatened to take my eyebrows—there had to be some compound in Signor Cristoforo's ink which made the wood burn even more merrily, with a bluish flame like a torch.

I went to the window, holding the burning roll as far from me as possible, hoping I could cast it down before it burned down to my oily fingers. I watched Brother Guido set down the boat and wrap his sodden cloak around his hands. "Drop it to me carefully, Luciana."

I did so, praying the fall would not douse the fire, but the torch fell like a comet with a flaming tail—and Brother Guido caught it skillfully and picked his way carefully down the rocks. I could not let him go without knowing. "What happened?" I yelled.

"I could not light the beacon. Too wet," he shouted briefly.

"So you're taking that flame all the way to the *cliffs*?" I screeched in disbelief. "It will never last till then!"

"I know," he yelled back. "Signor Cristoforo has another idea. I am to take the firebrand out to his ship, which he will set afire and sail into the fleet. For the Muda are hard by—a thousand ships, not half a league from here."

My mind boggled at the lunacy of the scheme. "You'll be killed! Both of you! The storm, the fire—"

He cut across me. "Better two than thousands." He set the boat on the churning sea, took the torch in his teeth, and fitted the oars in the rowlocks.

"Don't go!" I screamed. "Let them come! Why does it matter?"

He looked up at me one last time. "You know why it does."

I watched, helpless, as he struggled with the black mountainous waves, fearing that he would be dashed on the rocks; but he was a strong oarsman and pulled free of the wicked shoreline, the light getting smaller and smaller. At every stroke of the oars I feared that the torch would go out, feared that it wouldn't. I couldn't decide whether I wanted him to succeed in his task or fail and return.

The torch flickered, was dying. Then the boat leaped into flame—he had used something for kindling, to keep the flame alive. Now I knew he could not survive, and watched, appalled, as the lighted boat illuminated a larger scape, the dark, tall silhouette of a Genoese schooner, pulling the boat in with grapple hooks, smaller dots of flame breaking off from the burning bark as the sailors lit torches. Dark figures fired the sails; then the whole ship became a conflagration, for they must have soaked the canvases with oil. Shapes jumped and fell against the flame as all hands leaped into the water—Signor Cristoforo and his valiant crew. Then the fire ship, keeping a steady course, found the flagship of the Muda and one, then ten, then twenty, then a thousand ships caught and the ocean itself was aflame. Screams and confusion as the fleet burned and enough light for my desperate eyes to search for the little burning bark—as impossible as trying to see one twig in a burning hearth. But then, for the second time that night, I did see a human form burning, standing alone in the ocean on the burning curracle—a little island of fire. The figure stretched out his arms like Christ and shouted some words, before he dived into the waves.

I did as Brother Guido had bid me and began to pray.

50

The first day of spring dawned cold and drizzling.

Although the storm had blown itself out, the misty rain soaked my hair and clothes, in the place where Lorenzo's dream had died and my own had ended. He had wanted an empire,

I had wanted a lover. A great dream and a little one. Both dead.

More than dreams had finished their stories here. As I wandered on the beach in the silver dawn, charred bodies of sailors washed ashore, some Genoese, most Neapolitan. I set myself a grisly task—I turned every body with my foot, examined every bloated face for Brother Guido's features. My heart told me he had gone, but I had to be sure. I would not give up. My feet were numbed by the freezing tide washing over my shoes, but I barely noticed.

"Luciana!" A voice hailed me from the shore. I spun at once, but it was Signor Cristoforo.

"Come away," he said. "He is not there."

"I know."

He came to me, laid a hand gently on my shoulder. "In the end he had to set fire to the boat to keep the flame alive. I saw him jump—he had no choice—it was that or burn. We all did the same. But I think he could not swim."

"He couldn't," I choked.

"Better swimmers than he are dead this day. The fire, the storm, were too much for them, and him too."

I turned my eyes on him. "Bartolomeo?"

"He lives. But many poor souls did not—here and upon the mountain too. But Genoa won the day."

It seemed an odd phrase—for all appeared lost to me. I looked out to sea, fixing my eyes on the spot where I had last seen Brother Guido. "Did he say something?"

"Yes. He said, *The chaff He will burn with unquenchable fire.* He shouted it. Then jumped."

I nodded. Unable to speak. I suppose I should have been glad that he quoted the Scriptures at the end, before going to meet his God.

But I had rather he had sent a message to me.

Signor Cristoforo held both my shoulders. "He saved many more than were lost. Countless souls. He saved my city. I think . . . he must have been a very good man."

"He was," I whispered. My legs gave way and I sank to the shingle, swept away on a tide of grief.

He squatted beside me and looked out to sea. Charred hulls poked from the water like bergs, soon to sink forever, their masts and blackened pennants the last to go. So many, so very many burned-out ships, clustered on the horizon like a winter forest. "I came to say good-bye," he said.

I turned stricken eyes upon him. "You too?" He was the one friend I had left.

"I have been too long from the ones I love. If this last night has taught me anything, it is that it is time I saw my son."

"Diego?"

He smiled. "You remembered."

I turned back to the sea, beyond the wrecked fleet, off into the infinite, gray-blue yonder. "How will you live?"

"I think now Doge Battista may pay for my ship of fools, after the service I rendered the city, don't you? And if he does not, no matter. I will petition the rulers of Spain."

"Take this on Venice's account." I reached beneath my sodden robes and gave him the purse of fifty ducats I had stolen from my mother. His bulbous eyes popped further when he saw the gold flash, heard the chink of coins. "Don't you need it?"

I shook my head. Money didn't matter to me anymore. "Where will you go?"

"Portugal first, then the Azores, to my father and Filipa. And little Diego."

I sighed like the wind, for all that he had and that I had not.

"I would not prevent you. Go and be with your wife and child. Love and family is all that matters." I had forfeited both in one fateful night.

"I was about to say the same to you. Your mother awaits you at the doge's palace."

"My mother?" I had not given her a thought since Brother Guido had left my sight.

"Yes. She and your father and Ludovico il Moro were captured and brought to the city at dawn. They are my lord doge's hostages until they sign a treaty of peace, which even now is being writ by his scribes."

"What of Don Ferrente?"

"Turned for home as soon as the first ship burned."

"And Niccolò della Torre?" I asked with a catch in my voice.

"Who?"

"The lord of Pisa?"

He shrugged. "I have no word of him. Why?"

"No matter." I could not form the words, not explain the terrible irony that if I were to return to my life, I would be wed to the cousin of he who was lost to me, to be reminded every day that a better copy of this nobility once lived, once loved me. The cruelty struck me in the chest like a blow and I thought I would die too. Wished that I would.

"When you are ready, go back to your mother. You are the first soul she asked for, never thinking of her own safety. I think that she loves you. She is a lioness, granted; but you are the lion's child." I felt him kiss my forehead.

I could not look up. Could not lift my weary head.

"Godspeed," he said.

"And you," I whispered. But he had gone harborward and the wind snatched my words away from him.

I don't know how long I sat there on the freezing shingle. Rafts of wood and bundles of canvas nudged and bumped at my feet as the tide inched in. At length the treacherous sun broke through the clouds and dried me, warmed the pebbles beneath my legs. It was going to be a beautiful day.

Soon I must choose to stay and drown or rise and live. I heaved myself up, and as I did so, I felt the scratch of a parchment in my bodice. The *cartone* of the *Primavera,* which had found me love and lost it again. I took the thing out and cast it into the sea, as far, far as I could, and turned back landward before I could know where it landed. I did not want the thing anymore. But the tide would not allow me even this gesture. The thing washed back to me, soaked and dun like a dead sole, and flopped over my sodden shoe. I looked at it draped there, and thought then that it was the last thing he and I had touched together—'twas something he and I had shared. Perhaps one day I would be able to look on it again. I rescued it from the surf before the ebb could take it again—squeezed the water from it like a washcloth and turned to wander back to the Palazzo Ducale, not knowing what else I could do.

My options were limited. I could stay and work the stews of Genoa, fucking sailors until I was too old for them to want me, or I could claim my birthright and get a feckless *finocchio* of a husband into the bargain, like a worm that comes with the apple. Or die by my own hand and meet Brother Guido in the afterlife. Only I wasn't sure I believed in the afterlife, for all my convent education. And even if I did, the nuns had not neglected to tell me that suicides went straight to hell. As Brother Guido, who died to save others, like Christ himself, was surely going to walk straight into heaven, we would then be parted for all eternity. I hoped Brother Guido rejoiced with the angels that he believed in afresh.

Tears blurred my eyes and I all but lost my way. I passed countless families on their way to mass, anxious to give thanks for the fate they had escaped. Even the bells sounded joyful as they called the faithful in triumph. I was the only soul on the streets who did not wear a smile—not even the sight of the dames and children we had saved lifted my stony heart. I came at last to the huge striped palace with the great gates, knew that once I laid my hand upon the door I had made my choice.

I called to the guard and accepted my fate.

I was shown to an airy presence chamber, as if I were the Queen of Sheba—my fame had clearly spread and the city was in debt to me. I felt oddly guilty, as the guards and servants kissed my hands, for I did not merit this. Others deserved such thanks and praise, others that were gone. I was placed in a golden chair, given a cup of wine and asked to wait, told that the doge would be with me presently.

The door opened almost at once and another exalted personage was seated across from me, also to await the doge's pleasure. For him, though, there was no golden chair, no chalice. Just a bracelet of chains around his wrists.

The door closed again, and for a few, short, incredible moments I was alone with Lorenzo de' Medici.

51

He leaned forward in his chair and considered me. He seemed to bear me no enmity but just looked intensely interested. I met his eyes, for I had learned in the last hours that if you no longer have anything to lose, you no longer have anything to fear.

"Why did you want to stop me?" Those graveled, famous tones were completely in earnest, inquiring, wanting to know. "Why did it matter?"

I realized with a jolt that he echoed exactly my last question to Brother Guido, and I recalled his very last words to me. *You know it does.* Suddenly I knew why it did matter, so very much.

"Because in Genoa two brothers have a map shop by the

sea and dream of finding new lands. Because in Bolzano they eat dumplings called *Knödel* and dance like lunatics. Because in Pisa, there is a tower that leans but does not fall down, and every year four quarters of the city push a tree trunk over a bridge. Because in Venice they have built a city on water and make wondrous glass out of dust. Because in Naples you can buy a carving of the Nativity so real it's as if you're there, and at the next stall buy a human skull. Because in this land"—I had to steady my voice—"a man can love his city so much, he will give his life to have it stay the same."

I had to stop, fiercely blinked away my tears, not wanting him to see me cry. But the traitorous drops brimmed and spilled from my eyes and down my cheeks. The first tears I had shed since I was a baby in a bottle. He said nothing, but his granite eyes softened ever so slightly. Knowing I would never get the chance again, I questioned him in turn. "Why did you want to do it?"

"Because I wanted to make Italia great," he replied simply.

I lifted my stricken face to him. "It already was," I choked. "It already was."

The door to the ducal chamber opened. "My lord doge will see you now," intoned a liveried servant, clearly having difficulty in finding a single tone with which to address a friend and a foe. "Both of you."

We rose, and the Prince of Florence, incredibly, stood back to let me pass through first.

A strange sight met my eyes. Seated around the perimeter of the room were three figures.

Figura Uno: Ludovico il Moro, still in full armor, bloodied and beaten.

Figura Due: my father, without his ceremonial robes and *corno* hat, just looking like a sad old man. And:

Figura Tre: my mother, in a breastplate and riding gear, looking at first glance like an Amazon queen, but on closer inspection she looked old, as if she had cried the night through, this and many others.

My mother half rose from her seat at the sight of me, as if she would have run to embrace me, but a glance from the doge stopped her. Armed guards wearing the cross of Genoa on their tabards ringed the room with pikes and halberds glinting in the sun. Out of the paned windows I could see the *faro* and the brilliant sea, smooth and clear as if naught were amiss. I could hear the mew of the same gulls I had heard yesterday, before the world had changed.

The doge sat upon his scarlet couch, sifting through a document. Today he showed total self-possession. He had grown up in a night. Today he was not Cupid. Today he was a king.

"Ah, Lorenzo," he said. "Come. We are missing only your signature."

Il Magnifico approached the couch, his face as sour as a lemon. The doge passed him the quill himself, watched him struggle to write his mark with bound hands.

"Well," said Genoa's lord, when it was done. "That all seems to be in order. A confession and a contract in one—rarely is a treaty so simply achieved. I'd like to thank you all very much." He smiled sweetly round at the thunderous faces in the room.

My father, ever the politician, was the first to speak. "This treaty of peace, it will be . . . strictly sub rosa?" His voice was weak and cracked when he spoke—the voice of an old man.

"As secret as the plot that made it necessary," replied the doge pointedly. "History will not learn of these events, *if* you obey my terms."

"This is ridiculous!" burst il Moro in his blustering tones, unable to keep silent. "Are you really saying we cannot ever again face each other in armed conflict? There have been wars in Italia since the Romans and Etruscans, and before that too!"

The doge smiled. "My dear Ludovico. How you do love a war, do you not? Don't worry. I'm sure we all will meet in battle again, at field or sea. I'm sure there will be alliances made and broken from now until the end of time. But this is different." He waved the parchment. "This contract states that never again will an attempt be made to unify this peninsula and subsume the city-states into one empire. In support of this I am sending a copy, with all my seals intact, to His Highness Louis XI of France, Their Highnesses Ferdinand and Isabella of Spain, and His Highness Edward IV of England. As I am sure you will acknowledge, such a union of our states would be as threatening to their kingdoms as it was to my own duchy. If any of you, or your fellow members of 'the Seven,' should break this agreement signed here today, I will instruct my allies to break the seals and read what was writ here today, and to mobilize their forces against you. With my full support, they may ride their battalions through my duchy, as a gateway to yours. For to such a union Genoa will never agree."

He sat back on his couch and steepled his hands together. "Incidentally, I am sending a copy also to His Holiness Pope Sixtus in Rome. I have a feeling that his godly conscience will prompt him to ratify the treaty, don't you?"

He addressed the room at large, fully in control; the knowledge that the Holy Father had connived with the conspirators hung in the air, acknowledged but not expressed. The doge had caught all these fine nobles in his net like so many gaudy fishes—he alone could release them. And he did. "And now I give you leave to return in peace to your own kingdoms and principalities. As far as I am aware, you were never here. You will have safe conduct to the Torriglia mountains. After that, you must shift for yourselves." He stood, as if dismissing the company. "Rule well, and let us celebrate our differences, while remaining friends."

The exalted company rose to their feet as one, and the doge sat down again at once, pointedly taking up the treaty to read it over, as if he could not bear to be bracketed with these allies even in the simplest terms—if they sat, he stood. If they should stand, he would sit. Genoa would act now and forever alone. But the doge had not quite done. "Not you, Signor Medici," he said, not looking from his papers. Lorenzo did not turn but stood in the middle of the room, waiting to know his fate. We all looked on, not breathing.

"As for you, *il Magnifico*"—his voice bore the weight of irony—"I thank you very much for your *visit* to my city." The doge clearly wished to stop short of openly accusing Lorenzo of being the mastermind behind the alliance. "I hope the experience was not ruined for you by the *weather*. I see that *spring* has brought clemency and harmony to the climate." He waved a languid hand at the peerless view. "In return for my hospitality I'm sure you won't mind if we write off our outstanding debts to the Medici bank. I wouldn't want the origins of last night's events to become *public,* would you? And secrecy always has its price."

Il Magnifico looked as if he had a rotten fish below his nose. He nodded once, curtly, then looked the young doge in the eye.

"It is coming, you know," he said with assurance. "Someday, all our states will be one."

"Perhaps," said Doge Battista, and leaned close. "But not in *my* lifetime, and certainly not in *yours*."

It was the taunt of a young man to an older one. Lorenzo seemed to turn to stone, then the spell broke and he flourished and left, followed by the rest of his conspirators. My mother turned at the door and sent me a beseeching glance.

The door closed behind them all. "Signorina." The doge turned to me and drew me down beside him on the scarlet

couch. "Your services to this city are over. I offer you my gratitude and am forever in your debt." He kissed my hand, then
searched my face. "I hear your friend is dead and am truly
sorry. He was brave and steadfast and served God. Find your
example from him and not your family. Be a worthy heir to
your city, as I hope to be to mine. Now go and join your mother."
He took up his papers again.

I joined the rest as we waited in the presence chamber for
our carriages to take us home. I sat next to my mother and she
folded my hand in hers. I did not take it away. I looked around
the room at these rulers of men, those elected and those born
to power. In that moment I realized the ship of fools was not
sailing to Portugal this day. It was here. This room. Now I
knew the significance of Brother Guido's last, shouted prayer
as he burned. *The chaff He will burn with unquenchable fire.* But
it had all gone awry. It was the wheat that had been burned
away and the chaff remained.

I realized then that Italia wasn't great because of men like
these but because of men like the one that was lost.

· 10 ·

Pisa II

52

And so, by the end of the spring I was once again in Brother Guido's city. Once again I stood in the Campo dei Miracoli, at the doors of the great white cathedral, gazing on the great white baptistery and the great white tower that leaned but would not fall down. Only today I matched the white city.

It was my wedding day.

Today there was no painting in my bodice. Instead, for my own satisfaction, I put the green glass knife there—the neck-rim from the bottle I'd been in as a baby. Sharp and curled as a claw, it reminded me where I came from and where I was going to, and that there was always a way out. If suicides were damned, so be it. Damnation may be better than married life. I had seen enough lambs slaughtered in Ognissanti to know I could push the blade behind the windpipe and the blood would course down the white and gold, a satisfying exit, right there at the altar. They'd be talking about it for years.

My mother interrupted my thoughts. "Let me look at you." Resplendent in her favorite green, she wore her golden lioness half-mask today, with a hundred golden chains hanging from the nose to chin. She smiled at me proudly beneath it, as if naught were amiss. As if I were a favored daughter about to fulfill her heart's desire, not about to be shackled to a pederast whom I hated with the heat of hellfire.

I had not seen my intended since we had come to Pisa, where we were, by a strange twist of fate, guests of Lorenzo de' Medici at his riverside palace on the Lungarno Mediceo. A place I had once gone to with Brother Guido, and stolen a boat, to drift down the river of a thousand torches. The irony was not lost upon me; Brother Guido had left his own city in the manner in which he was to die.

I saw Lorenzo il Magnifico now and again, and he was the very model of courtesy. Neither he, nor anyone, referred to the events that had taken place in Genoa not four months ago. In all that time I had not once seen Niccolò. I understood he had taken an arrow in the leg at the Battle of Torriglia Pass and had gone to the mountains to take the waters and recover. My mother had assured me that all was well. (As if I were worrying about him.) "The marriage contracts are intact, despite recent—events . . ." It was the closest she ever came to speaking of it. "Except for a few minor alterations. It is true that the prince was injured in the battle, for he is, as you perhaps know, not an accomplished fighter. But his condition will not affect the wedding, it will take place *almost* as planned."

Yes, with my damaged husband carried in on a litter. *Madonna*. One thing worse than being married to an evil selfish man was being married to an evil selfish cripple.

Now, at the hour of my marriage, my mother pinched my cheeks, then adjusted my bodice. "There. You are lovelier than a summer day." I looked at her sharply, but there was no irony in her tone nor her eyes. She meant what she said and it was said with love. I shook back my hair, heavy with a thousand pearls and moonstones, and hitched up my bodice. Something felt different. I looked down between my breasts—the knife was gone.

"Mother," I called sharply.

She turned back, guilty, and I saw at once she had taken it. She had last touched that piece of Venetian glass when her hands had placed me in the bottle, with the bread and breast-milk. She had taken it, and with it, my way out.

I let out a gusty sigh, utterly defeated. "Very well." I knew now I must go through with the wedding, but it would not be for naught. "Grant me a boon then, as a wedding present, if I am to do this thing."

She came back to me. "Of course."

I said, slowly and clearly, "I want you to free Bonaccorso Nivola." I thought I would have to explain who the imprisoned sailor was, for my mother, as I told you, never noticed the little people. But she knew at once—perhaps he had been troubling her conscience too.

"Done."

And as she spoke the trumpets and timbrels sounded, and the great doors opened into the cathedral. I processed down the aisle on the arm of my mother, feeling, as I had done once before, that the great white pillars and the arching ribs above my head were bones, and I was trapped in the belly of a great beast. As we walked through ranks of cheering people I wondered if they were the same folk who'd cheered me a year ago, when I'd been here with Brother Guido, riding in a golden carriage with the doomed father of my betrothed.

My mother kissed my cheek as we reached the altar. "You'll be happy," she said. "Trust me." For the second time today I looked into her leaf-green eyes and saw no lies writ there.

And now I saw the back of my detested groom, broad and tall and clad to match me in white velvet and gold. I noted he did not even turn to greet me as the rest of the congregation did; he did not even possess the basic courtesies of a family of consequence. He was taller than I'd remembered; his hair curled like his cousin's had, but a little longer, the resemblance crueler than everything else. I felt as if the knife were in my throat after all, for I was bleeding to death.

He turned and I nearly fainted at a cathedral wedding for the second time in my life.

It was Brother Guido.

Really, truly he—living, breathing, smiling. He held me with the hand that wore a gold ring of the *palle* on his thumb.

He was thinner, his hair a little longer, clean shaven, with his sunburned skin golden against the white. I felt my heart fail with love and longing. The only true difference was that upon his ring hand the flesh was livid with burns; a desert of smooth, arid, healed skin stretched over the long bones. I wondered what other injuries were hid by the fine clothes, but did not care—I would love him, through and through, however damaged he may be.

I could not follow the service, could not breathe for the happiness that swelled in my chest. Could hardly hold my right hand up in the traditional Tuscan greeting, to my groom and guests. Could not look at the priest or heed his words, for I could not shift my eyes from my—could it be true?—*husband*.

I managed to murmur the responses, and we were wed.

I held his burned hand hard as we moved as one down the aisle. Caught my mother's eye, and she smiled at me from beneath her mask. Once outside we were able to speak at last as we threw handfuls of coins to the children. I had a thousand questions but began with two.

"What happened? Where is Niccolò?"

"Dead. He contracted gangrene in his leg, and so died of his battle wounds."

I remembered what my mother had said: *his condition will not affect the wedding, it will take place almost as planned.* Then she told me I'd be happy. I had to smile.

"I was the surviving heir of the della Torres," he went on, "and at last I was ready to inherit my city. As I told you of my time in the Bargello, things change in Tuscan politics all the time. The worm at the bottom of the dungheap can next day be king of the castle."

The children were jackdawing for coins around our feet, but we might as well have been alone in the world.

My husband tenderly tucked a golden curl behind my ear. "When I took Holy Orders I was young and untried. I loved the church and I loved books, but knew nothing of the world. You showed it to me. In Rome I fell out of love with the church." A cloud passed over his face. "But now I know that I may love God, and you, too, and that there is no need to choose. My church is no longer my church, but my God will always be my God; is now and forever shall be."

"But how . . . that is, how did you survive?"

'I jumped into the sea, for I was aflame, that much is true. But I clung to the mast of the flagship and held on for dear life; life that was infinitely dear since I had found you. The storm still raged around me, and once I almost let go from the pain, for my hands were badly burned and the salt brine stung like vinegar. But something made me hold on."

"Me?" I asked hopefully, knowing then the prayer I had offered from the *lanterna* had been answered.

He smiled. "In a sense. Perhaps we should thank your alter ego, the goddess Flora," said my husband. "As I swallowed the seas and fought for breath, I saw her form, *your* form, and the life and promise within, and the swell of a child at her belly, and I knew I had to live to see the spring. But in my vision, as on the *cartone,* she had no face, and I had to see yours again." He cupped my cheeks, as if to make sure that I was real. "At the same moment I saw the lights of the shore and washed up on the beach at Peglia. I made my way back to the doge's palace, a slow and painful journey, for by then I was in high fever: now burning hot, now freezing cold. I knew I was not out of danger, for if I was found on the cliffs by the loyal Genoese after the battle that had lately taken place, I would have been executed as an enemy deserter. But I came to Genoa at last, where the doge was more than happy to reward me for my services. He put everything at my disposal: his best physicians, and then when I was ready, clothes, horses, and a retinue. He told me that you'd gone to Pisa with your mother. He told me to pursue you, that I might dare to hope; but I needed no telling." He tightened his arms around me. "He's a good man, and will rule well, I think."

"I do too."

"And so it was that I came home to my birthright, and the palace that is rightfully mine. I redrafted the contracts with your father—but a change of name was all that was needed—and your mother seemed more than happy with what had come to pass."

I shook my head, amazed. It was too much to take in, too much happiness. He turned me round to look at him, and the crowd of children melted respectfully away, well pleased with their bounty. I looked into the blue, blue eyes of my Lazarus-husband, back from the dead; come from the Catacombs into the light—proof of the afterlife I had doubted and he had not. And we, we had come from darkness to light too—come from ignorance into knowledge; read the treasure map, solved the puzzle, and claimed the prize. But the treasure we had found was no jewel casket or trove of coins; it was beyond price. "What now?" I asked, not really caring, so long as we were together.

"A feast at the palace, and the . . . wedding night." A shadow crossed his face. "Of course, it is usual for the *bride* to be a virgin on the wedding night."

"I'll be gentle with you," I said, and kissed him in a manner that belied the words.

The field of miracles deserved its name that day. The sun set behind the leaning tower, the symbol of Guido's city—and mine—into a beautiful red sky. And the day began.

It was going to be a beautiful summer.

· II ·

1492

In 1492 three things happened.

Cosa Uno: I gave birth to a daughter whom we called Simonetta after the pearl of Genoa. Appropriately, the pearl in my navel, which had stayed determinedly put through all manner of adventures, popped out at Simonetta's birth, making her name a certainty. I sent the pearl to Bonaccorso Nivola, who had been freed at my mother's word and now lived peacefully with his family on Burano, while his grown sons fished the lagoon. I played with Simonetta constantly, told her I loved her every day. She was my weakness, the apple of my Eden. I was joined in this preference by my mother, who visited our palace much more after Simonetta was born, dandling the baby, feeding her comfits, bringing her toys and treasures from Venice to surprise and delight her. And the greatest gift of all: just being there and playing with her, reveling in the girl's growing beauty as her own faded. She found joy in every stage of her granddaughter's development, was there for her first steps and words. The child loved her too, and my mother had her second chance to be a *Vero Madre.* Sometimes they sit in the atrium of our palace, and I watch the old lady and the little girl play at marbles or skittles beneath the framed *cartone,* which hangs on the wall there. It is cracked and stiff with salt, all the vivid colors almost gone, bleached by the sea when I cast it into the Genoan tide. All the figures have dissolved away save one—my own. I don't know whether the extra pigments used to paint her garden of flowers had fixed the paints to the paper more firmly, but at any rate, Flora now stands alone in her ruined bower.

Cosa Due: Lorenzo de' Medici died after ruling Florence justly and well for nine last years of peace and profit. At the instant he died lightning struck the church of Santa Maria del Fiore and set the great dome aflame. Il Magnifico's dreams of empire died with him. But:

Cosa Tre: a certain Signor Cristoforo Colombo of Genoa sailed to the world's edge as he always said he would. There he discovered a new vision of *imperium*—the Americas, an empire destined to become the new Rome.

HISTORICAL NOTE

Italy was eventually unified in 1870. At the turn of the century, a modern monument called the Altar of the Nation was constructed in the heart of the new country's capital, Rome.

It is a marble monstrosity, which neatly obscures the views of the Capitoline Hill.

AUTHOR'S NOTE

The *Primavera* by Sandro Botticelli enjoys more interpretations than perhaps any other picture in art history. A number of them are examined at differing depths in this story. I am indebted to Charles Dempsey's scholarly interpretation of the painting in his work *The Portrayal of Love: Botticelli's Primavera and Humanist Culture at the Time of Lorenzo the Magnificent* and Mirella Levi D'Ancona's incredibly detailed botanical reading of the picture in her book *Botticelli's Primavera: A Botanical Interpretation Including Astrology, Alchemy and the Medici*. However, this book owes the most to the work of Professor Enrico Guidoni of the University of Rome. It was he who posited the idea that the figures represent Italian cities and suggested the painting concealed a Medici design to unify Italy. The professor's arguments can be fully explored in his work *La Primavera di Botticelli: L'armonia tra le città nell'Italia di Lorenzo il Magnifico*. I have respectfully named my most learned character, Guido, after him.

It should be emphasized, however, that this novel is a work of fiction, and that, with respect to the work of the scholars here named, any additions, omissions, or alterations of characters, events, or places are my own.

THE BOTTICELLI SECRET

by Marina Fiorato

About the Author

- A Conversation with Marina Fiorato

Behind the Novel

- "Botticelli and the Art
  of Reading a Painting"
  An Original Essay by the Author

Keep on Reading

- Recommended Reading
- Reading Group Questions

For more reading group suggestions
visit www.readinggroupgold.com.

ST. MARTIN'S GRIFFIN

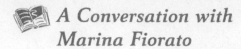

A Conversation with Marina Fiorato

What inspired you to write *The Botticelli Secret*?

The painting, first and last. It's been my favorite picture ever since I saw it in the Uffizi as a teenager. The scale, the color of it, and the intensity of detail really captured my attention, then and ever since. I've always found the figure of Flora particularly captivating; I find her expression deliciously intriguing. She really steps out of the frame. I've always wondered what she is thinking—and this book is my answer to that question.

What does *La Primavera* mean to you? What about it do you wish to reveal to your readers?

I read an article in the *Times* about an Italian academic named Enrico Guidoni who had come up with a new theory about *La Primavera,* and the meaning of each of the figures. There have been so many interpretations of the painting over the years, but this one struck me as being completely convincing. So it formed the spine of the novel. It's meaningful because I think it completely encapsulates that period of the Renaissance in almost every aspect—fashion, belief systems, patronage, symbolism, even botany. As to what I'd like to reveal to my readers the answer is simple: Italy!

You have already written about Renaissance Italy in your previous novel, *The Glassblower of Murano.* How, if at all, was the process of writing *The Botticelli Secret* different for you? Also, in crafting your story about Botticelli, did you stick solely to the facts? Or did you take any artistic liberties?

Writing *Botticelli* was a very different experience from writing *Glassblower*. For one thing, it's all written in first-person, from the point of view of Luciana, the model for Botticelli's Flora. Also, this novel is wholly set in the past, where as *Glassblower* had a split timeline between past and present. One of the major differences was the humor: Luciana is such a flawed, earthy character; the contrast between her demeanor and language and the more buttoned-up, erudite Brother Guido was a rich

> "I've always found [Flora] particularly captivating... she really steps out of the frame."

seam of comedy. Luciana's language is certainly more colorful than any I've ever used before—I miss her already!

Because this book is so dependent on its premise, I was much less strict with the facts than I've been with other works. I tried not to be overtly anachronistic—there are no digital watches!—but for *Botticelli* it was more important to stay true to the ethos and feel of the period than to be too pernickety about dates and details. So some people are in cities they may not have been in, or I've imagined events that may not have happened at all. I've always maintained that historical novels should not be taken as hard fact, but more of a jumping-off point for readers to research the period if what they read sparks their interest in history. I'd be delighted if that happens with my readers.

About the Author

THE PONTE VECCHIO

Why do you enjoy writing historical fiction? Why do you do you think readers are so drawn to historical novels?

L.P. Hartley wrote: "The past is another country, they do things differently there." I think this is exactly right and it's at the root of our fascination with historical novels. I find everything about the Renaissance period utterly absorbing; the people dressed differently, spoke differently, ate different things, and had different belief systems. When I open a historical novel I'm taking a trip to a different land, and, as with all journeys abroad, I'm as interested in how much we are similar as in how much we differ. People are people, after all; wherever, or whenever, they live.

Have you ever known a Luciana in your own life? Did you base her character (or others in this novel) on people you know? Please take us through the process of how characters come to life in your imagination— and on the page.

No, I don't know anyone like her, but I wish I did! I love her so much. She's a creature of contrasts—ignorant but not stupid, greedy but not grasping, selfish but loving, base but beautiful. The challenge was to try to make the reader like her despite, or perhaps because of, her faults. The key to Luciana's character is that although she has an internal monologue, that's also what comes straight out of her mouth. When she does flatter, or posture, it's immediately undercut by the fact that we know exactly what she's thinking. It makes her very human. I created Guido by trying to imagine a character who was the opposite to Luciana: he is educated, cultured, reticent, and speaks very wordily and with great propriety—no curse words for him! The novel is built on the tensions between their two personalities. Essentially, they have exactly the same core values. I have not really based any of the characters on people I know, but I've tried to make them neither completely villainous nor completely virtuous.

"When I open a historical novel I'm taking a trip to a different land."

Of all of the cities featured in *The Botticelli Secret*, which is your favorite?

One of the things I'd really like to get across the incredible diversity of all these cities, but that they all have so much to offer. In fact, one of the main messages of the novel is that Italy always was, is now, and ever shall be intensely regional. So in the spirit of that I'd have to confess to a soft spot for Venice, the city of my fathers, with Florence as a close second. If I'm to be allowed two answers, I'd say Venice in the winter, Florence in the summer!

MARINA AND HER DAUGHTER, RUBY

"Botticelli and the Art of Reading a Painting"
by Marina Fiorato

It's tempting to think that we're getting more and more sophisticated as we forge our way through the twenty-first century. We like to think that we can look back on the past and find it simplistic, or even primitive. But despite, or perhaps because of, all of our technologies, the images that fill our world today are actually reasonably simple. Photography must take some responsibility for the erosion of meaning within image—essentially the photograph captures a moment of life and, unless digital trickery is at play, there are no layers of meaning. It is just a literal snapshot of a scene.

During the Renaissance, things were vastly different. I first learned this lesson in a history class at school. We were studying Andrea Firenze's *Triumph of the Church* and the Church's use of art as propaganda. The fresco is a glorious and awe-inspiring piece, complete with a Christ in judgment, the gates of heaven, and a complete rendering of the Duomo in Florence. But what caught my teenage attention was a pack of dogs at the bottom of the painting. "Cute dogs,' I said to my teacher. "Not just that, she told me, "look closer." I did. There were a number of black-and-white dogs fighting with fewer brown ones. The black-and-white dogs seemed to be winning; they were on top of the brown ones, biting them or rolling them in the dirt. "*Domini canes,*" my teacher said. "*Hounds of God.* You'll notice that the black-and-white ones are overpowering the brown ones. They represent the Dominican monks, who had black-and-white habits, suppressing the Franciscan monks, who wore brown. The two orders often contested on points of theology."

> *"We like to think that we can look back on the past and find it simplistic, or even primitive."*

That did it. From that day forward, I was hooked. I began looking for hidden meaning in every painting I saw. When I first stood in front of *La Primavera,* I was fascinated. I became one in a long line of people to set eyes on that great panel and mutter to themselves, It must all mean something. What are all those flowers, those jewels? What are the trees? Why is Venus raising her hand? Why are flowers dropping from Chloris's mouth? What is Zephyrus's intention? Why does Mercury stir the clouds? And, most intriguing, why does Flora smile? For the next twenty years, I started to look, not just see; and began, in part, to understand that everything—*everything*—has a meaning.

The new millennium—which began with the horrors of 9/11—was a time for looking back, for looking forward, for looking for meaning. Those of faith and those with no faith at all were trying to figure out who they were and where they were going. So too were the citizens of Florence in Botticelli's era. They were heading toward the end of a century; they were fresh out of a war of ideology. Like us, they were dealing with civil unrest and shocking public violence. The Pazzi conspiracy saw Florence's first family brutally attacked in God's house, the Duomo. In the wake of all this turmoil, Botticelli painted his greatest masterpiece for the Medici family.

The head of the family, Lorenzo, surrounded himself with poets and thinkers like Marsilio Ficino and Angelo Poliziano—men willing to embrace Humanism, a philosophical movement that embraced Classical inspiration. Although Humanism wasn't necessarily at odds with Christianity, it's tempting to impose a pagan interpretation on *La Primavera.* The scholar Charles Dempsey, for instance, points convincingly to the pagan symbolism of the *La Primavera,* with particular reference to Venus, the goddess of April for whom the festival of Calendimaggio is still celebrated in Tuscany. Others, drawn irresistibly to that breathtaking, bewildering carpet of flowers in the painting, have taken to botanical interpretation. Scholar Mirella Levi D'Ancona has done painstaking work classifying every plant in the panel and identifying its significance, drawing some fascinating links to astrology and alchemy (and other so-called "heretical" sciences). And then there's Enrico Guidoni, with his startling notion that political empire building during the time was the inspiration for the painting.

All of these theories, or none of them, could be true. Unfortunately, we'll never know. A few short years after creating his secular masterpieces, Botticelli turned his back on his work and embraced God under the influence of fanatical preacher Girolamo Savonarola. In fact, it's possible that Botticelli was instrumental, or at least complicit, in the destruction of some of his own works in the infamous Bonfire of the Vanities. Botticelli had found another idol, and was seemingly, at the end of his life, deaf to the siren call of the golden world of the Medici.

Opinions or messages within the painting could in themselves, then, be transient. Taking this into account, perhaps *La Primavera* is a fleeting moment in time captured forever, a unity of briefly held beliefs detailed minutely in multiple symbols—as much a snapshot as a photograph.

This whole book is a speculation, an answer to that question I asked myself twenty years ago: Why *does* Flora smile?

"La Primavera is a fleeting moment in time captured forever, a unity of briefly held beliefs detailed minutely in multiple symbols."

 **Recommended Reading**

Marina's Favorite Historical Novels

Shield of Three Lions
and
Banners of Gold
Pamela Kaufman

Shield of Three Lions is a wonderful novel featuring, in my opinion, one of the most engaging heroines in historical literature. Alix of Wanthwaite loses her estate in the north of England and goes to petition the King for its return. The only problem is that Richard I is engaged with the Third Crusade. Alix follows the Lionheart all the way to Jerusalem disguised as his male page; what follows is a fantastically rich adventure— comedic, gripping, and romantic by turns. It's so well written that the sounds and smells and pageantry of the Crusades leap out of the page.

The follow-up to *Shield of Three Lions*, *Banners of Gold* sees Alix of Wanthwaite installed as Richard's mistress. Set amongst the courts and castles of medieval France, there's a fascinating power struggle between Alix and the King's redoubtable mother, Eleanor of Aquitaine. This story also features the wonderful Jewish character Bonel, who introduces questions of faith and tolerance into this medieval world.

Katherine
Anya Seton

This book is based on the factual relationship between Katherine Swynford and John of Gaunt. Anya Seton builds a complete picture of medieval England, from the pomp of court to the ignominy of the Black Death and the civil unrest of the Peasant's Revolt. At the center of it all is a beautifully drawn heroine who struggles constantly with the conflict of the desires of her heart and the fate of her soul.

The Name of the Rose
Umberto Eco

An intriguing mystery set within an incredibly detailed rendering of the monastic world. Brother William of Baskerville and his novice Adso could be the prototype for the modern "detective and sidekick" pairing, but this is much, much more than a murder mystery. This is not the easiest book to read, admittedly; but the wonderfully rich story investigates heresy, faith, and the medieval ideology in satisfying detail, and I found it provided an invaluable insight into the monastic rule.

A Traveller in Time
Alison Uttley

One of the original "timeslip" novels, this is ostensibly a book for children but has lots to offer the adult reader. Penelope slips back in time and finds herself at the ancient farmhouse of the Babington family just at the period when Anthony Babington plans to free the imprisoned Mary Queen of Scots. An engaging read, this book features a wonderful description of an Elizabethan Christmas.

My Lady's Crusade
Annette Motley

Back to the Crusades again—one of my favorite periods of history. Perhaps I'll visit it one day too! This time our heroine, Eden of Hawkhurst, travels to the Holy Land in search of her husband who has gone to fight for the Lionheart. This fascinating take on the Crusades is the only version I've read in which a significant portion is seen from the point of view of the infidel. Eden spends quite a lot of the novel in Damascus living in the house of a Saracen Emir, so it's a much more balanced picture than usual. There's a wonderfully romantic strand, too, as Eden finds herself in a love-hate relationship with a saturnine knight named Tristan de Jarnac.

Lady of Hay
Barbara Erskine

This is a fascinating read, a story split between modern-day and twelfth-century Britain during which King John was busy subjugating the Welsh barons. It's based on the true story of Matilda de Braose, the eponymous Lady of Hay, who is torn, both emotionally and politically, between a brutal husband, a courtly lover, and her mercurial King. What makes this book so interesting is that the device of time travel is achieved through the medium of hypnotic regression. So as well as being a satisfying read as a straight-up historical novel, it also asks questions about whether we have lived before, as it emerges that many of the modern characters knew each other in the past as well as the present.

The Leper of St. Giles
Ellis Peters

This is my favorite Brother Cadfael mystery. Although it is technically in the crime genre, I mention this book because it deals with the condition of leprosy in the Middle Ages and the treatment of, and attitudes toward, its sufferers. Brother Cadfael himself is, as always, an engaging and sympathetic character—the natural successor to Eco's William of Baskerville—and in this well-told tale he attempts to reunite a pair of divided lovers while befriending a mysterious leper who is not quite what he seems.

*Keep on
Reading*

Reading Group Questions

1. Few works of art are as celebrated as Sandro Botticelli's *La Primavera*. Keeping in mind that *The Botticelli Secret* is a fictional account of the story behind the famous painting, how did reading the book teach you about—or change your impression of—its subject? Has anyone in the group ever seen the painting in person?

2. What do you think of Luciana? Do you like her more, or less, for her brash conduct? Is a person's moral code something that's written in stone, or is it a result of varying circumstances? Do you think your code of conduct would change if *you* were poor and hungry?

3. Duplicity is an important theme throughout the book. How is Guido plagued by a feeling of duplicity? In which other characters do we see (or not see) duplicity? Can there be both positive and negative effects of a duplicitous nature?

4. Despite their differences, why do you think Luciana and Guido are drawn to each other?

5. Guido, as a man of the cloth, believes in God, whereas Luciana, as a woman of the streets, believes only in herself. Throughout the story, both beliefs are called into question. Do you think it's more important to have faith in God, or faith in yourself? Are the two mutually exclusive?

THE MONASTERY AT SANTA CROCE

6. Discuss the nine cities of Renaissance Italy as "characters" in the book. How is each portrayed? And what role does each play in shaping Luciana and Guido?

7. Do you believe that a picture is worth a thousand words? Can a work of art—a painting, or a book—ever truly capture a person's essence? Did Botticelli's portrait of Luciana, even as she sat as an archetype, capture hers?

8. The action in this novel is built around several secrets which Luciana and Guido unearth. Discuss the element of mystery in these pages. What types of narrative devices did the author use to keep the reader guessing?

9. *The Botticelli Secret* is about strength and frailty, truth and beauty, art and artifice. It is also about the ties that bind us to family—in all its glory and pain. How important is the notion of family to Luciana? Which relationships, regardless of the standard definition of "family," seem the most real to you in the book?

10. In the story, Sandro Botticelli is an artist but he's also a member of a powerful inner circle. What does *The Botticelli Secret* suggest about the role and function of art in the Renaissance era? Was it more or less political than it is today?

11. What do you imagine happens after the end of the novel? What do you think Luciana and Guido's life will be like now that they are free to be together, and Luciana knows her real identity? What truths do you think she'll learn about herself?

For more special features, photographs, and "secret trivia" about this book, please visit the author's Web site at www.marinafiorato.com.

"Marina Fiorato has beautifully recreated the bright, glittering world of the seventeenth-century glassblower, and nestled it surely within a compelling contemporary romance."
—Jeanne Kalogridis

Venice, 1681.
Glassblowing is the lifeblood of the Republic, and the glass-blowers of Murano are virtually imprisoned as they work. But one artist, Corradino Manin, sells his methods and his soul to protect his secret daughter.

In the present day, his descendant, Leonora Manin, finds new life and love in the city of Venice. But her fate is inextricably linked to that of her ancestors...

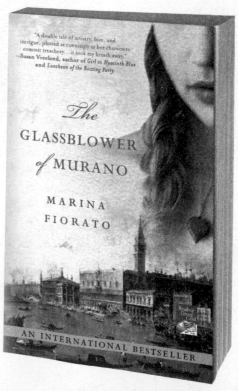

"A double tale of artistry, love, and intrigue, plotted as cunningly as her characters commit treachery...it took my breath away."
—Susan Vreeland, author of *Girl in Hyacinth Blue* and *Luncheon of the Boating Party*

The
GLASSBLOWER
of MURANO

MARINA
FIORATO

AN INTERNATIONAL BESTSELLER

St. Martin's Griffin

www.stmartins.com